TONY PARK

THE HUNTER

Quercus

First published in Australia by Pan Macmillan in 2014
First published in Great Britain by Quercus Publishing in 2014
This paperback edition published in 2015 by

Quercus Publishing Ltd
Carmelite House
50 Victoria Embankment
London EC4Y 0DZ

An Hachette UK company

Copyright © 2014 Tony Park

The moral right of Tony Park to be identified as the author
of this work has been asserted in accordance with the
Copyright, Designs and Patents Act, 1988.

All rights reserved. No part of this publication may be reproduced
or transmitted in any form or by any means, electronic or
mechanical, including photocopy, recording, or
any information storage and retrieval system,
without permission in writing from the publisher.

A CIP catalogue record for this book is available
from the British Library

PAPERBACK ISBN 978 1 78206 167 0
EBOOK ISBN 978 1 84866 788 4

This book is a work of fiction. Names, characters, businesses,
organizations, places and events are either the product of the
author's imagination or used fictitiously.
Any resemblance to actual persons, living or dead, events or
locales is entirely coincidental.

10 9 8 7 6 5 4 3 2 1

Printed and bound in Great Britain by Clays Ltd, St Ives plc

For Nicola

LONDON BOROUGH OF HACKNEY LIBRARIES	
HK12002677	
Bertrams	06/07/2015
THR	£7.99
	02/07/2015

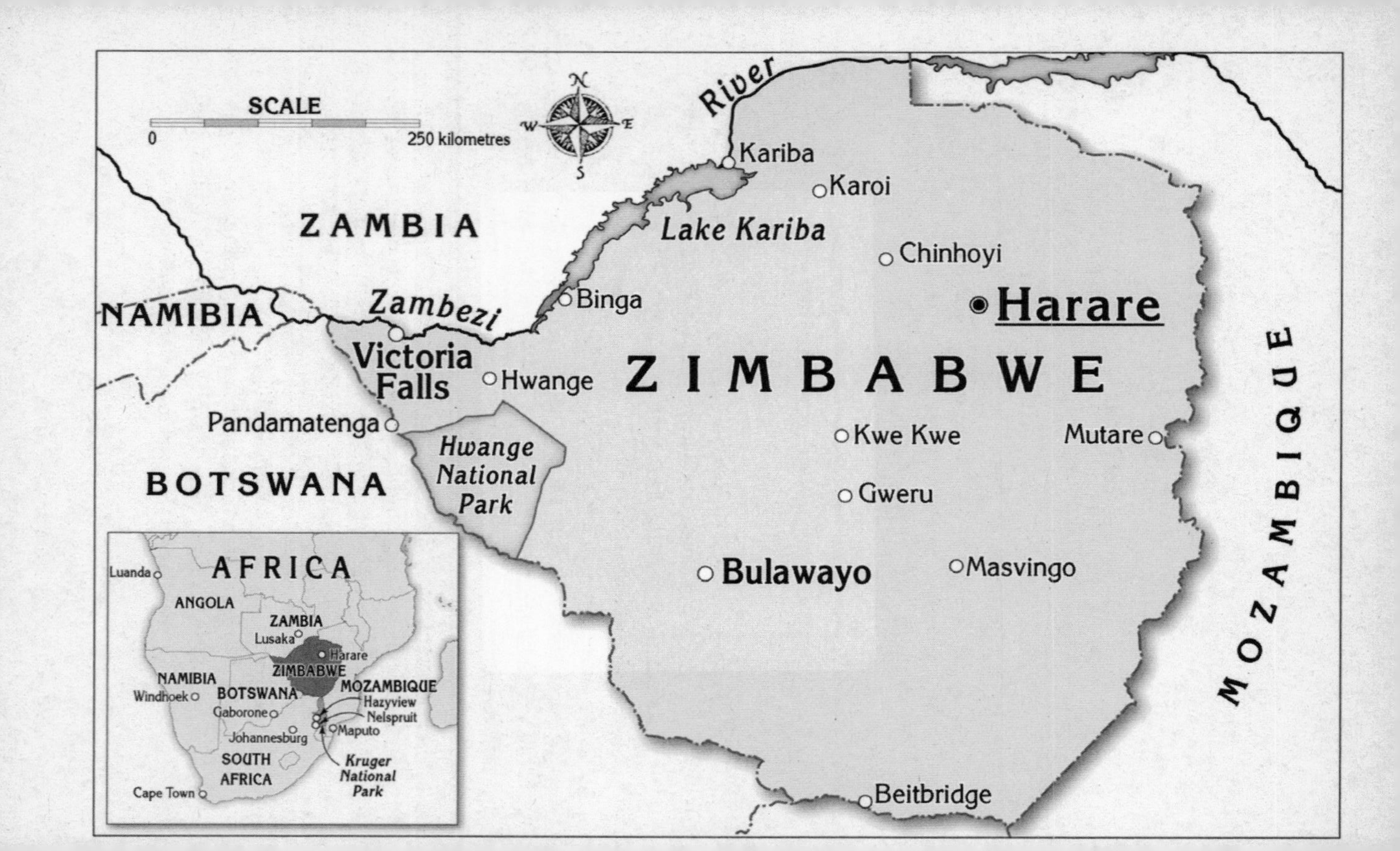
SCALE
0
250 kilometres
N
S
W
E
River
Zambezi
Kariba
Karoi
Lake Kariba
Chinhoyi
ZAMBIA
NAMIBIA
Binga
Harare
Victoria Falls
Hwange
ZIMBABWE
Pandamatenga
Hwange National Park
Kwe Kwe
Mutare
BOTSWANA
Gweru
MOZAMBIQUE
Bulawayo
Masvingo
Beitbridge
AFRICA
Luanda
ANGOLA
ZAMBIA
Lusaka
Harare
ZIMBABWE
NAMIBIA
Windhoek
BOTSWANA
MOZAMBIQUE
Hazyview
Nelspruit
Gaborone
Maputo
Johannesburg
SOUTH AFRICA
Kruger National Park
Cape Town

Prologue

Hazyview, South Africa, June 2010

Captain Sannie van Rensburg looked at the vultures in the trees and shuddered. *Only in Africa*, she thought. She took a pair of rubber gloves from the packet in the boot of her Mercedes and snapped them on.

Two officers, a man and a woman in the blue-grey uniforms of the South African Police Service, were standing over the body, and the latter kept glancing up at the vultures, her right hand resting on the Z88 pistol in the holster that perched on her rounded hip. Sannie greeted them.

Her new partner, Mavis Sibongile, exchanged muted greetings with the officers and hung back. Sannie stepped over the rocky ground, winding her way carefully between the stubby thornbushes, and made her way to the bundle wrapped in black builder's plastic that lay at the officers' feet. 'Who found her?'

'A woodcarver,' said the female officer. Sannie liked her braids. The officer pointed at a man squatting twenty metres away. The old man didn't look at her. 'He makes giraffes and lions and chickens for the tourists. He was in the *veldt* looking for a tree to cut down when he came across her.'

Sannie ignored the witness for the moment and knelt down beside the bundle. A hand – or, more correctly, the remains of a hand – protruded from a ragged tear in the plastic. Sannie saw the hyena spoor in the dirt. 'Were the hyena still here when the man found the body?'

The male officer called the question to the woodcarver, who responded in Tsonga. Sannie didn't need a translator. 'Yes, they were,' the man said. 'I threw some rocks at them and they ran off.'

'What time was this?' She peeled back some more of the plastic.

'Just after dawn.'

The hyena couldn't have been here long, she thought. If the nocturnal animals had been on the body all night they would have made short work of the plastic, and the woman wrapped inside. A Kombi towing a caravan slowed on the main road, the family inside staring at the parked police *bakkie* and the people in the bush. Four hundred metres up the road was the Phabeni Gate entrance to the Kruger National Park. 'I want this area cordoned off,' Sannie said to the uniforms. 'No more walking around here. We need to check for footprints.' She looked at her new partner, who was still hanging back. 'Mavis, come help me,' Sannie said.

Mavis was half her age, a university criminology graduate who had enlisted into the SAPS on an accelerated traineeship. Sannie had retired from the police before she'd turned forty, then returned as a police reservist to help cover manpower shortages in the Nelspruit serious and violent crime unit. Like an addict she had been unable to give up the job completely, no matter how destructive the drug, and she had allowed herself to be talked into returning to work fulltime as a detective captain in a mentoring role for new officers. Her husband, Tom, an Englishman, had also once been a police officer, but had now taken to running the family's banana farm with the vigour and optimism of one who had been brought up in a city all his life. He had been against her going back to work, but loved her enough to give up trying to talk her out of it when he realised he would never win that argument.

Sannie looked at Mavis's high-heeled boots. She would have to have a quiet talk to her, again, about appropriate clothing for this job. 'Help me unwrap her some more.'

Flies buzzed and took flight as Mavis dropped hesitantly to one knee and the two women started to unroll the body. Mavis gagged. *Poor girl*, Sannie thought. She would probably be sick. 'If you must be sick don't do it close to the crime scene.'

Mavis swallowed hard and nodded. A face emerged from the plastic; eyes wide and ligature marks immediately visible around the neck. She had been a pretty girl, perhaps aged nineteen or twenty, maybe twenty-one. She wore purple eye shadow and her curly hair had been cropped close to her scalp. There were gold hoop earrings, still in place.

'Her . . .' Mavis swallowed again, 'her wrists have been tied as well.' She held up the pulpy, bloody mess and showed Sannie the marks on the girl's skin.

'Naked,' Sannie said as they unrolled further, revealing more skin. '*Ag*, cigarette burns on her breasts.'

'Who does such a thing?' Mavis asked.

Sannie wanted to be home, right then, with her husband and her three children, not in this field of scrubby thorn and death. The carver was glancing over at them. 'Boyfriends, husbands, fathers, gang members, random rapists; it's our job to find out who.'

There were other lacerations and bruises on the breasts, as though she had been tied up, and perhaps beaten with something. Sannie shook her head. As she moved away more of the plastic she saw the coagulated blood and the first of the cuts. Beside her, Mavis stood and rocked on her high heels.

'I'm sorry . . .' She put her hand to her mouth and turned and ran.

Sannie steeled herself as she uncovered the woman's groin. The insides of her thighs were coated with dried blood. She saw the incisions and knew this had been more than a rape. Whoever had done this had tortured this poor girl and, by the looks of it, plunged a knife between her legs, inside her body. She fought back the rising tide of bile and, as much as she wanted again to be away from this evil, from this depressing job, she knew she could not go back to her home in the hills and live the life of a farmer's wife. No matter how many horrible things she saw, this was what God had put her on earth to do; that and raise her own children in safety and love her husband.

The politics of the job and the new South Africa dismayed her on a daily basis, and in a way she wished she could be like those who turned their back on it and said to hell with them all, but when she looked into the wide, pain-filled eyes of the dead girl and imagined her last moments on God's earth she knew she could never walk away.

'Clean yourself up, Mavis,' she called to her partner, who was bent double. 'We've work to do.'

1

Kruger National Park, South Africa, 2014

Hudson Brand watched the lion jump over the guardrail and onto the bridge over the Sabie River.

'Shoot,' he said.

'Shoot what?' the man wearing South African National Parks khaki behind the register in the Paul Kruger Gate office asked him.

'Nothing. It's a euphemism for shit.'

'You Americans are funny, Hudson, and . . .'

Brand didn't hear the rest of the man's sentence. He was already out the door of the gate office. 'Get back in your cars,' he yelled to some tourists who were oblivious of the big black-maned cat walking towards them from the other end of the bridge.

The lion was silhouetted in the dawn's half-darkness by the headlights of three cars that were following it along the bridge. At Brand's end, tourists checking into the Kruger National Park had faces and cameras pressed to the window of the thatch-roofed gate office, watching the lion's progress as it passed the last of the cars in the long holiday weekend queue that stretched from the office back a third of the way down the bridge.

Brand had been glancing out the window, checking on his lone client in the Land Rover game viewer while the national parks guy was processing his paperwork, when he'd spied the lion. His first clue that something was amiss was the cars that had stopped at the far end of the bridge. The Paul Kruger Gate was like rush hour at dawn every day, with staffers in a hurry to get to their jobs at Skukuza, the park's main camp situated twelve kilometres inside the reserve, and tourists in private cars and safari vehicles, like his, coming in for the day or overnight stays. No one stopped at the far end of the bridge without good reason. As a guide and a private investigator, Brand knew that changes in the natural pattern of things often signalled that something interesting – and potentially dangerous – was about to happen.

At first Brand thought the movement in the lead car's headlights was the big male leopard whose territory encompassed the bridge and gate, and the Sabiepark Private Nature Reserve across the river from Kruger. Brand had seen the big muscled tom, who had the bulk of a lioness, a few times on the bridge, and even on the main road outside the park when he'd been bringing guests in early. The leopard came and went from the protected reserve as he pleased and didn't give a damn about the rules or the people outside Kruger, some of whom would have gladly killed him to stop him eating their goats or dogs or whatnot. But this animal was bigger.

'There's a lion coming towards you,' Brand said to the nearest couple of tourists, who were standing nearby, poring over a map book on the bonnet of their rented Corolla.

'*Leone*?' said the man, who sported an Andre Agassi bandanna.

'*Si*,' Brand replied.

Mobile phones were drawn faster than six-shooters as word rippled down through the parked cars in the queue. Some people were jumping back inside, slamming the doors on their BMWs and Kombis, others were getting out. Camera flashes popped like far-off white phosphorous rockets, marking targets in the bush.

Brand's mobile buzzed in his pocket. He quickly checked it. There was a message from a fellow guide, Bryce Duffy, a young South African guy of English descent, originally from Durban. *I'm in the queue – check the lion on the bridge.* Brand looked up and found Bryce's Land Rover a few cars back in the slow-moving procession that was following the lion. Bryce must have spotted Hudson's vehicle parked near the office.

Brand double-checked his own vehicle and saw Darlene, his lone client for the day, climb down out of the game viewer.

'For crying in a bucket,' Brand said. He strode down the line of cars to where his game viewer was parked.

The lion was calling as he padded along the tarmac towards Brand. The low throaty rumble got to Brand every time; it was what kept him in Africa, what made this continent, and not the place where he was born, his home. Part of the attraction, too, was the edginess of this part of the world and the fact that danger could and did rear its head with no notice. Like it had now.

'Darlene, please get back in the truck,' Brand called as he picked up his stride.

Amateur photographers were piling back into their cars as the king of beasts sauntered past them, hardly deigning to dignify his laughably lesser subjects with a glance. He had other things on his mind; food most likely, perhaps sex. *No wonder I love lions*, Brand thought.

Darlene was holding her tiny digital camera out at arm's length. The inbuilt flash kept popping off but the lion, who Brand could now recognise as Pretty Boy, a member of the Mapogo coalition, was still too far from her for the flash to be of any use. Pretty Boy was maybe a hundred metres from Darlene, but he was closing fast with that effortless, distance-covering fast walk that lions had.

Darlene looked back at Brand. She was thirty-five, newly divorced, bleached blonde and blue-eyed, with a California tan and a rack that Brand thought looked promisingly natural. 'Get in the truck,' he ordered her.

Darlene gave him a thumbs-up and an expensive smile. She didn't get the urgency or realise how quickly Pretty Boy could cover the ground between him and her.

Brand kept walking towards her, pointing to the truck and using the queue of cars as cover. He didn't want Pretty Boy taking a bead on him as the only biped still moving on the bridge. Brand was sure that as long as no one did anything stupid Pretty Boy would just keep on walking briskly by, and then peel off into the bush once he reached the statue of *Oom* Paul Kruger. The old president's big fat face with its leonine beard somehow still managed to dominate the entry and the name of South Africa's flagship reserve, despite the fact that every other Afrikaner name was busily being changed throughout the country.

But this was the Kruger Park, and Brand knew well that people on holiday and even those who worked here, living cheek by jowl with the Big Five and possibly feeling a false sense of security, did some stupid things. As if to prove him right, a car raced onto the bridge, its driver seemingly oblivious to what was happening up ahead. It was a VW Golf with dark tinted windows, and even from the other end of the bridge Brand could hear – and feel – the thump of deep bass speakers from inside. Brand assumed this was a national parks staff member, who would have a pass they could use to leapfrog the queue of tourists' private cars and open game-viewing trucks like Brand's.

'Shoot,' Brand said.

Darlene was grasping the side ladder to haul herself back up into the game viewer, but she was still holding her camera in one hand. She looked up at the bridge when she heard the sound of the speakers and the speeding engine, and saw that Pretty Boy was now a whole lot closer.

The staff car saw the lion, at last, and hit his brakes. Rubber painted the tar surface and the little car fishtailed as it skidded. Pretty Boy looked over his shoulder and gave an angry roar.

Darlene's digital camera clattered to the roadway and she lost her footing, her rubber sandal slipping on the bottom rung of the ladder as she tried to climb faster, but with only one hand on the ladder. Her feet touched the ground again.

The car had come to a halt, but Pretty Boy had decided it was time to fight rather than flee. Lions were like that, Brand mused. Catch them on foot and ninety-nine times out of a hundred they would see you first and get up from their daily snoozing and run away. Surprise one, or corner one, and the instinct to kill took over from the urge to retreat.

Pretty Boy vented his anger at the hapless driver and Brand reckoned he could see the little Golf rocking under the acoustic onslaught.

Brand found himself running – something he knew he should definitely not be doing in the vicinity of a fully grown lion – and Darlene looked like Brand felt in his nightmares. He had the same dream often; he was back in Angola, trying to run from a smoking, ambushed Ratel armoured vehicle, while the Cuban-manned T-54 tank slowly traversed its turret for the killer shot. His legs always felt as though they were encased in lead, and when he pointed his R5 at the tank commander the trigger never worked.

Darlene looked from the lion back to Brand and did what he was doing – she ran.

Brand was running towards the lion, which was stupid enough, but what Darlene was doing was suicidal. Brand saw Pretty Boy's head flick from the car to the woman. The big beast flattened his ears back, tensed and lowered his whole body, like an aircraft carrier jet pilot bringing his engines up to full power just before the catapult flings him down the deck.

Darlene only had the chance to run four or five metres. That was because she ran slap bang into Brand. He had darted between a Discovery and the front bullbar of his Land Rover Defender game viewer. Brand feared for a moment Darlene might knock him over, but he caught her, grabbed her forearm and pulled her behind him.

Pretty Boy launched, and Brand felt that in all of his twenty-five years of being a safari guide he had never come so close to losing control of one or more of his bodily functions. He had seen lion charges and kills plenty of times over the years – enough to know he never wanted to see a maned missile aimed at him, on foot.

The urge to flee was as strong in Brand as it was in any other creature being preyed upon in the bush. His mind, however, told him he could not run from Pretty Boy because if he did then he, or most likely Darlene, would be dead within seconds. Also, the lion would be killed if it took out a human.

Brand fought the urge to run and raised his arms high above his head and roared back at Pretty Boy as the lion charged him with the speed of a rocket-propelled grenade. As he had on a few other occasions in his life, Brand thought he was dead; never this scared, but dead, for sure.

Just as the Golf had slid to a crazy halt, so, too, did Pretty Boy. The lion stopped no more than a metre from the couple, and when he roared Brand felt the sound waves shake him like a spindly sapling in a gale. He felt Pretty Boy's hot breath wash over him. Darlene screamed as she clung to Brand's back, and he felt her face burrow into the weave of his khaki bush shirt. Around him he was dimly aware of voices, and the blinking of camera flashes.

As he waited to die Brand had the sudden thought that if Pretty Boy killed them now then he and Darlene could at least go to their deaths knowing their last moments would go viral, and if someone in the queue had the presence of mind to turn on their video camera then they would be enshrined forever as YouTube's most viewed and stupidest victims.

Pretty Boy roared again and Brand called back until he was hoarse, though he knew he could not compete with the king, the top of the food chain.

'Go on, get!' Brand croaked. Then, because Pretty Boy was a South African lion, he added: '*Voetsek*.'

Pretty Boy suddenly seemed to notice the crowds of people and the camera flashes. He shook his head and trotted away, across the grass and into the bush behind the statue of Paul Kruger's head.

A Land Rover roared up and stopped beside Brand. Bryce Duffy was grinning. 'Gutsy move, Hudson. You OK, *bru*, or should I get you a spare pair of shorts?'

Brand exhaled. 'A bottle of bourbon and a pacemaker wouldn't go astray.'

*

Like many old soldiers, Brand was an easy sleeper, but a light one. He had taught himself to grab some shut-eye whenever the opportunity presented itself, whether in pouring rain or the heat of the African day. By the same token, the smallest of noises would bring him alert instantly, sometimes searching for the rifle he no longer carried, all his senses pre-programmed to cry out 'danger'.

At the sound of the gentle, hesitant knock on his door his eyes were open. He got up, dressed only in boxer shorts, and padded over to it.

'Hudson,' a woman's voice whispered.

Brand coughed. He had tried to give up smoking many times over the years, and had been free of tobacco for four weeks, but one of the camp's guests, another of his erstwhile countrymen, from Virginia, had produced a cigar after dinner. Brand hadn't been able to say no. Alcohol, women and tobacco had always been his weaknesses.

'Can I come in?' said the voice, a little louder now in case he was still sleeping.

For a moment Brand considered feigning slumber. That would have been the right thing to do, the professional course of action, but Darlene had taken a foolish risk coming to him in the dark alone.

He opened the door. 'You shouldn't have walked here without a security guard. You *know* how dangerous this country can be.'

Darlene was an animal nut and Brand's job that day had been to take her into the Kruger Park for a five-hour game drive, followed by a transfer into the neighbouring Sabi Sand Game Reserve, to a luxury lodge called Leopard Hills. She'd wanted to maximise her time seeing Africa's wild animals.

It had taken them an hour, though, over breakfast at the Skukuza Golf Club, to recover from the meeting with Pretty Boy on the bridge. After that Darlene had moved from her spot in the first tier of seating behind Brand to the front passenger seat beside him for the rest of their game drive. They'd laughed, eventually, about the lion, and he'd shown her more, as well as buffalo, rhino, zebra, giraffe and a variety of antelope before they'd left the park and driven into the private reserve.

Brand had lunched with Darlene at Leopard Hills. The lodge was set in a pile of granite *koppies* overlooking a waterhole, where a giant bull elephant had drunk while they ate on the viewing deck under a market umbrella. He'd then accompanied her on the afternoon and evening game drive in a Leopard Hills Land Rover. Ordinarily he might have skipped the drive, preferring to let the lodge's guide take the reins, but he was feeling a connection to Darlene. Perhaps it was shared adversity, the thrill of surviving a near-fatal moment, he thought; or perhaps it was her perfume and her legs.

At dinner they'd put away a four-course gourmet meal and too much beer, wine and Amarula liqueur, which should have rendered them both unconscious by this late hour. But Brand knew that surviving danger did strange things to the human body, especially the libido. It gave men and women strength and stamina beyond their normal capabilities and, when members of the opposite sex were in close proximity it brought on a powerful urge to procreate, or at least go through the motions.

'I'm too scared to sleep alone,' Darlene said.

She had lingered at the entrance to her own suite after dinner, standing in the dark while the lodge's security guard waited patiently for them to say goodnight and scanned the bush around them with a torch in search of night-time predators and buffalo. Darlene had thanked Brand, again, for rescuing her that morning, and turned in. In truth, Brand knew the credit for their survival lay with Pretty Boy Mapogo. The lion could have killed him, or her, or both of them before any firearm could have been located in the gate office or the glove compartment of some tourist's Audi to stop him. Pretty Boy had charged and Brand had stood him down, but Pretty Boy had made the call that it wasn't worth his while killing the defenceless humans.

Brand believed the lions in the Kruger Park and elsewhere in Africa were taught, probably by their mothers, what they could and couldn't eat. Poor Mozambican illegal immigrants walking across the park in search of a new life in South Africa: yes. Rich white foreign tourists and heavily armed game rangers: no. Pretty Boy had let them live, but now that Darlene had slipped back to his room, he wasn't going to give the lion all the credit.

'Come here,' Brand said, his voice rough from the cigar. He fancied he saw her shiver a little in the moonlight, despite the night's heat. She had changed into shorts and a T-shirt. Brand knew he should call the security guard and have the man walk her back to her suite, but instead he led her inside. His curtains were open and beyond the balcony he could see a sky studded with stars.

The king-size bed was encased in starched white cotton of a high thread count whose cool crispness contrasted nicely with the scarred skin of his back and the warm softness of Darlene's breasts as she pulled off her T-shirt and snuggled up to him.

'You saved my life,' she whispered in Brand's ear as he enfolded her in his arms.

'It was the lion,' Brand confided to Darlene in between deep, sensuous kisses. 'He did the smart thing and overcame his initial urge to kill us.'

'I have urges too,' she said into the side of his neck as he felt her hand move down between them.

Darlene's body was lean and angular, her muscles firm. Her body felt sculpted, the artist some part-time surfer or ex-Marine personal trainer cashing in on the housewives and divorcees of Orange County. There was a hardness to her. Brand recalled that she was an executive in an IT company of some sort. He was sure she went about her business with the same single-mindedness and methodical efficiency as she was now using in going after him.

Her hands were on him, then her mouth and, wanting to prolong the experience, Brand brought her face back to his and kissed her deeply as he opened her with his calloused fingers. In the moonlight he could see her eyes, and the tear that formed at the corner. Her sexual aggression was a mask; she was still shaking inside. He kissed the teardrop away. 'You're safe, now.'

'It's not the lion,' she whispered, and turned her head on the pillow. Brand stopped touching her, hovering above her on one elbow.

'Am I your first, since the divorce?'

Darlene nodded. 'I've never been with any man other than my husband in all my life.' A new tear formed and rolled down her cheek.

Brand took her chin between his thumb and forefinger and turned her pretty face to him. 'You're beautiful, Darlene, and he was a fool to lose you.'

She started to speak, but Brand let go of her chin and put a finger to her lips. He felt the taut muscles of her thighs ease as he moved his other hand down her body. It would have been easier for Brand if hers was just another case of khaki fever, but there were other issues at stake here and he did not want to hurt her.

What would it have been like, he wondered, as he kissed her again, to have been with just one woman? The African fish eagle mated for life, as did the dainty little steenbok, so the concept was not without precedent in his world in the African bushveld.

'Please,' she said, and that was all he needed to hear.

2

'My name is Linley Brown and I'm a drug addict,' I said to the group.

'Hi Linley,' came the ragged reply, which echoed slightly in the empty church near Sandton City, Johannesburg's shopping mecca. The eight others were mixed in every sense of the word; there were men, women, blacks, whites, an Indian and a coloured. The demographic ranged from an eighteen-year-old boy who had sold his body to pay for his habit to a well-dressed matronly Afrikaner housewife. We were the Rainbow Nation of substance abusers, and our poisons – coke, heroin, prescription painkillers (my drug of choice), tik and crack – mirrored our rich cultural diversity.

I saw my eyes in theirs: sometimes glazed, sometimes fidgeting from side to side, pupils dilated, others like pinpoints. I saw the hopelessness and the belief, probably wrong, that this time they would make it; this time they would get clean. I checked my watch. This was the lunchtime 'express' meeting, giving those of us with jobs time to get back to work and the shopaholics a chance to feed their other addiction after cleansing themselves, for an hour, at least.

'It's been sixty-three days since I took my last painkiller,' I said. I saw the rentboy roll his eyes, as if a pill-popping white woman in her early thirties didn't have the right to be here among the hard-core users, but everyone else smiled or nodded or murmured an encouraging word or two.

'Do you want to tell us how you've progressed?' asked Mark, the convenor. He was a good-looking guy, late twenties, and a reformed cocaine addict. He had nice eyes, and I could tell by looking at them that he had succeeded. The pupils were normal, the whites clear, but there was a soft sadness to him, as if he would carry forever the burden of the sins he had committed to feed his addiction, even if he was now free of his demons and helping others to exorcise theirs.

'OK, I think. I still have nightmares about the car crash that killed my friend, in Zimbabwe, but like I said last time, in a funny way that's what forced me to come here, and to take control of my life.'

'I know it's hard for you, but tell us a bit more about that day,' Mark said.

I nodded and took a deep breath. 'I was stoned at the time the car burned. We were in the hills between the Dete Crossing turnoff and Binga, heading to Lake Kariba to catch a houseboat.'

I sniffed and looked around the group. The rentboy was inspecting his fingernails, but most of the others were leaning forward on their chairs, perhaps grateful to hear a tale as sad, and possibly sadder, than their own. 'My best friend, Kate, was driving my car; we were taking it in turns. We were on a bridge and a warthog came from the other side. Kate swerved to miss it and lost control and we went over the edge, through a section where the guardrail was missing. My car was ancient, from the 1950s. It had been my grandmother's and it didn't have seatbelts. I was in the back getting us drinks from the cooler box when we went off the bridge. Kate was knocked out and trapped behind the steering wheel.' I drew a breath and screwed my eyes shut, but it was no good. 'We were carrying a plastic container of petrol in the boot, which you're not supposed to, but there were fuel shortages. There was a fire. I got out, went to her side to try and free her. There was nothing I could do for her, but . . .' I opened my eyes and felt the tears flow down my cheeks.

'Go on,' said Mark. His eyes were searching mine, to see if I was under the influence of something. My lapse in concentration as I experienced yet another flashback to the burning car had no doubt set off some alarm bells.

'The thing is, I can still see her body behind the wheel of the car. I can still smell her burning.' I looked down at my nails to focus my thoughts, not wanting to hold those dark eyes any more. I'd had the French tips done that morning, as I had a job to go to straight after the narcotics anonymous meeting. The varnish was flawless and my shoes were new, pinching slightly, but gorgeous. I smoothed the silk of my dress, which cost more than that bitchy little rentboy could make in a year.

'I have the need for the drugs, the craving, always. I wonder if it will ever go away.' I looked to Mark and around the circle of others on their hard-backed chairs in the musty-smelling place of worship and was not encouraged. The matron looked at the floor and the rentboy at the ceiling. This was not America; there were no high fives or 'praise-the-lord's or 'you can do it, girl's. This was the new South Africa, Mandela's tarnished dream personified in we nine, plus Mark, as we faced one new problem one day at a time. I didn't want to be in South Africa, I wanted to be home in my native Zimbabwe, but there was no money north of the border. Like three million other Zimbabweans I had headed south to *eGoli*, Johannesburg, the city of gold. This was where the money and the work was, and too many people in the dwindling white community in my home country knew me for me to be able to stay there and work among them.

'As well as thinking about the car crash I've also been going over, in my mind, some of the things my addiction caused me to do, or at least things that happened when I was stoned.' This time, when

I looked at him, the rentboy's eyes were downcast. I felt sorry for him then. I had done the same as him, though not on the street. I had done disgusting things for drugs, things I would never have imagined myself doing, and perhaps our lives, our backgrounds, weren't that dissimilar in other ways. When he looked up I gave him a little smile; if he wouldn't support me then at least I would try and be supportive of him. He nodded in return. 'I hate myself for some of the things I did. I want to erase that part of my life, but I know I'll never be able to.' I looked at Mark. 'Perhaps there is something I can do; some sort of penance that would atone for my sins?'

'I'm not a priest, and not even overly religious, though I do thank the church and the local minister for letting us use this place for our meetings. I can't tell you to go and say ten Hail Marys to ease your conscience, Linley, but you do have to look forward. That's something I can tell you from experience. You've made the decision to change your life and to move on. You need to define yourself by your future life and the choices you make from now on, not by your past.'

I nodded. It was easy for him to say; Mark was a merchant banker whose employer had taken him back once he had got himself clean. He wore an expensive suit and I knew he drove the latest model Audi. My clothes were a disguise, not a reflection of my way of life or my bank balance. In fact, I had nothing, not even the insurance payout, which the brokers back in England were taking their sweet time processing. When the money came through I would leave South Africa for somewhere else on the continent – I fancied Kenya because I'd never been there. I would lead a good, clean, honest life, free of all my demons, both chemical and human.

There was nothing else I could add. I looked at the diamond-encrusted Cartier watch I was wearing and my silence cued Mark to ask if anyone else wanted to contribute to the meeting.

At the end, as we all rushed back to our day jobs, someone came up behind me and touched my arm. I spun around. It was the latte-skinned boy who probably still sold himself. He took his fingers off me. 'Sorry. I just wanted to say . . . well, I mean, like, I think I know what you were talking about in there.'

'It doesn't matter whether we take pills or tik or stick a needle in our veins, we're all in there for the same reason,' I said. He looked down again. It was my turn to touch him, on the arm, my finger connecting with his hard bicep. He kept himself in shape and I hoped he wouldn't succumb to his habit again and risk the damage to his physical and mental health that came with it. 'We can *do* it, right?'

Johnny looked up at me and I saw his eyes start to glisten. I always looked at people's eyes before any other part of them. I could tell, now, if a person was honest or dishonest straight away, but I'd had to learn this the hard way. '*Ja*, Linley. We can. And whatever you did,' he forced a smile, 'it's not nearly as disgusting as some of the things I've had to do.'

It was good he could laugh about his past, which might also still be his present. I smiled for his benefit, but there was too much darkness in what I had done and what had been done to me for me to ever make it the subject of a joke. I resolved not to be judgemental of him or any of the others in the group again. 'You'll be fine. We'll all be fine.'

But I didn't really believe that.

*

In the undercover car park at Sandton City I pushed the alarm thingy on the key ring and the lights on the new Mercedes convertible flashed and the door locks clicked. I looked behind me to make sure no one was following me, and eased myself into the low-slung status symbol.

The forward edge of the leather seat was cool against the skin behind my knees, below the hem of my dress. I liked the feeling, but not the smell; it brought back too many bad memories. This wasn't my car; I couldn't afford something like this. It was a loaner from

Lungile's brother. I plugged my iPhone into the cord and dialled Lungile's number.

As I reversed out of the car park spot and drove out onto the street she answered and I used the hands-free. '*Howzit.*'

'Hi, girlfriend,' Lungile said.

I heard traffic in the background. 'You're finished at the salon.'

'Yes, and I look a-*may*-zing, if I do say so myself.'

I envied Lungile her self-confidence, even if was sometimes just for show, or for my benefit. She had her own troubles, mostly her seriously ill mother's medical bills. 'I've finished my meeting; I'll pick you up outside the hairdressers in about ten minutes. OK?'

'*Yebo.*' Lungile hung up.

I smiled, properly, for the first time that day. Lungile was amazing and I loved her. By the time I started school in 1986, Zimbabwe had been independent and black-ruled for six years. The president, Robert Mugabe, had been doing terrible things to the Matabele people in his first few years of office, wiping his political opposition from the face of the earth, but I was too young to know about any of that.

Unlike my parents I went to school with black kids all my life. I remembered seeing Lungile for the first time when I was packed off to high school to board. My father was against me boarding, but my mother put her foot down, for the first and probably only time in her life. Lungile had the most amazing, perfect afro I had ever seen, and when the teacher asked us all what we wanted to do when we finished school in six years' time, Lungile said she was going to run for parliament and eventually become president. Most of the class laughed. I was a shy, scared kid with limited horizons – I said I liked the idea of working in a bank, like my mother had before she met my father – but Lungile just smiled at her mockers as if to say, just you wait and see.

But my best white friend and I both liked her and by the end of first term Linley Brown, Kate Munns and Lungile Phumla were known as the terrible triplets.

I stopped at a robot, as the locals called traffic lights in South Africa, and glanced into the rear-view mirror, not to look for potential car hijackers but to check my makeup. We were going to a big job, Lungile and I, and both of us were dressed and made up to impress. Image was everything in this city of status and designer must-haves. My throat suddenly felt thick as I saw the younger me, minus the encroaching crow's-feet, and remembered the three of us laughing and playing pranks on the intractable girls of both colours who could not see beyond the divisions of the past to a new, fun, funky future in Africa. The only time I'd ever truly been happy in my life, except for the brief time I'd spent with my one serious boyfriend, George, was at boarding school. I blinked. Damn it, I did *not* need tears now. Lungile *should* have been in politics – our country needed someone smart and full of love, like her – and then she would not have been forced into doing this kind of job. But there was no work for her in Zimbabwe and nothing in South Africa, other than what we were about to do, that would pay for her mother's chemotherapy.

I looked away from the mirror, out at the traffic. A guy in a *bakkie* tried to catch my eye, but I ignored him and floored the accelerator, trying to outdistance my memories. But they were there, behind me, always.

'Oh, Kate, I do miss you,' I said aloud.

*

Given the right circumstances Lungile could have been a supermodel if the whole president of Zimbabwe thing didn't work out. She was tall, slim and fine-boned, and the four-inch patent leather red heels she wore made her tower above the two men who walked past her and turned their heads for a second glance. Her hair was straightened today, lacquered into perfectly sculpted bangs. Her lips shone with fresh gloss; she was the picture of a well-to-do black diamond trophy wife, right down to the impressive rock on her left-hand ring finger.

I stopped the Merc and she folded herself into the sports car. Outrageous shoes aside – for these were her trademark – Lungile was dressed in a demure grey skirt, matching business jacket and white blouse. She did, in fact, look amazing. '*Howzit, sisi?*'

'*Lekker*,' I said, but felt less than great. The meeting had shaken me, as it always did, and I wondered if I could stay away from the pills once I had some more cash in my purse. I couldn't truly make a clean start with the money I made from the day-to-day work Lungile and I did so well together; I needed the insurance payout to set myself up again and I'd been surprised to learn it took months, not weeks as I had hoped, for a claim to be processed and paid. I smiled for Lungile's benefit, but I also knew that once I had a big enough stake I would have to say goodbye to my friend. We loved each other, as long-term friends do, but I was smart enough to know that if we stayed in close contact it would only be a matter of time before Lungile's high-living, partying lifestyle led me back to my recent excesses. She needed to end this gig as well, and I hoped me disappearing might force her to try her hand at something better.

Rosebank was one of Johannesburg's old-money suburbs. Here the wealthy lived in fortified mansions, eschewing the relative safety of a sprawling gated *kompleks* in favour of high walls topped with electric fences, as well as big dogs, and armed response security. A sign on the street warned me that men with guns were but a call away.

'Here it is, number twenty-two,' I said. Lungile was quiet now. When we worked she was the consummate professional, not the brash party girl she was the rest of the time.

She checked her watch. 'It's one thirty; the real estate agent should have packed up and left half an hour ago.' Lungile reached into the cramped back seat of the car and grabbed the red cushion decorated with a vinyl cut-out of a rhinoceros I had bought at Mr Price that morning. She undid the single button of her jacket and then her blouse, placed the cushion against her belly, then buttoned up again.

I indicated left and drove up the short drive to the electric gate. Its bars ended in sharp spikes at the top and these were crowned with wires promising several thousand volts of electricity. A Rhodesian ridgeback ran up to the bars and started barking.

Fixed to the wall beside the gate was a Pam Golding real estate 'FOR SALE' sign, with professional pictures hinting at the wonders that lay beyond the fortress walls. In the lower right corner was a mug shot of the agent selling the property. His name was Frikkie. I dialled the mobile phone number under his name and he answered. It sounded like he was in his car, on hands-free.

Like most whites from Zimbabwe I had friends and relatives living in Australia and I'd visited the country a couple of times. I fancied I could do quite a good imitation of a South African living among the diaspora down under. 'Frikkie, *howzit*, I'm outside number twenty-two, at Rosebank. I'm over here on holiday from Australia and I'm really interested in buying in this neighbourhood. My husband and I have had enough of Australia – it's too boring and over-regulated.'

'*Ag*, no, but I'm sorry,' Frikkie said, 'I'm on my way to another house showing. The open house for number twenty-two finished at one o'clock. Can we maybe make a plan for me to meet you there tomorrow?'

I already knew Frikkie's schedule – it was easy to deduce from the advertised listings on the property company's website – and he was busy for the next three hours at least. 'Sorry, but I've got to fly back to Sydney this evening on the six o'clock flight. I was just out shopping with a friend of mine and we passed this place on the way. From the pictures it looks ideal. My husband told me not to leave South Africa without making an offer on something and, well, I'm worried I'll be in trouble now, Frikkie.'

There was a pause as he deliberated. The South African property market was flat and there was nothing like the sound of a foreign accent and the promise of overseas cash to get a real estate agent's pulse pumping. 'I'll have to call the owner. Maybe the maid can let you in if she agrees.'

'That would be so good of you, Frikkie.' I gave him my mobile number and hung up. While I waited I reached out the car window and pushed the button on an intercom mounted on a pole.

'Hello?' said a voice from inside the house.

'Is the madam home?' I asked into the intercom, knowing full well she was not.

'Ah, no. She is not back until five.'

'We want to come inside and look at the house.'

'Ah, no, it is not possible,' said the maid, her voice distorted by the tinny speaker.

My phone rang and Lungile winked at me. '*Howzit*, Frikkie,' I said, recognising the number.

'Fine, and you? OK, the owner, Mrs Forsyth, says you can go inside and have a look. She's calling the maid now.'

I thanked him and promised I would call him back to let him know what I thought of the place.

A woman in a brightly printed pinafore emerged from the house and walked down the long curving driveway. Her accent had sounded Zimbabwean and she looked like a Shona; it wouldn't be unusual for Mrs Forsyth's maid to be from the same bankrupt country as Lungile and me. We all did what we could to survive. The woman went to the ridgeback and grabbed it by the collar, silencing it, then pushed a remote and the spike-topped gate rolled open. I drove up the driveway and we got out of the car while the maid closed the gate. My heart changed gear; this was almost as addictive as the pills.

'Hello, how are you, my name is Patience,' said the maid, who was sharp-eyed and stick insect-thin. 'The madam says I am to show you around.'

'*Kanjane*, sister,' Lungile said to the woman, then continued on in Shona. Lungile was Ndebele, but had learned the politically dominant tribe's language far better than I had at school.

The maid's face softened a little and she smiled as she replied in the same language. Like me, Lungile had immediately recognised the woman's accented but precise English. It helped ease the situation a little, for all of us.

Patience led us into the house and the ridgeback, sensing all was OK, nuzzled me as I walked. I held out my hand and let him sniff me, then patted his head. 'Hello, beautiful.' He panted with pleasure as I stroked him.

The home was even nicer than the pictures on the sale board had indicated. Patience led us through a grand reception area with a marble floor out to a central courtyard dominated by a swimming pool. All of the bedrooms faced onto the pool. The furniture was typical Joburg – big and over the top. I would have gone for something more minimalist. It was interesting, visiting so many other people's homes, learning about their tastes and their secrets.

I walked around the lounge and let Patience show us the home cinema room. Mostly the home looked like it had been decorated and furnished by a professional designer; there was little in the way of family photographs or the clutter that had always been a part of my family home, growing up in Bulawayo. Behind a bar, though, I saw something that made me stop. It was a plaque bearing the Maltese Cross badge of the Rhodesia Regiment, which was manned by national service soldiers during the Bush War. My father had served in the regiment. Lungile's father had been a guerrilla leader; such were the ironies of life in our country. I mused silently about how very different my life would have been if Lungile's father had killed mine.

'Is the madam from Zimbabwe?'

'Yes,' said Patience.

'And the boss?'

'Ah, he is dead, of the lung cancer. Just last month.'

Lungile and I exchanged glances, then she put her hand to her mouth. 'Oh my God, sorry,' she mumbled. 'I think I'm going to be sick.'

Patience's eyes widened. I patted my stomach and pointed to Lungile's. 'It's the pregnancy.'

'Ah, shame,' said Patience.

'Toilet,' gargled Lungile.

The maid nodded and led her briskly down the corridor.

'I'll just look around a bit,' I said, but Lungile was running now, and Patience was trying to overtake her and give her directions to the bathroom in Shona.

I found the master bedroom and went to work. The one bedside table's drawers were empty so I went to the other. In the top drawer was an expensive man's watch, which I dropped into my shoulder bag, along with a last-year's model BlackBerry, which had probably been replaced by a newer model when Mrs Forsyth's contract had come up for renewal. Either that or, like the watch, it was her late husband's.

I went to the walk-in closet and started going through the drawers there. In the second was her jewellery box. I tipped the contents into the bag. On the opposite side were the late Mr Forsyth's clothes. She hadn't got around to donating them, or perhaps she couldn't bear to part with them. I wondered if he had served with my father – it was a big unit, but it was possible – and not for the first time in recent memory I hated myself.

Perhaps the Forsyths had left Zimbabwe at independence, in 1980, or even earlier, for they had obviously done very well for themselves here in Johannesburg. There were no pictures of children or grandchildren, so I imagined they were childless. I forced myself to stop thinking about them, and what the impact of what I was doing would be on someone recently widowed.

I heard a toilet flush, and then the sound of Lungile and Patience chatting.

Next to the master bedroom was a study with a charger cord snaking across the glass-topped desk, but no laptop. I opened the top drawer of the desk and found the new model MacBook, which joined the other loot in my bag.

'*Tatenda*,' Lungile said to Patience, thanking her as I joined them in the lounge room.

'I think I've seen enough,' I said. Lungile nodded and thanked Patience again, as did I. I said goodbye to the dog, ruffling him under his chin. 'Look after your mom tonight,' I whispered to him.

'I will open the gate from in here,' Patience said.

Lungile and I walked out, keeping our pace measured but brisk as we went to the Merc and climbed in. I started the car, and as we drove towards the gate it began to roll open. Lungile fished into my shoulder bag and grabbed a handful of treasure. The diamond stud earrings, gold necklaces and other clearly valuable bits and pieces from the jewellery box glittered in her hands.

'Check,' she said, holding it up.

I eased my foot off the accelerator as she let all of the jewellery slither back into the bag, save for one gorgeous piece set with the biggest rocks I had seen in a long time. 'Wedding ring,' I said. I felt nauseous, the shame bubbling up inside me and fighting to come out. I swallowed.

Lungile nodded.

'Shit. She probably leaves it at home when she goes out shopping because of bloody crime.'

'Ironic.' Lungile laughed, but I hadn't meant it as a joke. I was almost at the gate when it stopped moving, halfway, then changed direction and began closing. Lungile looked back over her shoulder. 'She must be onto us!'

'Fuck!' I accelerated.

Lungile was looking out the back window. 'We're not going to make it. The maid's probably calling the armed response guys now!'

The panic rose up inside me, but I could not stop the car. We would be trapped. I had a pistol in the bottom of my bag, a puny little .32. It was for self-defence, ironically, against carjackers and other criminals. I had never, and repeatedly promised Lungile and myself that I would never, use a gun in the commission of one of our crimes. I hated myself enough for what I was doing, and I would rather be arrested than harm one of my targets or a policeman.

'Give me the gun,' Lungile said.

'No.' I snatched the bag from between us and put it under my legs.

I braced myself for the coming impact. The nose of the Mercedes made it through, but the gate closed on my side of the car. Metal on metal made a maddening screech as the whole right side of the sports car fought against the closing barrier. I revved the accelerator hard, fighting for our escape, and we squealed through, suddenly released like a champagne cork. I slammed on the brakes.

Lungile was wide-eyed. 'What are you doing?'

'Give me the wedding ring.'

She closed her fist around it and glared at me. But either she softened or she realised we were not leaving until she gave it to me, because she opened her fingers and I plucked it from her palm.

I could see through the mangled gate Patience was now running down the front steps of the mansion to check on our progress, mobile phone clamped to her ear as she yelled into it. There was a mailbox slot in the wall next to the intercom. I walked to it and popped the wedding ring through the slot then turned and ran back to the car.

I put my seatbelt on and stood on the accelerator, sliding the rear of the car out into a right-hand turn. I zoomed up the quiet, leafy street, the engine howling as the automatic gearbox screamed and propelled us up to one hundred and thirty. When I took the next right I eased off a bit. I didn't want to draw unnecessary attention to us, but I knew the bare metal scrape marks down the side of the car would be an instant giveaway once Patience or the Forsyths' security company put the word out.

'Taxi,' Lungile said.

Ahead of us a minibus taxi had pulled over to pick up a gardener in green overalls, his work finished in some rich family's home. I passed it then pulled over and we both got out. The taxi started moving again and Lungile stepped out onto the road and flagged it down.

I grabbed the bag of loot and went to her side. The driver stared at us incredulously; a black diamond and a *kugel* hailing him was probably a first. He leaned out of his window, looking Lungile over from head to toe. 'Where to, sister?'

'Anywhere but here,' she said.

He looked at the banged-up car and grinned. 'Climb aboard the love bus.'

Lungile and I squeezed our way in among the dozen domestic staff and the driver took off. I glanced back and saw flashing lights as a security company car rounded the bend behind us. As I continued to crane my neck I saw them slow and stop beside the Merc.

Lungile punched me on the shoulder. 'Man, that was close.' She laughed.

'Too close.'

Hip-hop thumped from speakers in the roof above us, the beat not keeping pace with my heart.

3

Hudson Brand woke an hour before dawn, as he always did. As a safari guide his working day typically began at first light, or just before. This was the time of day when the predators – lion, leopard, hyena and so forth – were most likely to be on the move, finishing their night's hunting or making use of the cool hours of light to have one more go at killing something.

Before the first tourists rose, however, there was work to be done. In some camps he had guests to wake, doubling as a waiter cum personal valet and delivering tea or coffee prepared by the kitchen hands. More than once he had crept out of a guest's tent or chalet to quickly shower and don a fresh uniform before starting his pre-dawn chores.

But Darlene had come to his room, so he carefully lifted a spray-tanned arm off his chest and slid across the bed until his feet touched the polished cement floor. 'Darlene, wake up. You need to get ready for your morning drive.'

She groaned.

Hudson grinned and shook her. 'Come on, now, sleepyhead. I'm going to grab a shower.'

He walked through the en-suite bathroom, savouring the warmth of the underfloor heating on his bare feet, then through a sliding door to the outdoor shower enclosure on the verandah. The outdoor shower was Africa's gift to the civilised world, he thought, a successful marriage of first world plumbing and the African sky, which, day or night, was always a treat to behold. Hot water from a shower head the size of a dinner plate encased and protected him from the pre-dawn chill and, as always, it was a mission for him to turn off the tap and return to the cool of the morning. Brand towelled himself dry, then swore silently as he heard the call of a woodland kingfisher.

It was still months before the first of these beautiful, bright blue and white birds were due to return to this part of Africa. They spent the winter in Kenya then heralded the start of summer when they arrived in Kruger, but this one was calling from inside.

'Phone,' Darlene mumbled as he walked back in.

He picked up his mobile from the bedside table and snuffed out the bird ringtone by pressing the green answer button. 'Hudson Brand.'

There was a delay on the line, and the voice, when it came, was faint, but he recognised the English accent as soon as the caller started to speak. 'Hudson, hi, it's Dani.'

Brand held the phone in the crook of his shoulder as he pulled on his green shorts and zipped them up. Darlene rolled over and checked the time on her phone as he padded past her and back out onto the verandah. A hyena whooped somewhere on the tree-studded plain below.

'What was that?' Daniela Russo asked, before he'd even had a chance to reply.

'Hyena. It's early, Dani, as in before dawn.'

'Yes, I know. It's even earlier here, still dark, in fact. I wanted to catch you in case you were going out on a game drive.'

She knew Brand had gone back to guiding, in South Africa, after his last case. 'Good guess. I've got to go, Dani. Have a nice –'

'Stop that. Listen to me.' Dani was a lawyer of Italian and British descent, with the body of a dancer and the tone of a school principal.

Brand told himself he didn't need Dani, nor what she was no doubt going to propose. He was about to set off on four days in the African bush with a group of tourists that included a particularly fetching divorcee who made love like a snarling lioness on heat. From Leopard Hills he was taking her to a new camp set up by an Afrikaner friend of his, Gert Pols, in the Timbavati Game Reserve to the north. Gert was running a fly camp, a mobile tented affair that could be set up anywhere on his concession, and the plan was that the guests would go out on walks in the bush every day.

'I'm still here,' he said to Dani, 'but I really do have to go in a minute.'

'I've got another case for you, in Zimbabwe.'

'I'm not interested.' In the course of the last investigation Brand had done for Dani he had stepped on some important toes and found himself incarcerated in Harare's Chikurubi Prison for a week – not a pleasant place to be. He was in the bush, about to go on a walk, and he didn't want to be anywhere else, least of all Zimbabwe. Brand heard a noise behind him and turned to see Darlene, her hair tousled, standing at the mosquito mesh door with a white sheet wrapped around her like a Roman goddess ready for round two in the local orgy.

'Come back to bed, Hudson, it's still dark.'

'What was that?' Dani asked down the line.

'A local bird,' Brand said.

'I need you,' Dani said.

Normally those three words worked like a charm on him, but not this time. 'No.' If the walking safari went well, he wanted to do more work for Gert. He preferred tracking animals to people any day and wanted to make the most of the rest of the dry season, the best time for walking, before the rains came.

'I'll pay double your normal fee.'

His mouth was dry and his voice ragged from the cigar, which had seemed like such a good idea at the time. Dani worked for insurance companies, so if she was doubling his fee she had to be taking a loss or making next to nothing. She managed a stable of insurance scam investigators and he was her dark horse in Africa. In spite of himself, he was curious. 'Why double?'

'It's not just an insurance company this time. There are also family members here in the UK who want the death investigated,' she explained.

'Ah, double dipping,' Brand said. That made sense. Dani had not made the serious money she had by being overly generous to her employees.

There was a pause on the other end of the line, thousands of kilometres away. All he had done was accuse a lawyer of being mercenary; he knew she wasn't the pouting kind. Something else was in play here, he thought. 'It happens to be a friend of mine who's involved; that's the family connection.'

Brand checked his wristwatch. It was ten after five. He'd found Dani's call intriguing, but the wild was calling. He looked along the verandah at the sound of the sliding door. Darlene had walked over to the outdoor shower, not bothering with a towel or a robe. She winked at him as she turned on the water.

'No, sorry, Dani; like I said, I'm busy.' Darlene was facing him, soaping her breasts.

'Triple.'

Brand had made up his mind, rightly or wrongly, and he was not the sort of man who changed it on a whim. Also, he didn't like Dani thinking he could be bought. He could, of course, and what she was offering was about five times what he would likely make in the next two weeks, even if the tips were good. 'Goodbye, Dani.'

'Please, Hudson. For me.'

Dani had once come to South Africa to assure herself and the insurance company she represented that he was on the up, and not likely to fleece her clients like so many of their policyholders were doing. He'd taken her on safari, across the border into Zimbabwe, to Mana Pools in the Lower Zambezi Valley, one of his favourite places. As forthright as Dani was it turned out she was scared of insects – not the lions that growled and the hyenas that prowled their campsite at night – and therefore ended up spending several evenings in Brand's dome tent for protection. It was a holiday romance, though; she'd told him there was no way she could live in Africa. For his part, Brand had been to London once and had no desire to visit again.

Brand sighed. Darlene turned off the shower and pouted. She walked back inside and then turned to wink at him over her shoulder as she pulled on a purple thong and then green cargo shorts. Dani had cost him enough time this morning. His mind was made up. '*Fambai zvakanaka*,' he said to Dani. He had taught her the farewell before she left Zimbabwe. It meant, in Shona, go in peace. He ended the call.

'I'd better be moving along,' Darlene said, pulling on her T-shirt as Brand walked back into the suite. 'Don't want to get you in trouble or anything.'

He kissed her. 'It's fine. And thank you.'

Darlene put a hand on his chest and looked up into his eyes. 'No, thank you. For saving me.'

Brand melted, just a little bit. 'Go on, git.' He slapped her playfully on the butt and she grinned and walked to the door. She opened it and looked theatrically from left to right, then waved back at him and headed to her suite.

Brand shaved, then combed his hair and brushed his teeth, regarding his lined self in the mirror as he did. He thought again about Dani's call. The case was unusual, and not just because of the amount of money she was offering. The whole personal connection thing was interesting to him. Brand didn't say no to her offer just because he was busy or because he had landed in prison the last time he'd investigated an insurance fraud claim in Zimbabwe. He liked investigation work for all the wrong reasons – it gave him a thrill of a different kind from the rush he experienced when he faced down a lion or a blustering elephant on a walk. Here in the bush he would be walking with dangerous game, but on the streets of Zimbabwe, or wherever Dani's case would lead him, he would be among humans – creatures that lied and cheated and stole and murdered, mostly for money.

He had hunted men before, in Angola, but he had never hunted animals. Brand had turned his back on war, gladly, for the solace of a peaceful life in the remnant patches of unspoiled Africa, but he missed the thrill of the hunt. He wanted to go in peace, yet he had let Dani lead him back into the business of stalking prey. He didn't like that she could make him do that, or engender in him second thoughts, albeit brief, about a four-day walking safari. He held his own gaze for a couple of seconds, then shook his head. No, he had made the right decision when he refused her offer. He walked out of his suite and surrendered to the incomparable beauty and tranquillity of the African dawn.

*

They saw a leopard on the morning game drive, a young female perched atop a termite mound, keeping watch for her mother, who was out hunting.

Darlene was in awe of the sighting and she clutched Brand's hand tightly as she feasted her eyes on the beguiling cat. As they left the leopard she kissed him on the cheek and the Leopard Hills guide, who had chosen that minute to glance back at them, winked at him. At least she wasn't married, he thought. Gossip moved faster than a bushfire in the Sabi Sand.

After breakfast back at the lodge Brand drove Darlene to their next stop, Gert Pols's camp, Zebra Plains. It was a three-hour drive, out of the Sabi Sand and via the R40 through the sprawling town of Bushbuckridge and then back into the Greater Kruger Park through the Timbavati Game Reserve to the north. They arrived in time for lunch.

Gert's operation was run on a shoestring, to help him build up the capital he needed to market himself and improve his facilities. Darlene had told her travel agent back in the States that she wanted to walk in the African bush, from a tented camp, and Gert's start-up suited her budget and her needs.

Gert, however, was in Cape Town on business, and could not be there to escort the walks Darlene and the other guests in residence would be going on. For that reason he'd asked Brand not only to handle Darlene's transfer, but to accompany his other guide, Patrick de Villiers, as the second rifle on the game walks.

Lunch was served under canvas at Zebra Plains, in an old open-sided army tent, the kind in which Brand had spent many a night in South West Africa and Angola. It was rustic, to the say the least, compared to the air-conditioned luxury of Leopard Hills, but Darlene seemed to be enjoying the change of atmosphere.

Scattered about, as though washed ashore from a nineteenth-century shipwreck, were old steamer trunks, now employed as side tables to deeply upholstered leather lounges. Gert had at least made some effort with the furnishings, to give the place a faux-colonial feel.

The other five guests at Zebra Plains all knew each other. They were two couples, one South African and the other Australian, and a single woman also from the other side of the Indian Ocean. The South Africans, like many Brand had known over the years, had emigrated to Australia. 'But we love the bush so much, and we miss the Kruger terribly,' the wife, Sunelle, said to him from across the table.

'And they give us a Yank to take us around our own country,' the husband, Keith, said, followed by a big laugh to let Brand know he was just joking – partly.

Brand sized up Keith, who he would have picked as a stockbroker even if Gert hadn't already filled him in. His South African accent was almost gone, but he would still fancy himself an expert on wildlife and the bush, Brand guessed. Brand's strategy for dealing with clients who thought he knew nothing because of where he had been born was to draw on his knowledge of trees. From an early age as a safari guide Brand had studied every tree book he could get his hands on, reasoning that trees, after animals, birds, insects and reptiles, were about the last thing on any bush-lover's list of things to know.

The single woman, Sharon, who was older, fuller-figured and blonder than Darlene, waved off Keith's jibe. 'Well, Sunelle did tell me all safari guides were good-lookers, so I've got my value for money already.'

Brand forced a polite smile. He would be friendly and attentive to all the guests and do his best to continue sleeping with Darlene without making it obvious to the rest of the group or showing her undue favouritism. The only person he wasn't sure how to handle, although he knew him well, was the other guide.

Zebra Plains was different from most other lodges in the Timbavati and the Sabi Sand in a couple of aspects. Firstly, it specialised in walking safaris, rather than driving guests around the bush looking for wildlife. It was modelled on successful trails camps run by national parks rangers in the Kruger Park, where guests walked both in the morning and afternoon, from a fixed rustic camp in the bush. The clientele Gert was aiming for were experienced safari-goers who wanted something more than a mad dash from one animal sighting to another.

'*Howzit*, all,' said Patrick de Villiers. Twenty years younger than Brand, with the bow-legged swagger of a bodybuilder, Patrick doffed his cap with one hand, put his right foot up on a vacant chair and rested the butt of his .375 rifle on his knee. 'Right, who's ready to go find some man-eaters?' His left hand, the wrist festooned with copper, elephant-hair and plastic save-the-rhino bracelets, drew a long, fat, brass-encased round from the bandolier on his belt. He worked the bolt on the rifle and proceeded to load the bullet, and four more. As he closed the breech for the last time, he said: 'Let's roll, the Land Rover's waiting.'

Brand dabbed his mouth with a linen serviette. 'I'll just go to the bathroom, Patrick. I'm sure the clients might like a final pit stop as well.'

Patrick gave a snort. '*Ja*, I know how it is for you old-timers. Don't worry, folks, there'll be plenty of stops to answer the call of nature on this walk, I'm sure.'

Brand excused himself from the guests at the table and took his rifle to the bathroom located near the dining platform. He disliked Patrick; the man was a racist and a bully, but he'd had to work with him before. This, however, was the first time he had walked with the man in the bush and already he was worried on a number of counts.

First up, Patrick should have been at lunch with the clients. Brand didn't know whether the younger man had used the midday break to sleep, or if he thought himself above the need for a meal before an afternoon's walking. In any case, Brand believed the guide should have been at the table getting to know his guests and briefing them about the walk ahead.

Secondly, and more concerning, Patrick had made a show of loading his rifle at the table. It was purely for effect, Brand supposed; the simple action of loading rounds into the breech always conveyed a strong message to safari guests that they were heading out into a land where there were many things that could maim or kill them, and it behoved them to listen to the man with the gun. What worried Brand was that Patrick had said the vehicle was waiting, so they would presumably be driving somewhere. When Patrick had started loading his rifle Brand assumed they would be walking out of camp, because a rifle was not normally carried loaded when driving, for safety reasons.

'All right,' Patrick said, drawing himself up to his full height, which was about a foot lower than Brand's, 'we're going to take a short drive and then we'll walk from there. I'll brief you on board the vehicle.'

They followed Patrick off the platform to the front of the lodge, where an open Land Rover was parked. Patrick laid his rifle in a cradle fixed to the dashboard.

'Aren't you going to load your rifle, or have you done it already?' Darlene asked Brand as they allowed the couples to climb aboard first.

Brand turned to her. 'No. I have to hold mine between my knees while we drive. Patrick's is fine, resting in the gun rack.' It was a lie, but he didn't want to alarm Darlene or undermine Patrick in front of her or the other guests. The chances of Patrick's weapon somehow misfiring if it were jolted out of its cradle were negligible, but all the same it was standard practice not to drive around with a loaded weapon sitting in front of you. It was another basic rule that Patrick had either forgotten or ignored. Given Patrick's age, Brand suspected he was guilty of the latter, not the former.

Brand made sure the clients were all settled in the back, then climbed into the front passenger seat next to Patrick. As Patrick drove, at a speed Brand felt was too fast for the road, he began to explain to the guests the format of the day and the rules of the walk. They would be out for about four hours before returning for dinner. Patrick would lead and Brand would walk second, explaining things and pointing out anything of interest. They were to walk in single file, Patrick said, and, most importantly, no one was to run if they encountered dangerous game.

'What is he saying?' Brand heard Sharon ask from the rear of the vehicle. Given the rush of the air and Patrick's tendency to talk while looking straight ahead over the folded-down windscreen, it was no wonder she had missed much of the briefing.

Brand swivelled in his seat and reinforced the rule that under no circumstances should anyone run if they encountered a dangerous animal, even if it charged them. When he turned to face forward again he saw that Patrick was glaring at him. He would, Brand hoped, learn to become a better guide in the future, but in the meantime he didn't want anyone, least of all himself, getting killed because of Patrick's slapdash briefing.

The Zebra Plains property was, Brand thought, a truly beautiful piece of land. With no other vehicles allowed to traverse the area they walked in, it seemed as though they had the whole continent to themselves. The dirt track they bounced along ran through a savannah of golden grass. Herds of zebra and wildebeest, skittish things at the best of times, took flight at the sight and sound of their high-speed progress. Brand wondered why Patrick hadn't parked the vehicle and begun the walk already. The fact was that it was hard to have good game viewing on a walk. Most animals would detect the approach of a human, particularly a group of tourists, stumbling through the bush, and run off long before the guides had a chance to pick them up. Had they already been walking they might have been able to get closer to the grazers that had just fled from Patrick's hard revving of the diesel engine.

Perhaps, Brand thought, he was being unnecessarily critical of Patrick, but on second thoughts he didn't think so. Sharon and Darlene, both newcomers to the continent, seemed over the moon just to see a zebra, and could not know they were in the hands of a rank amateur. Brand heard Sharon curse because she couldn't get her camera out quick enough to photograph the zebra, but if Patrick heard her, he ignored her. He took a left turn and they headed downhill, towards a line of tall trees that Brand knew marked the course of a river.

'We've got a better chance of seeing lion and buffalo in the riverbed. They'll be in the thick stuff as it gives them cover and shade,' he said over his shoulder to the guests.

Brand looked at him. What Patrick had said was essentially correct, and in his peripheral vision he saw the clients in the back nodding enthusiastically. They had hundreds of square kilometres of stunning open country to roam, where they would probably come across giraffe and impala and other relatively benign animals and, perhaps, if the wind was in their favour and the guests not too noisy they might get a sighting of a pride of lions far off before they detected the humans and moved away. But it seemed to Brand that Patrick was intent on arranging an assisted suicide for himself and presiding over the manslaughter of the rest of them. He had to say something.

'Maybe this open country would be a bit easier on the folks,' he said quietly. Brand knew very well that Cape buffalo might be lurking in the riverbed ahead, which was precisely why most game walks tended to cross riverbeds quickly rather than spending any more time than was absolutely necessary *in* them.

'Did you hear that?' Patrick looked back at the guests. 'Hudson thinks you're all too weak or old to walk along the river line. Who wants to see a lion?'

'We do!' they called back in unison.

Patrick glanced at Brand and out of the side of his mouth said, 'I can take you back to camp if you're chicken.'

On the walks Brand had led, in peacetime at least, he avoided danger and did not go into thick bush deliberately with the intention of seeking encounters with the Big Five, save for white rhino which were easy to track, relatively docile and usually favoured open grassland in any case. Perhaps Zebra Plains marketed itself differently, promising guests adrenaline-charged thrills and near-death experiences, but he doubted it. He resolved to call Gert when they got back to camp and alert him to Patrick's behaviour. In the meantime, he rose to Patrick's childish challenge. Whatever Brand did, Patrick seemed intent on putting his clients in harm's way, and Brand now felt some moral obligation to try and make sure they all returned from this afternoon's walk alive. 'No, I'm coming along.'

Patrick stopped the vehicle and, to his credit, quickly reiterated the key parts of his briefing. Brand loaded his rifle. 'Keep up with me, Yank,' Patrick said to Brand as he set off.

Brand thought it odd that Patrick was forging ahead. Patrick, Brand knew, was a freelance guide like himself, but he'd had more to do with Gert's camp than Brand had. Brand had assumed that he would have been out front, tracking, and that Patrick would be in the second position, looking after the guests. That was how he would have arranged it. Brand was the hired hand on this occasion and as such he shouldn't have had a speaking role. But perhaps Patrick guessed, correctly, that if Brand was number one rifle he would have chosen a safer route, and one with less potential to deliver hefty tips. Brand always made a point of telling people on a guided safari walk that he was *not* looking for big game, and explained his reasons why.

Brand slipped into his role as the commentator for this walk. 'We're here to look at the small things as well as the big animals – spider webs, tracks, insects and trees,' he said. 'Your safety is our number one priority so we won't go out of our way to find dangerous game.'

Brand could sense Patrick bridling as the other man moved off, down a sandy bank into the thick bush and towering sycamore figs and fever trees that lined the banks of the largely dry river. Brand said a small prayer and held his rifle across his chest, at the ready.

Patrick, Brand observed, was not unskilled as a tracker or guide. He moved carefully and quietly and tested the wind by allowing a handful of fine sand to run slowly from his closed fist. He led them so that the wind was in their faces and he insisted they keep the talking to a minimum. If he wanted to walk them into an encounter with a surprised and ornery buffalo or a protective lioness and cubs then he was going about it the right way.

Brand called a halt and deliberately allowed his voice to carry as he showed the guests the shell of a leopard tortoise. A hole had been pecked in the hapless creature's back and Brand explained that the ground hornbill, with its long, strong, black beak was one of the few creatures that could crack the tortoise's armour.

'Can we move on, if you're finished with the dead tortoise?' Patrick said, not trying to hide his impatience.

Asshole, Brand thought. Patrick's skilled tracking paid off, though, when he picked up a herd of elephant feeding ahead of them and called the tourists forward without alerting the elephants to their presence. They crouched in the riverbed, in the shade of a towering jackalberry tree, and watched the giant creatures for a while, peaceably munching on foliage around them. They were oblivious to the humans, until the auto-focus beep on Darlene's camera alerted the herd's matriarch. The elephant turned to them, flapped her sail-like ears and shook her head. At her signal, a rumbling from her belly, the herd gathered and moved away from the people, out of the riverbed and deeper into the surrounding bush.

Patrick glared at Darlene. 'Can't you silence that?'

'Sorry.'

Brand was astounded Patrick would address Darlene in such an abrupt manner.

Darlene fiddled with some buttons on the camera. 'I don't know how. Maybe I shouldn't take any pictures.'

'Here, let me have a look,' Brand said to her. As a guide he had developed a basic understanding of cameras and photography early on and as a private investigator he found his knowledge of light, shutter speeds and lenses was a bonus during surveillance work. He found the settings menu on the camera and was able to cancel the beeping noise. 'All done.'

Darlene laid her hand on his and smiled up at him. 'My hero.'

Patrick was up and moving again, so Brand made sure everyone was fine and they carried on along the riverbed, keeping to the shade of the trees along one side. Ahead of them, the near-dry watercourse curved around to the left.

Patrick pushed ahead, outstripping the rest of them. As he approached the bend, he stopped and dropped to one knee to study the sand. Brand stopped the group. He waited a few seconds, checked there was nothing coming up behind them, then told Darlene and the others to stay put. He walked up to Patrick. 'What is it?' Brand asked.

'People,' Patrick whispered. He licked his lips. 'No one else walks this part of the concession and I haven't been here for two weeks. These are fresh.'

'Poachers.'

Patrick nodded. 'There are plenty of rhino along here. We often see them in the riverbed. I'm going to follow them.'

'Are you fucking crazy?' Brand couldn't believe what he was hearing. 'We've got clients with us. Let's call this in to the reserve's security people. We need to get the guests out of here. You said it yourself, these tracks are fresh.'

'Just as I thought, you're gutless,' Patrick said.

There was bold, and there was insane. If Brand had been alone, or if it had just been him and Patrick, he probably would have followed the tracks. He hated poachers, and was incensed that in this day and age rhino were still being hunted for their horn so that rich Vietnamese businessmen could impress their friends by serving up ground horn as a party drug – they claimed it prevented hangovers.

'I'm taking the tourists back to the truck. You do what you want,' Brand said.

'So you're not going to back me up?'

'We can come back later, Patrick.'

Patrick shook his head, stood up and moved forward. Brand was furious; he backtracked to the guests. Patrick had been nothing but a dangerous liability since the moment he'd loaded his gun at the dining table.

'What's going on?' Darlene asked him.

'Patrick's just checking something out. We're going to move slowly back the way we came.'

'Why?' she asked. Patrick had moved around the bend and was out of sight.

A burst of three gunshots, fired on automatic, echoed down the riverbed. Darlene screamed. 'Everybody behind that rock,' Brand said, motioning to a boulder a few metres away from them. He turned to look up the river, his rifle in his shoulder.

'Help!' yelled Patrick. He emerged, running around the bend towards them, eyes wide and arms and legs pumping. His hands were empty.

Brand heard voices, men calling in Portuguese, which meant they had to be Mozambicans, from across the border on the other side of the Kruger Park. Someone was telling another person to hurry up. It was the language of his youth, taught to him by his half-Portuguese, half-Angolan mother. A man dressed in a green shirt and shorts and carrying an AK-47 came into view, holding his rifle at the ready. He aimed at Patrick's back and Brand saw the man's surprise as he caught sight of him.

Brand didn't have time to think. His reactions had been honed in combat, decades earlier, but they were still razor sharp. He squeezed the trigger. The heavy projectile, designed to take down a charging buffalo or elephant, hit the poacher in the chest and sent him flying backwards. Patrick ran past Brand.

'How many?' Brand asked his back. Patrick said nothing.

'Hudson, what do we do?' Darlene cried as Patrick charged past her and the others.

'Get back to the truck. Follow Patrick.'

Brand swore under his breath as he worked the bolt of his Brno and chambered another round. He wanted to run too, but his training told him he couldn't. The poacher would not have been alone. He moved forward, hugging the bank of the riverbed, where the trees cast shadows that might give him some concealment. If there were more coming he needed to buy the tourists – and Patrick – some time. He gripped the stock of his rifle tight. His heart thudded; he'd been here before and he felt the calm settle over him, stilling his urge to flee.

As he came around the bend, where Patrick had foolishly been, he saw the carcass of the rhino. Two men were kneeling on the far side of the butchered grey bulk; one was sawing frantically. '*Foda, foda*!' the other man swore and raised his weapon, a heavy-calibre bolt-action hunting rifle similar to Brand's. Brand was quicker and squeezed off a shot. The gunman fell back, dropping his rifle and clutching his shoulder. The man with the saw got up and ran. If he was armed he had dropped his rifle on the other side of the carcass.

'*Pare aí*!' Brand called, but the man refused his order to stop where he was. Brand stared down the sights of his rifle, placing the blade in the centre of the running man's back. He breathed through his nose, his chest rising and falling. The adrenaline was supercharging his system and the hunter's instinct, the primal killer within, was screaming at him to pull the trigger.

The man on the ground who had aimed at him was screaming in pain. The mist cleared from Brand's eyes and he lowered the barrel of his weapon. He could not shoot an unarmed man in the back. He jogged forward, passing Patrick's abandoned rifle and a long scuff mark in the sand that told him the younger guide had probably tripped and fallen when the first poacher had fired at him. He came to the carcass and saw the second poacher lying on his back. His rifle was on the ground next to him and Brand picked it up and tossed it further out of reach. He frisked the wounded man, who clawed at him in his pain, but Brand smacked his hand away. He was clean. Brand knelt and ripped the man's shirt off his back, balled it and pressed it against the wound in the man's shoulder.

He placed the man's hand on the makeshift dressing. '*Manter a pressão sobre isto, seu bastardo.*' The bastard nodded and kept the pressure on the shirt to stem the flow of blood.

4

Captain Sannie van Rensburg sat opposite Hudson Brand in the small interview room in the Skukuza police station, at Number 1 Leopard Street. The building was near the post office, on the staff village side of the fence that separated the administrative area from Skukuza Rest Camp, the largest camp in the Kruger Park.

'Nervous?' Sannie asked him.

He stared back at her. She remembered the first time she had interviewed him, four years earlier, while the FIFA World Cup was still in full swing. Given the euphoria and hype of the event, the news media had barely reported the case of the prostitute who had been raped and murdered. Sannie had picked up Brand in the Kruger Park, where he'd been driving a group of British soccer fans. Brand had been angry when she had shown up at Lower Sabie Rest Camp, where he and his clients were having brunch. He had tried to tell her he couldn't leave his tourists stranded.

'A woman has been killed,' Mavis had yelled at him.

Sannie had laid a hand on her young partner's arm and gently remonstrated with her afterwards about making a scene in front of people, but Sannie had brooked no protest from Brand. He'd called Tracey Mahoney and she had sent another guide into the park. The Brits had seemed content enough to sit on the deck at the Lower Sabie restaurant drinking beers at eleven in the morning until their replacement guide arrived. Sannie and Mavis had driven to the same station where they were now, with Brand in the car.

'What's this about?' he'd asked, and she could smell the stale alcohol on his breath across the same interview table where he sat now, in the police station. His eyes had been bloodshot then, his skin paler than its normal coffee-coloured hue. She'd thought he could be handsome if he wasn't so hungover.

'Nandi Mnisi.'

'Who?'

He'd seemed genuinely confused but, Sannie had reflected at the time, a killer didn't need to know the name of his victim, and as Nandi had been a working girl she had probably used an alias.

'The prostitute you were seen dancing with last night, in a pub in Nelspruit.'

'Which one?' Brand had asked.

'Which prostitute or which pub?' Sannie had replied.

'Pub.'

She'd told him and he'd nodded. 'I was there. I danced with a lot of people.'

'One in particular.'

'Says who?' he retorted defensively.

She hadn't told him, but they'd got lucky and had received an anonymous tip-off. The most important period in a murder investigation was the first twenty-four hours and Sannie had to keep her excitement in check. It was her first murder case in a long time and adrenaline was kicking in. 'I have information that you were seen dancing with Miss Nandi Mnisi last night around midnight, and that your vehicle was spotted stopped on the side of the road between three and four hundred metres from Kruger's Phabeni Gate entrance on the road to Hazyview at around five am this morning.'

Brand had rubbed his hand up and down his face. 'I'd ask for a lawyer if I was guilty of anything.'

She had shrugged. 'You have the right to have an advocate present, but it will be simpler if you just tell me what happened.'

'Simpler for who?'

She'd said nothing, which was often the best course of action in an interview. Brand eventually sighed, breathing more alcohol in her direction, and filled the void. 'I danced with a few women last night; there was a big party after the game. This morning I had to be in the park early. I wanted to avoid the queues and catch an extra half hour's sleep at the gate before the coach carrying my clients for today's game drive showed up.'

'Why did you stop by the side of the road?'

He'd looked at the ceiling, then at her. 'So I could throw up.'

'Were you *babelaas*, or did you see, or do, something that made you sick?'

'Yes, I was very hungover, no I didn't do anything, other than hurl. What happened? Who was killed? Was it this Nandi Mnisi?' Brand demanded.

'Yes, her body was found this morning. Ring any bells now?'

He closed his eyes, thought for a moment, then opened them. 'Red dress, spangly, very short and tight?'

Sannie nodded. 'The victim was wearing a red dress.'

'Covered in blood,' Mavis had shot from behind her. Sannie silenced her with a look.

'I didn't kill anyone. But yes, I was dancing with a girl in a red dress, until my girlfriend cut in.'

'What's her name?'

'Hannah van Wyk. I went home to her place.'

'What time did you get there?'

He'd looked at the ceiling. 'Late. To tell you the truth I can't remember exactly.'

'Don't worry, Mr Brand, we'll be contacting this Hannah van Wyk.'

'Knock yourself out. Hey, look, I'm sorry about the girl, really I am, but every minute you waste here grilling me is another minute that this case is cooling off,' he had said.

His tone had rankled her, giving the impression he knew more about investigations than she. 'Don't tell me how to do my job.'

She and Mavis had called Hannah van Wyk and the woman had confirmed that Hudson Brand had spent the night with her; had gone home with her in fact and left her place at about half past four in the morning, after just two and a half hours' sleep, to get to the Kruger Park. The man was a menace and should not have been driving foreign guests in the park while still drunk, but that was of less concern to her than catching a killer. She had impounded his vehicle and executed a search warrant, taking the clothes he'd been wearing at the bar the night before. His game viewer was clean and his clothes showed no trace of Nandi's DNA. There was no physical evidence to connect him to the scene, other than his vomit by the side of the road, which he admitted to leaving there. There were no footprints near the location of the body, but Brand was a safari guide and knew a thing or two about tracking, so could have removed any sign of his presence. The bottom line was that she did not have enough evidence to charge Brand with, and she had eventually released him.

And here he was again. Sannie looked at Brand now, across the desk from her, four years on. He was sweating a little.

'Nervous?' Van Rensburg asked him again.

Brand wiped his brow. 'Hot.'

Van Rensburg looked through the file in front of her. 'Patrick de Villiers says the poacher fired first and that you ran away. You didn't back him up, like a partner should.'

Brand leaned back in his chair. 'We're not partners. He got too far ahead of the group and went off following the poachers' tracks on his own. I warned him not to.'

Van Rensburg nodded. 'I'm sure you did the sensible thing, but was it the right thing, morally?'

She knew she was goading him, playing on his male ego. She hoped that he would fall for it.

'My first duty was to the tourists in my care, and that should have been Patrick's first duty as well.'

'He says that you ran, ignoring the tourists.'

Brand scoffed. 'And you believe that?'

She shrugged and closed the folder. 'The other witnesses, particularly a Miss Darlene Jones, say you were concerned about them. Miss Jones spoke very highly of you indeed.'

Brand looked back into her eyes but said nothing.

'For the record,' he said eventually, 'I didn't run anywhere. I was moving the tourists back towards the vehicle, but when I heard the shot I moved forward to check on Patrick. He'd dropped his rifle and he ran straight past me and the tourists.'

'He says he was shepherding them to safety.'

Brand shrugged. 'Are you saying this wasn't a righteous shoot?'

Van Rensburg shook her head. '*Righteous*? Only an American would describe a killing in such a way. But no, as of now there will be no charges laid against you or De Villiers, but there is still a national parks investigation to be carried out and your licences as guides in South Africa will be suspended until the outcome of that inquiry.'

Brand rolled his eyes. 'Great.'

'You killed a man and wounded another, Mr Brand. You don't seem too remorseful or disturbed by that.'

'It's not the first time.'

'I know. I've been checking you out since I first interviewed you, over Nandi's death.'

'I'm flattered,' he said. 'And a little disturbed. I didn't know I was still the subject of an ongoing investigation.'

'I'm confused.'

He raised his eyebrows.

'You're half American, half African. Your father was an oil man and your mother was a local woman, half Portuguese, half Angolan.

The old regime classed you as a "coloured" when you obtained South African citizenship in 1990, after you were discharged from the army. Why on earth would a – what would you call yourself, an "African American" or an "American African"? – fight for a white apartheid regime's army?'

'Good question,' Brand said.

'That's why I asked it. You were with 32 Battalion; that buffalo head tattoo on your arm is proof of that. I knew a couple of guys who served with them; it was a multiracial unit, with mostly white officers and black Angolan soldiers. There were also a few foreign mercenaries, like yourself.'

'Mercenary seems like such a harsh word.'

She smiled. 'One of the guys I spoke to told me he remembered you, that the word was you were ex-CIA, but you'd done something wrong and ended up in Africa without a job, which was why you joined 32.'

He shrugged. 'Folks do love a good spy story.'

'Were you CIA, Mr Brand?'

'My past has nothing to do with the shooting of a poacher in the Kruger Park.'

'But you were a mercenary, trained as a killer. I've been doing some reading. The Angolans called 32 Battalion *os terríveis*, the terrible ones. Anyone with a reputation like that could easily cross the line between soldier and psychopath. They might think nothing of raping and murdering a woman. Are you unwell, Mr Brand? Is it something to do with your service in Angola? Did you do things there you were ashamed of; do you secretly want to relive them? When we interviewed Hannah van Wyk back in 2010 she told us that you had confided to her that your parents had split after your father brought your family back to America from the oil fields in Cabinda province in Angola, leaving your mother to raise you alone. Life must have been tough. You must have been an outsider.'

He said nothing. He closed his eyes, tight, for a second, then opened them. He leaned forward, elbows on the interview table.

'My father was a right-wing Republican and my mother hated the communists. She had Angolan cousins who were fighting for Holden Roberto's FNLA and later Unita, the anti-government, pro-western rebels. I went to Angola on business and my work there dried up; I met my cousins and I served with Unita for a while. I'd served in the US Army, Rangers, and when I met some high-ranking South African military advisers they offered me a job. Unita couldn't pay me, but the apartheid regime could. At the time I think I hated communism more than apartheid.'

'I understand.' She nodded.

'I was being ironic. I was stupid.'

'Both ideologies crumbled, yet the wars fought in their name left many men broken, physically and emotionally. My late husband served on the border, and it affected him deeply.' There was a moment of silence between them.

'What are you thinking about?' Van Rensburg pushed. 'What are you remembering?'

He shook his head. 'Nothing. You know I didn't kill that girl you found near Phabeni in 2010.'

'I don't know anything at all, Mr Brand. I know there's a killer on the loose and that you were at the scene of that crime around the time it happened. Just because I didn't have enough evidence to arrest you doesn't mean I don't think you are guilty.'

'You had no evidence.' Brand pushed back his chair. 'If that's all, I'll be on my way.'

Mavis moved slowly out of his path. Sannie van Rensburg looked back over her shoulder without getting up. 'I'll be in touch with you again, Mr Brand. You can count on it.'

It had been a long day. Sannie and Mavis drove back to Nelspruit, and by the time they had finished their paperwork and Sannie had backtracked home it was well after dark.

Sannie and Tom's banana farm was on the R40 in the hills just outside the small town of Hazyview, about an hour's drive from her work at Nelspruit. She had been brought up on the farm, then had moved to Johannesburg, where she had met Tom, her second husband, and they had returned to the country, ostensibly for a quieter life.

'You're late,' Tom said by way of greeting as she walked into the farmhouse. Beyond the deck, the lights of Hazyview sparkled in the gloom. When she was growing up these hills and valleys had been dark at night, sparsely populated save for a few farming families, but things had changed in South Africa. The breakdown of the restrictions of the apartheid era had brought new settlers to the area, many of them illegal immigrants from across the nearby border with Mozambique who were looking for a better future. The tourism sector had boomed, with the Kruger Park, just a dozen kilometres away, drawing visitors from around the world once South Africa had returned to the international fold.

'I was interviewing the guy who shot the rhino poachers. Did you hear about it?'

'It was all over Jacaranda; my only contact to the outside world is an easy-listening FM radio station.' Tom drained a beer and got up, walked past her to the refrigerator and got himself another. 'Wine?' he asked as an afterthought.

They hadn't even kissed. 'Yes, please,' she said without enthusiasm. The kids were in bed and she had missed yet another dinner with them. She resented Tom's surliness, but the thing she – they – had feared was happening, more and more. Her decision to return to policing was taking a toll on the family. Sannie was tired of justifying herself, tired of snide remarks and full-blown arguments. She set the case docket down on the kitchen bench top.

Tom nodded to the thick folder. 'More work?'

Tom had never been happy about her decision, but she was her own woman. She had raised her first two children solo for several years after her first husband, also a policeman, had died, so Tom didn't get to call all the shots in her life. Now that her youngest, little Tommy, the son she'd had with Tom, had started school, she wasn't tied to the farmhouse. Sannie knew her husband worried about her every time he said goodbye to her, but while Nelspruit had its moments it was not as dangerous as working in Johannesburg.

'*Ja*. That murder investigation, from the time of the World Cup. The guy I interviewed today was a suspect back then.'

Tom raised his eyebrows. 'That American fellow? What's his name?'

'Brand.'

He slid her drink across the bench top to her. 'Christo got in trouble again today. He slapped another boy; the teacher called me.'

'And that's because I work late?'

He ignored her sarcasm. 'No, I just wanted to tell you. I'm OK disciplining him, but it would have been nice if you'd been home tonight.'

Sannie heard loud and clear what Tom was leaving unsaid. Christo was not his natural son. Tom obviously felt she needed to be around more for her older children, given the difficult ages they were entering; Christo was thirteen and her daughter two years younger. But Sannie wanted to yell back at her husband, *I also need to be here for Nandi Mnisi, who was brutally raped and murdered.*

'There's nothing on TV,' Tom said.

She wondered if that was a peace offering, a hint of intimacy. If so, he had a funny way of going about it. The frequency and intensity of their lovemaking had dropped off sharply since the first year of their marriage, since her return to the job.

'I don't get time to review cold cases at work. There's too much day-to-day stuff, and not enough people or resources,' she said.

He tipped his bottle of Windhoek Lager to his lips and took several gulps. 'I'm tired, anyway. There's still the farm to look after.'

Men, she thought. It was as if he thought she spent her days at a desk doing her nails. It was so unfair. He *knew* what policing entailed and he seemed to think that because he was through with it that she should be too. Yes, her family was the most important thing in the world to her, but had he completely forgotten what it was like to make a difference to a community, to a country? Crime, whether a murder in a field in Hazyview or corruption at the top levels of government, was the number one problem in her country, and she, for one, wanted to do something about. Couldn't he see that?

'I won't disturb you,' he said, draining his beer. 'I'm going to bed to read.'

Sannie took a breath, trying to control her anger. They fought more often these days – hell, they hadn't fought at all in that first year. She didn't want raised voices waking the kids. She would look in on them before she went to bed.

Sannie picked up the murder case docket and took it outside, through the sliding screen doors, onto the timber deck. It was a nice night, not too chilly. She sat at the wooden picnic table and sipped her wine as she opened the docket. She would go through the death of Nandi Mnisi again for – what would it be – the hundredth time?

She read the notes and transcripts from the initial interview with Brand, and with the woodcarver. Hannah van Wyk's testimony in relation to Brand's alibi was there as well. Perhaps it would be worth visiting her again. Sannie knew the pair were no longer together and time apart may have softened any misplaced loyalty that Van Wyk may have shown to Brand. With the lack of evidence implicating the American guide, and no other leads, her next strongest theory was that the rape and murder had been perpetrated by a foreigner. South Africa had been awash with tourists from all over the world back then, drawn by the FIFA soccer World Cup. Australia had played Serbia on the day of the killing and she had contacted police authorities in those countries to see if there had been any similar killings on their turf. Of course, there had been soccer fans from scores of other countries too, but none of the internet and other searches she and Mavis had done periodically over the years had turned up similar crimes.

It was time to try again, she thought. She made a note to email the Investigative Psychology Unit tomorrow, to put in a request to talk to someone there about running a search on similar crimes since the last time she had checked. There would be no time, but she would have to make time. She knew this docket inside and out and she was sure she and Mavis had overlooked nothing. She needed a break, even if that break was news that another woman had been killed in similar circumstances. Sannie closed the docket and finished her wine; Tom had only poured her a small glass, perhaps thinking she would come to bed sooner rather than later. He was half smashed judging by the cluster of empty bottles he had left out on the kitchen bench for the maid to tidy up tomorrow. Sannie opened the fridge and poured herself another glass, a bigger measure.

She went back out to the deck, sat down and re-opened the docket. She began to read, again, from the beginning. She must have missed something, other than her children's day and her husband's love.

5

Brand nursed a Castle Draught in the Pepper Vine bar at Hazyview. His mobile phone sat on the table in front of him, next to the copy of the *Lowvelder*, which had a picture of him standing over the body of the slain poacher on the front page; the shot had been taken by Keith, the South African-turned-Australian tourist.

Hannah van Wyk walked over and changed the ashtray. 'Cheer up, it could have been worse. The poachers could have shot *you*.'

Brand raised an eyebrow. 'At least one of them still has a job.'

Life had thrown a lot at Hannah in her thirty-five years. She was still attractive, though she had the flinty edges of a woman used to living nearly as hard as the customers she served. He'd described her as his girlfriend when Van Rensburg had taken him in for questioning in 2010 and when he'd spoken to Hannah after the interview she'd been surprised at his use of the word. 'I never pictured you as the boyfriend type,' she'd said.

'The same cop interviewed me today as in the murder case.'

'Oh.' He saw how she gripped the cloth tighter in her hand.

'It's OK, we didn't talk about the old case – much – and not about you at all.'

Hannah gave a short nod. Their relationship was over, in a sexual sense, but their secret would bind them forever, or until she let it out. Hannah had told Sannie van Rensburg when she'd called in at the bar that she had driven Hudson home from the nightclub on the evening Nandi Mnisi was murdered, and that he'd been with her all night until he'd left for the Kruger Park. It wasn't true. Hannah had grown tired of his carousing and had driven herself home at one o'clock. Hudson had stumbled into her bed around three in the morning and been gone an hour and a half later. She had lied for him; other guides who had seen Hudson being picked up by the police at Lower Sabie had already been gossiping and SMSing their friends and word had filtered quickly to the Pepper Vine that Hudson was being questioned in relation to the murder of the prostitute. When Van Rensburg had asked her about Hudson's whereabouts the night before, she'd told the lie to cover for him. She had told him, afterwards, that she knew he was not the sort of man to commit such a crime, but in the days that followed she had kept her distance from him. They were still friends, though they had never made love again.

Then an old flame had come back into her life and Brand had been happy for her, for a short while. Sadly, for Hannah, her former beau had overdosed on heroin six months after they had reunited. Hannah took the dirty ashtray back to the bar.

Brand looked at his phone. He did not want to make the call, but he knew he had to.

It was two days since he had killed one poacher and wounded the other. His licence was still suspended, but even if it hadn't been he had no work. This sort of thing happened every time a guide discharged their weapon, but he was confident he would be cleared by the parks board, just as Van Rensburg had closed her case on the shooting, if not on the murder during the World Cup. A couple of other guides had told him there was misinformation being spread about the shooting on Facebook. Patrick was out there spinning his version of events, saying Brand had run like a chicken and left him hanging.

Brand had spoken to Gert Pols about what had gone down at Zebra Plains and Gert had not seemed overly surprised by the chain of events. Brand thanked him for not warning him about Patrick and his strong desire to get himself and the guests killed while walking in the park. 'You'll be fine,' Gert had said, laughing off Brand's sarcasm. 'The investigation will clear you. I'm finished with Patrick, though. He's a cowboy and he's cost me money.'

The safari had been cancelled, the guests traumatised by the death of the poacher and how close they had come to danger. Gert had organised with Tanda Tula, a tented camp in the Timbavati, to take Darlene and the others. They would be staying in luxury, at Gert's expense, and if they were still keen for a walking safari after their experience they could do one from Tanda Tula's field camp.

His hand shook a little as he raised the beer to his lips, remembering the moment when he had pulled the trigger. He wasn't nearly as cool now about the shooting as he had been when Van Rensburg had questioned him; he'd had time to think about how close he'd come to getting shot. Darlene had broken down in tears after the shooting, but she had left him with a kiss. He was pleased she was safe, but he knew he'd never see her again, and now he was out of work and out of money.

He recognised most of the half dozen or so other patrons in the open-air bar but he drank alone by choice. He didn't feel like socialising. Brand decided that as soon as he finished this beer, his third, he would go next door to *Oom* Kallie's butchery, buy some *boerewors* for his supper and drive home. But first he knew he should make the call.

The afternoon sun was slanting into the courtyard where he sat at a table under an umbrella. Most of the Pepper Vine was open to the elements, except for about a quarter of the pub's drinking and eating area, including the bar and kitchen and the big flat-screen television where they showed the rugby, which was under a tin roof. Normally in this familiar setting Brand would have been feeling pleasantly mellow. Instead, his stomach was knotted and he gripped the glass too hard. The gate to the courtyard, the entry to the pub, squeaked.

'Ag, look who it is. The great white chicken himself. *Howzit*, Hudson.'

Of all the people he did not want to see right then, Patrick de Villiers's elder brother, Koos, would have been close to the top of the list. Unlike his sibling, Koos was a banana farmer, with hands the circumference of an elephant's hind foot, and the build, brains and temperament of a Cape buffalo. Brand had seen Koos demolish men and furniture in other bars, over matters so trivial that no one could recall them the next day. Brand had a premonition just then that people would remember why Koos had done what he was surely about to do.

Brand drained his beer and dropped sixty rand on the table top, more than enough for the cost plus a tip. He stood and nodded, 'Fine, and you, Koos?' Not that he really cared.

Koos stopped in the courtyard, between Brand and the exit. The conversations around the pub had fallen away. 'I'm fine, but my *boet* Patrick is not so *lekker*, man. He's lost his job. That *poepol* friend of yours, Gert, just fired him. He didn't even wait for the investigation.'

Brand shrugged. 'Sorry to hear that, Koos.' Brand took a step towards him, stopping just out of swinging range, but Koos didn't move aside. Brand sighed.

'My brother says you didn't back him up.'

Brand didn't really want to get into the detail of how much Koos's little brother had fucked up that day, but he did think it worth explaining some of his own actions for the slow learners like the farmers, and the gossipmongers at the surrounding tables.

'Your brother put his own life and, more importantly, the lives of our clients at risk by following the poachers' tracks. We should have just pulled back and called it in.'

'He's a brave *oke* and you put him in danger by not going with him.'

Brand could see there was no way he was going to win this argument, but he pressed on anyway for the sake of his audience. 'He was stupid. He panicked and ran when the poacher fired at him and he dropped his weapon. He's only alive because I killed a man.'

'He lost his job because of your cowardice.'

Brand squared up to the rough-hewn farmer. 'I've got no beef with you, Koos.' As Brand tried to get around him Koos sidestepped to block him and shoved him in the chest. *So this was how it was going to be*, Brand thought. 'I do not want to fight you, Koos.'

'Typical American; you start a war then you don't know how to end it. You're not leaving without a broken bone.'

Brand considered arguing the toss with him; the only war he had been in had been a largely South African one, in Angola, but he guessed the irony would be lost on Koos. The farmer had bully written all over him, and Brand had encountered his fair share of them over the years. Koos was bigger than him, and maybe twenty years younger, but Brand had learned a trick or two in the border war, and in more than a few bar-room brawls since.

'Let me past, Koos,' he said, giving the man one more chance.

'Make me get out of the way, *boy*,' Koos said.

Brand took a deep breath and clenched his fists beside him. 'Let's take this outside.'

Koos backed to the gate that led out to the dusty car park. Several of the bush bar patrons rose from their seats to follow the two men out and enjoy the spectacle.

'Where's your chicken-shit brother?' Brand asked Koos. He was ready for him and he wanted him angry. Hopefully he would lash out with a predictable sucker punch that Brand would dodge before kicking him in the balls.

'Here.'

Brand made the cardinal mistake of turning towards the sound of the voice. As he did so a massive fist collided with the left side of his face. Brand glimpsed Patrick as Koos's blow felled him. As they said in the South African Army, no plan survived the first contact with the enemy.

Rolling in the dirt to get away from the kick he knew was coming, Brand scooped up a handful of gravel. When Patrick danced over to him he reared up like a black mamba and flung the grit in his eyes. It was an afternoon for falling for old tricks so Brand made the most of this one and smashed Patrick square in the nose. As satisfying as that was he could not fight on two fronts at once, and Brand screamed as Koos's fist slammed into his kidneys.

Patrick spat blood. As Brand squared up, painfully, to Koos, he saw Patrick pull something from the back pocket of his shorts. Brand hoped it wasn't a gun, as he had left his at home. Koos lashed out with a hook that Brand managed to dodge, but Koos escaped Brand's cross as well. The farmer's next punch was quicker than Brand's and Brand's head snapped back as Koos's fist found his chin. Brand spun around and aimed a kick at Patrick. The younger brother didn't try to move, instead holding out his hand. Too late, Brand saw that he held a taser.

Brand faltered and Patrick caught his half-formed kick and zapped him with a jolt of electricity. Brand collapsed, and Koos's buffalo-hide boot found its mark, in the side of his chest.

A Land Rover game viewer vehicle pulled up close to the scuffle, its sudden stop sending a cloud of dust washing over the three men. Brand groaned. Through a haze of pain he registered Bryce Duffy, the guide he'd last seen with the lion on the bridge, climbing down. 'Hey, get off him!'

'Taser . . .' Brand croaked. But the warning wasn't necessary. As Bryce approached, Koos sucker punched him in the face with a single blow from his massive fist and Bryce fell backwards.

Brand was still on the ground and the De Villiers brothers weren't of a mind to let him get back up again. The beating was bad, but would have been worse – for him and Bryce – if a gunshot hadn't gone off.

With one eye half closed and his head ringing Brand wondered if one of them had produced a gun and fired at him and missed. Surely the second shot would find its mark. Koos kicked again, hard and sharp into Brand's gut, and another boom sounded. He backed off. Brand rolled painfully onto his side and saw Hannah van Wyk standing at the pub's entry gate, a lick of smoke curling from the barrel of her sawn-off shotgun.

The De Villiers boys retreated to Koos's *bakkie* and drove off, leaving a defiant cloud of dust in the wake of their spinning tyres. Hannah helped Brand and Bryce to their feet and asked Brand if he wanted to go to her place.

'Thanks,' he coughed, and spat blood into the dirt of the car park, 'but I should get back to the place I'm house-sitting. Bryce, are you OK?'

Bryce was gingerly feeling his nose. 'Yeah. You just can't seem to stay out of trouble, can you, Hudson?' He began to laugh then winced with the pain.

Hannah fussed over Brand, ignoring the younger man. 'But Hippo Rock's thirty-five kilometres away, Hudson. Are you sure you can manage? You look like you're about to pass out.'

He turned away from her and spat again. He probed a tooth with his tongue. It was loose. 'I'll manage.'

She looked doubtful. 'I'll follow you; make sure you get home OK.'

It was her call. Brand shook hands with Bryce, apologised for dragging him into the melee, then eased himself into the driver's seat of his Land Rover while she went and fetched the keys to her Toyota *bakkie*. They left Hazyview and drove through the ever-extending and almost interconnecting township settlements between the town and the Paul Kruger Gate entrance to the national park, where he'd had the encounter with the lions and Darlene. It seemed like weeks, not days ago.

He was probably a little concussed, because just before Mkhulu he nodded off. It was just as well Hannah was following him home; the blaring of her horn woke him as he began drifting off the tarmac onto the gravel verge of the road.

Because of the nature of his work, both as an investigator and a safari guide, and perhaps because Brand had long ago realised he would never truly settle down, he was something of a nomad. He was living in a house at Hippo Rock, a wildlife estate on the banks of the Sabie River overlooking the Kruger Park. There were a few such estates on the border of the reserve, where the privileged lived or kept holiday houses set amid bushland and roaming animals.

The house he was staying in was owned by a South African goldmine manager who had emigrated to Australia. He didn't get back to the country of his birth nearly enough but didn't want to sell his house in the bush either. Brand had guided the man as a client a couple of years earlier and the pair had struck up a friendship. They had come to an agreement that Brand could stay in the house in Hippo Rock if he kept it maintained.

Brand came and went from the house depending on where he was working. He signed in and lifted his arm in a painful salute to the gate guard and as he drove into the estate, with Hannah still tailing him, he felt a little sad to know he would soon be leaving again.

When they reached the house Hannah got out of her vehicle before Brand could ease himself free. He leaned on her bony shoulder as she walked him to the door. 'Want me to come in?' she asked.

'I'm,' he coughed, 'fine. But since you've come all this way at least let me get you coffee or a beer.'

'Precious can look after the bar for a little while longer.' Hannah helped him along the stone-flagged hallway to the master bedroom. He lay down on his back and closed his eyes. Hannah fetched a bowl from the kitchen and returned to the bedroom's en suite. She filled it with hot water and brought soap and a facecloth.

Hannah set the bowl down on the bedside table and paused to open the curtains. Across the timbered verandah was the view of the Sabie River Brand cherished and coveted. The waterway was shrunken by the long dry winter, but was still beautiful, gurgling its way around pink granite boulders. An elephant snorted trunks full of water from the edge of the far bank and the sight of him did nothing to harm Brand's recovery. Gingerly he undid the buttons of his bloodied bush shirt and winced as he tried to remove it.

'Here, let me.' Hannah moved to the bed, eased off the shirt and tut-tutted at the patchwork of bruises underneath. When even her gentle fingers made him nearly cry out he knew there were some cracked ribs. 'You'll have to go to the doctor. But I'll clean you up a bit.'

She dabbed at the cuts on his cheek and his lip and each touch seemed to hurt more than the last. 'You men are such pussies when it comes to pain.'

Brand regretted his attempted laugh. 'What would you know?'

'You should try childbirth.'

There was so much, he realised, that he didn't know about her, and they hadn't been together long enough for him to find out. 'You never told me.'

'Whenever I asked you if what people said was true, you always said you didn't want to talk about your past, that you had come to South Africa to fight in the border war, so I thought you wouldn't want to know about my previous lives.'

Lives. He nodded. She rummaged in his bathroom again for some sticky plasters and Betadine and then continued to torture him as she returned to her nursing duties. In a brief moment of respite she got up again and sifted through some of Brand's dirty bush clothes until she found a bottle of Scotch, the cheap kind. Hannah poured two generous glasses.

'Thanks.' He clinked glasses with her. The liquid warmed him as it washed over his ragged nerve endings.

She sipped her drink. 'I should have killed Koos. He tried it on with me one night, after closing. I kneed him in the balls.'

'That was my plan.'

Hannah looked away from him.

'Did you go to the police?' Brand asked her.

She laughed. 'Here? He would have bought them off. Besides, the cops are too busy with rapes and murders. They don't care about some farmer backhanding a barmaid.'

Any thoughts Brand might have had about getting some payback on Koos de Villiers for how he and Patrick had ambushed him were now overwhelmed with his desire to hurt him, badly, for what he had done to Hannah. 'Well, thanks again for saving my ass.'

'What are you going to do now?'

Brand shrugged, and it hurt. 'I can't work until the parks board investigation clears me for shooting the poacher.'

Hannah nodded. 'Watch out for Koos and Patrick. They're not finished with you yet. I know them. They're bad.'

'So I gather. I did get an offer of some work in Zimbabwe. I turned it down because what I really wanted to do was go on that walking safari.'

She tutted again. 'Zimbabwe. Isn't it dangerous up there, man?'

He braced himself for the pain as it was his turn to laugh. 'Not like Hazyview.'

She smiled and he thought he saw her obsidian eyes soften just a little. 'I do need to get back to work. Precious is a good girl, but she'll be busy robbing me blind while I'm here.'

Brand reached out and put his hand on hers. Hannah leaned closer to him and kissed him on the cheek. That also hurt, but he manned up and didn't wince.

She pulled back from him, as if having second thoughts about what she had just done. 'Is it guiding work you're going to do in Zimbabwe?' she asked quickly.

'No. Hunting.'

'Ugh, I hate hunting.'

'People, not animals.'

'Oh, that's all right then.' Hannah stood and smoothed her short denim skirt. 'I must go. Be careful if you go to Zimbabwe, Hudson. I wouldn't want anything bad to happen to you.' She went to the bedroom door and walked out without looking back.

Brand found his phone in the pocket of his discarded shirt. Miraculously, it had survived the beating and kicking of the brothers De Villiers. He scrolled through the recent numbers and found Dani's in London. He pressed the call button. Brand let the phone ring a few times then hung up.

Gently, he eased himself back onto the bed, the phone by his side. Afternoon sunlight slanted in through the sliding glass doors that led to the deck outside. He should have been walking in the bush in this golden hour of the day, not lying here, feeling like shit.

Brand didn't have long to wait. The phone gave its kingfisher call and vibrated on the bed. He picked it up and held it to his ear, too tired and sore to even say hello.

'I take it you don't have enough funds to call the UK?' Dani said by way of greeting.

Poor Dani, Brand thought. She was so wrapped up in her work that she would call him straight back on a Saturday. She should have been out in the beer garden of a sunny pub or strolling in a London park, or whatever it was people in England did for fun.

'How did you guess?' The truth was, he didn't have enough credit on his phone to speak to her from his end, and his current bank balance would barely cover the cost of a call if he drew the cash out.

'I know you're not a big believer in the internet, but you're currently trending.'

'What the hell does that mean?' Brand croaked.

'I'd tell you to google yourself, but you'd probably think that was a euphemism of some sort.'

'I like it when you talk dirty to me. It's your accent.' Brand thought he heard a titter.

'Seriously, Hudson, you've made the news on several continents in the last few days. I read all about the poacher, and the lion, and that poor American woman who was nearly killed twice. She looked like your type.'

Brand groaned, inwardly and outwardly. Just three nights earlier

Darlene had been slipping between crisply ironed sheets to act as his personal hot water bottle. 'I had to kill the poacher.'

'Whatever. I take it you are now in a position to accept the assignment we discussed.'

'I am,' he said.

'You're assuming I haven't found someone else.'

'I'm assuming it would take you longer than three days to find someone who can investigate a possible fake death certificate in Zimbabwe. I'm also assuming that you knew I would relent, one way or another, and end up taking this case, and that you probably guessed I didn't really have back-to-back safari bookings coming up.'

The suppressed titter again. 'We know each other well, Hudson, but now, down to business. I'll email you the file, but the basics are you're looking for a Zimbabwean female, Katherine "Kate" Elizabeth Munns, born 14 May 1980.'

There was a Windhoek Lager coaster on the bedside table. Brand slid it from under the empty bottle of the same brand and took a pen, which Koos's toecap had cracked but still worked if he held it carefully, and wrote down the name. 'White?'

'Yes. Don't sound so surprised,' Dani said. 'Crime knows no colour bar.'

Brand knew that, but this was a first in the niche business Dani and he had carved out. Several million Zimbabweans, black and white, had left their country since the country's economy had begun to spiral out of control in 1998. President Robert Mugabe's bid to cling to power by sanctioning the invasion and confiscation of white-owned commercial farms had tipped Zimbabwe's economy from the relatively prosperous and self-sufficient end of the scales to the wheelbarrow-loads-of-cash-needed-to-pay-for-a-loaf-of-bread end. In fact, for a few years there had been no bread. Although the situation had stabilised with the entry of the opposition Movement for Democratic Change, or MDC, into the government, and a switch from the valueless Zimbabwe dollar to the greenback, the fact was that Zimbabwe was being kept afloat largely by remittances sent from expatriate Zimbabweans to their relatives still living in the country.

And crime. Zimbabweans, Brand had found, were a practical people who could turn their hand to pretty well anything, including theft and fraud. Crime in Zimbabwe generally didn't include the senseless violence that characterised the farm murders and carjackings of South Africa, but was rather more creative and bloodless.

'I guess it was only a matter of time before the whites cottoned on to the idea of faking their own deaths to claim their insurance payouts,' Brand said.

'Exactly.' And that was the scam that had brought Dani and he together and made them both some tidy fees, mainly from two insurance companies in the UK that now used the services of her law firm to investigate suspect claims. So far the eight cases he had investigated had been claims lodged by the beneficiaries of policies taken out by black Zimbabweans living in Britain. Typically, the policyholder, with premiums fully paid up, would take a 'holiday' back home to Zimbabwe and meet with a tragic end – on paper. The seven fraudsters Brand had uncovered (one of the claims had been genuine) had paid two different crooked doctors for faked death certificates, as well as other bribes to obtain false police reports.

The causes of death were varied; Brand had encountered a drowning, three motor vehicle accidents, all with the same police officer investigating, as well as the same doctor pronouncing death, and a very imaginative head-kicking by a donkey. The beneficiaries tended to be spouses or other close relatives. The final case had involved a person dying of malaria three days after entering Zimbabwe. It didn't take a medical doctor or a genius to label that one as suspect. Unless the woman in question had picked up malaria somewhere in the UK, it should have taken at least a week for the disease to incubate and manifest itself.

'How did Miss Munns allegedly meet her end? Or was it missus?' Brand asked Dani.

'Miss. Car accident – again – on the way to somewhere called Binga.'

'That's on Lake Kariba, the western end. What made the insurance company suspicious?' Despite what Dani had just said about the colour bar, the fact was that Kate Munns did not fit the racial profile for Zimbabweans faking their own deaths.

'Her sister. That's the personal involvement I have in this one. Anna Cliff, Kate's sister, is a chum of mine.'

Chum. That was why he liked talking to Dani. Half a world away she was witty and charming; in the flesh she was beautiful, but very high maintenance. 'Did you declare your interest to the insurers?'

'Of course. But as I'm not undertaking the investigation itself they don't mind.'

'Who was the beneficiary of Kate's policy? I'm guessing it wasn't her sister,' Brand asked.

'Correct.'

'Parents?'

'No, they're both dead. If the claim is paid an old school friend of Kate's, Linley Brown, who is still living in Zimbabwe, will get the money.'

Brand thought about that for a moment. There must be a stronger connection than 'old school friend'. Kate Munns was thirty-four and single. Who in that demographic took out a life insurance policy and – potentially – faked their death so their pal would get rich? 'I'm trying to follow this, but my head is hurting.'

'Spend the afternoon in the pub, did we?' Dani sounded like a disapproving schoolmarm.

'Yes, but I didn't get much drinking done. OK, so, the sister . . .'

'Anna. Do try and keep up, Hudson.'

'Right, Anna, is pissed that Kate leaves the money to her lesbian lover from her school days instead of to her.'

'I had similar thoughts.' Dani paused, and Brand thought he heard her sipping something. Tea, he imagined. He remembered her lips; thin and soft. 'But Anna and her husband are very well off. The insurance payout is two hundred thousand pounds, not, as you Americans would say, chickenfeed, but Anna's husband, Peter, is a Harley Street cosmetic surgeon; she doesn't need to work and they pay more than that every year for a new car each. No, Anna thinks Kate was running away from something, or someone, and faked her death more to disappear than for the money. And, for the record, Anna says Kate was as straight as they come.'

Brand ached everywhere, and needed beer, painkillers and sleep, but his mind was ticking over. He didn't know these people, but Dani knew some of the cast of characters in this twisting tale. 'Does Anna know the friend, Linley?'

'Only vaguely. There's a six-year age difference between the sisters; Anna left for the UK while Kate was still at boarding school back in Zimbabwe. She remembers meeting Linley once, when she was home on holiday, but that's it. She didn't even know Kate had stayed in touch with the girl, though we do have a picture of the two of them together, perhaps from a few years ago.'

In one sense, it was a straightforward case. Brand knew the system well enough now in Zimbabwe that he could check out the bona fides of the death certificate and police reports within a couple of days. With luck he might even find that one of the same crooked cops or doctors he had come across in the past was involved. The insurance companies he and Dani worked for invariably did not prosecute fraud, although they refused payment when it was proved. They didn't want publicity about scams reaching the UK press in case they damaged the company's reputation. Brand thought it might be good for investors and policyholders to see that a company didn't tolerate fraud, but the corporate spin doctors in London were uniformly of a view that some publicity was bad publicity. Brand had hoped that the local police and medical boards in Zimbabwe might take action in the wake of his investigations, but he knew at least one of the doctors who'd faked certificates was still practising and a couple of the cops were still on the job. Zimbabwe's justice system was the best money could buy.

'If I do find out the death certificate is fake, what then?' he asked Dani.

'There are two parts to this case,' Dani began. 'There's the interest of the insurance company – the claim would be denied, of course – but there's also Anna's personal interest in the case. She really wants to find her sister, and find out what's going on in her life that might have made her fake her death – if indeed it was faked.'

'She wants to hire me to find Kate, if she's still alive?'

'I've given her your details, Hudson. Obviously if Kate is alive the insurance company, my client, will simply wash its hands of the matter and cancel the claim. But Anna just wants what's best for her sister. I'll leave it up to her to contact you with further instructions on her behalf.'

Brand had experienced many moments in the bush when he could sense that danger was close before it reared its horned head, snarling teeth or forked tongue. There was nothing mysterious or spooky about this extra sense; he reasoned it had developed simply because he was in nature's grip day after day. If he couldn't see a warning he might hear it, or smell it. The signs were there, one just had to let one's existing senses hone themselves, over time. He heeded this ability, and exercised caution, but he savoured the tingling sensation in his fingertips and the tightening of his chest when the signs appeared. It was, he had to admit, part of what kept him in Africa.

Clients sometimes asked if he, as an American, had a love affair with Africa, but he would tell them he did not. 'You cannot,' he would reply, 'love a place where poverty, crime, corruption and illness are so much a part of the fabric of day-to-day life. I am not in love with Africa, I am addicted to her.' He felt the symptoms of that addiction now, coursing from his heart out to his fingertips, that sudden jolt of fear mixed with excitement and anticipation, masquerading as adrenaline. It was the same when he had hunted men, in Angola.

'I'll take the case,' he said to Dani.

'I knew you would.'

*

Brand awoke the next morning with a hangover that sharpened the residual pain of his beating. The pills and booze had given him temporary relief after Hannah left, but he had answered the call of nature in the middle of the night and been greeted with the sobering sight of blood in his urine.

He walked to the kitchen and even the soles of his gritty feet hurt. He tidied the litter from his evening's excess. No orange juice had mysteriously appeared in the fridge overnight; instead he was faced with his last three bottles of Castle Lager and one of Miller Genuine Draft. He chose the Miller, as to his mind it was a better breakfast beer and, like him, an American Brand now owned by South Africa. He gulped down two Panado tablets from the kitchen drawer and found a banana that was bruised almost as badly as he.

Brand showered, sipping the cool beer as he let the hot water pummel his aching flesh. After he'd dried off and dressed he finished the second half of the banana and, reluctantly, set about closing all the curtains in his friend's bush lodge, shutting out the sight of the river. He packed his duffel bag, turned off the gas hot water geysers and spread the dust sheets back over the bed, the lounge suites and the dining table, then closed and locked the door behind him.

He loaded the duffel into his battered Land Rover Defender. It was an old diesel model, slow compared to more modern vehicles, but reliable. He would travel north towards Zimbabwe through the Kruger Park, he decided, as the view was better and he wouldn't have to worry about being overtaken by a continuous stream of traffic or being sideswiped by one of the kamikaze minibus taxis through Bushbuckridge.

The beer had awoken his craving for cigarettes, but fortunately he had none with him. He drove to the entrance gate to the Hippo

Rock estate and told the Shangaan security guard, Solly, that he did not know when he would be coming back. As he turned right onto the R536 towards the Paul Kruger Gate, Brand thought about the last insurance investigation he had done for Dani; the one that had landed him in prison in Harare.

The alleged deceased was the son of a prominent politician from the ruling ZANU-PF party. Brand's investigation had led him to the politician, a junior minister, and on confronting him Brand immediately realised the man was none too happy about him investigating the circumstances of his son's untimely demise. He rightly feared that Brand exposing the boy's sham death would rebound on him and his political aspirations.

Brand had been staying with friends in Borrowdale, a leafy suburb of Harare inhabited mostly these days by ageing white farmers who had been kicked off their lands. He'd been out to dinner with his friends, an old farming couple, but had become engrossed in a conversation with a thirty-something divorcee. His hosts had headed home but Brand had stayed, chancing his luck over a couple of Amarula Dom Pedros. Despite his best efforts, however, the woman got a call to say her youngest child was throwing up, so she cut short what could have been a beautiful thing and headed home.

It had been February, the middle of the wet southern African summer, and the lateness of the hour, the Land Rover's weak headlights, the drizzle and a low fog that clung to the road combined to make visibility next to nothing as Brand had driven back to his friends' house.

He'd taken it slow because the city's roads were dangerous at night in the best of conditions. People walked on the ill-lit streets and, as the country's numerous police roadblocks were only manned in daylight hours, illegal goods were moved in broken-down cars with no lights.

As he'd slowed at a blacked-out set of traffic lights, a man stepped from the darkness and waved his hands in front of Brand. He stood on the brake and stopped, just missing him. Before Brand could yell abuse at the man a gun was thrust through the open window beside him and into his temple.

'Keep your hands where I can see them. Get out of the vehicle,' said a man in a balaclava.

The man who had leapt out in front of the car like a startled impala came to the gunman's side. 'Search him, he's probably armed,' said the one with the pistol.

Now how could he have known that? Brand had wondered. In South Africa it might be a fair assumption that a white man driving at night would be carrying, but in Zimbabwe the gun ownership rules were very tight and there weren't many firearms on the street – one of the few benefits of living in a regime presided over by a paranoid dictator.

At the gunman's insistence, Brand had got slowly out of the Land Rover and assumed the position, with hands on the car roof and legs spread. The decoy had now donned a balaclava too, but Brand reckoned he'd had a good enough glimpse of him in the headlights to identify him again, if he lived to inspect a line-up. He felt hands running under his armpits and around his waist. 'He's clean,' the man said.

'What now?' Brand asked. The electricity was out in this part of Harare, par for the course at the time, so there were no streetlights and no passing traffic. 'My keys are in the ignition. Take it, but I must warn you the injectors need servicing.'

'Funny man,' said the gunman, before pistol-whipping Brand on the side of the head. He staggered but didn't fall. The gunman's assistant pulled Brand's hands behind his back and cable tied them together. The plastic bit into the flesh of his wrists. 'Get in the truck.'

Brand had been led down the street to a shiny new black double-cab HiLux. The assistant opened the rear door and shoved him in. The gunman slid in beside Brand, keeping his pistol, a Russian Tokarev, jabbed against his ribs. The other got into the driver's seat and dropped the clutch as he sped off.

'What do you know about Tatenda Mbudzi's death?' pistol man asked him.

'He died in a car crash, right?' Brand said.

'That's not what you told his father, the comrade minister.'

It occurred to Brand that either this was a very dumb criminal, giving away the fact that he was in the employ of the politician Brand had interviewed, or that he had no intention at all of letting Brand live once he had gathered just how much he knew and, probably, who he had told about what he had learned.

'I've emailed a full report to the insurance company that Tatenda had his policy with.' In fact, he hadn't got around to doing his electronic paperwork on the case and he had been unsuccessful in even connecting to the internet with his laptop for the week he had been in Harare.

'Bullshit,' said the man. 'We've been monitoring your emails.'

'Now you're the one who's bullshitting. We're in Harare, not Houston.'

'Your FNB cheque account is overdrawn again.'

This was getting worse, Brand thought. 'Who are you, Charlie 10?' Zimbabwe's Central Intelligence Organisation – CIO, abbreviated by locals to Charlie 10 – was the equivalent of American's CIA.

The gunman chuckled. 'Does it matter who we are? I'm the one with the gun.'

'I also called the insurance company in England to tell them to contact the police here if I don't check in every twenty-four hours.'

The gunman laughed out loud this time. 'Your network's been busy all day. We can't even bug people in this country the phone service is so shit.'

They drove through the darkened city, the intermittent slap of the *bakkie*'s windscreen wipers the only sound for a while above the soft purr of the engine. Harare was a jumble of shantytowns interspersed with suburbs of grand but fading colonial homes and ostentatious new mansions built as ziggurats of greed by the ruling political and business elite. They skirted the town centre and headed out on the southern road towards Masvingo and South Africa, past Coke Corner, named after the soft drink factory situated there. Beyond that they passed knots of soaked people thumbing hopelessly for a lift, and closed on the sprawling fields of graves Brand had often glimpsed on his way into and out of this crumbling city.

Turning in through the gates in the ruined wire fence a security guard in an overcoat and woollen cap just nodded at the black *bakkie* as it bounced along the access road. Brand had the terrible feeling these two were regular visitors to the cemetery. Like other graveyards he had encountered in sub-Saharan Africa this one resembled the aftermath of some terrible battle. Beyond the older stone slabs and headstones were hectare after hectare of simple earthen mounds. Thanks to HIV/AIDS and every other ailment known to mankind the life expectancy of the average adult male in Zimbabwe was thirty-eight. Photos pinned to simple wooden crosses and the cellophane wrapping from bouquets of flowers were all that passed for markers and monuments here.

It took them some time to drive to the outer edge of the field of death, the rear of the truck fishtailing more than once on the slippery, muddy track. The driver finally stopped and got out. He dragged Brand out of the vehicle and held him while the gunman slid down from the new-smelling vinyl seat. 'Get the shovel.'

The driver opened the cargo area of the truck and took out the tool. He came to Brand, turned him around and with a knife he produced from somewhere slit the plastic tie binding Brand's wrists. His fingers throbbed in pain as the blood returned to them, making it agonising even to grip the shovel. His boots squelched in the mud and he felt that the damp had wet the hem of his long cargo pants. Brand wore shorts for maybe three hundred and sixty days of the year, and it was only because he was in Harare at night, on a rainy evening, that he had chosen trousers.

'Keep well back from him in case he tries to hit one of us with the shovel,' the gunman said. Damn, Brand thought, had this man seen all the same movies as him? 'Dig.'

Brand chose a spot for his own grave next to that which was marked with a cross and a photo of a smiling young man in a white dinner jacket and black bow tie. He wondered if the photo had been taken at a wedding, perhaps the man's own? Brand hoped the bride had not become infected with whatever had killed the groom, but that was why the cemetery was bursting at the seams. He started to dig, the blood-red clay sucking in the blade of the shovel then holding it fast.

'Faster,' said the gunman.

A jackal whined in the night nearby, and Brand tried not to think about what it was doing there. He shovelled the damp earth to the side and began working up a sweat in his long pants and long-sleeved T-shirt. He straightened for a moment and wiped his brow.

'Don't worry, you have eternity to rest.' The gunman planted his boot between Brand's shoulder blades and he had to use the shovel to stop from pitching forward. The gunman was getting cocky. Brand resumed digging. He could yell for help, but it had seemed to Brand the cemetery security guard would take his time responding, if he responded at all. No, this would have to end the other way. 'Deeper,' said the gunman.

Brand dropped to his knees. He stopped digging again, his hand in the small of his back. 'I'm not as young as I used to be.'

The gunman laughed behind him and, as he had hoped, pushed him again with his foot, harder. Brand let the wooden shaft of the shovel slip from his grip as he tumbled forward onto his hands and knees. If the gunman was smart, Brand thought, he would finish it now and shoot him in the back of the head. Brand heard the man's shoes talking to the sucking mud as he changed his stance, but he had deliberately fallen on the shovel.

'Don't you want the shovel back?' Brand asked, not looking up. 'It's got your fingerprints on it.'

'Pass it up, but stay down on your hands and knees,' the gunman said.

Brand looked up. The other man, the one who had driven, was standing at his head, perched on the edge of the grave. Brand reached under his body and slid the shovel up, shaft first, for him to take. The man grabbed hold of the wooden handle.

'No, get him to put it on the side,' said the gunman behind him.

But he was too slow. Brand yanked on the blade and for the briefest moment the driver instinctively held on to the shaft. Brand saw him teeter and sprang up and snatched his trouser belt with his left hand. With all his strength he hauled the other man over and down on top of him. At the same time, Brand twisted his whole body, using his hand on the man's belt as a fulcrum. Brand heard the silenced Tokarev's muted bark and the bullet grazed across the upper part of his chest, from shoulder to shoulder, before thudding into the mud.

The gunman's next shot went into the driver's body somewhere as he writhed and punched at Brand. The driver screamed and arched his back. He was not dead, but he was hurting. Brand ignored the man's kicking and clawing and reached down to his right ankle. The wet hem of his cargos had ridden up, making it fractionally easier for him to draw the little .32 semi-automatic from the ankle holster he had velcroed to his leg before going out.

Using the wounded driver as a shield Brand rolled and fired a double tap, two shots at the gunman. The gunman fired again and the bullet went through the driver's chest and into Brand's upper right shoulder. The shot killed the driver, but Brand was running on adrenaline and didn't even register the hit. The gunman cried and staggered backwards. Brand had winged him, but he was still very much alive. Brand rolled the dead weight of the driver off him, but stayed low in his makeshift foxhole. He raised the shovel's head above the edge of the grave and it clanged painfully in his hand as a bullet ricocheted off the metal. He raised his gun hand over the rim of the hole and fired twice more, blindly.

Brand had fired to keep the other man's head down, and as soon as he'd loosed his second shot he vaulted up and over the edge of what was now the driver's grave and slithered on his belly in the mud to the next grave. The rain started to increase and he felt it pattering hard on his back as he peered around the mound of fresh, damp earth.

The gunman raised his head above the burial mound he was hiding behind and Brand was surprised to see that he was no more than three metres away. He squeezed the trigger and although the CIO man had lowered his head on seeing him, the fresh earth piled at the top of the hummock he was lying behind was not packed nearly hard enough to stop even Brand's puny .32-calibre projectile. Brand hadn't seen the hit immediately, but he later realised the bullet had entered the man's head via his nose and then bounced around inside his cranium, killing him instantly.

Brand waited thirty seconds, or perhaps thirty minutes – he couldn't remember now – for the adrenaline to subside, and to make sure the gunman was dead. He had barely registered the wound in his shoulder – the one across his chest was just a graze – but it throbbed painfully now as he stood, his pistol loose in his right hand, and walked across to the dead CIO agent. He rolled him over with his boot and the man stared past him to the cloudy sky above. The rain washed away the blood in rivulets that followed the pronounced contours of his face, down his cheeks and into his open mouth. Brand searched him and pulled a phone from the inside of the black vinyl bomber jacket. He noticed the man's scuffed shoes. He had been a tool of a brutal regime that had bled his country dry in order to line the pockets of the ruling elite, and this guy was wearing cheap shoes made of imitation leather.

Figuring the CIO would trace the call he dialled Dani's number in the UK, which he knew by heart. 'It's me,' he said when she answered.

'Hudson,' she asked, her voice slow from waking. 'Are you all right?'

'No.' Brand told her what had happened as a result of him gathering the evidence he needed to prove Tatenda Mbudzi had faked his own death. 'I know the insurance company won't like it, but I need you to go public about this case, straight away. Issue a media release to the expatriate Zimbabwean online news media saying Tatenda, son of a government minister, is alive and a fraud.' A number of Zimbabwean news websites were watched by government and opposition alike and fed the fledgling independent press inside Zimbabwe, which was making a comeback after years of suppression by the president.

'It's against our protocols, going public,' Dani said. 'This is a matter for the insurance company and its client, and the local police now.'

'I know all that, and you and I both know nothing will happen to Mbudzi. Hell, Dani, you've got to go public with this – get it out so that everyone knows that we know about Mbudzi. Otherwise his father is going to have me killed before I can get out of the country. He'll probably rub out the doctor who issued the fake death certificate, if he hasn't already.'

Dani paused while thinking his proposed strategy through. 'I'll talk to the insurance company. What are you going to do?'

'I'm going to the American embassy, but I don't have their number. I need a doctor.'

'Hudson! You didn't tell me you were hurt. How bad is it?'

The phone beeped. Either the signal had dropped out or the CIO agent had run out of pre-paid airtime. Brand had certainly just cancelled the man's account for good. He tried Dani again, but the call failed to connect, so he dropped the phone on the dead guy and headed for the cemetery gate. Brand figured that when the agent's buddies checked the phone they would see he had called the UK and, even if Dani didn't deliver via the media, they would at least know that someone else apart from Brand knew about the minister and his crooked son.

Brand found the keys to the truck in the driver's jeans. He floored the accelerator, the car slipping and skidding on the muddy cemetery roads, but as the entry gate came into sight he saw through the slapping of the wiper blades the flashing lights of a police car. There was nowhere he could go. As he pulled up he saw the security guard smiling as two officers approached the car and hauled Brand out. They grabbed his wrists, raw from the plastic ties, and snapped cuffs tightly round them.

'I want to make a call,' he had said to the member in charge, the term for the officer commanding the station at Southerton, where they took him.

The senior officer shrugged. 'The landline is not working and there is no Zesa to charge my cell phone. Sorry for that.'

Brand knew that Zesa, the Zimbabwe Electricity Supply Authority, was local slang for electricity, which was all too often not working in the city. He waited two hours in a cell for a doctor to arrive at the station to check his shoulder wound. The man was a Nigerian, and when he mumbled his name, Brand, light-headed from blood loss, was momentarily gripped by the fear that it might have been the same quack who'd issued Tatenda Mbudzi's death certificate.

'Are you here to kill me?'

The doctor had smiled as he drew up a syringe. 'No, I am here to help you.'

The doctor had been true to his word, and he patched Brand up well enough for him to be moved to Chikurubi Prison, the country's most notorious, and dumped in a cell made for five men but inhabited by ten. By the next morning, after a sleepless night, he was covered in lice from lying on a piece of cardboard on the floor.

A US consular officer arrived, and shook his head when Brand was led into the interview room. The man, who said his name was Peters, slid a copy of the *Daily News*, one of the independent newspapers in Zimbabwe, through the bars separating them. Tatenda's faked demise was all over the front page, as was the news that the CID, the police criminal investigation division, had found and arrested him.

'The police are saying it was two muggers who hijacked you,' Peters said. He was half Brand's age, dressed in a blazer and chinos.

'Bullshit. They were Charlie 10; they wanted to know what I knew about Mbudzi and who I had told.'

'You're not licensed to operate as a private investigator in Zimbabwe,' Peters said. 'The authorities take a dim view of people trying to do their job for them, especially foreigners.'

Brand held his tongue. Peters was right. But the money Dani paid for a few days of investigating work was better than he could make in a month of guiding. He asked Peters what he should do.

'You're in court later today. The murder charges are being dropped. The police don't like the CIO and the opposition is cock-a-hoop about getting Mbudzi's head on a platter. Plead guilty to the charge of carrying a firearm without a licence and you'll get a fine.'

Despite the lumps and bumps and bites all over him, and the bullet wound that needed proper treatment and a clean bandage, Brand had started to feel quite good about himself and what he had achieved, even though it had almost got him killed.

'And leave Zimbabwe straight away, and don't ever come back,' Peters had said.

But that was exactly what Brand was about to do, only three months later. He drove across the Sabie River on the bridge where the lion Pretty Boy had nearly had Darlene and him for breakfast. He tried not to think about her as he checked in at the office and obtained a permit.

'No guests today, Mr Brand?' the same national parks man who'd been on duty that day asked.

'You heard, I guess.'

He nodded and stamped Brand's permit. 'Good for you. These poachers are evil.'

Brand slid his new weapon, a nine-millimetre SIG Sauer – the Zimbabwean police had never returned his .32 – across the counter and filled out the firearms declaration he handed him in return. The man placed his pistol in a canvas bag and closed it with a lead seal that would be broken when he left the park.

Brand went back out to his Land Rover and, after showing his permit to the security man at the boom, passed through the gates into the park.

On the twelve-kilometre drive to Skukuza he saw a pair of white rhino and a breeding herd of nine elephants, including a couple of tiny calves. The sight of these animals, in particular, helped ease Brand's mind. The elephant and the rhino were both hunted, poached to extinction in some parts of Africa, yet when left to their own devices they were no threat to man or other creatures. There was an innocence, a simplicity, about these lumbering giants that made him want to stay there, in the Kruger Park, and hide among them forever.

The two CIO men in the Harare cemetery had not been the first men Brand had killed, but he had hoped they would be his last. He put the Land Rover in gear and left the elephants, unable to look at them any more. He felt the darkness start to engulf him. He fought it, as he always did, but it seemed his vision started to blur at the edges and he felt the terrible weight of the things he had done in his life bearing down on him, as if this invisible force from within was crushing him from every angle.

He blinked at the morning sun and tried to ignore the pain in his beaten and booze-drenched brain. What was he doing here, in this paradise? he asked himself. What right did he have to be alive? He stopped the truck again, pulling over onto the verge beside the road. His pistol sat on the passenger seat, next to him, in its canvas bag. Brand looked at it for long, lonely minutes.

'What can you see?'

Brand looked up from the bagged firearm and out the driver's window. Slightly below him, in the passenger seat of a Hyundai Atos, a miniscule rental car, an attractive brunette of about nineteen was looking up at him expectantly. The young man behind the wheel next to her peered up at him through the tiny windscreen. 'Are you looking at an animal?' the man asked.

The accent was Dutch, or maybe German. 'We want to see a zebra,' the girlfriend added.

'A zebra? Not a lion or a leopard?' Brand countered.

'No, we have seen them,' she said, 'but I just want to see a zebra. I think it is my favourite animal and it would make me happy to see one. I have been looking for the past nine days and have not seen one.'

Brand resisted the urge to ask if she'd had her eyes closed the whole time, but game viewing could be like that. He knew that if he really wanted to see a particular animal or find one for a client, and deliberately went looking for it, then he would be unlikely to find it. If he told himself, or a paying customer, that he could never predict the future or know exactly what a mobile animal with a mind of its own was up to or where it was likely to be, then fate would, hopefully, take a hand. He felt the blackness of his mood ebb slowly away. He had just been thinking about leaving this place, this time, this life, when this wide-eyed tourist had reminded him of a young man who had come to Africa in search of a war and instead been seduced by the peace and the inestimable beauty of nature.

Brand remembered how excited he had been, all those years ago, when he had seen his first zebra. He was battle-hardened by then, having experienced the mixed elation and horror of surviving his first combat. He was drinking hard, living hard and loving hard to keep the first of the many nightmares at bay, and he and some army buddies had gone to the Kruger Park on a weekend pass. Instead of stupefying himself with alcohol, as he'd fully expected he would, he was hypnotised and hooked by the simple sight of birds and animals living as their maker had intended, free of cages and safe from hunters' rifles.

'Follow me,' Brand said. 'I'll find you a zebra.' In fact, he'd seen a herd grazing in open country no more than a couple of kilometres back towards the gate. There was a pretty good chance they were still there and the Dutch couple, with their untrained tourist eyes, had simply missed them.

He found the zebra in a matter of minutes and the Dutch pair were over the moon. The guy passed him a sixpack of Heineken, which Brand gladly accepted. He *could* have picked up some more freelance guiding work, perhaps in Zimbabwe or in South Africa once his licence was reinstated, but Dani's job would pay better, and in any case there was more to him going back to investigating than the cash.

Brand drove through the thatched entry gate to Skukuza, over the ridiculously bumpy rumble strips and past the main reception building. He headed down to the restaurant and park shop, where he parked, grabbed his laptop out of the Land Rover and nodded to a couple of the other guides he knew who were waiting while their clients raided the shop for wooden giraffes and more safari clothes. He walked past the bronze statue of two kudus fighting, towards the cafeteria.

He bought a Coke and sat down at an empty wrought-iron table overlooking the Sabie River. A *dagga* boy, an old male buffalo, wallowed in the brown shallows on the far side of the shrinking waterway. Mouse birds flitted in the grand old sycamore fig tree that cast its welcome shade over him. In the distance was the disused railway bridge that used to carry steam trains to the Indian Ocean coast, through what was now the Kruger Park. The line had been decommissioned and ripped up decades ago, collisions with wildlife being too regular. It was probably one of the few times in history, he decided, where nature had won out over people in the ongoing battle for space and supremacy.

Brand opened his laptop and tethered his phone to connect to the internet. The signal here at the camp was 3G, faster than at Hippo Rock where any attachments in Dani's messages would have taken him too long to download. He took his reading glasses from the pocket of his bush shirt and sipped his Coke while he waited for the machine to boot up.

The buffalo looked at peace, in seventh heaven in fact. He was too old to run with the herd any more and had probably been left to his own devices in an enforced retirement. Often these old bulls roamed in packs, a handful of grumpy old men content to ruminate all day and gore to death anything or anyone that pissed them off. Brand liked them.

When the email program opened and finally finished downloading he saw that in addition to the usual spam there was the file Dani had promised, a separate email from her with an attached photograph, another that included a chain of correspondence between Linley and the insurance company, and messages from Anna and Peter Cliff, the sister and brother-in-law of the possibly late Kate Munns.

6

Anna Cliff sipped her sauvignon blanc and looked up through the glass roof of the conservatory at the pale grey clouds. Another English summer that had not failed to disappoint had faded into a bleak autumn.

In Zimbabwe the long dry winter would be coming to an end, the days becoming hotter and heavier before delivering the gift of rain. Spring was a season in name only, merely a sweltering build-up to the wet season. Unseasonably, yet poignantly, it had rained prematurely for Kate's cremation in Bulawayo.

Early spring rains, the old people said, were a portent of drought and death. Anna walked through the lounge room to the kitchen bench and pressed a key on the laptop's keyboard, waking it up. Her email program refreshed but there were no new messages. She wondered if this waiting, this hoping, was any good for her.

Peter was supportive, but she wondered now if he was just being indulgent, and if he would eventually tell her to come to her senses and forget this business of investigating Kate's death.

Their old family doctor, Geoffrey Fleming, had met Anna and Peter at the airport. She knew from the death certificate that Geoffrey had identified Kate's body. Anna had been surprised when

Geoffrey had called her, when she was still in London, to say that he was helping Linley Brown organise the funeral.

Geoffrey had taken her hand in both of his. 'I am so sorry for your loss, Anna.'

Fleming drove a rusting double-cab *bakkie* and had apologised for the state of his vehicle. 'Everyone's doing it pretty tough here these days. I have several patients, especially the elderly, who can't pay me. An African lady gave me a chicken – still alive – the other day.'

'Thanks for all you've done,' Anna said. He had aged well, she thought, still handsome, with his thick hair now silver.

'Linley made most of the arrangements, but it's a shame she can't be here for the service.'

'Yes,' Anna said. 'She contacted me via email. I don't really know her and didn't know she and my sister were so close. I want to see her, doctor.' She didn't feel, even at her age, that she could call him by his Christian name. 'Do you know where she is?'

He looked at her and shook his head. 'I'm so sorry, Anna. All I can tell you is that she's in South Africa.'

'Is she a patient of yours?'

'She was, but I have no idea where she's living at the moment.'

'Is there no way I can see my sister?'

Fleming swallowed and cast a glance at her as he drove. 'I'm so sorry, Anna, but her body was . . . well, there's no other way to say it, it was incinerated. It will have to be a closed casket service.'

Anna fell silent for a moment. 'I just can't understand why Linley couldn't stay, at least for the funeral?'

Fleming returned his concentration to the road. 'As she was a patient I can't tell you too much about her, but she's gone to South Africa for a type of treatment.'

Fleming braked and slowed for a donkey that had ambled onto the road. Anna had caught herself planting her foot on the floor of the pick-up's cab, searching for a brake, not used to being back on an African road.

'It couldn't have waited?'

'I'm hesitant to say "life and death", but Linley was not well, emotionally, after the accident. An opening appeared and she had to fly to South Africa.'

The kindly doctor's words had irked Anna. The woman had done a bunk, but was quite happy to take Kate's insurance money.

'How are you, Anna?' Fleming had asked.

'I'm perfectly fine. Why?' She'd tried to keep her reply calm, matter-of-fact, but she could feel her hackles rise and perspiration prick at her underarms.

He'd looked at her again with those blue eyes, still as piercing and questioning as they had been when she and Kate were children. 'Coming home, back to Zimbabwe I mean, must bring back some memories.'

'Naturally.'

'Well . . .' He looked back to the safety of the road. 'If you wanted to chat, some time, over a cup of tea, I'm a professional listener.'

'As I said, doctor, I'm perfectly fine.'

She hadn't spoken to Dr Fleming again that trip other than to exchange some small talk after the cremation. She'd spent the three days in Bulawayo in a daze, and then had flown back to London. She wondered in retrospect if she would have been capable of arranging anything.

She heard the growl of Peter's Aston Martin as he pulled into the driveway.

'Hello,' he said a few moments later as he dropped his keys on the hall table.

He was ten years older than she, and greying now, but he was still the handsomest man who had ever looked at her more than twice. He came to her and she kissed him on the cheek. 'How was work?'

'All right, I suppose. I don't know if she told you, but Sam brought Jessica in today and asked if I'd do a breast augmentation for her. Can you believe it?'

Anna shook her head. 'Ridiculous.' Samantha was a tennis friend, and Jessica, Sam's daughter, was just sixteen. Anna and Peter had never had children; she had never felt the urge and now wondered if their marriage would have been different, better perhaps, if she had pushed to conceive when they were newlyweds.

Peter went to the drinks cabinet and fixed himself a Scotch. 'Why the sad face?'

'I was thinking about Kate again.'

'Have you heard from the private eye that Dani put you on to?'

Anna shook her head. 'Not yet. I've been checking the email all day.'

'Anna . . .'

'I know, I know,' she said. 'It's all probably a waste of time, but it just doesn't feel right.'

'Of *course* it doesn't feel right. Your baby sister died in a horrible accident; there's nothing OK about that.'

He was being irritatingly rational, which annoyed her more than anger would have. If she were rational she would let it go, but instead she was becoming obsessed with Kate's death. And she was drinking more. It was all Dani's fault for going on at Sam's birthday party about people from Zimbabwe faking their deaths.

No, Anna chided herself, it was not Dani's fault. True, when she had heard Dani explain the way expatriate Zimbabweans were rorting their insurance policies she had reached for the idea like a failing alcoholic snatches back a bottle, but it was not Dani who had made her feel uneasy about her sister's untimely death.

'I could *feel* it, before Dani said anything. I know she's alive, Peter.'

She braced herself for a dressing down, but the corners of his mouth drooped and he tilted his head a little. 'I can tell you, as a doctor, that sometimes things happen in the operating theatre or in people's cases that I can't explain in scientific terms. I and other colleagues have seen patients pull through or go into remission when the odds and the science were against it, and I've heard of people dying from no other cause than a broken heart. I can't tell you to stop being foolish if this is something you believe in.'

'We've got to find out the truth, Peter.'

He sighed. 'Yes, we do.'

*

Brand ordered another Coke from the waitress as he studied the electronic files Dani had emailed him. He shifted his chair to stay in the shade of the thatch-roofed *lapa* and saw as he did so that the buffalo was still wallowing in the shallows of the river.

Dani had made file notes of conversations she'd had with the insurance company, and with her friend, Anna Cliff. Dani had questioned Anna about her sister's financial affairs. Her notes, spare and terse, just like Dani herself, read: *Kate had rented a flat in Islington. Until three months before her travelling to Zimbabwe she had held the same job for the previous ten years as a human resources manager with a brewing company. Accepted an offer of voluntary redundancy following merger with another company. Had plans to travel the world. No car loan or other outstanding debts that Anna was aware of.*

That, Brand figured, was a 'no' in answer to his mental question about whether the claim would have been treated as suspicious by the insurance company. Kate Munns didn't owe anyone a huge amount of money – not anyone who'd left a paper trail at least – and she should have been looking forward to some extended travel. She did not seem like the sort of person who needed to disappear off the face of the earth, or who needed the two hundred thousand pounds her life was insured for.

Brand rubbed his chin. There were, he knew, other reasons why someone outwardly secure – financial and mentally – might need money to disappear. Problem gamblers and, to a lesser extent, drug addicts were good at keeping their vices hidden from family and friends and both could find themselves in need of sizeable amounts of cash. He turned back to Dani's notes.

Anna Cliff said her sister appeared in 'relatively good spirits' the last time she saw her, before Kate's trip to Zimbabwe. Kate had booked a return ticket to Zimbabwe, but had made no plans to go further.

So this was not the beginning of the round-the-world tour. Brand took out a bound notebook from the pocket of his bush shirt and, under the heading 'Kate Munns' made his first note, to ask how long Kate had planned on staying in Zimbabwe.

Dani's file continued: *When quizzed what 'relatively good spirits' meant, Anna said Kate had appeared distracted and somewhat anxious at the airport, when her sister dropped her at Heathrow. Anna quizzed Kate about this and her sister replied that she was having second thoughts about her plans for travel, and even her trip to Zimbabwe. She said she was missing her job more than she expected and felt that in the current unsure economic times she should be trying to find another rather than going abroad and spending her redundancy payout.*

Brand had spent his life drifting so couldn't quite understand why someone who had been forced out of a desk job, and given money, would be so eager to find another one too soon, especially if the person involved was financially secure. But then, he had little experience of the corporate world, nor financial security for that matter.

He craved a cigarette while he read and reached instinctively for his other breast pocket before remembering there was nothing there, and that he was supposed to be giving up again.

The words didn't tally – was it possible to be in good spirits while also distracted and nervous? Was Anna Cliff trying to read too much into her sister's mood in order to reinforce her own suspicions that Kate wasn't dead, but rather in hiding or running away from something? What did Kate have to run from?

Anna said her sister had had three short to medium term relationships, all with men. She said her sister was heterosexual and felt sure she would have known if there had been another side to her sex life.

Typical Dani, Brand thought. Going straight for the jugular, but he didn't completely trust the lawyer's neat tying up of this aspect of her questioning; no one really knew all about anyone else's sex life. He had done a little of this sort of investigation when he had lived in Harare, tailing spouses of clients who believed their other halves were cheating on them. It was dirty work, and not in a good way, and, to Brand's mind, not worth the money. He wondered if Kate's 'short to medium term relationships' meant she'd had trouble committing, or if she had just chosen the wrong men.

Brand wrote a second entry in his notebook: *Relationship with Linley Brown.* His initial gut instinct that there was more going on between Kate and Linley than Anna thought, or would admit, was still his strongest theory for why Kate would make her friend her beneficiary, if not for why she might want to disappear from her normal life in London.

He stretched, and his cracked ribs curtailed the movement. It still didn't stack up. This was the twenty-first century. People didn't fake their deaths to cover up their sexuality, and if Kate had wanted to run off with her boarding school lesbian lover she'd had the cash to do so, for a while at least, until her redundancy payout ran out.

Brand tapped his pen on the page of the notebook.

Attached to the email file was a scanned PDF of Linley Brown's claim on Kate's insurance policy, and a copy of Kate's last will and testament, which named the same Linley as her executor. Brand read the will first. It seemed Kate had few possessions. There was no car – Brand assumed she might have had a company car until she lost her job – and her cat, Ingwe, which meant leopard in various African languages, was left to her sister, Anna. Linley inherited the proceeds of her cheque and savings accounts. *How much?* Brand wrote on the next line in his notebook.

Linley Brown's address was a street in Burnside, Bulawayo. Brand knew the area vaguely; he'd lived in Zimbabwe in the early nineties working as a guide after the Angolan border war had died down and before he'd started as an investigator. Even though he had fought for the apartheid regime, he hadn't wanted to live in South Africa under its racial laws. Until Mandela took power in 1994 Zimbabwe had been the hotspot in the southern African tourism market for overseas visitors. He'd had a girlfriend who lived in Hillside before emigrating to Australia. He used to visit her every few weeks when he had leave from his job at The Hide, a private game lodge on the edge of Hwange National Park. Hillside had once been full of young white families with old money, but now most of its inhabitants were white pensioners with little money. Linley Brown's bank account details for transferal of the insurance payout were, however, in South Africa. Brand wrote down the account number, and Linley's address and phone number in Zimbabwe.

He closed the scanned PDFs and opened the next file, a saved email chain from Linley Brown to and from the insurance company Kate had her policy with. Linley's first email was asking why it was taking them so long to pay out the policy. A little cold, he thought, but perhaps two hundred thousand quid meant a lot more to a woman in Zimbabwe than to Kate's stay-at-home sister and her rich doctor husband. The reply in the chain assured Linley her claim was still being processed, and was subject to normal due diligence and verification. The process, the sender explained, could take up to three months.

Linley's second email was even terser and pointed out that she was experiencing extreme financial difficulties. She also advised the insurance company that her contact number had changed. The new number started with +27, which Brand knew was South African. Brand copied the new number into his notebook then tapped the end of his pen against his chin.

He was about to head north into Zimbabwe to try to prove or disprove Kate's death. It was unusual, but not unheard of, for him to have to interview the beneficiary of an insurance claim; more often than not they were living in the UK, where the policy had been taken out. The document trail would probably prove whether

Kate had faked her own death or not – it usually did – but the additional factor in this case was that whether Miss Munns was dead or alive, it seemed the family would most likely want to contact Linley Brown.

Brand disconnected his phone from the laptop and punched in the number from the email. It rang then went straight through to message bank:

'*Howzit, you've called Linley. Sorry, I can't take your call, but please leave your number and I'll get back to you just now.*'

'Ma'am, good morning, my name is Hudson Brand, I'm the local South African assessor for the company holding Kate Munns's life insurance policy. I'm sorry for the loss of your friend, but I have some papers for you to sign so we can expedite your claim and I'd be much obliged if you could call me back.'

Brand left his number and ended the call. Calling himself an assessor was being a little liberal with the truth, but he would draft and print out an affidavit for Linley to sign to cover the other lies he had just left in the voicemail message.

He returned his attention to the remaining emails and attachments, which had downloaded in full before he had disconnected. The other documents included a death certificate, which Brand noted was signed by a Dr Geoffrey Fleming of Bulawayo, and a police report of the fatal accident that had claimed the life of Kate Munns. It had been filled in by a Sergeant G. Khumalo of Bulawayo police's traffic department, who was the investigator.

Brand read the scanned handwriting, which was neat and slightly girlish. He wondered if G. Khumalo was male or female; there was no way of telling.

I arrived at the scene of the accident, 23.5 kilometres from Dete Crossing on the road towards Binga at 1143 hours. A lorry carrying maize meal was parked on one side of the road, heading west, and the burning wreckage of a 1956 Austin A40 was in the riverbed on the north side of the bridge in the gorge. A white female, who I subsequently identified as Miss Linley Louise Brown, was sitting in the grass with her head in her hands, crying. Miss Brown, as I now know her, said to me, 'My friend is dead – she is in the car.' The driver of the lorry, whom I identified as Mr Goodluck Nyati, was sitting beside his truck, smoking a cigarette. I walked along the bridge and down the embankment to the still smoking car and confirmed there was the badly burnt body of a person in the driver's seat. The person was clearly dead. The ambulance was in attendance and I told the driver to recover the body. I went to interview Miss Brown. She was distraught.

Brand pictured the scene. In his years of living in Africa he had formed the opinion that the most dangerous activity a person could embark on in this continent was not to fight in one of her perennial wars or to walk on foot among big game, or even to go out at night in Johannesburg; it was simply to get behind the wheel of a motor vehicle and turn the ignition key. While South Africa and other African countries made the world news now and again because of crime and conflict, the hidden killer in Africa – aside from malaria, the number one cause of fatalities – was bad driving. He'd seen old cars still on the road in Zimbabwe, including diminutive Austins with their rounded bodies, and the chance of surviving a crash in one of these was less than in a modern vehicle.

Goodluck Nyati, the police officer's report outlined, had not been the cause of the accident, though he had come close to becoming the second fatality. Rounding a bend as he came down the hill from the direction of Binga he had been confronted with the sight of the Austin bursting into flames below him. He had swerved, instinctively, as a fireball washed up and over his cab, and then had overcorrected.

Mr Nyati recovered his wits and ran to the guard railing, part of which was missing where the other car had gone over the edge. The railing on most of the northern side was washed away in a flood earlier this year. He saw Miss Brown, dazed but alive, screaming and waving for help in the riverbed. He went down to the river, but the force of the heat and flames made it impossible for Mr Nyati or Miss Brown to free Miss Munns.

Linley Brown had told Sergeant Khumalo that her friend, Kate, had lost control of the car when she'd swerved to miss a warthog that had wandered onto the bridge.

Miss Brown said that she had been in the backseat of the car, retrieving drinks from a cooler box. Her friend, Miss Munns, had not been restrained as given the age of the vehicle it was not required by law to have seatbelts or airbags.

The report noted that Linley Brown had suffered some abrasions and minor bleeding to her head, where it had connected with the interior of the car.

Brand closed the police report – he would re-read it later – and went back to his inbox. He opened the next message, which was from Anna Cliff.

Dear Mr Brand,
My friend, Dani Russo, who I believe you know, has told me you will be investigating the insurance claim lodged by Linley Brown, a friend of my late sister, Kate Munns. I have read a good deal online lately about people faking their deaths in Zimbabwe and making fake insurance claims. I have no idea why my sister would want to fake her own death, or why she would want to leave the proceeds of an insurance policy to her school friend. I know by now you will probably think I am mad, or just a grieving person who refuses to accept the death of her sister, and there is probably little I can say here that will convince you otherwise. However, I don't believe I can put this matter to rest until I make sense of what happened in the accident that allegedly killed my sister.

Linley Brown was not at my sister's funeral so I never got to meet her. I do live in the hope (however ridiculous) that my sister's body was not in the coffin that was cremated in Bulawayo and that she is alive, somewhere, guarding her privacy with a new identity for some reason. I have read how doctors and police can be bribed to say anything in Zimbabwe and I am aware from Dani that this is the line your investigation may take. If you do find that my sister is alive then naturally I would want to find her – I would want you to find her – and if she is, indeed, dead, then I would also like to discuss with you the possibility of you tracking down Linley Brown for me so that I can at least speak with the last person who saw my sister alive. I know you may think I'm crazy, but I need your help, Mr Brand, and you come highly recommended.

Yours sincerely,

Anna Cliff

Brand did not think she was crazy. He understood the pain of loss, the unwillingness to believe. He had seen the bodies of most of his friends who had been killed in action and, in a way, that made it easier to accept the loss. His mother, however, had died while he was in Africa. She had been one of the reasons he had volunteered for Angola, and it pained him to learn that she had passed and been buried while he was there, in the country of her birth.

Linley Brown should not be hard to find, he thought. If her emails were a true indication, she was in desperate need of the payout. He would find her and he would tell her how much Anna Cliff needed to talk to her.

Linley's absence from the funeral didn't ring true, Brand thought. There would have to be powerful reasons why a friend close enough to benefit from another's death would not even attend the service. Linley would be nursing the survivor's particularly painful wound to the heart of living when a friend had died. Brand knew that pain, and it was one he had run from, seeking refuge in drink and women. Nothing helped, he had learned, except the sort of confrontation and forgiveness that Anna Cliff was searching for.

He would hold off replying to Anna, he decided. He would wait until Linley Brown called him back, and there was no better place to while away a few hours or days than the African bush.

There was one more email from Dani to open, which said, simply, *Picture* in the subject line. When he opened it he saw it was a forwarded message sent from Peter Cliff to Dani. Cliff's brief text informed Dani that he had found the attached photo at Kate's home on her refrigerator door. It was a print from *perhaps a few years ago* according to the sender; he had scanned the image in order to email it. *Linley is on the left*, the message concluded.

Brand looked at the two women. Both were blonde, attractive and smiling, but that was where the resemblance ended.

He closed out of the email and the mail program, shut down his laptop and touched his finger to the brim of his Texas Longhorns cap in a salute to the old buffalo wallowing in the mud. He pictured, briefly, Kate Munns's body blazing in the wrecked car as her best friend looked on, helpless.

Brand hoped that when his end came it would be quick, and that there would be no friends around to see it. It was time for him to hit the road again, if only until Linley Brown called.

7

When I switched on the phone again, to see if Lungile had had any luck buying the dresses, it beeped to tell me I had a message. I ordered another latte from the Shona waitress in the Mugg & Bean at the Broadacres shopping centre, next to the Cedar Lakes walled housing estate where Lungile and her brother rented a house.

I didn't recognise the number of the missed call, but it was South African.

'*Ma'am, good morning, my name is Hudson Brand*,' it began, the man's accent a mix of South African and American English. I listened to the rest of it and when I saw there was nothing from Lungile I switched the phone off again. Cops track people by their mobile phones and while I had no reason to suspect they had my number, I played it as safe as I could. If Lungile had been arrested for something stupid she might have given it to the police.

'*Tatenda, sisi*,' I said to the waitress, and she smiled wide. It was nice seeing someone from my country – someone I wasn't robbing – even if I couldn't be there right now. I wondered if Beauty, as her nametag read, was as desperate to get home and start a new life as I was.

I thought about the message on the phone, the accent of Mr Hudson Brand. His name sounded like a cross between a fighter plane and a washing machine.

'Are you still OK?' Beauty asked, checking on me not a minute after she had delivered my coffee.

'Fine, thanks.' I folded the copy of *The Citizen* in half so that the grainy security camera picture on the front was no longer visible, and so it wasn't obvious to the waitress that I had been reading and re-reading it several times since I had arrived in the cafe.

Glamour girls strike again, screamed the tabloid's headline. The theft of the widow's jewellery was only our third job in Johannesburg, but already the police and the media had discerned a pattern. It was why Lungile was out shopping, and why we were going to have to change our modus operandi. The story on the front page told of the 'attractive and well-dressed' women who had talked their way into another Joburg mansion on the pretext of wanting to buy it, and fleeced the owner. The lady whose ring I had popped back into the letterbox was pictured, holding a photo of her recently deceased husband, next to the shot of Lungile and me making for the car – eyes deliberately downcast in case of this sort of thing. The article didn't say anything about my good deed, returning the wedding ring.

Turning my mind back to Hudson Brand and his raspy accent that reminded me a little of Denzel Washington, I opened my netbook, connected to the free wi-fi, and googled him.

The only Hudson Brand I could find seemed to be a safari guide, not an insurance assessor, and he had his own collection of press clippings, beginning with: *Safari guide kills rhino poacher.* There were several versions of the same story, from just a few days ago. One of the articles noted that Brand was born in America, and that tallied with the drawl, possibly southern, that I'd heard on my voicemail, but the job description was all wrong. There was a picture of him, dressed in bushveld khaki and a sweat-stained cap. He had a nice smile and the perfect, even teeth of an American. He was either deeply tanned or there was some African somewhere in his background. He was old, but still good looking, for sure.

I hit the back arrow and scrolled down past the stories. There was another entry that made more sense. *Minister's son faked his death – insurance company decides not to press charges.*

'Aha,' I said out load.

Beauty looked over at me.

'I'm fine,' I said to her.

In the body of the news article, from the *Daily News* in Zimbabwe, I read that a man called Tatenda Mbudzi had faked his death and been exposed by a private investigator, Hudson Brand, who had been wounded in an attempted car hijacking. There couldn't be two men in Africa with a name that preposterous. Hijackings were very rare in Zimbabwe, so I wondered if Mbudzi had been trying to run interference with Brand's investigation. There was another article from a newspaper in South Africa dating from 2010 which said police had interviewed *local safari guide and private investigator Hudson Brand* in relation to the rape and murder of a woman near the Kruger Park.

So, Brand was an investigator, not an assessor, and possible murder suspect. But I had nothing to fear from Brand – Kate Munns was dead and cremated. I still cried, at night, when I thought about how bad it was that I couldn't be there to say goodbye to a woman I loved. I wondered if Anna was behind this apparent investigation, if she could not accept that Kate was gone. All of the paperwork for the claim was perfectly in order.

My coffee was getting cold as I sat there thinking about what to do next. I didn't want to see Brand, or to answer his questions, and nor should I have to. I was entitled to the money and I did not want to go through the ordeal of telling someone else again how I burned my hands banging on the closed window as I watched a human being go up in flames like a Roman candle, or how the smells of cooked flesh would stay with me forever.

I resented Anna's interference, if it was her, or her domineering husband, Peter, if it was he who was questioning the claim. I decided I would email the insurance company, saying I had heard from their investigator, Brand, but advising them to email me any additional papers they had for me to sign.

Beauty came and took the cup and asked if I wanted anything else. 'Just the bill, please,' I said.

The Mugg & Bean was filling with the lunchtime crowd and the owner would be grateful for my table. I decided to take the copy of the newspaper with me, in case Beauty took another look at the blonde on the front page I had been staring at before she brought me my drink.

My phone beeped and vibrated with a message.

Hi girlfriend. Have found the most FABULOUS outfits for us in the Oriental Plaza. See you at home. I fixed up the bill and, before leaving, decided to make one more call. I dialled a number in Zimbabwe.

'Dr Fleming's surgery, good morning,' a woman said on the end of the static-plagued line.

'*Howzit*, it's Linley Brown here, one of Dr Fleming's patients, how are you?'

'Fine, and you?' she said.

'Fine. Please can I speak to the doctor?'

'Ah, but he is on his way out just now.'

I heard a soft voice in the background asking who it was. The receptionist, not doing a good job of muffling the mouthpiece, said, 'Linley Brown.'

'Linley,' said Geoffrey Fleming a second later. 'You just caught me – I'm here at reception on my way out to a house call. How are you, my dear?'

He was so old-fashioned, addressing me that way, but I liked him and he'd been good to me. He'd cared for me when others hadn't. 'Fine, doc, fine. Well, a bit worried in fact.'

'Really?' I pictured his kind, lined face, the still-thick silver hair, and his outdated horn-rimmed glasses. As bad as things got with me, as low as I went, I always felt better just seeing him. 'Did you go to the program I referred you to?'

'I did.' I felt a little swell of pride as I said it, hearing the conviction in my voice. 'And,' speaking more softly so the businessmen and housewives sitting around me couldn't hear, 'I've been going to the Nar-anon meetings, like you suggested.'

'Good, good. But what's wrong?'

'Doc, have you been contacted by an investigator about the insurance claim?'

He coughed, clearing his throat. 'No. Why do you ask?'

'There's a man here in South Africa, an American by the name of Brand, Hudson Brand, who says he's an assessor for the insurance company. He wants to meet with me and for me to fill out some papers. Does that sound normal?'

Again, the pause, as he processed the information and my question. 'I don't know. To tell you the truth I haven't had a lot to do with overseas insurance companies, but you'd be aware of these scams with people faking their own deaths, Linley.'

'Doc, I don't want to go through what happened again, not with anybody. I don't know if I can take it. I need the money – I have to tell you, I need it desperately – but I just want this to all be over.'

'I don't know what to tell you,' he said. 'If he calls me I will tell him what happened, and the truth: that the last time I spoke to you, you were in South Africa. He obviously has your number, so it really is up to you whether you meet him or not. I'm sorry, but I do have to go now. I'm glad you finished your program, and do please stay with the meetings – they may seem awkward at first, but they will help you.'

I wasn't as sure as he was, but he had confided in me that he had been through Alcoholics Anonymous twenty-something years ago and hadn't touched a drop of booze since. That was some feat in Zimbabwe, where alcohol was cheaper than bottled water and the tap water was usually undrinkable.

When Doc Fleming ended the call I felt as though I had been cast adrift. I still had Lungile, though, who had always been like the third sister in our gang at school. I loved her to bits, although I wasn't sure Doc Fleming or my sponsor at Nar-anon, Mark, would approve of me keeping company with her or her sleazy brother. I left the restaurant, stopped in at Woolworths to buy some pasta for dinner, then walked out of Broadacres onto the busy Cedar Road.

A car hooted and some guy called something unintelligible but no doubt filthy at me as I walked the short distance to the entrance of the housing complex.

'Afternoon, madam,' said the Malawian security guard. He recognised me by sight now and knew I was staying with Lungile and her brother. 'You know, madam, it is not always safe to walk around here, even in the daylight.'

I shrugged and pushed my sunglasses up on top of my head. 'What am I going to do? The Porsche is in for a service.'

'Madam?'

'Never mind, Benjamin, but thanks for the advice.'

I could have asked Lungile to come fetch me from the Mugg & Bean, but the walk, as short as it was, had given me time to collect my thoughts. I'd walked everywhere in Bulawayo, even as a kid, and the heightened sense of security in Johannesburg, whether misplaced or not, was one more thing I didn't like about the city.

Once through the gates I was struck, again, by how orderly and calm the estate was. The houses were arrayed in cul-de-sacs and avenues around wide expanses of manicured grassland with water features and a clubhouse. The dwellings were mostly mock Tuscan, or mock Balinese, or mock something else. A woman in shorts and T-shirt pushing a pram said hello to me in Afrikaans as I passed her. I could have walked or run around the estate, but on the couple of times I had tried it I had felt like a caged animal, or an inmate in a prison, albeit a nice Tuscan prison. The whole place reminded me of a model railway set village, with walls topped with razor wire and an electric fence. Lungile had told me the security was good here; there were no break-ins and the only crime on the estate was neighbourhood teenagers stealing from houses for fun or to score some cash for weed or booze.

Crime was everywhere, and it didn't matter if you were in Johannesburg, Harare or London. I thought that if I felt uneasy running around inside the walls at Cedar Lakes, then how would I handle prison? I needed to get myself straight, in every sense of the word, but I also needed to eat.

The deep thump of a slow bass line reached out through the rendered mustard walls of Lungile and Fortune's rented house as I walked up the drive. Lungile must have been watching for me, as she opened the door to greet me.

'Check!' she screeched, holding up a long black dress.

'I love it. How are you?'

'I'm fine, girlfriend, fine, fine, fine.'

The cloying odour of marijuana followed her out onto the *stoep*. I had never acquired a liking for the stuff. I grew up in a conservative house and even when Lungile smuggled some into school I found it didn't really do a lot for me, other than make me feel paranoid. That was an unwelcome side effect, and I enjoyed the high I got from my prescription pills much more.

Lungile wiggled her ass as she sashayed into the marble-tiled reception area, still holding the dress in front of her. Her brother, Fortune, appeared from the kitchen in a shiny tracksuit and bling, a packet of Salticrax crackers in one hand and a *zol* in his mouth.

'*Kanjane*, sister,' he mumbled through the dope smoke.

'Fine.' I wasn't his sister and I didn't like the way he looked at me sometimes, like he was now, as though appraising me from head to toe. He was several years older than Lungile and still single, a would-be gangster and a player. I hadn't known him when we were at school and had only met him when I came to Johannesburg.

While Lungile had been out hunting for dresses I had been for a job interview, for a post as a secretary to a real estate agent in the shopping centre next door. It would have been perfect for me, as I could have walked to the shop. Even if Benjamin the guard didn't approve, the commute was still safer than my current line of employment.

Lungile set the garment down on the purple leather couch, which her brother had bought and I hated. The backs of my knees stuck to the cushion as I flopped down on the monstrosity and sighed.

'How did the interview go, or need I ask?' Lungile asked.

She wasn't being smart; I could hear the sympathy in her voice already. 'My Afrikaans is not so *lekker*, it seems.'

'There should be a law against that – not being able to get a job because you can't speak the no-longer official language of this country.'

I shrugged. 'Babe, I just don't know what to do.'

Fortune leaned over the back of the couch and waved the joint he'd been smoking in front of me. 'How about a little of this to help ease the pain of rejection?'

I coughed. 'No thanks.' His cologne smelled even worse than the weed. What I wanted came in a little plastic bottle with a childproof lid. Fortune would probably know a doctor who could be bribed to write me a script and he wouldn't tell his sister if I asked him not to.

No, I chastised myself. Then he would want a favour. I bunched my hands into fists by my side.

'Sauvignon blanc?' Lungile suggested.

I nodded. I should have been going cold turkey, but I couldn't, not after the call from the safari guide cum private investigator. Lungile brought a glass from the kitchen and poured the pale golden liquid into it while I held it. I took a deep sip. It certainly didn't hurt. I looked up at her. 'Did you see *The Citizen* today?'

'Glamour girls!' Fortune started doing an impromptu dance on the marble. 'Glam, glam, glam, glamour girls.'

'Enough,' said Lungile. 'Yes, I saw it. Are you worried?'

I took another drink. 'A little. You can't really see our faces and I'm glad you told me to always wear those big Paris Hilton sunglasses, but it felt like everywhere I went today people were reading that bloody newspaper and looking at me.'

Lungile sat down beside me and put her hand on my knee. 'Well, *no one* is going to be looking at you after the next job. Come try on your new outfit.'

As crazy as it sounds, I felt safe with Lungile. I knew, however, that what we were doing was wrong and the life I was leading was reprehensible. I wanted nothing more than to go straight, but I felt like I was trapped in a downward spiral. I'd been cursed, denied the innocence and freedom and choices that so many other people took for granted. When my money came through, I told myself for the thousandth time, I would make amends to the victims of my crimes and I would become a good person. For now, though, I let Lungile top up my empty glass and I silently prayed that I'd made the right decision not to meet with Hudson Brand and that my claim would be rubber-stamped once he found out that Kate's death certificate and the reports of the accident were all legit.

8

The bull elephant trumpeted and shook his massive head, producing a dust cloud that enveloped him like a smoky aura.

Brand held his ground as the bull flapped his ears. The elephant took a couple of steps towards where Brand was parked in his Land Rover, by the Klopperfontein waterhole in the far north of the Kruger National Park. The front ranks of a phalanx of thirsty Cape buffalo were churning the already muddy waters into glutinous goo while the elephant turned his attention to the vehicle.

The early rain had come and gone and the temporary burst of green grass and leaves had dried to desiccated gold and brown once more. Early rain was an illusion, a promise of bounty, but Brand had long ago learned that if something seemed too good to be true, it usually was.

Finding out that Linley Brown had a South African mobile phone had also been a glimmer of false hope. In the two days he had spent winding his way leisurely from Skukuza to the north of the park he had called Linley's number six times and SMSed it three. Still he had received no reply from her. This could mean a number of things, he thought as he watched the elephant barge his way back into the herd of buffalo. The bull thought this was his waterhole and he was determined to try and scare off anyone or anything that tried to suggest otherwise. Brand had seen the mock charge directed at his Land Rover for what it was, and so, too, did the buffalo, who gave some low bovine moos and shifted around a bit, but otherwise kept pressing their point men into the mud, ignoring the feisty young bull's blustery rants.

Brand took a stick of chilli beef biltong and bit into it. He washed the heat from his mouth with a swig of Windhoek Lager while he watched the buffalo and the obstreperous young male elephant face each other down. Linley could be somewhere without mobile phone coverage. Such places were becoming fewer and farther between in South Africa, but they did exist. Alternatively, if she was using a pre-paid SIM card she could just be out of credit. It had happened to him often enough.

But it didn't make sense. He was her lifeline to two hundred thousand pounds and all she had to do was call him. If she was suspicious of the creative semantics he'd used in his voicemail message, introducing himself as an assessor rather than an investigator, then that could mean she had something to hide.

Brand drained his beer, which was getting warm in any case, and tossed it with the other empties in the passenger footwell. If this was a scam it was more elaborate than the others he had investigated. There had been no sham funeral in the case of Tatenda Mbudzi, or the others, but according to Dani's file Anna Cliff and her husband had flown from the UK to attend a cremation and had taken home Kate's ashes – or someone's ashes. That sort of shit, Brand told himself, was harder to fake, but not impossible. Could a crematorium be on the take? It was Africa, after all, and he imagined weirder things happened in the rest of the world when it came to the business of getting rid of bodies or making people disappear.

One thing that had definitely vanished without a trace was his bank balance. Brand had been counting on the walking safari and the tips he'd hoped to earn. In a way, Linley Brown's refusal or inability to return his calls was good news for him. He had hoped, for expediency's sake and the sake of Kate's sister, Anna, that he could meet Linley and wrap this case up in South Africa without having to cross a border. However, if that happened he would only have been able to charge Dani for a day's work, in all good conscience, but the longer Linley delayed him the greater the need for him to travel north into Zimbabwe. By doing so he would start racking up some hours and days that he could bill Dani for, and thus make up the shortfall in funds.

Brand disconnected his phone from its cigarette lighter charger and pressed the dial button to call the last number he had tried.

'*Howzit, you've called Linley . . .*'

He ended the call, not even bothering to leave another message. The hell with it, he thought, it was time for him to go to Zimbabwe and start earning some of Dani's money.

*

'Thanks, Dani, bye,' Anna said. She re-tied her dressing-gown belt, which had come loose.

Peter looked up from his copy of *The Times*, folded beside his morning tea and toast. 'Encouraging news?'

Anna sat down and picked up her cup of tea. It had gone cold. 'I don't know. She said her investigator, Brand, emailed her from South Africa to say he was about to cross the border into Zimbabwe and should be in Bulawayo late today or early tomorrow. She says his email access will be limited from there; I could have told her that.'

'Don't fret. There's nothing we can do from over here. By the way, last night, after you went to bed, when I was up reading some papers online, I checked out your Hudson Brand. Seems he's a safari guide as well as a private investigator.'

'Really? Well, it would have been nice if he'd replied to my email. Perhaps he was too busy out in the bush telling tourists zebra jokes.'

Peter smiled and went back to his tea. 'He made the news after killing a poacher.'

'Good for him. I just wish there was more I could be doing. I suppose this Brand fellow doesn't want to have much to do with us until he can find out through his own sources if we're barking up the wrong tree.'

'Hmmm, perhaps.' Peter sipped his tea. 'You know, it was a shame we could only spend such a short time in Zimbabwe for the funeral.'

Peter had had a full surgical schedule at the time, and even with some re-jigging they had only managed to get away for four days, including travelling time. 'You mean we could have done some checking of our own?'

He shook his head. 'I'm not saying that, but it was all so terrible; it must have been awful for you having to make such a rushed visit back to the place where you were born, and having no time to look around again.'

Peter was right. The trip was a blur in her memory. She had pictured herself going back to the bush to stay in a safari lodge or travel to some new, exotic destination if and when she returned to Africa. She had never dreamed she would have to go to cremate her sister.

It would be hot and dry there now. She closed her eyes and her ears to the drumming of rain on the conservatory's glass roof, and tried to conjure the smells of her childhood: wild sage, dust and the musty scent of elephant borne on an open-furnace wind.

'I wonder if it might help,' said Peter, bringing her back to the reality of rain-swept London.

'A trip back to Zimbabwe?'

He took off his reading glasses and put them in his top pocket, closed his paper and stood up from the table. 'Maybe not just Zim. What about Botswana, South Africa? Wherever you want to go. A proper safari.'

She looked up at him. 'There's nothing like the bush soothing what pains you, my granny used to say.'

Peter took his suit jacket off the back of the chair and put it on.

'Will you be home late this evening?'

'I'll try not to be,' he said.

She waved goodbye to him and contemplated another day of waiting for news that would probably not come any time soon, thanks to the unreliable phone and internet connections in the country of her birth.

Her laptop was on the kitchen bench. Anna opened it and boiled the kettle to make herself a fresh cup of tea while the computer booted up. She poured the water and took the drink to the counter, where she perched on a stool and entered the words 'hudson brand safari guide' into Google.

Anna found the stories Peter had mentioned about Brand killing a poacher while on a walk, and read with more interest his success in proving a government minister's son had faked his death in Zimbabwe; he seemed to know what he was doing as an investigator. Next she clicked on a hit from what looked like Brand's own webpage, Brand Safaris.

It was slow to load, so Anna opened the bottom kitchen drawer and found her hidden pack of cigarettes and lighter under the tea towels – somewhere Peter would never, ever find them. She opened a window and felt a cold gust of damp air. He would probably still be able to smell it when he came home, but she didn't care. She needed the nicotine hit. A picture of Brand, wearing khaki and standing with one foot up on the bumper of an open Land Rover came up on the screen. He had stubble on his chin and a pistol in a holster on the belt on his short shorts, which revealed dark brown legs.

She exhaled towards the window then waved at the smoke with her hand as the wind blew it back inside. Brand's website advertised personalised escorted safaris throughout southern and East Africa, and day drives into the Kruger National Park from his base in the town of Hazyview. His biography said Brand had worked as a guide in Zimbabwe, Botswana and South Africa, and by special arrangement in East Africa, in Kenya and Tanzania. There was nothing on the website about his work as a private investigator.

Anna thought about what Peter had suggested over breakfast. She did want to go back to Africa. She started to wonder what the mocha-skinned man with the crooked grin and blue eyes would think of her. Even if he did find that Kate had died in the car crash – the most likely outcome – she still wanted someone to find Linley Brown for her so that she could talk to Kate's friend. Anna didn't care about the money, but she wasn't satisfied that any medical condition, short of the need for open heart surgery, could have kept a woman away from her best friend's funeral. No. Something was up with Linley Brown and Anna wanted – needed – to confront her.

She went to the fridge and took their combined social calendar down from its magnetic hook, then opened her copy of Peter's surgical schedule, which he kept updated for her remotely from his work laptop. In the unlikely event Kate was alive and in hiding, Anna wanted Brand to find her and, if she was dead, she needed Brand to find Linley. Brand was a safari guide, so whatever the fruits of his investigation he could probably put together a private tour for herself and Peter. With luck she and Peter might even be in Africa at the same time as Brand found something for them. She was paying the man, indirectly via Dani, and directly if he agreed to do the follow-up investigation for her, so she thought she may as well get her money's worth out of him.

Anna finished her cigarette and her tea, put the cup in the sink and went to the bathroom. She turned the shower on to let the water warm up, then slipped out of her robe. Stepping in, she added some cold and tilted her face to the shower's rose.

She squeezed shampoo from the bottle into her hand and as she massaged it into her hair she closed her eyes and thought about the plan for a safari. It would be fun, and whatever came of Brand's sleuthing, Peter was probably right – it would also be good for her.

Through the foggy glass of the shower door Anna looked at her reflection in the bathroom mirror. She kept herself in good shape, going to the gym three days a week and watching her weight, but for what? She and Peter had no sex life.

Anna washed her chest and under her arms, then felt her breasts, as she did regularly, for lumps. She found herself lingering, though, her fingers brushing a few more times than was necessary over her nipples. They responded to her touch and her thoughts, and started to harden.

Looking away from the mirror so she wouldn't see the manifestation of the colour she felt in her cheeks, she turned her mind to exactly what it was she wanted.

She and Peter had been to a luxury safari camp on an island in Lake Kariba, in Zimbabwe, for their African honeymoon after their wedding in Bulawayo. Anna forced the memory of Kate as her teenage maid of honour from her mind and directed herself back to the hot, steamy October afternoons when she and Peter had used the outdoor shower, open to the elements, at the rear of their safari tent. It was like skinny-dipping behind closed doors – liberating and arousing, but with no risk of anyone seeing them. Peter had been as he always was, a considerate, adept lover who seemed to enjoy putting her pleasure before his. For a while, for the first time in her life, everything had been perfect. Then, one day, when she found out what he was really like, the intimacy between them had ended.

She imagined the setting now, the sounds and smells of the African bush enveloping her along with the water, and a man opening the door of the outdoor shower. Anna's hands moved down over her belly to the tangle of hair at the apex of her legs, a finger pushing between the folds of skin, finding the other part of her that was hardening, for the first time in too long. She looked over her shoulder, eyes closed, and pictured the man there. Not her husband, but a tall man with skin the colour of the rich brown heart of mopane wood, undoing a bush shirt and unbuckling a gun belt, his shorts sliding to the stone floor.

Her back was to him, a false, futile show of modesty as his left arm snaked around her, drawing her forcefully to him, pressing her against his muscled belly and the hard shaft. His calloused finger replaced hers, readying her with one hand while he gathered her wet hair into a ponytail with his other and yanked it back, hard. He kissed her exposed neck, drawing the skin between his teeth, then whispered something filthy in her ear, what he was about to do to her.

Now, as in the vision played out behind her closed eyelids, she steadied herself against the wall of the shower with one hand. She felt his knee knocking her legs apart, sensed herself pushing her backside towards him, arching her back, displaying herself like some wild creature on heat, ready to be mounted.

Anna felt him enter her, one stroke, uncaring, commanding, taking possession of what was offered to him. She felt the coarse stubble burning her cheek as he talked dirty to her, all the way through to her climax.

She shuddered, suddenly unsteady from the waves of guilty pleasure that rolled through her body and the hot steam engulfing her, both robbing her of breath. The soap slipped from her free hand and she eased herself to her knees to retrieve it, and to let the shaking subside. At last, she opened her eyes to find the lost soap, but in doing so she caught sight of her pathetic reflection again. A lonely, rich housewife who had lost the little sister she never really knew well enough, the last blood member of her family. The tears pricked at her eyes and she coughed from the cigarette she should not have smoked.

In truth, Anna Cliff did not know what she needed in life, other than that she was not happy being who she was, where she was, doing what she was doing right now. Perhaps her considerate if romantically inattentive husband was right; maybe the answer was back in Africa.

*

'Oh, I don't know. I still can't make up my mind,' the young woman, stage name Bambi, real name Emily, said to Peter Cliff as he washed his hands in his surgery. 'I know I can make more if I have bigger boobs, but I'm scared.'

'There's a minute risk with any surgery, of course, but you've no reason to be *scared*,' Peter said. He buttoned his cuffs and sat down behind his desk. Emily listed her occupation as 'dancer', leaving out the 'lap' bit. It was her fourth consultation and she was still dithering about whether or not to go ahead with a breast enhancement. Emily had been referred to him by a colleague.

'Giles told me you were the best,' Emily said, tucking in her blouse and sitting down again in the chair on the other side of his desk.

Peter's time didn't come cheap although Giles, an orthopaedic specialist, was loaded, so Peter consoled himself that his friend wouldn't mind paying for his mistress's indecisiveness.

'Giles wants me to get the operation,' she said.

'Yes, but the important question – the only question – is, do you want it?'

She forced a little smile with those pouty lips. 'I want him to be happy, and he's ever so good to me. Sometimes, though, I . . .'

Peter crossed his legs and waited.

'Well, you know, sometimes I wish he was a bit more like you. A little more concerned about what I want.'

'Read this,' Peter said, and slid across his desk a brochure that detailed the ins and outs of the sort of surgical procedure Emily was considering. She reached as if to take it, but instead put her fingers, with their shiny red nails, on his.

'Giles said I should thank you, properly.'

Peter snatched his hand away. 'That's very nice of you, Emily, but you've said thank you already. You can thank me by paying the bill.'

She seemed suddenly emboldened, her embarrassment gone. Peter assumed she knew exactly how to get men to do what she wanted. Despite her youth she no doubt had a wealth of experience in getting men to fork over tipping dollars at whatever strip club she worked at.

Emily stood, put her palms on either side of the blotter advertising a drug company's wares, and leaned forward. Her breasts were close and he smelled her sweet, girlish perfume. Her long, straightened hair brushed his cheeks and he sat, unable to move for the moment as she moved her mouth to his left ear and gently bit the lobe. 'He told me to give myself to you, but I want you anyway,' she whispered.

Peter put his hands on the edge of his desk and pushed, propelling himself backwards on the rollers of his office chair, out of her reach. 'I'm a married man, Emily. And I do not, under any circumstances, get involved with my patients. Sorry.'

She pouted and tilted her head. Along with the spoilt child expression he thought he saw a flash of anger in those brown eyes. She was used to turning men away, but not to being spurned. Peter wondered if the business about Giles telling her to have sex with him was true – he would have words with him if it was – or if she was getting sick of Giles and was in the market for a new doctor sugar daddy. 'That's nice.' She straightened and took her overcoat off the back of the chair. 'Sorry from me too.' She turned and walked to the door of the consulting room and, as she put her hand on the knob, looked back over her shoulder. 'But I meant the bit about wanting to.'

Peter pulled himself back under his desk and exhaled as Emily closed the door. He had more important things to worry about than randy strippers.

He checked his watch; even with the flirting he had finished Emily's appointment with ten minutes to spare. He pulled the computer keyboard to him and switched from the patient records software to his internet browser. He googled Hudson Brand and scrolled down the hits to the man's webpage.

He sized up the guide cum private eye from his picture. 'Arrogant prick,' he muttered. He clicked on the tab that said 'Book a safari'. On the page that came up were the details of a travel wholesaler that handled bookings for Brand's tours in Africa, and which had with branches in the UK, America, Australia, Germany, France, Portugal and Spain.

Peter clicked on the link to an email address for the UK operator and typed a short message, saying he wanted a quote for a three-week safari guided by Hudson Brand around Zimbabwe, Botswana and South Africa. He included a line claiming that Brand had come highly recommended by friends who had used his services as a guide, and that he wanted no one else. He made sure to sign off the email as 'Dr Peter Cliff', as he knew for most people this conjured up images of a man with money to burn, and guaranteed a prompt reply.

As soon as he hit send Peter got up and walked out to reception. Emily was at the counter paying her bill. She looked over at him and winked and he knew he had failed to stop his own blush. He looked around the waiting room and recognised his next patient. 'Mrs Hyland. Come through, please.'

9

I typed an email on my iPhone as Lungile drove our new car, a BMW sedan, through the leafy streets of the Houghton Estate, one of Johannesburg's most exclusive neighbourhoods. Nelson Mandela had lived here in his final years. The car was hot – Fortune's work – but it had been re-sprayed and sported the plates from a wreck.

The email was addressed to the person at the insurance company in England who was supposedly processing the claim:

Dear Miss Johnson,
I was contacted here in South Africa, where I am currently staying on business, by a Mr Hudson Brand, who claimed he was an assessor for your company, and needed to meet with me and get me to sign some papers. I made some enquiries with your affiliate here and was told no such assessor existed. Given the high rate of crime in this country I was immediately suspicious. Also, from further contact I have had with other people in the insurance business I have learned there was nothing regular about Mr Brand's request. Can you please clarify who this man is and why it is taking so long to process my late friend's claim, and fulfil her wishes, as outlined

in her will. If there are additional declarations which I need to sign then please email them to me and I will reply accordingly.
Regards, Linley Brown

The mesh-covered slit I was looking through was annoying and I had to tug it, again, to make sure I was hitting the right key to send the message.

'You look good in black.' Lungile gave a muffled laugh from inside her own burqa. She had bought the kind that concealed us completely. She had even found us gloves so that no one would know if the women under the outfits were black, white or brown.

'I'm sweating like a pig in this thing,' I said. 'Turn up the air con.'

We needed to leave Johannesburg, especially after the front-page exposure our last job had elicited, but Lungile wanted one more go at the big end of town before we relocated our operation. I had laughed when I had seen the special dresses she had bought for our next job; it really was a stroke of genius.

I wondered if it would be a one-off. If the home owners we were about to rob connected the two women in burqas to the loss of their belongings then the media and the police would probably connect the case to the 'glamour girls' in a matter of minutes. Perhaps Muslim women in traditional dress would be banned from open house viewings as a result, and we certainly wouldn't be able to risk trying the same trick twice.

That was fine with me because I definitely, positively, wanted this to be my last job with Lungile. My money was surely close to coming through, despite what the Brand guy got up to in Zimbabwe. There was no reason for me to think otherwise, but I just did not want to meet him in person. Lungile's brother, Fortune, had fenced the loot from the widow's house and while it was not as much as Lungile had hoped for – it never was, and I was sure Fortune was taking more than the twenty-five per cent commission he claimed he skimmed – I at least had enough money in my bank account now to buy food and a few items of new clothing, and to contribute to Lungile's rent. We would, however, need some more cash if we were to relocate, as there would be up-front payments to make on a new house.

I felt another pang of guilt over the anguish we'd caused the widow on our last job. Maybe the phone I'd stolen had been her husband's. What if the loss of it had brought her grief to the surface again? I resolved, as I had before, that when my money came through I would find my victims and try to do something for each of them, to repay them in some small way for any hurt I'd caused them. I was never meant to be a career criminal; the feeling of shame was eating me from the inside out and I wanted this ride to stop.

I wondered what it was like for Muslim women to wear this get-up every day. What did they wear underneath it? I was wearing a pink Lycra running top and short black exercise shorts and I was boiling. Did they wear nothing at all? I was made up, but my makeup felt grimy in the heat and my hair was plastered to my face.

'Are you still thinking of leaving me and flying to Kenya or wherever when you get your money?' Lungile asked me.

'Yes.' I was glad I couldn't see her face. I hoped she wouldn't continue her thieving without me, but I knew she probably would. She couldn't pay her mother's hospital bills on the wages of a domestic or waitress, which would be about the only line of work she could pick up as an illegal immigrant.

I detected a shrug under the folds of Lungile's burqa. 'I'll miss you.'

All I really wanted was a life free of drugs and hassles and, for a while at least, men. I wasn't turning gay – though life might have been easier if I could – but after my last relationship I needed to get away, and a new country was a good start. I had stopped after four glasses of wine the night before, and I was proud of myself and my newly found willpower. Lungile had carried on and started twerking in front of the TV, and for a little while I felt nervous, angry even, that I hadn't reached the same point of release. I wanted to mix a couple of pills with my drink, badly, but I held off, made some black coffee, then went to bed.

I asked myself again what I was doing here, sweating nervously, wiping my hands on the material of my disguise before I had to put my gloves on. I was telling myself the insurance payment would come soon, and if I lived on noodles and *pap* I could have survived without thieving any more. But Lungile had pleaded for me to come along, and I was excited by the novelty of her brazen plan to hit Johannesburg's millionaires again. I didn't feel like we were female Robin Hoods, but I did take some consolation from the fact that everything we stole would, if the owners were sensible, be replaced by their insurers, and that no one would ever be harmed as a result of our raids. Also, Lungile's mother needed her cancer treatment.

I knew it was a thin justification, but despite my feelings of guilt and conviction that I had to stop, I was addicted to the thrill of stealing almost as much as I was to prescription drugs. My precarious mental state was balanced on such justifications. I had blurred too many lines in the past couple of years and I didn't think I knew the difference, really, between right and wrong any more. So much of what I did was legally or morally unjustifiable that I had constructed an elaborate web of excuses for my actions – love, lust, addiction, drugs, adrenaline, Lungile, him – it was always the fault of some other person or substance or condition, never me. It would all change, I told myself again, when my money came through. Until then, I had to eat.

'There's the house,' Lungile said.

I saw the over-sized real estate agent's sign in front of the security gate and had a flashback to the last job. Part of me wanted to tell Lungile right then to keep on driving and to forget all this. What the hell, I would get a job as a phone sex operator, a car park guard, anything to avoid breaking the law again. But for some reason I couldn't do it, so I held my tongue.

As Lungile turned into the drive, I noticed an Eskom *bakkie* parked across the street. I guess power failures and the theft of copper electricity cables didn't only happen in the townships and poorer suburbs of Johannesburg.

The estate agent waiting to greet us was a man, solidly built with a spiky grey crew cut that was running to a mullet in the back. His jacket was buttoned, stretched across a beer belly, and as we got out he ran a finger around his collar. I wondered if he was new to the job.

'Morning, ladies,' he smiled as we eased ourselves awkwardly from the car.

'Good morning,' I said, in what I hoped was a passable Middle Eastern accent.

'Welcome.' He had a clipboard in one hand and pulled a plastic biro from his shirt pocket with the other. I glanced down and saw that the black shoes beneath the slightly frayed charcoal cuffs had a mirror sheen. I knew it was spit and polish rather than patent leather because the sides of the shoes merely gleamed instead of shone. 'Now, if you don't mind, ladies, could I perhaps get a name and cell phone number from you?'

This was standard procedure among the agents we dealt with and Lungile or I always bought new pre-paid SIM cards before each job so that if someone tried to call us just after the viewing we could reply, thus establishing we hadn't given fake numbers.

'Fatima el-Khouri,' I said.

Lungile waited while I spelled it out for the agent, then did the same when she gave her name.

The man coughed as if clearing his throat. 'Ladies, I don't like to sound rude, but you don't perhaps have some ID do you? I understand and respect your traditional dress, but we can't be too careful these days.'

'You mean these women who rob the houses?' I asked, disappointed he couldn't see my theatrically raised eyebrows.

'Just standard procedure,' he said quickly.

Bullshit, I thought, but I reached into my real Gucci handbag and took out Fatima el-Khouri's ID book. 'Is one enough or do you need both?'

'No, no, no,' he said, scribbling down Fatima's ID number. 'The one will be fine.'

I willed myself to breathe more slowly and I was now very pleased he could not see the sweat rolling down my face or my chest rising and falling. When Lungile had outlined her plan for us to dress as Muslim women I had insisted that we go mall-trawling in Johannesburg until we could find the handbag of a suitable target to lift. Fatima had, in fact, not been wearing a burqa but a rather fetching Prada suit when I spied her in a cafe in Sandton Square. Indeed, I complimented her on her outfit as I lowered my open-bottomed shopping bag over her Gucci number and then picked both up and walked away, holding tight to the two sets of handles. Finding her ID in the bag later, I used it to buy a new SIM card, registering it in her name under the RICA regulations which were designed to prevent criminal activity using mobile phones; I got a laugh out of that.

Lungile and I set off, joining half a dozen other women inspecting the six-bedroom, six-bathroom pile. When the theft was noticed the agent would give the police the list of names and numbers. My number would ring out, but even a tiny amount of surface scraping by the laziest of detectives should uncover the report of theft the real Fatima el-Khouri had no doubt submitted by now. The ladies in the burqas would be obvious first suspects.

Be calm, I told myself as I entered the first of the bedrooms. It was a teenage boy's, if the bikini-clad model on the wall and the cricket bat in the corner were any indication. On the desk was an Apple MacBook, an iPad and an iPhone.

I looked around the room and its adjoining en suite, then poked my head back out into the corridor. Lungile was asking the agent something, and glancing at me over his shoulder. I couldn't see her face, but I knew she was thinking, *Get on with it* as I returned her blank stare.

Slung across my torso, under the burqa, was my voluminous beach bag. I went back into the boy's room and started to lift the hem of my disguise. I stopped and cocked my head. I heard nothing, but an alarm bell was trilling inside my mind. Instead of grabbing the loot I lowered my hem again and walked out into the lounge room.

Lungile was pretending to admire the couches and some art on the wall while the agent talked to a woman about council rates and projected rental income. He made no move to look over his shoulder at what Lungile or I might be up to. I knew Lungile was staring at me, but I couldn't read her face. I shook my head and walked into the master bedroom.

On one of the bedside tables was a man's gold watch.

'Come on, who are they kidding?' I whispered to myself inside my veil.

Quickly I went through the motions of viewing the other rooms. Just as I thought, there were three more laptops on desks in bedrooms and a study, along with a new-model BlackBerry and a couple of iPods. When I slid open the drawer of the writing desk in the home office there was a wad of two-hundred-rand notes.

'What are you doing?' Lungile hissed. I hadn't seen or heard her come up behind me – I had no peripheral vision in the burqa. Meanwhile a dozen bells were ringing in my head now and I was sweating profusely under the black garment. 'Have you got *anything* yet? There's stuff just lying around,' she persisted.

There was, indeed, a good range of very portable, valuable consumer goods on show in this house, ripe for the taking. 'Let's go,' I said to her.

'What is wrong with you? At least let me take that laptop. We'll get a couple of thousand rand for that, easy.'

'No. We're leaving.'

I heard her groan in her burqa. 'You're getting cold feet.'

I grabbed her arm and moved her to the door of the home office. 'Unless you want to end up being a party favour at Sun City I suggest you come with me *right* now.' I was using the nickname for Johannesburg women's prison, not suggesting Lungile and I might end up at the casino.

Out in the lounge room the burly estate agent was tugging on his collar again and studiously avoiding us, as he had done since he had taken down my fake ID details. I wondered if they were being checked right now.

'Goodbye,' I said to him, taking his attention from the would-be buyer. 'House is nice, but not big enough for family.'

'Really?' He raised his eyebrows as he tried to peer through the gauze covering my eyes.

'Big family.'

I forced myself to walk slowly to the front door. If he had checked us out already there would be a police *bakkie* blocking the gate in about thirty seconds. It looked clear, though, as Lungile and I got into the BMW.

'Are you going to tell me what's going on?' Lungile asked me. '*Eish*, did you see all that stuff lying around just waiting to be taken?'

'Just drive.'

'All right, all right, but what's wrong?'

I ignored her for the moment and watched the Eskom *bakkie* as Lungile indicated right after we passed through the security gate and turned up the street. There were two men in the cab, and I was sure there'd been only one when we'd arrived. Perhaps the other had been in the back, or maybe, if they really were Eskom workers, one had been working in one of the houses. The *bakkie*'s indicator light flashed and in the wing mirror I saw it pull out into the street behind us.

'Shit.'

'*What?* For heaven's sake.'

'We may be being followed.'

Lungile tilted her head to check her rear-view mirror. 'The Eskom dudes?'

'Yes.' The electricity authority *bakkie* was on our tail, and closing the gap.

'You think they're undercover cops?' She was trying to sound cool, but failing.

'Yes.'

'But how?'

I was annoyed that she hadn't spotted the trap herself, so I explained: 'You said it yourself, there were, like, gadgets everywhere in that house. Show me the teenage boy who leaves home without his phone and iPad and I'll show you a police sting.'

'*Eish*,' she said again.

It was all too obvious. Sometimes in the houses we visited silly people would leave a laptop on a desk, just so the buyers inspecting the house knew that the room was meant to be a home office, but generally when we lifted phones and computers we had to rummage through desk drawers. Most of the phones we stole were actually last year's model or older, consigned by their owners to a drawer when they updated their phone plans and received the latest BlackBerry, Samsung or iPhone. No one actually left a working new-model phone at home on a bench top or desk. The trap had been laid and we had very nearly taken the bait.

'Did you check that Neanderthal real estate *oke*?' I said.

Lungile nodded in her burqa. 'Bull neck, not used to wearing a tie. It all fits now.'

'Yes, police. And I gave him a stolen ID book.'

'What do we do?' she asked me.

Damn good question. I checked the wing mirror again. One of the electricity workers was talking on his phone. 'Turn left. Now!'

Lungile stepped on the brakes, swung the wheel without indicating, and then accelerated. Behind us the driver of the *bakkie*, taken by surprise, laid some rubber of his own as he overshot the turnoff and skidded to a halt. I could see the passenger gesticulating and talking as the driver reversed in order to take the corner. 'Go, go, go!'

Lungile geared down and planted her cheap canvas and rubber shoe on the pedal. The BMW lurched forward like a grateful racehorse released from the starting gate. We hit a speed hump and my head connected with the low roof. I ignored the pain and looked over my shoulder. The electricity company truck was blowing black smoke as they tried to catch up; they were definitely cops.

'Go left up ahead, the mall's just around the corner.'

Her black cowl nodded. Lungile took the turn and ran a red light, to the honking outrage of the driver who had just started to nudge forward. The next turn was the entrance to the mall, beneath the Game store sign. 'Come on, come on,' she said as she punched the button to get us a parking ticket. As the boom came up I could see the Eskom *bakkie* coming through the traffic lights.

Lungile pumped the accelerator as she dodged shoppers and trolleys and took a corner at speed. She raced up to the next level, pulled the handbrake and drifted into another turn, only stopping when she expertly slotted the BMW into an empty space. She was a hell of a driver. As we climbed out of the car we were ripping off our disguises. I went to the back and popped the boot. From inside I lifted the stroller and unfolded it. Once I was done I rolled and bundled our burqas into the pram and we both put on hats we had also stowed in the boot. I pulled mine low over my eyes.

'Let's get away from the car. Quickly,' Lungile said. I pulled the sunshade with its mesh panels over the stroller and did up the zips.

'Come, Precious, we have shopping to do,' I said in my best imperious Johannesburg trophy wife voice.

Lungile smiled, hiding her nerves better than I, and said: '*Yebo*, madam.'

I heard tyres squealing and made a snap decision as the *bakkie* swung into view. Instead of heading into the shopping mall I strode past the line of parked cars towards the truck, my arms moving across my body like a power walker's. I thought that if the cops saw us walking away from the car they would try and stop us and question us; they wouldn't be expecting us to head towards them. Behind me, Lungile pushed the baby carriage, dressed in a lightweight Pick 'n' Pay maid's uniform. After our last close call we had decided to don extra disguises under our other costumes, just in case. The cops in the *bakkie* skidded to a halt next to the BMW.

I heard doors opening. 'Hey, excuse me! *Mevrou*?'

Slowing, I looked over my shoulder. '*Ja*?'

'Did you just see two women dressed all in black, like in Muslim clothes?'

'Burqas?'

'*Ja*, I think that's what they're called,' said the man, who was wearing an Eskom uniform.

'Why, did they not pay their electricity bill?' I drawled.

Behind me my maid tittered.

'We're police. Where did they go?'

'They went into the mall. They were running. Now please stop shouting or you'll wake my baby.'

'Sorry for that,' the policeman said, touching a hand to his Eskom baseball cap.

The other cop was out now and he tried the driver's side door of the BMW. Lungile still had the keys, but hadn't locked the car. He reached in and hit the boot release. The one who had spoken to me checked the boot and, seeing no burqas inside, he and his partner jogged off into the mall.

'That was close,' said Lungile as she drew up beside me. I increased the pace of my power walking and she pushed the pram containing our disguises until she was panting.

'Too close,' I said. The police were on to us and were running sting operations to try and catch us. We needed to stop this now, or move to another location, like Spain.

'Close, but fun. Can we do it again?' Lungile said.

After a moment we both started laughing as we walked through the car park entrance and into the sunshine, poor, but free.

10

This corner of Zimbabwe had not had the early rains that had brought a first flush of green back to the bush in the south of the Kruger Park, near where Hudson Brand had been housesitting.

The grassless earth was baked red under the clear sky and burning sun, the trees bare of any leaves. Heat haze shimmered off the narrow, recently patched road and goats nibbled on rubbish tossed from passing cars. Brand hoped that when the rains did come they would be heavy and sustained; this country needed a break more than others.

He had crossed the Limpopo and queued his way through both sides of the Beitbridge border crossing in two hours – not bad timing for one of Africa's most infamously congested and chaotic frontiers. His Land Rover was South African registered and a few years earlier this would have guaranteed that every cop on every one of the fifteen roadblocks between the border and Bulawayo, an average of about one every twenty kilometres, would try and shake him down with a bogus fine or a request for cigarettes or a simple demand for cash, but not this time. Brand had smiled and exchanged pleasantries with all the cops and they had asked for nothing other than to see his driver's licence or the temporary import permit for his vehicle. He hoped it was a sign that the authorities had been ordered to lay off tourists. If Zimbabwe was ever going to bounce back it would probably be a recovery led by holiday-makers, with South Africans leading the charge.

The little towns he passed through – West Nicholson, Colleen Bawn and Gwanda – boasted stores with stock in the windows and people on the streets ready to buy. When the economy had all but collapsed during the years of hyper-inflation there had been nothing to buy.

The Land Rover's old diesel engine hauled the vehicle slowly uphill through Esigodini, but reaching the plateau on which Bulawayo was situated brought a measure of relief to the old girl. Brand stopped for another roadblock and checked his watch. 'Good afternoon, how are you?' he asked the young policeman.

'Ah, I am fine. May I see your driver's licence?'

'Sure.' Brand had his wallet on the seat beside him in readiness and he handed over the licence. 'Say, you don't know where I would find Dr Fleming, do you?'

The policeman looked up from the licence. 'Dr Fleming? He is in Hillside. He delivered my second child. It was a difficult birth. Are you ill?'

Brand nodded. '*Yebo*. I have a sore stomach. What street is he in?'

'He is a good doctor. You will find him in Weir Avenue. He will make you a better man.'

Brand doubted that, but thanked the policeman and took a can of Coke from the cooler box in the back and passed it to him. Once through the roadblock, he pulled over and entered the street into his GPS. He was still about twenty kilometres outside town. Brand's stomach was rumbling, not sore, but he was of the view that he could wrap this job up sooner rather than later. It had occurred to him that since he was in Zimbabwe, away from the controversy of his last job in South Africa, he might try and pick up some freelance guiding work. He would contact the owners of The Hide, the lodge on the edge of the Hwange National Park where he had worked before, to see if they could take him on for a spell.

Brand knew Bulawayo well; he had conducted investigations there in the past and had spent time in the city on leave from his work in Hwange. He liked the orderliness of the town's rectangular grid of streets. Those running one way were numbered, which made them easy to navigate, while the streets crossing them were named after heroes of the revolution – Robert Mugabe, Herbert Chitepo, Josiah Tongarara and so forth.

Despite the country's economic and political woes Bulawayo always seemed to Brand to be able to muster some sense of civic pride. The people here were Ndebele, formerly known as the Matabele, and they had always opposed Mugabe's ruling Shona. There was a feeling of stubborn defiance in the population.

He bypassed the turnoff to Hillside for now and headed instead to the government offices in the centre of town. The purple jacaranda blossoms were out and they compensated for the fading paint and run-down look of some of the once stately buildings. Bulawayo was a mix of old colonial architecture, hotels with wide covered verandahs and stark 1960s blocks of low-rise flats and offices. The streets were wide enough to turn a bullock cart in the old days, and today the centre strip was crammed with parked cars. Many of the models were ancient and those moving belched smoke; this was a country where nothing, least of all cars, was thrown out until it died. It wasn't unusual that Kate Munns and Linley Brown had been driving what would have been a collector's car anywhere else in the world. Here it was still a perfectly usable, legal means of transport even if it wasn't required to be fitted with seatbelts.

Brand turned into 10th Avenue and found a parking spot near the corner of Lobengula. The building he wanted, the Bulawayo Provincial Registry, was in front of him, part of a cluster of government offices in the grounds of the old Drill Hall, an imposing white Victorian structure that had been built for the old British South

Africa Police. The towers of the city power station loomed behind the buildings. A young boy leading a blind man wearing a threadbare suit and holding a tin cup and a stick zeroed in on him as he got out of the Land Rover.

'Hello, sir. I will watch your car,' said the boy.

'Sure,' said Brand. In South Africa he was never worried about someone stealing his old beast of burden – thieves there preferred Toyota *bakkies* to Land Rovers, but here in Zimbabwe wheels were wheels. He took his daypack containing his camera, passport and other valuables, and left his other bag in the truck. As he approached the government precinct he saw a line of people stretching out of the compound and along 10th Avenue.

'What are these people waiting for?' he asked the boy with the blind man.

The youth wiped a snotty nose with his finger, then ran it down his stained shirt. 'IDs, birth certificates, that sort of stuff.'

'They're queuing for the registry office?' Brand asked.

'Yes, sir.'

It was just as he feared. Last time it hadn't been nearly as crowded. 'Is this old man your father?'

'Grandfather,' the blind man interrupted. 'His father is dead, of tuberculosis.'

'How'd you like to make fifty *yusa*, pops?' Brand asked, using the local slang for US dollars.

The old man frowned. 'What do you want? Not my grandson.'

'No, of course not. I need you.'

The old man nodded. 'I understand.'

Brand, together with the man, whose name was Isaac, and his grandson, Joshua, walked along the queue and through the gates into the grounds of the Drill Hall, then over to the steps of the Provincial Registry Office.

'What are you doing?' a big man in the queue asked gruffly. He wore a ZANU-PF baseball cap in the gaudy colours of the ruling party.

'This man is old and blind,' Brand said, 'and he needs a copy of his son's death certificate. His son was the father of this small boy.'

The big man harrumphed. 'Let him through,' said the woman standing next in line.

'Thank you.' Brand took Isaac's arm and Joshua followed him to a walled cubicle at the head of the queue. Brand repeated the lie to two more people along the way.

The woman sitting behind the table in the cubicle was filling in a form. She didn't bother looking up.

'Cecelia, right?'

She raised her eyes and took a moment to recognise him. 'Ah, the American man.'

'Good afternoon, how are you?' he asked in Ndebele.

'I am fine, and you?'

'Can't complain.'

She put down her pen. 'Who is this old man?'

'A friend. I'm helping him. He needs to check a death certificate.'

Cecelia looked at Brand dubiously. 'Didn't I read about you getting into trouble, in Harare?'

Brand shrugged. 'You can't believe everything you read in the newspapers, especially in this country.' He didn't need her getting cold feet. 'About the death certificate for my blind, elderly friend . . .'

'You were locked up in prison, weren't you? Something about exposing a crooked *mashona* government minister's son?' Cecelia Ndlovu leaned across the counter, adopting a conspiratorial air. 'You know we don't criticise the government or the president; it is an offence.'

'Of course,' Brand whispered.

'But, well done.'

The blind man smiled. Brand was relieved. 'Cecelia, I've written the name of the deceased person on a piece of paper here.'

Just as he had done last time, he slid a folded piece of A4 paper across the counter to her. Inside it was not only Kate Munns's full name and date of birth, but also a crisp, new fifty-dollar bill. Cecelia gave no sign of even seeing the cash as she slid it beneath the bench top and into a small pocket near the waistband of her blue skirt. She studied the name. 'This Munns is a friend of this old man?'

'Of course,' Brand said. The blind man sat quietly, his hands folded in his lap, his stick between his knees and his tin cup by his right foot. The boy looked around, studying the people queuing for the various, tortuous rites of officialdom.

'I remember this one. Car accident.'

Brand raised his eyebrows. 'You knew her?'

Cecelia shook her head. 'Not personally, but I remember when it happened. I am from Binga, originally; my mother was on a bus and passed the scene. She saw the car burning. A couple of days later it was in the *Chronicle* that the white woman had died.'

So, Brand thought, he had a potential witness to the aftermath of the crash, which appeared to have actually happened. 'Can I see the death certificate?'

'Of course.' Cecelia went through a door and returned with a ledger book. She flicked through the certificates and stopped when she found the page. 'Here we are, Kate Munns, died 19 May.'

She turned the folder around and Brand checked the certificate. 'Can I get a copy of this?' It was the same date listed on Sergeant Khumalo's sudden death docket and investigation report.

'Ah, sorry, but the photocopier is broken.'

Brand wasn't surprised; if it hadn't been that then the electricity would have been off. He took out his phone and switched on the camera. 'Do you mind?'

She shrugged and he focused on the certificate and took a picture. The certificate was signed by Dr Geoffrey Fleming and dated the day after the crash. The case was turning into a slam dunk, assuming Sergeant Khumalo and Dr Fleming checked out. 'Thanks, Cecelia. Say, you do know what I'm investigating, don't you?'

'You are not looking for the death certificate of this blind man's friend. You are looking for people who fake their deaths,' she said matter-of-factly.

'Do you have other people checking certificates for the same reason?'

She nodded, and closed the heavy folder. 'Yes. There was another man, a local, doing the same work, for an insurance company in Australia. He uncovered a doctor selling fake certificates, just as you did in Harare.'

'Dr Fleming?'

'No, no, no. Not him. He is well known in Bulawayo. My mother goes to him, even though he charges a lot of money. He is a very honest man.'

'Do you remember the name of the other doctor who was selling the certificates? What happened to him?'

'It was a she,' Cecelia said. 'There was an investigation and the police came and took the certificate as evidence, but nothing happened and she is still practising.'

'How come?' Brand asked.

Cecelia smiled. 'In Zimbabwe if you have enough money you can buy anything, even your freedom. The police are paid and a prosecution docket and evidence mysteriously disappear. It happens all the time.'

Brand knew it happened and wasn't all that surprised, and he had to smile at the irony of Cecelia tut-tutting about bribery when she had just palmed a fifty to show him the death certificate file. 'Do you remember the name of the doctor?'

Cecelia looked at the ceiling for a moment, trying to recall. 'No, I can't think of it. It was something foreign, something European, I think.'

'Tell you what.' Brand tore a page out of his notebook and wrote on it. 'This is my Zimbabwean phone number. If you think of that doctor's name or you can find it, please call me. You can just hang up as soon as you ring so you won't have to pay for the call, and I'll call you right back.'

'I'll see what I can do.'

'I'd *really* appreciate it,' Brand said. It would be worth another fifty to get the name of a crooked doctor in Bulawayo in case he had more investigations in the future. He could also give the doctor's name to Dani and she could have her insurance companies run a check on recent suspect life insurance claims.

Brand and the old man and his grandson left the building and went back outside to the Land Rover. Brand thanked his accomplices and gave the young boy some cash. 'Be careful. If you go looking for the dead, you may find them,' said the old man as Brand gently shook his hand.

He drove off, away from the queues, and found a coffee shop. He ordered coffee and a toasted ham and cheese sandwich with mustard and while he waited for his lunch he dialled the number for Dr Geoffrey Fleming's surgery in Hillside, spoke to a receptionist, and was pleased to hear that the doctor could fit him in for a consultation in an hour. In his experience this was the best way to interview a doctor, on his or her time, with a fee paid. If he called explaining who he was and why he wanted to see the doctor he might be fobbed off.

Brand lingered over the meal. As he ate it he remembered the time in the not too distant past when none of these ingredients had been available in Zimbabwe. Although the dollar had brought some stability, times were still tough. Few of the people he saw walking past the plate glass window looked prosperous or well dressed. People were still just hanging on in Zimbabwe, hoping for real change, but the government was doing precious little to stimulate the economy. A recent law requiring all foreign companies investing in Zimbabwe to be fifty-one per cent locally owned had ensured that very few outside businesses could be bothered investing in the country. Unemployment was still high. Even doctors were doing it tough enough to take bribes, or perhaps that was just plain old-fashioned greed.

Brand read a newspaper – more tales of government corruption and a supposedly last-ditch scramble by politicians and party faithful for the remaining white-owned farms – and then paid his bill and headed out.

He turned the smoking Land Rover around and retraced his route into Bulawayo back out towards Hillside. The GPS guided him, but Brand found he remembered the way quite well. His girlfriend had lived in Percy Avenue, which was off Weir. He turned into the street and began searching for a plaque or sign that would identify the doctor's surgery. The houses were mostly surrounded by walls but while some had one or two strands of electric fencing on top there was nowhere near the level of security he would have encountered in Johannesburg. Through gates he glimpsed Japanese four-by-fours and late-model BMWs. There was still money in Zimbabwe and Weir Avenue looked relatively prosperous.

He drove to the end of the road and back again and still he could not find an indication of where the doctor lived. The address the insurance company had for him was a post office box. He was wondering what to do next when he noticed a woman in a green maid's uniform and headscarf walking along the side of the road carrying a plastic shopping bag. Brand pulled over and greeted her. 'Which one is Dr Fleming's house?' he asked, after exchanging the ritual pleasantries demanded by African culture.

She looked over her shoulder and pointed to a whitewashed wall on the corner of a cross street. 'It was that one, but he now lives in the cottage behind the big house. You turn there,' she said, twisting her hand to indicate he should go down the cross street.

'Thank you.'

Brand turned the Land Rover around and indicated into the cross street. He came to a green metal gate in the whitewashed wall with *Dr G. Fleming, MD* engraved on a brass plaque next to it. Brand pressed the button in the intercom on a pole beside the gate.

'Dr Fleming's surgery,' said a tinny voice.

'Hudson Brand, here for my appointment with the doctor.'

'Come through, please.' The gate started to roll open.

In a tight courtyard there were four cars parked close to each other. Brand could see now that a fence separated this plot and a small beige-painted brick house from an older, grander residence which fronted onto Weir Avenue. He parked the Land Rover and walked into the cottage.

'Mr Brand? Good afternoon.'

The receptionist handed him a pen and a form to fill out and he sat beside a heavily pregnant woman and ticked and crossed the boxes. It was a necessary formality if he was not to frighten the doctor. When he was finished he leafed through a battered copy of *National Geographic* while the pregnant woman went in for her consultation and, eventually, a man older than Brand expected came out and called his name.

Brand took the doctor's hand and met a strong grip. The man had alert blue eyes that searched his as he said, 'Mr Brand, I was expecting you.'

Brand followed him into the surgery, realising he had lost the element of surprise. 'I take it Linley Brown's been in touch with you.'

The doctor waved him towards a chair and sat down behind his desk. 'I don't talk about my patients, but I had heard you would probably be contacting me about Kate's death. Why did you book an appointment?'

Brand leaned back in the chair. 'If I'd called you and told you I was an investigator, what would you have done?'

'The same thing I'm going to do now, I expect.' The doctor checked his watch. He was handsome, grey-haired, straight-backed. Brand looked around. There was a picture of a boat on the wall, along with a fine shot of a painted dog, and a stuffed orange and black striped tiger fish with vicious teeth.

'You're aware there have been a number of cases of people faking their own deaths to claim on insurance policies abroad, especially the United Kingdom.'

Dr Fleming nodded. 'And you think I'm the type of person who would sell a fake death certificate?'

'Please don't take offence, doctor, there is no "type" when it comes to crime, in my experience.'

'I'm sure. Well, you know I signed Kate Munns's death certificate. I identified the body positively by the presence of a pin in her pelvis. I'd learned from Linley that Kate'd had a car accident in the UK and I was able to email her surgeon to get the details. Kate's childhood dentist had long since left Zimbabwe so there were no dental records I could check here. So, what makes this case a suspect one?'

Brand debated how much to tell the man, but Fleming was a step ahead of him already thanks to Linley Brown, so Brand figured it was best to come clean. 'Kate's sister raised a red flag with the insurance company. She thought it was odd Kate would make an old school friend the beneficiary of her insurance policy.'

Fleming sipped from a teacup. 'I've heard of odder things. From what I saw of Anna and her husband and learned of their life while they were here for the service, they seemed well off, financially. I wouldn't have thought they'd be overly worried about not getting Kate's insurance money.'

'From what I hear you're right, and they're not interested in the money. What can you tell me about Linley Brown?'

'You seem a smart man, Mr Brand, and all Americans I've met seem to have a good working knowledge of the law and medicine thanks to too much television. You should know I'm bound by patient confidentiality.'

'So she's a patient?'

'Very funny, Mr Brand. You know she's been talking to me; that's how I knew who you were and why you were coming to see me.'

Brand didn't feel like the doctor was being belligerent, more like he was involved in a game of chess with him, and was waiting for his next move. 'Let me ask the question in a different way. What do you know of the relationship between Linley Brown and Kate Munns?'

Fleming stroked his chin again. 'I delivered both of them, watched them grow up. They were good friends, and quite a bit younger than Anna. Linley's an only child. They were very close, but I'm as likely to speculate on my patients' personal lives with a stranger as I am to release details of their medical conditions.'

'So, you don't think it's unusual, then, that Kate made Linley the beneficiary of her policy.'

The doctor shrugged. 'Perhaps Kate thought Linley would have a greater need for money than her sister.'

It still didn't gel, Brand thought. He opened his notebook and flipped back a few pages. 'Kate Munns was . . . thirty-four years old. She should have been a long way off dying, so why should she care about her best friend's financial position in, say, another forty years or so? Is Linley in financial trouble now?'

'I don't know about that.'

'But surely you must see where the evidence is pointing; Kate makes her friend a beneficiary because she's living in Zimbabwe, perhaps penniless or just eking out a living like many folks here, but if she lives to a normal age then Linley won't see any money until she's seventy.'

Fleming said nothing.

There was something else Brand wanted to raise, but he suspected the doctor wouldn't answer. 'How many single thirty-four year olds do you think would even bother to take out a life insurance policy?'

'I'm sure I have no idea.'

'Kate had no children, no spouse, no dependents at all who would need caring for if she died.'

Fleming took off his glasses and pulled a tissue from the box on his blotter. As he cleaned the glasses he looked at Brand and rocked back in his office chair. 'All I can tell you, Mr Brand, is that for whatever reason Kate took out a policy and, as per her wishes, Linley should receive that money. The other thing I can tell you, quite categorically, is that there was a car crash on the Binga road and that Kate Munns was killed.'

Brand checked his notebook again. 'And she was cremated.'

'As per her wishes.'

Fleming sighed and put his glasses back on. 'I know that Anna must think that her little sister is still alive, and that she has faked her death and that she and Linley are living it up in Mauritius or the Seychelles or something like that.'

It was Brand's turn to say nothing.

'But it's not true. I pronounced that poor girl dead and I saw Linley after the accident.' Fleming took another two tissues and blew his nose. He looked away from Brand. 'Now, if you'll excuse me.'

Brand was reluctant to get up, but it seemed as though the old doctor was fighting to stay in control of his emotions. Brand figured the guy would be no stranger to death after maybe forty years as a doctor, but clearly this case had shaken him up. 'One more question, if I may, doctor.'

Fleming blew his nose again and looked back at Brand through red-rimmed eyes. 'Go on,' he said in a soft voice.

'Did you see Kate Munns at all before her death, on her last visit to Zimbabwe?'

He thought about the question for a moment. 'Doctor–patient confidentiality extends to the grave, Mr Brand.'

Brand nodded. 'I'm sure it does. But this question of why someone with no dependents and the rest of their life to look forward to would take out a policy and name a friend in trouble as the beneficiary still has me puzzled. A UK insurer wouldn't issue a policy to someone with a pre-existing condition, but I was wondering, if someone went to their old family doctor in Zimbabwe and, say, confirmed they had a terminal illness, maybe they might consider an assisted suicide and try to cover it up as a road death, in order to help their friend.'

Fleming's eyes widened. 'By driving themselves off a bridge? I could think of more efficient ways to commit suicide and make it look like an accident, and I dare say a bright young woman like Kate could as well.'

In spite of his line of questioning, Brand had been thinking the same thing. Another theory was forming in his mind. It was a long shot, a combination of several of the what-ifs he had canvassed with Dr Fleming and Dani. The doctor checked his watch. There seemed to be nothing in Kate's recent life that pointed to a problem that might force her to abandon her life in the UK. Brand had a thought. 'You knew Kate Munns and her sister from the time they were born. What was their upbringing like? Was it a happy home?'

Fleming stiffened visibly in his chair, just for an instant. Instead of looking at Brand he opened a diary on his desk and flicked through it. He looked up a couple of seconds later. 'My next appointment is overdue. Naturally I'll sign whatever paperwork you wish, in order to complete your investigation,' the doctor said.

'You didn't answer my question.'

'You said the previous question was your last,' Fleming said. 'And as I said before, doctor–patient privilege extends beyond the grave. If you want to know about the Munns girls' childhood you'd have to take that up with Anna, though I doubt she'll have much to say.' The doctor pushed back his chair and stood. 'Now, if you please, Mr Brand.'

'Much obliged,' Brand said. 'I'll be in touch if I need anything else.' He got up and let himself out of the surgery, putting on his cap on the way out. Behind him he heard Dr Fleming sniff and wipe his nose again.

11

Brand drove his Land Rover back into Bulawayo to the police traffic department. It was in the same complex of government buildings as the provincial registry, in the grounds of the Drill Hall. He walked up to the charge desk in the main office, greeted the female constable on duty and asked if he could see Sergeant G. Khumalo from the traffic department.

'Goodness, she is in the compound, doing police clearances.' The constable went back to her copy of the Bulawayo *Chronicle*, the government-controlled local newspaper.

So, the sergeant was a woman. Brand walked outside again and looked at the sky. Grey clouds were forming, but not enough yet to block out the sun, which burned down on him ferociously. Bulawayo was up high, like Johannesburg on the South African Highveld, and it often seemed to him that little bit of variation in elevation made a big difference to the impact of the sun's rays. Closer to the sun, closer to the rain clouds, perhaps closer to God.

His mother had been a staunch Catholic, a legacy of her Portuguese father, but Brand had chafed at being forced to go to mass every Sunday as a child. The war in Angola had put paid to any residual beliefs he might have taken with him into adulthood.

Had Kate Munns really killed herself to help a friend in need? Perhaps the sister, Anna, would know of Kate's views on euthanasia. Suicide might void her policy; he would have to check that in the fine print, but if she had staged her own death then Dr Fleming might have been persuaded to turn a blind eye if he suspected something. Perhaps Kate had killed herself in some more traditional manner, such as gassing herself in her car or slitting her wrists, and the evidence had been concealed by Linley in a fiery crash after pushing their vehicle off the bridge. Cars didn't usually burst into flames, despite what Hollywood thought, but carrying plastic jerry cans of petrol in the boot of a vehicle made it a more likely scenario. Brand had seen signs at service stations in Zimbabwe warning that this was an illegal practice, but everyone in Zimbabwe had lived through fuel shortages in the past, so many people still carried a container – legal or not – just in case.

While Dr Fleming had played his cards close to his chest Brand had no doubt the doctor and Linley Brown had been in contact. Reading between the lines, the woman was in trouble of some sort.

In a car park in the police compound twenty or so people were queuing to enter a small timber shack, known locally as a Wendy House because the prefabricated dwelling resembled a child's playhouse. There was precious little shade and the queuers pressed against the shack's walls under the asbestos eaves or held newspapers or satchels over their heads to ward off the sun's rays.

Brand walked to the office door, which bore a sign saying *CID – police clearances*. In order to take a motor vehicle out of Zimbabwe drivers had to get a clearance certificate from their local police station verifying they were the legal owner of the vehicle, or that they had permission to be driving it. In theory, a police officer checked the vehicle's chassis and engine numbers against the registration papers and the driver or owner's licence to ensure stolen vehicles were not transported out of the country. In practice this scheme had been reduced to an exercise in queuing and paying. As with most enterprises in Zimbabwe it was also a way for smart operators to make money; at some garages you could pay someone to take your papers and queue for you.

Brand leaned around a man waiting to enter, knocked on the wall and said to the policeman sitting behind a desk, 'Excuse me, good afternoon.'

The plain-clothes officer looked up, clearly annoyed. 'Get to the end of the queue.'

'Sorry, I don't want a police clearance, I'm looking for Sergeant Khumalo.'

The man tossed his head. 'Out back. She is at lunch.'

Brand thanked him, nodded an apology to the driver whose clearance he had interrupted and walked outside and around behind the Wendy House. Under a tree three men and a woman sat around an improvised charcoal brazier made from a cut-down oil drum. A pot of *sadza* bubbled on the radiator grill grid. The female police officer stirred the pot with a wooden spoon while the men smoked and talked.

'Sergeant Khumalo?'

The woman looked up at him. 'Police clearances are on the other side of the office. You must queue.'

'No, I'm looking for you. I have some questions about a vehicle accident you attended a little over two months ago.'

Khumalo glanced at the pot. 'I am about to eat.'

'It's important. Perhaps I can have five minutes of your time in private? Or I could buy you lunch.'

One of her male colleagues said something in Ndebele. Brand had a working knowledge of the language, which was a derivative of Zulu. It sounded to him as if the man had said, 'Order a steak'. Khumalo smiled.

'I don't accept gifts or bribes,' she said, loud enough for the others to hear.

Brand shrugged. He had no reason to doubt her. He'd found that in Zimbabwe and other African countries female police were far more likely to be efficient and less likely to be on the take than their male counterparts. It wasn't a hard and fast rule, but Goodness Khumalo did not have the look of an overfed cop whose diet was subsidised by bribes.

'Then perhaps your personal code of honour extends to helping put to rest the concerns of a family who lost a loved one in a terrible car crash,' Brand said.

Khumalo pursed her full lips. 'Five minutes.' She stood and stretched. 'There is a takeaway shop across the road. Maybe you can buy me a Coke.'

So much for not taking bribes, Brand thought, although it seemed Khumalo was going to come cheaper than Cecelia, the registry clerk. 'Deal.' They walked out of the gate. 'Do you remember the death of a woman called Kate Munns, killed when her car went off a bridge on the road between Dete Crossing and Binga?'

Sergeant Khumalo nodded. 'Yes, a bad one. But then they are all bad. The driver, Miss Munns, was not wearing a seatbelt because she was in an old car and she was knocked unconscious and trapped behind the wheel when the fire started. Her friend watched her burn. She was stupid to be carrying petrol in plastic containers in the back of the car.'

Brand nodded. That explained the fire. They crossed the street and Brand asked the policewoman what she wanted.

'Coca-Cola.'

He ordered one for each of them and the shop assistant reminded him they had to drink them on the premises as the glass bottles were refundable, and worth money in Zimbabwe. Brand took a sip; the stuff tasted better out of a slightly scratched, curvy bottle, and the taste and the glass reminded him of his childhood in America. Cold Coke was about the best of it.

'I'm investigating a claim on the dead woman's insurance policy.'

Khumalo nodded and sipped from her bottle. 'It's not uncommon in this country for people to lodge fake claims. Some police officers will sell real forms which are fraudulently completed, but not me. And I don't take bribes to write false reports.'

Just Cokes for information, but there was a difference.

'I'm not suggesting you would,' Brand said. 'I'm more interested in the circumstances of the crash.'

'The insurance company asked for a copy of my report. It was sent, so I am assuming you read it,' Khumalo said. Her tone was haughty now, slightly miffed that Brand was questioning her integrity. Her blue uniform was crisply ironed, although Brand noticed her skirt was fraying at the hem. Her flat lace-up shoes were polished so that the toecaps gleamed.

They took a seat on plastic chairs outside the small cafe. Office workers and other police streamed in and out, emerging with styrofoam containers of *sadza y nyama*, mealie meal with a meat sauce, and fried chicken heads and feet, which Brand knew were called 'walkie talkies' in South Africa. When he was growing up, in Texas, his mother would sometimes make traditional African food for him, but only when no one else was around. 'I did. It was very thorough. You interviewed the passenger of the car, Linley Brown.'

'Yes, she was understandably upset. I was working at Binga at the time, relieving another sergeant whose wife had died; I had set up a radar trap about ten kilometres up the road and I was on my way back to the station. I was first on the scene, even before the ambulance.'

'Where was Linley Brown, the passenger?'

'She was sitting by the car. I remember her hands were burned and she was nursing them; she had been banging on the window of her friend's door. The door itself was jammed and she couldn't get back in via the rear passenger side where she had exited because of the fire.' Khumalo looked down at her own hands, seemingly inspecting the chipped polish on her bitten-down nails.

'You identified her when you took her statement?' Brand took out his notebook and pen.

She looked up at him again. 'Yes.'

'How?'

'I checked her driver's licence. Afterwards I asked to see some other ID and she showed me her passport.'

'So you've no doubt she was who she said she was.'

Khumalo nodded. 'The driver's licence was old – the girl in the picture was much younger – but the passport was her, for sure. It was recently issued and the picture was of her, no doubt. Also, when I checked later at the morgue, they said the doctor, Fleming, had examined the remains; he identified a pin in the dead woman's pelvis that matched an operation Miss Munns had been through. We found her handbag in the car. Everything was badly burned, but the British passport of Kate Munns was in there, burned but the name was still recognisable. I collected it and it was later sent to the family in the UK.'

'What kind of passport was Linley Brown carrying?'

'A green mamba – Zimbabwean.' Khumalo drained her Coke and checked her watch. 'I need to go if I am going to eat my *sadza* and get back to work on time.'

'Just one more question.'

'All right.'

'I can see you were very thorough in your investigation, but I was wondering – that passport, could it have been a fake?'

She looked at him and he could see her mind ticking over. She was young for a sergeant, maybe mid-twenties, and attractive, with her carefully braided hair piled up high in a bun so as to not get in the way. He wondered if she was a party member, or if she had achieved her rank simply by being good at her job. He had meant what he said about the thoroughness of her investigation; she had taken the time to verify Linley's ID documents.

Goodness shrugged. 'It is possible, I suppose. I saw no reason to run the number.'

'I agree,' Brand said quickly, 'you cross-checked her ID, but I need to cover off all bases, and the family of Ms Munns wants to contact Linley Brown to get some closure.'

The sergeant nodded. 'That is such an American word. It doesn't really happen here very often, closure.' She looked around her, as if to check no one was in earshot. 'Our troubles never end.'

Brand kept quiet. He knew she was wavering and he didn't want to push her. She would be the sort who would think of herself as by-the-book and thorough. He had planted a suggestion in her mind, but it was up to her to make the decision. He might be able to pay someone in the immigration office in Bulawayo to check a passport number, but it would be quicker and easier for a police sergeant to do it for him.

She stood. 'All right, Mr Brand. I will check the passport number for you.'

'That's much appreciated, ma'am.' He reached into his pocket.

Khumalo held up a hand. 'Don't go doing me any *favours*. I don't want your money. But if this is a case of fraud, of any sort, I will follow it up. I want to be a detective.'

'I was just reaching for my card.' He handed it to her. 'I'll share any information I get, if it looks like this case is fishy.'

She looked at it and smiled. 'Hudson Brand, safari guide and private investigator. You track criminals as well as big game?'

'That's the general idea, ma'am.'

'All right. I am hungry. I will call you later today, perhaps tomorrow.'

He touched his hand to his cap and watched her walk across the road, back to the police compound. She was smart and diligent.

Brand's phone rang but before he had taken it out of his pocket it stopped. The number was a Zimbabwean mobile phone. He called the number back and Cecelia from the Provincial Registry Office answered.

'Cecelia, it's Hudson Brand. How are you?'

'Fine. I found the name of that doctor you wanted.' Her voice was faint, as though she was whispering.

'Who was it?'

'Can you come, in half an hour? There is something you should see. I don't want to talk about it over the phone.'

He heard a man's voice and figured there was someone else in the cubicle, perhaps a supervisor. 'OK. I'll see you in thirty.' He ended the call.

Brand didn't want to use his laptop in public, sitting in his Land Rover, so he walked down the street to an internet cafe and paid the young man sitting behind the counter for fifteen minutes' worth of time. The assistant repositioned his headphones and went back to whatever game he was playing.

Brand logged into his email program and open a new message with the subject line 'Good news', from the wholesaler who represented his one-man business in the UK, Wayne Hamilton.

Hi Hudson, good news. I've just taken a booking for a three-week safari around Zimbabwe, Botswana and South Africa for a couple from London. The guy is a doctor, so expect a big tip, or a free prostate examination. Details and dates to come, but I've taken the liberty of assuming you're free next week after reading about your exploits with the poacher in Kruger. Regards, Wayne.

Smartass, Brand thought. He had a suspicion he knew who the doctor and his wife were, so he typed a short email back to Hamilton asking for the names of the clients.

While he was waiting, he googled Linley Brown and Kate Munns. He turned up no hits in Zimbabwe or South Africa for Linley, although there were a couple of stories in an accountancy firm's corporate newsletter quoting Kate as the human resources manager and some news reports of her death in the car crash. There were no photos of either woman. He tried Facebook, but the only Kate Munns and Linley Brown he could find of approximately the right age were both, coincidentally, in Australia, the former in Melbourne and the latter in Perth. Neither was a match.

The computer pinged and Brand went back to his webmail program. It was a reply from Wayne Hamilton. *Pax are Dr Peter and Mrs Anna Cliff*, said his message.

Brand was mildly annoyed. He hadn't completed his investigation and the Cliffs were already practically on their way to Africa. If Kate was, in fact, dead, then they would want him to track down Linley Brown. Proving the claim was legitimate would expedite Linley's insurance payment and that meant one of two things: he could either use the news that she would receive her money as a means of getting her to contact him face-to-face, or she would get her money and disappear. He suspected the latter would be the case as she had not fallen for his white lies the first time around.

He was likely to be placed in a quandary, one which Dani might have to adjudicate since he reported to her and not to the insurance company. If Kate was dead and Linley was the rightful beneficiary of her policy then he had a duty to report that finding to Dani as soon as possible. If she delayed telling the company in order to buy her friend and her husband more time to get to Africa and try to track down Linley, then that was Dani's call.

Brand's phone rang again. He didn't recognise the number, but it was local. 'Brand.'

'It's Sergeant Khumalo.'

'That was quick. I thought you'd still be at lunch.'

'I am eating at my desk. You aroused my curiosity, but I'm afraid I don't have anything of interest to report. The passport is genuine and it was issued to Linley Brown three months ago. My contact at the department of immigration says it was a replacement, the original was stolen.'

'And you're sure the woman in the photo was the woman you interviewed at the scene of the accident.'

'I already told you that.'

'Right, sorry,' he said.

'I'm sorry, too,' she said, her tone softening. 'I was hoping this might be a case I could investigate.'

'Well, I meant what I said before. If I find anything untoward, I'll let you know. It will be a matter for the Zimbabwean police if there is any evidence of fraud.'

'I'd appreciate that, Mr Brand. Goodbye.'

He checked his watch and logged off; it was time to see Cecelia again.

Brand drove his Land Rover back to the Provincial Registry Office, nodded to the same boy and his blind grandfather and asked them if they could actually watch the vehicle this time. He made a mental note to invoice Dani for car park guards and bribes.

He walked into the musty-smelling room and saw Cecelia. The queue was shorter at this time of the day. She looked up from a form she was scanning, spotted him and waved to him to come to the head of the line.

'Hey, you are not finished with me,' a woman with a baby tied to her back with a wrap said indignantly.

'You need to fill in the blanks in this form. Go away and do so, then come back to me. This man was here before and we have business.'

Yes, and I'm paying good money to jump ahead of you, Brand thought to himself. The young mother looked miffed, but snatched back her form and went to a desk at the edge of the room. Cecelia took the same ledger book she had shown him earlier from the side of her desk and looked behind her, in case a supervisor was hovering there. She opened the book and leafed through till she found the file she was looking for. 'The doctor's name is Elena Rodriguez.'

'Cuban?'

Cecelia nodded as she flicked through the folios. 'Yes. They come here because there is nowhere else they can practise. I have a daughter, but I won't take her to a Cuban, only Dr Fleming. Here, this is what I wanted to show you.'

Brand took his reading glasses out of the pocket of his safari shirt. Cecelia was glancing around again as he looked where her finger was pointing. It was a death certificate, like the others in the file, and he read the printed name *Dr Elena Rodriguez* below an illegibly scrawled signature.

'Have a look at the name of the deceased.'

He shifted his gaze and whistled softly through his teeth when he read the name: *Katherine Elizabeth Munns*.

'Same date of birth, as well,' Cecelia said. 'But look here, this certificate is dated 16 May, three days before the death in the car accident. It says, *Cause of death, cerebral haemorrhage*.'

Brand processed the information. The odds that there were two women with the same name, born on the same day, who died in the same town in Zimbabwe three days apart were infinitesimally small. 'Did you file this certificate?'

'No, I was on leave then. I only came back the day before the other certificate was issued.'

Brand rubbed the stubble on his chin. 'What do you know about this Dr Rodriguez?'

Cecelia shrugged. 'She is the one the police investigated, but as I said, the case was dropped. I've never met her. The police also questioned myself and some of my colleagues at the time. Dr Rodriguez must have a contact here in the registry, but I don't know who it is.'

'Two death certificates,' he said out loud, as he pondered the new information.

'Should I call the police?' Cecelia asked.

He guessed she had not told her supervisor about her discovery in case she was asked what she was doing going through the records. Brand saw the mix of worry and guilt on her face; as a private investigator he'd seen that look many times when people were caught out.

'I don't want to get you in trouble, Cecelia,' he said, playing on her fears. She nodded. 'I have a contact in the local police who I can give this information to, anonymously. She'll probably come and ask you for the certificate, but you don't have to say how you came across it.'

'Thank you. But what does this mean? How can this woman die twice?'

'That's a very good question.'

*

Dr Elena Rodriquez's surgery was on the ground floor of a run-down four-storey walk-up apartment block on the edge of Bulawayo, in Fife Street. The flats above had old sheets for curtains and broken window panes. Her offices didn't look much better from the outside.

When he entered, a woman at the reception counter looked up from reading a newspaper and raised her eyebrows. Half a dozen patients sat on old kitchen chairs around a coffee table laden with torn magazines.

A high-pitched scream came from behind a closed door. A girl of no more than six turned wide dark eyes at her mother, who patted her on the arm. The girl did not look reassured, particularly when the noise came again, louder this time.

'Can I help you?' the receptionist asked.

'I'd like to see Dr Rodriguez, if possible.'

Again the woman raised her eyebrows. 'You're not a regular patient here.'

'I know.'

She sighed, reached for a clipboard and passed a form over to him to complete. 'Fill this in.'

Brand filled out the form; he used his own pen as none was offered, then reached into his pocket and felt for the twenty-dollar bill he had put there. Careful not to let the other patients see, he slipped it under the form, with just the edge of the note visible as he passed the clipboard back to the receptionist. 'I really am very unwell and need to see the doctor as soon as possible.'

The woman said nothing. Brand sat down and picked up the same *National Geographic* he'd been pretending to read in Dr Fleming's surgery. Ten minutes later everyone in the waiting room looked up as the sound of raised voices carried from the other side of the door behind the receptionist. A moment later it was flung open and a man emerged carrying a sobbing child, a girl about the same age as the one waiting. A woman, the mother, Brand guessed, turned as she entered the waiting room. 'No bloody anaesthetic. I just can't believe it.' Brand saw the fresh bandage on the girl's foot.

A woman in a soiled white coat emerged, tucking a stray strand of dark hair behind her ear. 'I do best I can, Mrs Hall, and I warn you before the procedure.'

The mother put her hands on her hips. 'Yes, well, how was I to know how much this was going to hurt my daughter?'

'How you think it feel if you stick needle in your foot and sew?'

Brand held his smile in check. The doctor passed the receptionist a piece of paper and she said, 'Fifty dollars,' to the mother.

The mother looked at the father, who shrugged. 'I don't get paid until next week, babe.'

The mother turned back to the doctor. 'I'm sorry, doctor, not only do I feel we should not have to pay you when you used useless painkillers to operate on our child, but we do not have fifty dollars at the moment. Send us a bill and we'll pay next week.'

The doctor shrugged. Brand noticed how the coat sagged on her slight frame. She looked almost like a child playing dress-ups, with her sleeves rolled at the wrists. Her dark hair was tied back in a ponytail and her eyes, while dark-rimmed, were nonetheless attractively large, the whites contrasting with her olive skin. 'You want to know why I have no proper anaesthetic?' She looked around the forlorn people in their frayed clothes in the waiting room, 'because most people here like you will not pay me. Good day, Mrs Hall. Change your daughter's dressing daily, but don't come to me for bandage; this one was almost my last.'

As the couple and their daughter left, the receptionist passed the clipboard to the doctor, lifting the form Brand had completed as she did so. 'Mr Brand? Come this way, please.'

Brand felt the eyes of the other patients on his back as he followed the diminutive doctor through the door.

The paint on the walls of the corridor they followed was peeling and Brand smelled the unmistakable odour of mice. The room the doctor led him into, however, was freshly painted. She went to a stained basin in the corner and washed and dried her hands. 'Take a seat, please,' she said over her shoulder.

He sat on a chair similar to those in the waiting room, its foam stuffing exploding from a wound in its vinyl upholstery. The doctor sat behind her desk and crossed a leg, giving him a glimpse of denim skirt and rubber flip-flop. The leg was thin, but the calf shapely.

'Thank you for seeing me at such short notice,' he said.

'Twenty dollars will buy you that. You heard what I said out there.'

He nodded. 'How can you practise if your patients won't pay you?'

'Only the poorest of the poor come to me, Mr Brand. If you have money you go to another doctor. What is matter with you?'

'I'm in a bad financial position,' Brand said, testing the waters.

Dr Rodriguez tucked a strand of black hair behind her ear. 'I am sorry, I do not understand. My English is not so good, but you pay money to go to head of queue and now you say you have no money? What business is this of me?'

He liked her accent and the way she mangled her words. 'I have a fully paid-up life insurance policy in South Africa, and a daughter living with my ex-wife in Durban,' he lied. 'I'd like to put my daughter through varsity, but I don't have the money, and neither does my ex.'

'I still no understand how I can help.' She looked at her watch.

'I think you do, Dr Rodriguez. I need to die, or, to be more accurate, I need you to issue me a death certificate.'

Elena looked over her shoulder towards the door to her room, as if expecting someone to break in as soon as she said something. 'I no know what you talking about. Please leave, Mister Brand. To issue death certificate for someone who is living is crime.'

'Now, keep your hat on, doctor. You issued a fake death certificate for a friend of mine, Kate Munns.'

'I do no such thing.'

'I saw the death certificate.'

She leaned back in her ageing office chair, which squeaked in protest. 'Kate, she die in a car crash, but I no sign death certificate.'

Brand reached into his shirt pocket and took out his phone. He clicked on the camera icon then went to the gallery and opened the picture he had snapped before leaving the registry office. Brand passed the phone to the doctor and she zoomed in on the picture of the certificate.

Her face paled a shade. 'Where you take this picture?'

'Provincial Registry Office. Today.'

'My God. Is not possible.'

'It is. If you told someone to pull the phony certificate, doctor, you paid the wrong person.' Brand recalled Cecelia saying she had been away from work that week; perhaps her crooked colleague was also inept.

'Who are you?' she asked him.

'I'm an investigator for the insurance company that Kate had her policy with.'

'Please leave.' Dr Rodriguez started to stand and Brand placed a hand on her forearm. She shook him off but sat down again. 'Have you told police?'

'Not yet. Maybe you can tell me what happened and we'll take it from there.'

She checked her watch again. 'Not here, not now. I have real sick people to treat. You must let me see the people in the waiting room and then we can talk, tonight, perhaps.'

Brand knew Dr Rodriguez could be across the border in Botswana within an hour if he let her out of his sight, and then he would probably never see her again. He thought of the policewoman, Sergeant Khumalo, eager to put the first notch in her budding trainee detective's belt. Then Dr Rodriguez reached across to him and put her hand on his and squeezed it. 'Please, give me this afternoon. These people have no one, and then I attend a clinic for mothers and babies from five to seven. Where are you staying?'

Brand hadn't booked a room, but he usually stayed in the same place when he came to Zimbabwe's second city. 'The Bulawayo Club.'

She nodded. 'I know it. I will come, and explain. I want to tell you what happen, and why. One thing you must know, however, from start, is that Kate she is dead. Dr Fleming sign death certificate and he is good person, not like me.'

Brand wavered. He had the photo of the death certificate signed by Elena Rodriguez, which said Kate Munns had died of a brain haemorrhage, and it predated the one Fleming had signed and which the insurance company had in its possession.

The doctor slumped in her chair. 'You can call police now, if you want, and no one will see those people in waiting room. Or, you can wait for me to tell you what you want to know. After that you can decide what to tell police. But please, give me chance to explain.'

He looked into her dark eyes and tried not to be moved by her pleading look. 'What do you know about Linley Brown?'

A smile formed on her lips. He had thought he had her, but now the tables were turning. 'I know all about her. I tell you, tonight. Maybe you buy me dinner – my last before police come take me away, or send me back to Cuba.'

He couldn't stop the smile this time. She probably wouldn't show, but he wasn't the police. Elena Rodriguez put her hand on his again and raised a foot to run her toes up the inside of his calf muscle. 'Please,' she whispered, and that settled it.

12

Brand sipped a brandy and Coke at the long bar of the Bulawayo Club and looked at his watch for the third time. He wondered if Elena Rodriguez was in another country by now.

'I sorry I late.'

He swivelled on his stool at the sound of her accent and was surprised at what awaited him. She was wearing a black sleeveless cocktail dress that ended mid-thigh and long black leather boots with high heels; they didn't suit the sticky weather but Brand thought the doctor looked as sexy as hell.

Her hair was teased out and she brushed a strand behind her ear, as she had done in the surgery that afternoon. 'You going to say something?'

'You look different.'

'I take that as compliment.' She opened her black patent leather purse and took out a packet of Zimbabwean Newbury cigarettes. 'Want one? You can smoke in here. I not sure how long they allow this; two year ago women were not even allowed in this bar, so rules do change, sometimes for better.'

'I'm trying to give up.' Seeing her fossick in her bag some more he took the Zippo from his pocket, rolled the wheel on the fabric of his chinos and held the flame to her. She leaned forward to light her cigarette and he smelled perfume. He didn't smoke any more, but he still carried his lighter; he'd had it since Angola and never went out without it.

'*Gracias*.' She blew a stream of smoke upwards and it twisted its tendrils around the slow-moving ceiling fan. 'You look surprised still. You think I not come?'

'I thought you'd come wearing your baggy doctor's coat.'

She laughed and picked a speck of tobacco from her smooth, even white teeth. When she ashed the cigarette into the heavy stone ashtray the bartender slid across to her Brand noticed she had painted her nails blood red. 'You going to order me drink?'

'Of course. What would you like?'

'Cane and Coke. Is closest thing here to Cuban rum; cheap and potent. You been to Cuba, Mr Brand?'

He ordered the drink, and another for himself. 'Please, call me Hudson. No, I haven't, but I did try some Cuban rum, once, in Angola.'

She nodded. 'Aha. You fight there in the war?'

'Yes. South African Army.'

'Let me guess.' She drew on her cigarette again and when she placed it on the rim of the ashtray he saw the fresh circle of lipstick, the same shade as her nails. 'Three-two battalion? Buffalo soldiers.'

He took the drinks from the barman and passed the cane and Coke to her. They clinked glasses. 'How did you guess?'

'You speak like American, but you look like you got some Portuguese, maybe black African in you. Three-two was South African mercenary battalion, with Portuguese-speaking officers and black Angolan traitors to revolution.'

Brand smiled. 'How do you know so much about South African military history?'

'I was there, as nurse. Angolans were short of doctors so Cuba sent assistance. I assist with some surgery in field and decided I want to be doctor when I finish my army service.'

'You don't look old enough to have served in Angola.'

She laughed. 'Now *you* flirting. I was nineteen.'

'I wasn't much older. I can't for the life of me think now why I was keen to find a war somewhere in the world.'

Elena leaned close to him and he could smell her perfume again as she lowered he voice theatrically. 'I can't for life of me think now why I wanted to help my socialist brothers and sisters in that shithole.'

He laughed. 'I'll drink to that,' he said, and they clinked glasses again. 'We were both fighting for long-forgotten causes. You wanted to create a socialist utopia in Africa and I was a part African American helping defend a system that oppressed black people and doesn't exist any more. I read recently that Luanda has the most expensive hotel rooms in the world, thanks to the interest of oil and gas company executives fighting over somewhere decent to stay.'

'There nowhere decent to stay in Luanda. It like Zimbabwe, only worse.'

She drained her glass and finished her cigarette and he ordered her a fresh cane and Coke and lit her second cigarette. He smelled the smoke and felt the craving. 'You sure not want some?' She uncrossed her legs then crossed the other one, giving him a glimpse of smooth thigh.

'You were going to tell me about Kate Munns.'

She stubbed out her cigarette after just a couple of puffs. 'What I tell you is, how you say, off the record, as far as police go, OK?'

He shrugged. He wasn't in Zimbabwe to do Sergeant Khumalo's job for her. 'It would be unusual, doctor, for the police to go to the insurance company and subpoena my report, but it could happen. For their part, the company rarely presses charges when fraud is uncovered.'

Dr Rodriguez pursed her lips; she was sexy even when she was vulnerable, he thought. 'Call me Elena. To tell you truth, I can probably buy my way out of a prosecution. There not enough doctors in

Zimbabwe. Just don't make their job easier for them than it needs to be. In any case, no crime committed this time.'

'What do you mean, "no crime"? You sold Kate Munns a fake death certificate.'

Elena looked at the floor in a moment of contrition, then back at him. 'You see my surgery. You hear that family complain that I no got drugs.'

He nodded.

'I have something to show you.' She opened her purse again and pulled out a sheet of paper.

Elena passed the page to Brand and he saw that it was an invoice from a South African pharmaceuticals company. The total at the bottom of the list of various drugs, some of which Brand recognised as painkillers and antibiotics, was twenty thousand rand, or about two thousand US dollars.

'Kate pay me two thousand dollar for my services.'

He didn't need to ask what those services were. If he believed her, she was telling him she had used all that money to buy drugs for her patients. Playing Robin Hood didn't excuse crime in the eyes of the law, but Brand had some sympathy for her.

'I not sorry for anything I do in life,' she said.

He saw the defiance in her eyes, and something else. She had been to war, as he had, and seen the horrors of a struggle consigned to the irrelevant section of history. She wasn't cowed by him or his investigation. 'Tell me about Kate. What was she running from?'

Elena sipped her drink and shrugged. 'I not know. All I know is money not for herself alone. She have friend with drug problem, addicted to painkillers.'

'Linley Brown?'

'Yes, that one. She come with Kate to my surgery. Linley like many people in Zimbabwe, just hanging on, you know?'

He nodded.

'Plus, she need to go to rehab in South Africa and that cost long bucks.'

It was interesting hearing African slang coming from a sensual Cuban mouth, he thought, then forced his mind to stay on the job. 'OK, but why did Kate need to disappear from her life in the UK, forever? This can't just have been about a friend in trouble; this was about her changing her life for good.'

Elena stirred her drink with her finger then licked it. 'I not know. I ask her, as I have same suspicion as you. But in this kind of *service* you not ask too many questions, you know?'

He could imagine. 'So, you wrote Kate a false death certificate, saying she had died of a brain haemorrhage, and the certificate was lodged at the Provincial Registry Office.'

She sipped her drink again, but said nothing.

'And then there was a car accident three days later, in which Kate really was killed.'

This time, Elena nodded. 'I am amazed when I read it in the *Chronicle*, local newspaper. You know, is sad that this girl is really killed. I ask around and find out Dr Fleming is friend of family. I call him – that old man he no like me – and I ask him if he sign death certificate. He ask me why I want to know, but he say yes, he identifies Kate positively from pin in her bones, you know? He very honest man, that one.' She looked down at her drink and added, softly, 'Not like me.'

Brand nodded. It was tragically ironic that Kate had been killed just a few days after receiving her death certificate. Perhaps, Brand speculated, the girls had been celebrating their good fortune as they made plans for Linley to lodge a claim on the life insurance policy once Kate's will was read.

'You going to tell police about me?'

Brand thought about his answer. As attractive as Elena Rodriguez was, she had committed a crime and he had told Sergeant Khumalo he would keep her up to date with his investigation. Elena had broken the law in Zimbabwe by selling the fake certificate, but the crime had gone no further; if Linley had not used the bogus document to lodge the claim then the payout that she was now awaiting *might* still be approved. On the other hand, Brand knew insurance companies were always looking for an excuse not to pay. The moral dilemma he now faced, about whether to hand Elena over to Sergeant Khumalo, was made more difficult by Elena's perfume and the way she ran her tongue across her teeth every now and then. The insurance company, he knew, would not want to press charges, which was something in Elena's favour. Goodness Khumalo, however, would want nothing more than to see the good doctor in cuffs and in court.

Elena reached out and put a hand on his on the bar. 'Please, don't make this harder for me, or easier for the police. Like I say, I can buy my way out of prosecution, but I have little money and what I do have I need to buy drugs and medical supplies. Anyone who live in Zimbabwe and say they have not broken one law is liar. Please . . . Hudson.'

He looked into those sad, ambushing eyes, and he wondered how many fake certificates she had issued, how many hundreds of thousands of pounds she had helped people defraud from overseas insurance companies. There had been at least one attempted prosecution of Elena, according to Cecelia. Perhaps she did spend all the proceeds of her criminal endeavours buying stuff to help her patients, or perhaps she was just a good liar. He slid his hand out from under hers.

She put her hand back in her lap, beneath the bar, pouted, then looked at him. 'I can pay you.'

'I don't need your money.' In fact, he did, as this case would be short on billable hours now that it was drawing to a close, but he did have the uncomfortable prospect of a safari with Kate's sister and brother-in-law in order to keep his bank balance out of the red.

'I no mean to offend you.'

'No offence taken. This is Africa, after all.'

She smiled at that. He couldn't judge her, he decided, but nor would he take her money to keep her name out of the investigation.

He could use a good contact in the Zimbabwe police, an up and coming detective such as Goodness Khumalo, but did he have the heart to hand the doctor to her? 'Are you still in contact with Linley Brown?'

'No,' Elena said.

'What did you make of Kate?'

She frowned. 'I no understand.'

'How did she act? Was she nervous; did it seem like she was scared? Did she have any real medical problems?'

'We have thing called doctor–patient confidentiality. Maybe you hear of it?'

'Elena, you're hardly in a position to assert your moral authority over me.'

She looked away, along the bar, and when she turned back to him he saw that her cheeks had coloured with a mix of anger and embarrassment. 'She nervous, of course; she and me about to break law. I ask her if she want to talk about why she want to disappear and she say it none of my business. She say her friend, Linley, has drug problem and this Linley she nods, but says very little. Kate ask me if I can give some painkillers, OxyContin, for her friend, to keep her going until she can get to rehab, but I have to just laugh at that. You know I no got any drugs.'

Brand nodded. He still couldn't fathom why Kate would think she had to disappear from her life in the UK in order to fund her friend's recovery. No, Kate Munns had needed not only money but a new life. He knew the only person who could fill in the gaps in this story was Linley Brown.

'I would buy you a drink, except I got no money. If you got no more questions for me, maybe I go now.'

'How are you going to bribe your way out of a police prosecution if you can't afford a drink?' he asked her.

She opened her cigarettes – something she clearly did have money for – and shook one out. Brand lit it for her. 'If I no got money there are other ways to change men's minds.'

'I happen to know the investigating officer will most likely be a female.'

Elena inhaled and winked at him as she released the smoke to the ceiling fan. 'I think I can change woman's mind as well.'

'Bartender, same again, please,' Brand said.

*

'Coming, coming,' Brand croaked. The pounding on the door of his room at the Bulawayo Club was reverberating around the inside of his skull. He coughed and checked his watch on the bedside table. It was nine o'clock.

He opened the door and saw the maid and her cleaning trolley. 'Sorry, I'll be out in ten minutes. I overslept.'

Brand found the light switch and flicked it on, illuminating evidence of the chaos of the night before. The heavy curtains kept the daylight out and muffled the sounds of traffic on the street outside, but he rarely slept this late. He sat down heavily on the bed.

The sheets were scrunched and rumpled, revealing the mattress below. His safari shirt and chinos were by the door. He needed water, but the glass beside the bed was empty. Elena had brought him water, somewhere around three in the morning, he recalled. He could smell her, on the bed, on him. He coughed again as the night's events replayed themselves on the screen of his tightly closed eyelids.

He had bought her dinner, even though he could ill afford the expense, in the open-air dining area in the courtyard in the centre of the club; Dani would pay, he had told himself. They had drunk more while waiting for their food, then split two bottles of wine with the meal. Elena had gone back to cane and Coke after that and he had matched her, drink for drink.

When the waiter, eager to close the dining room, had asked them if they wanted coffee or dessert, Elena had said, 'Let's have coffee in your room.'

He wasn't naïve. They had got along well over dinner, relating stories of their shared time in Angola, serving on different sides of the war, and on three or four occasions she had leaned across the table and again punctuated a point by placing her hand on his and touching his leg with the pointed toe of her boot.

She had played with her hair and some of her jokes and stories of her work had been unashamedly sexual. He liked her laugh, and he had flirted back at her. By the end of the main course the calf of her left leg was resting against his right and he was being drawn into those dark, sad eyes across the candlelight.

They had left the dining room and walked up the sweeping staircase past paintings of long-ago members of the Rhodesian colonial gentry. He loved the high ceilings, the airy rooms, the polished floors of this anachronistic man cave, but right then he was fixated on Elena as she walked up the stairs in front of him, her bottom at his eye level. On the first landing he had, on impulse, reached up and taken her black ponytail in one hand, checking her pace. Elena had thrown back her head, groaned, then turned. Brand kissed her, hungry, hard and deep. Breathless, she had broken the kiss and led him up the stairs. 'Which room?'

'Four.'

'Hurry,' she had whispered hoarsely in his ear.

She was clawing at his back, kissing his neck as he fumbled with the key in the lock. Inside he had pinned her against the wall and lowered his mouth to the small breast she freed for him from her cocktail dress. His hand had gone between her thighs, pulling aside her pants as he ran his finger across her hard little nub, parting the slippery, puffy flesh. Elena had bitten his shoulder. He rubbed the skin now as he opened his eyes in the room, and, looking down, saw the red marks her teeth had left.

Brand found a pair of shorts in his duffel bag and hopped, one-legged, into them. He needed to be out of the room by ten. On the wall he noticed a smudge of makeup, where Elena had turned her face, her cheek brushing the white plaster as he kissed her throat, lifted her, and entered her. He'd taken a free packet of condoms from the box in the men's room of the club, during dinner. The first time had been fast, almost brutal, as she wrapped her legs around him and reached under his untucked shirt to rake his back with her red nails. As he turned he caught sight of the scratch marks in the mirror.

As she came she had bitten the inside of his lip, drawing blood, and he had let out an animal groan as he tasted it and lifted her higher up the wall. She reminded him of a lioness, hissing and fighting as he took her, then sashaying past him, lifting her dress over her head as she walked to the bed, enticing the male into the act once more. As he had leaned against the door, catching his breath, she had bent over in front of him and wiggled out of her pants, then planted her booted feet apart, hands resting on the mattress, and looked back over her shoulder at him. 'Again,' she'd said.

She had ridden him, still dressed only in her boots, and after that he had finally dozed. Elena had woken him, though, lapping at him, coaxing back his arousal, and he had looked down and wrapped his hands in her dark hair.

Their bodies had been slick as he rolled her over and entered her, slower this time, kissing her as he rested at the end of each stroke, deep inside her. She had scratched him some more, urging him to move faster, and he had surrendered to her seemingly insatiable passion.

She had lain beside him, nuzzling against his chest as he had fallen asleep, exhausted from their exertions and his travels and still sore from his beating at the hands of the De Villiers boys. He remembered now that she had got up when it was still dark. Just a chink of pale pre-dawn light had shone through the curtains. She was standing in front of the mirror, zipping up her dress. He'd looked at her and she at him, saying nothing as she sat on the bed and pulled on her boots, which she'd discarded after their second round. She had let herself out of the room and he'd fallen back to sleep.

Brand opened the curtains to let in more light, buttoned his shirt and took his phone from the breast pocket. He dialled Elena's surgery and greeted the receptionist. 'Is Dr Rodriguez free, please? I'm a friend of hers.'

He heard voices in the background, an overflowing waiting room, he guessed. A child was crying. 'I am sorry, but Dr Rodriguez did not come to work today and I have many people waiting to see her.'

'Thank you.' Brand ended the call.

She would be across the border by now. Perhaps she didn't have enough money or guile to bribe the police in Zimbabwe, or maybe she, like the late Kate Munns, just wanted to disappear from her miserable life.

He had let himself be taken for a ride; not a bad ride, but a ride nonetheless. He picked up his phone again and scrolled through the numbers until he found Sergeant Goodness Khumalo's. He dialled it.

'It's Hudson Brand here, sergeant, how are you this fine morning?' He coughed.

'Fine. Better than you, I think?'

'All good here.' He coughed into his hand again and saw Elena's empty cigarette pack by the bed. He had caved in and smoked a few with her between bouts of lovemaking, and that accounted for the rasp in his voice and the foul taste in his mouth. The remains of one of hers sat in the ashtray, the red ring of her lips still visible.

'How can I help you, Mr Brand? Do you have some information for me?'

'I've confirmed Kate Munns really is dead, but you might want to go to the records office and pull the death certificates issued by a Dr Elena Rodriguez.'

'That name is familiar.'

'Let's just say that the good doctor has come to the attention of the Bulawayo police in the past. She sells fraudulent death certificates.'

'But you said Kate is really dead?'

'I did, but she bought a fake certificate three days before she unexpectedly had the need for a real one.'

Goodness paused for a second. 'The woman faked her death and then died in the accident. Serious?'

'I think if you pull some other death certificates Dr Rodriguez signed you'll find some interesting claims. If you do turn up some irregularities I'd appreciate a return favour as I might be able to follow up with the insurance companies abroad.'

'I think we may be working together in the future, Mr Brand,' Sergeant Khumalo said. 'I look forward to talking to the doctor.'

'OK, bye.' Brand didn't want the policewoman to know Elena had most likely crossed the border by now, and he didn't want to explain how she'd had the time to make good her escape. But it was probably a leg-up onto the first rung of the promotional ladder for Khumalo.

Brand brushed his teeth, packed his bag and left the room. He went to the club's office, on the ground floor, to pay his bill.

Brand needed something greasy to take the edge off his hangover. He turned into the car park of the Holiday Inn, left the Land Rover and walked into the Spur steakhouse. The familiarity of the Wild West-themed chain restaurant and the knowledge that the menu was the same wherever he went in Africa was a welcome break from the chaos of the real world outside.

He ordered a cheeseburger from the waitress and checked his emails while he waited. The first was from his UK travel contact, Wayne Hamilton. Peter and Anna Cliff were on their way to Zimbabwe.

13

It was a nice house, Captain Sannie van Rensburg thought, the kind of place she would like to live in, if she and Tom ever decided to sell the farm, or if the government bought it off them.

Sannie looked out the plate glass windows of the house in Steiltes, a suburb perched in the hills high above Nelspruit, and took a moment more to admire the view over the city and the valley below.

'Nice place,' said Mavis.

'*Ja*. And nicely dressed ladies who robbed it.'

'You think it's the same pair who were doing the thefts around Sandton and Houghton? The Glamour Girls? Salt and Pepper?'

Sannie didn't like the media's habit of giving criminals nick-names; Salt and Pepper was the latest. She felt it trivialised and even glamorised crime in the eyes of impressionable young people. But Mavis had matured into an experienced detective and she read the newspapers and checked internet news sites every day, keeping abreast of crime not only in the local area but also nationally. Sannie had the same thoughts about the well-dressed female bandits.

'Could be. Or maybe a copycat,' Sannie said. 'Robbing houses that are open for viewing is hardly a new type of crime, but the MO is similar to the others, and the perpetrators are two women.' In the kitchen the owner of the home, a matronly woman with permed hair, a white pants suit and gold sandals, was giving the estate agent hell for not keeping an eye on the people who came to inspect the house, which was for sale.

'Did you get the full list of what's missing?' Sannie asked her partner.

Mavis opened her notebook. 'Two laptops, a cell phone, some cash from a bedside table drawer, and a Rolex watch.'

'Not a bad haul. If it is the same pair they might have simply shifted their operation from Joburg to the Lowveld because the police were closing in on them.'

Both Sannie and Mavis had read the *Sunday Times* story the previous weekend about a couple of women in burqas who had attempted to rob a house in Houghton. The journalist had inside information that the police had mounted a sting operation, but the women escaped after showing a stolen ID.

'Mavis, you need to track down whoever was handling the earlier cases when we get back to the office. See what we can get on these two; descriptions, security camera footage and the like.'

Mavis's eyes widened. 'Maybe we can mount our own sting?'

'Maybe.' Sannie thought that if it was the same two women they wouldn't be fooled easily. The owner of this house had told them that she had made a point of telling her husband and sons to hide all their valuables. The agent said the white woman of the pair had engaged him in a detailed conversation about the house and he assumed her partner had then done the searching and the stealing. As in the other cases she had read about, one of the pair did the distracting and the other the thieving. Sannie had asked the agent if the woman had flirted with him, and he had blushed, giving her a truer indication of the nature of their 'detailed conversation'. He was able to give them a good description of her; a very good description. 'But for now we must issue a warning to all the local real estate agents in Nelspruit, today.'

'*Yebo*,' Mavis said.

Sannie's BlackBerry buzzed and she checked her emails. 'Interesting.'

'What is it?' Mavis asked.

'You know I contacted the Investigative Psychology Unit, about the woman who was murdered during the World Cup?'

'Yes; our first case together. I'll never forget it, and I think it's great you won't let it go.'

Sannie did not think it was great that they had been unable to catch the killer. 'They found another female prostitute dead, identical MO, in Cape Town six months ago.'

'Wow. That kind of rules out your chief suspect, though, doesn't it?'

Sannie looked out over the valley towards White River and the haze-covered hills beyond. 'I don't know. That depends on whether or not Hudson Brand was in Cape Town last February at the time of the woman's death.'

*

Mavis and Sannie worked on a flyer containing an artist's impression of the two women who had robbed the houses in Johannesburg, and whom they suspected may have been responsible for the theft in Steiltes, and Mavis emailed it to all of the agents in Nelspruit.

At five o'clock Sannie left the office and Mavis went for a drink with one of the uniformed sergeants, Vusi Baloyi. Sannie didn't know how serious it was between them, but Vusi was single, and a good-looking guy, and as far as Sannie knew he was a good cop. She just hoped Mavis, who had become a friend as well as a partner, would find someone who was her intellectual equal.

Sannie drove out of Nelspruit on the R40, climbing to White River and the forest-covered hills beyond. The gum and pine trees gave way to bananas and it was with a mix of guilt and excitement that she drove past her home. She should be on the *stoep* of the farmhouse with Tom and the three kids now, having a Savanna cider and listening to how their day had been. Instead, she pushed on towards the town of Hazyview. She wasn't deliberately excluding Mavis from the investigation of the dead prostitute, but as the person she needed to talk to was so close to her own home she had decided to make the unannounced drop-in by herself.

She wondered where Hudson Brand was now; she hadn't heard if his suspension from guiding had been lifted following the shooting of the poacher. Tracey Mahoney would know; she used him often as a freelance guide in her local safari business, and had employed him during the 2010 FIFA soccer World Cup.

Sannie slowed behind a mine truck and waited at the three-way stop at the intersection of the R40 and the R538, then turned left. She passed the Rendezvous shopping centre and waited at the robot to turn right onto Portia Shabangu, at the Blue Haze shopping mall. Minibus taxis taking workers back to the townships and informal settlements beeped and cut in and out around her. Hazyview had been a one-store town with hippos roaming the streets at night when she was growing up, but now it was a bustling, congested hub for the safari and farming industries.

Sannie turned into the R536. She stopped at another four-way, by the man selling metal warthogs and a menagerie of other hand-crafted souvenir animals, and glanced past *Oom* Kallie's butchery to the pub where Brand's former girlfriend worked. She would pay Hannah van Wyk a visit if she couldn't find out where the guide was staying at the moment. She had heard around town that even though the pair had broken up after the murder investigation Brand was still a regular at the Pepper Vine, which Van Wyk managed. Sannie wondered again if it was worth grilling the woman once more about the alibi she had provided for Brand.

Sannie turned left before the bridge then right into Tarental Street and left into Goshawk Ridge. Outside a black steel gate she hooted her horn and heard dogs barking from the other side. A gardener slid open the gate and Sannie, seeing that the small yard in front of the house was crammed with safari game-viewing vehicles and people movers, switched off her engine in the driveway, locked her car, and walked in.

Tracey Mahoney came to the barred security door. 'Captain Van Rensburg? Hello, can I help you?' she said in the London accent she hadn't lost in twenty years of living in South Africa.

'Good afternoon, Mrs Mahoney. How are you?' Sannie said.

'Fine.'

Sannie remembered that Tracey had been very protective of Brand in her earlier investigation. She didn't know if Tracey had a genuine regard for the American, or if she resented one of her stable of guides being involved in a murder investigation. Publicity over the case would not have helped her business. 'Perhaps I could come in.'

Tracey didn't move, at first. A Jack Russell stood protectively by her feet growling, while a large black dog of indeterminate parentage barked behind her.

'Dufus, shut up!' The black dog turned and walked away. 'Oh, very well. Come in. But I have to go pick the kids up from their friends' place in fifteen minutes.'

'I'm sure it won't take that long,' Sannie said. She followed Tracey inside, to a room off to the right of the front door that had been converted into an office.

Tracey sat down in her office chair behind a computer desk. 'This is about Brand, again, I assume?'

'Yes,' Sannie said. 'Do you know where he is now?'

'Zimbabwe. The parks board's still investigating the shooting of the poacher. You must have seen it in the *Lowvelder*.'

Sannie nodded. 'I interviewed him.' She remembered seeing his picture on the front page. One of the many things that disturbed her about the American was how handsome she found him. She was utterly devoted to Tom, but there was something about Brand that made women stop and talk to him. Perhaps it was the very arrogance and self-assuredness of the man that she found so irritating that was also, subconsciously, part of his charm. 'I saw it. What's he doing in Zim?'

'I'm not his keeper and, at the moment, not his employer,' Tracey said.

'No, but he was working for you six months ago, wasn't he?'

Tracey looked at her computer, ostensibly checking an email that announced its arrival with a ping. 'Was he?'

'That's what I'm here to ask.'

Tracey picked up her cigarette from the ashtray, took a drag and blew the smoke not directly at Sannie, but not away from her, either. 'Yes, I think so.'

'Can you check where he would have been working on 12 February?'

Tracey sighed and swivelled in her chair so she was facing the computer again. 'I keep all my bookings on a diary on here.' Her fingers moved across the keyboard and Sannie leaned forward to see the screen as Tracey clicked on February's bookings.

'Well, he wasn't here, if that's what you want to know, in case you're trying to pin another murder on him. Have a look.' Tracey moved the flat screen so Sannie could get a better look. 'There, see, he was on a tour. He took a family of Germans through the Kruger on the fourth; they drove down the Zulu War battlefields and stayed at Fugitives' Drift on the sixth, then did Durban on the eighth, the garden route for a few days, then Cape Town.'

'So he was in Cape Town on the night of the twelfth?'

'That's what it says here. Hope you're satisfied.'

Sannie felt her heart rate increase and a jolt of adrenaline shoot out to her nerve endings as she jotted the details of the itinerary in her notebook. The truth was she had hoped she would find that Hudson Brand had been on safari in the Kruger Park, not in Cape Town, on the night another prostitute had been raped and murdered.

*

Brand watched the herd of elephants break into a trot as they smelled the water. A cloud of white dust rose behind them as they headed through the shimmering heat haze towards him.

The thatched roof over the viewing platform at Nyamandlovu waterhole protected him and the three other visitors from the sun, and the fact that the hide was raised on stilts, a few metres off the ground, allowed them to make the most of the breeze, although that, like the rest of Hwange National Park, was hot and dry.

'Lion,' Brand said.

'Where?' said the man seated in the rickety wooden chair next to him.

They were Australians, two young men and a woman. Brand thought they might be from an NGO, or the embassy in Harare; they had that earnest, clean-cut look about them. Brand gave them a reference, off the big acacia on the far side of the pan that had somehow survived decades of ravaging by elephants to grow to maturity. Sometimes life held on, even in this harsh, thirsty Kalahari sandveld.

The Australians finally found the lion. Brand raised his binoculars and studied him again. He was a fine specimen, a male in his late prime, about ten years old, he thought. The elephant herd's matriarch raised her trunk as she caught the lion's scent, but even his presence was not enough to deter her and her family from their desperate mission to reach the water.

The pan, or waterhole, was a greasy grey colour, a slurry of water and mud churned together by countless elephant feet and the hooves and paws of myriad other creatures. Some nervous zebra, their legs dirtied by the sludge, took fright and galloped away. The lion padded on, ignoring the herbivores and the elephants.

This was what Brand lived for, not the paying tourists or the occasional thrill and spill of an investigation. This, for him, was peace and paradise; sitting in the shade watching Africa's wildlife play out their daily drama of life and death. It was better than television or a movie, and the ending was never as predictable as a book's.

Brand had emailed Dani from Bulawayo, telling her that according to the police and her doctor, Kate Munns was definitely deceased.

He had a day before the Cliffs were arriving, and his Land Rover was slow and noisy to travel in, so he had decided to break his journey to Victoria Falls and camp in Hwange National Park for a night. He had arrived in the park in the afternoon, checked in, and then driven the ten kilometres to Nymandlovu platform.

As the sun entered the belt of dust above the horizon the landscape was bathed in an unearthly, eerie pink gold.

The lion was at the waterhole, gingerly moving close to the edge of the pool, clearly not liking the feeling of getting his dessert plate-sized paws wet. He looked almost comical as he shook each front foot before eventually crouching, his tail curled, to lap at the water.

The elephants had made straight for the source of the water, which was a pipe through which water trickled into a concrete trough that would have then spilled over into the wider pan if the pachyderms weren't so intent on sucking it straight from the outlet. Somewhere nearby an ageing Lister diesel engine *tucker-tucker*ed away, sucking the life-giving liquid up from the depths of the dry sandy earth.

Brand opened the cheap plastic cooler box beside him and took out another Zambezi Lager. The ice had long since melted, but the water gave a semblance of coolness to the beer. He popped it and took a long draught, then wiped his mouth with the back of his hand.

The elephant matriarch trumpeted. She raised her trunk again and left the cluster of her family stealing the water from the pipe. There was a tiny calf amid the forest of grey legs and the old cow was clearly nervous about the presence of the lion who, in reality, was posing no threat to any of the animals. She took a handful of paces towards the lion and he looked up at her approach.

For a moment he glared at her defiantly, but as she carried on around the edge of the waterhole, closing on him, he stepped back from the ooze and started trotting. Emboldened, the cow chased him, her tail sticking out and her ears back as she trumpeted again. The lion broke into a run and headed for the tree line.

'So much for the king of beasts,' one of the Australians said.

Brand had watched the scene play out countless times. Elephants hated lions, as did buffalo, and both would turn on lions to chase them away from their young. In reality, it was no picnic being the king. Male lions were chased out of their prides when they reached sexual maturity and then spent long, often lonely years in the bush fending for themselves. If they were lucky they would survive and eventually challenge a male or a pair of brothers for dominance of a pride and enjoy a year or two of protecting their family and mating while their lionesses did the majority of the hunting. But all too soon they, too, would be challenged, and if not killed by the young usurpers they would be cast back out into the bush, to die of starvation if the wounds inflicted in the coup didn't kill them first.

Brand could identify with the old male. The De Villiers boys had sent him on his way and he had no woman, no family to speak of. He was past middle age with barely a dollar in his pocket; no one to feed him and no one for him to protect. In his own way, though, he was happy.

The male lion started to call, his deep, rumbling roar echoing across the plain that had been pounded flat by thousands of elephant. He had someone after all, Brand thought, perhaps a brother or perhaps still a pride. He was not alone.

Brand finished his beer as the elephants moved from the trough and fanned out around the muddy waterhole. Having slaked their thirst they were now snorting up trunkloads of ooze to spray on their backs and under their bellies. Once dry the black crust would protect them from the sun's rays and the itches of ticks and other parasites. Brand took his cooler box and walked down the timber stairs to his Land Rover, climbed in and started the engine.

He opened another beer and drove slowly back to camp. The sun was red as it neared the treetops and he stopped to watch it perfectly silhouette the long neck of a giraffe that grazed on an umbrella thorn. It was a quintessential African picture, and it reminded him why he was here.

He would meet Anna and Peter Cliff tomorrow and drive them around southern Africa, on a safari and a most likely fruitless search for Linley Brown. He wondered if Dani had told the sister and brother-in-law what he had learned about Kate, or if she was leaving that to him.

Brand raised his beer to the giraffe, and to a young woman who had thought she could pull off a fraud by cheating death.

'Goodbye, Kate Munns, whoever you were.'

14

To Brand's surprise, his mobile phone beeped in his pocket as the female ranger lifted the green and yellow striped boom gate and he drove back into Main Camp, which was, as the name suggested, the main rest camp in Hwange National Park.

He trundled past green-painted bungalows to the sandy, mostly empty camping ground. A trio of South African-registered Land Cruisers, fitted with rooftop tents, awnings, and every camping gadget imaginable, were laagered up around a fire and Brand smelled the greasily tempting aroma of sizzling *boerewors*.

When he found a place to park, under a mopane tree, he took out his phone and checked the screen. He had two missed calls. There had never been mobile phone reception in the park on any of his previous visits. He had only left the phone on to use as a clock.

There were other signs of progress in the camp, small indicators that Zimbabwe might be extricating itself, slowly, from the economic and political mess that had plagued it for years. Checking in to the camp he had noticed people in the garden of the Waterbuck's Head bar and restaurant, which had been closed for the past ten years due to Zimbabwe's disastrous economic climate and the lack of visitors to the park. But now it seemed tourists were returning to Hwange.

Brand got out of the Land Rover and opened the rear door while he dialled to check his voicemail. The first message was from Sergeant Goodness Khumalo.

'*Hello, Mr Brand. I checked with Dr Rodriquez's surgery and her receptionist said she had to leave the country urgently. I hope that wasn't because your investigation tipped her off. Goodbye.*'

Elena had escaped, and had probably cost him a good contact in the Bulawayo police, but Brand knew he would probably see neither of the women again. The second message was from Dani.

'*Hudson, hi. I've transferred the money into your bank account. You should be able to access the funds tomorrow. I spoke to Anna Cliff. As you thought, she is going to hire you to track down Linley Brown. Good luck with that. I've informed the insurance company that your findings are that Kate Munns is dead and the death certificate issued by Dr Fleming is valid. I've mentioned the fake certificate to the company and they have asked me for legal advice on their position. It's tricky – they are unlikely to want to involve the police, and if they don't then they may have no choice but to pay up. Will advise in due course, but this will inevitably delay payment to Linley Brown while the insurers faff about. Oh, I didn't get a chance to catch Anna and tell her your news about the fake death certificate. Thought I'd leave you to tell her that bit. Should make for an interesting first night around the campfire. Ciao.*'

Brand sighed and put his phone back in his pocket. He slid a canvas-covered mattress from the back of the Land Rover and undid the leather belt holding it rolled tight. He tossed the released mattress onto the roof of the truck. Next he took a compact travelling mosquito net and climbed up onto the roof via the front bumper bar and bonnet. He shook the net out and, reaching up, tied the piece of string at its apex to a low-hanging branch, then tucked the net in around the mattress.

Climbing back down again he opened another bottle of Zambezi. With the beer in one hand he dragged a stack of fresh-cut mopane wood into a cross-hatched configuration. Brand set his beer down, reluctantly, on the cement-and-brick *braai* and packed kindling and dry yellow grass into the well he had left in the centre of the firewood. Then he lit it with his Zippo. The parched fuel caught immediately and before he had finished his beer the fire had taken hold and the wood was blazing.

As well as his cooler box he had a forty-litre camping fridge that ran off an auxiliary car battery. From it he took a piece of rump steak he had bought before leaving Bulawayo. It was the last of his food. He would need to shop in the morning for the safari he was taking Peter and Anna Cliff on in Victoria Falls, before their plane arrived. Also, he needed to pick up a bigger vehicle from a guy he had worked with in the past, who ran a travel company in the Falls. There was much to do.

For now, though, he pulled a fold-out camping chair from the back of his truck and sat down with his beer to watch the flames turn the wood into coals he could cook on. Some people called a campfire bush television; Brand certainly had no need for the real thing, even if he could afford one.

For the moment he put off thoughts of the news he would deliver to Anna Cliff: that for some reason Kate had wanted to disappear and fraudulently obtain a good deal of money for her friend and/or herself. He wondered if the sister would come up with the answer. She would certainly want to track Linley down and this safari holiday would degenerate into a person hunt, with two amateurs tagging along with him. It would not, he predicted, be a pleasant trip.

A jackal gave its high-pitched whine out beyond the rusting, falling-down camp fence. Further off was the low rumbling of a lion, perhaps the male Brand had seen at Nymandlovu. In the shadows beyond the fire a shape was moving. Brand put his hand to his face to shield his eyes from the worst of the light and caught the slope-backed silhouette of a spotted hyena patrolling the perimeter. The smell of his steak would rouse its curiosity.

Brand was not scared of hyena. They were brazen, but cowardly when confronted. Another gave an eerie, *woo-oop* call, and the one on patrol responded. These were the sounds he loved, not the honk and whine of city traffic nor the rumble of jet aircraft overhead. The moon was rising and a shooting star blazed a trail across the dark purple sky.

He thought again about Kate Munns. 'Who were you?' he asked the flames as he prodded a log back into the fire's jaws. 'Why did you want to leave your life?'

Money, love, sex and drugs were, in Brand's mind, the motivators for most bad behaviour in humans. Kate's friend, Linley, apparently had the drug problem, but Brand couldn't believe one person would go to such bizarre lengths to help a friend. There were other ways to raise cash. No, there was more to Kate's attempted disappearance, and maybe even her eventual death.

Perhaps Linley Brown had decided she wanted all the insurance money, and not just whatever Kate was going to split with her – if indeed that had been their plan. Kate would have been dead to her family and friends in the UK, but she still had a new life to get on with. Maybe, Brand thought, Kate survived the car wreck, but Linley decided, on the spur of the moment, that she would be better off if her friend really did die. That would certainly account for Linley's absence from the funeral and her unwillingness to confront anyone who knew Kate or who was investigating her death. What that meant, though, was that if he did track Linley down, as Anna would undoubtedly pay him to, then instead of finding a sad young woman and offering a tearful reconciliation and closure, they might walk straight into the path of a cold-blooded murderess with money to protect. If they cornered her she might be as dangerous as any wounded animal Brand had ever encountered.

The hyena called again.

*

The next morning, Peter Cliff picked up his bag and his wife's at Victoria Falls international airport and loaded them onto a trolley with a wonky wheel.

They had taken a night flight from Heathrow to Johannesburg's O.R. Tambo Airport in South Africa, then made a connection to Zimbabwe. Despite the fact they had flown Club with British Airways he had not been able to sleep in the business class bed from London and had only dozed fitfully on the second leg.

Anna's friend, Dani, the lawyer, had texted her overnight and on arrival they received the message that the safari guide, Brand, would have 'news' for them about Kate, though Dani stressed that she was still most definitely deceased.

Unable to control her curiosity, Anna called Dani from the terminal while Peter was fetching the bags. When he pushed the trolley over to her she was ending the call. 'Well?' he said.

'She won't say. It's infuriating, Peter. I just wish she would spill, but she says it will be better if this man Brand tells us the news and puts it in context.' Anna sighed with exasperation.

'We'll see him soon enough.'

Anna checked the tiny padlocks on the bags. 'Well, at least the bags haven't been broken into.' On their trip to Zimbabwe for the funeral their luggage had been tampered with and Anna had lost her camera. The Zimbabwean police had blamed the baggage handlers at Johannesburg airport. All African countries liked to blame immigrants and citizens of neighbouring countries for crime.

Peter knew that what had pained her most was not the loss of the compact Nikon but the fact that there were some snaps of Kate on it which Anna had not yet downloaded to her computer. Her last and most recent images of her sister were lost forever. He missed Kate too, and while he was having reservations about trying to track down this Linley Brown he knew it had to be done, for Anna's sake and for his.

Brand was dressed in safari shirt and shorts. He was tall, taller than Peter by about six inches, and his arms were coffee-coloured and muscled.

'Hello, I'm Anna,' his wife said, and Peter thought she was almost flirting with the man.

Brand touched the brim of his hat. 'Sorry for your loss, ma'am.'

'Peter Cliff.' He shook hands with the American, squeezing his as hard as he could. Despite the size of the other man's hand his grip wasn't as brutal as Peter had expected; it was firm, but not crushing.

Brand looked him in the eye. 'Good to meet you, Peter.' The voice was deep, gravelly, and Peter suspected Brand was a smoker. He was curious about the man, but not cowed by him.

'Likewise, I'm sure. It's been a long flight.'

Brand nodded. 'It's a couple of hours' drive to the game lodge where you're staying tonight, but you can have a nap when you get there if you like.'

'I said a long flight, not that we're old-age pensioners.'

'No offence meant.'

Brand moved to take over the trolley, and Peter decided to let him. 'None taken.' Brand pushed ahead, leading them through the single-storey terminal building.

'Mr Brand – Hudson – Dani said you have some news for us, about Kate.'

The American nodded, signalling he had heard the question, but said nothing. He led them outside and Peter felt the pitiless burn of the African sun on his bald crown. His hat was in the daypack on the top of the luggage. 'Hudson, can you please get my hat out of my daypack?' Peter said.

The safari guide stopped, but didn't look back. 'The blue one?'

'Yes, that's the one.'

Brand reached over the handle of the trolley, hefted the daypack, swivelled and passed it to him. Peter hadn't really expected the man to unzip his bag and ferret for his hat, but he did want to see what reaction the request would provoke. Some people fawned over Peter because he was a doctor and others went out of their way to treat him like a common man, perhaps thinking that was what he wanted. The truth was, he didn't want to be judged by what he did, but who he was. He knew he was behaving childishly, but this man had irked him from the moment he'd met him, and while Peter knew why this was, it still annoyed him.

Peter regretted his deliberate arrogance as he fumbled with the bag while Brand stepped out, increasing his stride and pace towards a tan-coloured Land Cruiser, forcing Anna to break into a shuffling trot to keep up with him. Peter gave up, stopped and took out his floppy bush hat, watching his wife chase after the long-limbed guide.

The car park was crowded with minivans and safari vehicles similar to Brand's. The vehicle had a custom-built stretched cab and three side doors along the flank closest to them.

Anna put her hand on Brand's arm as he opened a door and lowered a fold-out step that gave access to three seats behind the driver and front passenger's positions. Peter felt a prick of anger and strode over to them.

'Hudson, please, what is it that Dani wanted you to tell us about my sister? This really can't wait,' Anna said.

Brand pulled the brim of his hat down a little, shading his eyes as he looked down at Anna. 'I wanted to wait until we got to the lodge, maybe until you had a drink in front of you.'

'I don't need a stiff gin to hear bad news.'

A snort caught in the back of Peter's throat, but the American didn't notice it. Peter was as curious about the guide's news as Anna. 'Yes, we don't need you to sugar-coat it.'

Brand turned to him, looked at him, then took off his hat and moved his dark-eyed gaze back to Anna. 'You might not want to hear this.'

She put her hands on her hips and glared up at him. 'For God's sake, tell me.'

He exhaled slowly. 'Your sister *did* plan on faking her own death, and paid a doctor in Bulawayo two thousand dollars for a false death certificate.'

Peter saw Anna's eyes and mouth widen in shock and he felt his own heart lurch. 'So, she's . . .'

Brand held up his big hands, palms out. 'Ma'am, she *is* dead. I've verified that with the police and a doctor who I believe. Your old family physician, a man by the name of Fleming.'

'Dr Fleming delivered us both as babies,' Anna said in a quiet voice. 'You're sure?'

Brand put his hat back on. 'We can stand here in the sun, ma'am, or we can go to the lodge and discuss this.'

Anna looked at him and Peter breathed a little easier. It had been tempting, he thought, to cling to the fantasy that Kate was still alive. Anna had had her hopes raised and dashed in the space of a few words. She reached out and put her hand on a side pillar of the truck to steady herself.

'Ma'am . . .'

She flicked her head. 'Stop calling me that. My name is Anna, and we're going to be spending the next three weeks together.'

'I know this is a shock.' He took her elbow and Peter went to his wife and held her other arm, taking her back from the handsome safari guide. Around them other tourists were being loaded into their vehicles and parents were loading the bags of children back from boarding school into four-wheel drives. Brand lifted their bags into the car.

They climbed up into the truck and Brand closed their door, then got in behind the wheel and slammed his own door, a little too hard, Peter thought. The man was probably annoyed at Dani leaving him to break the news that she had obviously kept to herself. Peter and Anna had taken the seats immediately behind him. Peter took off his hat and mopped his brow with it. The air was heavy and the air conditioner, while rattling, was struggling to cut through the humidity.

*

'Tell us, Hudson, please.'

Brand glanced back at the Englishman. He had rimless glasses and a face that never saw the sun. He was also clearly feeling the heat; he now took a handkerchief from his cargo pants pocket and mopped his brow. Peter Cliff had tried to crush his hand when they'd met, and Brand had felt that male-versus-male impulse before, so he had relaxed his grip.

Then there was the business with the hat. Brand liked to let his clients know that he was their guide, not their slave, as soon as the moment presented itself; rarely did it come so soon and so crudely as it had when Peter had asked him to fetch his hat from his bag. He wished Dani had told them about Kate, and that they'd had the good sense to wait until they got to the lodge before they pushed him for the information. Anna Cliff might not need a drink to hear the news, but he sure as heck could have used one to deliver it.

He glanced back at her. She was a pistol. Short women were like that, no-nonsense and full of attitude and at the same time shyly vulnerable. She was angry and upset, and on the verge of punching the back of the seat or bursting into tears. As a man, he couldn't tell which.

Brand left the car park and turned right onto the main road that led back to Bulawayo, and South Africa beyond. Habitually, his eyes swept left and right as he drove, looking for a kudu that might leap out from the trees, or an elephant he might show to the couple to distract them from the inevitable news of Kate's duplicity. 'I don't know the whole story, the why.'

'It's all right. Just tell us what you do know,' Anna said.

She would have to hear it sometime. He told her about the forged death certificate he had found at the Provincial Registry Office in Bulawayo. When Anna quizzed him about the doctor he told her about his interview with Elena, up until the part where they'd torn each other's clothes off.

'Did this Dr Rodriquez say *why* Kate wanted to fake her death?' Peter Cliff asked.

'No.' Brand turned to look back at Peter again, and even as he did so caught the flash of grey from the left in his peripheral vision.

The warthog darted in front of the Land Cruiser, its tail pointing skywards like an aerial. Brand braked and the two passengers reached out with their hands to stop themselves slamming into the seats in front of them.

'Sorry about that, folks.' He changed gear and accelerated again, cruising past the cops with the speed camera he knew were just up the road. 'It seems that just three days after your sister bought her fake death certificate she and her friend Linley were then in a real car accident and, unfortunately, Kate died.'

'Unfortunately,' said Anna.

Brand waved to another guide he recognised by sight in a Land Cruiser coming towards him. He knew the questions that would come flooding from Anna Cliff, but he had no more answers for her, only a few half-baked theories. He said again, 'I'm sorry for your loss.'

'I didn't lose her; she ran away, faked her death and then apparently died.' She began to cry.

'Anna . . .' Peter said.

Brand thought it was as if Peter was admonishing her for sniffing in public, for allowing her stiff upper lip to tremble. He had not taken to Peter, and he would have to spend a long time cooped up with him in a vehicle with poor air conditioning. He wondered if Dani would have told Anna about the fake death certificate if Anna had opted to stay in the UK.

'What reason did my sister give Dr Rodriguez for wanting to fake her death?' Anna asked again.

'Dr Rodriguez was big on doctor–patient confidentiality. Probably wise given her line of business. If she knew, she wouldn't tell me.' Brand wanted to remind Anna, subtly, that her sister had been embarking on a criminal enterprise, with intent to defraud an insurance company.

'I want to talk to her.'

'She has left the country. She was worried I was going to contact the local police,' Brand said.

'And did you?'

'I did. They'll look for her, but I don't think she'll be coming back to Zimbabwe any time soon. If the police start investigating I'm sure they'll find this isn't the first time Elena's issued a fake death certificate.'

'Elena?'

Brand coughed. 'Dr Rodriguez. This is forestry land we're passing through now. Those trees with the bark that looks like pale grey camouflage are Zimbabwean teak. It makes great furniture, and good coals to *braai* on.' In the rear-view mirror he saw Anna fold her arms and sit back in her seat, her face set in a scowl. She wasn't interested in the trees of Zimbabwe, or his attempts to change the topic of conversation. He did feel guilty about Elena, but he doubted she could have told them more about Kate's motives.

'I want to find Linley Brown, now more than ever,' Anna said.

'Yes,' echoed her husband.

Brand nodded. He had seen that coming and he wondered if Dani had held off telling Anna the news about the fake death certificate in case Anna had had a change of heart and decided to stay in England.

There was little more Brand could tell the couple for now, and they drove on in silence, Anna and Peter absorbing the news and, presumably, pondering Kate's motives. When they came to the coalmining town of Hwange, Brand pulled into a service station to let the couple stretch their legs. An old steam railway locomotive, a relic of another time and another country, when Zimbabwe had been Rhodesia, was slowly rusting away on a plinth.

'Your itinerary includes an afternoon game drive through the national park, but I'll understand if you want to skip it,' Brand said.

'No,' said Peter, 'we'll stick to the itinerary. Anna was looking forward to seeing Hwange National Park again, weren't you, dear?'

'I suppose.'

They got back in the truck and Brand turned to the couple. 'For what it's worth, I find that when I'm down some time in the bush helps me.'

Anna sniffed and dabbed her eyes with a tissue. 'Sorry. Yes, I suppose you're right, Hudson. The bush is the one thing I miss about this country when we're back in England.'

He felt for her. She was a pretty woman, coming to terms with shocking revelations about her sister, and her husband was an asshole. Brand shelved his feelings, though, and went back to business. He drove a short way down the main road, then took a right at a sign that read *Hwange National Park Sinamatella Camp.*

'Hwange town, as you probably know, has always been tied to coalmining, but you'll see up ahead there's a new mine here; this one's open-cut and run by the Chinese. It's not a pretty sight.'

The tar road gave way to gravel, the surface lined with compacted coal waste. A water tanker drove towards them, spraying to keep down the dust, but Brand knew this would also create a sticky black mud that would spatter the side of the Toyota. A vervet monkey darted across in front of them, and Brand slowed so the Cliffs could see the rest of the troop.

'The poor little things; they're supposed to be grey but they look almost black with soot,' Anna said.

Brand didn't like driving this way, but he thought it didn't hurt to let tourists see how Zimbabwe's rulers were replacing the old days of white colonialism with new masters from Asia's booming economies. The road took them through the open-cut mine's operations. A hill was being carved away and steam curled from fissures in the coal. Workers in black-stained overalls sweated in the midday heat haze.

'My God, it's like a scene from hell,' Anna said.

'Yes,' agreed her husband.

Soon, however, they were driving through bush again as they crossed the outer border into the national park. Brand hoped the miners' insatiable need for coal and the country's short-term need for foreign currency didn't result in the mine spreading, but he wasn't confident. After about thirty kilometres of bouncing along the corrugated surface they arrived at Sinamatella Camp. Brand left the Cliffs in the truck while he went into the office and paid the woman at the desk entry fees for the vehicle and three people, then got back in and drove them a short distance to the camp's restaurant. They passed a row of green-painted lodge buildings, but there were no cars parked outside any of them; visitors to Hwange were a rarity because of the country's economic and political problems.

Anna climbed down out of the Land Cruiser. 'I'm sorry for sounding so harsh and irrational when we first arrived.'

'It's OK,' Brand said. 'I know how hard this must be for you. But if I can find Linley Brown, or some more answers, I will. The question is, do you still want to go on safari, or do you want to go straight back to South Africa?'

Peter got out of the vehicle and the three of them walked up to a covered verandah. The camp was situated on a mesa that overlooked a sprawling plain covered in golden grass and leafless acacias. The Sinamatella River wound its way like a snake below them, from left to right. The restaurant behind them had been closed for years.

They took in the view while the Cliffs pondered their options. 'What do you think, love?' Peter asked his wife. The man had been adamant that they go on their game drive, but perhaps now he was having reservations.

'I don't know. I remember this place from my childhood; it was so busy here all the time, but nothing's the same any more, is it?' She looked from the view to Brand, her face crestfallen. 'What do you think, Hudson?'

'I'm making enquiries in South Africa already. I can't hurry them along, and our being there won't make the wheels turn any faster. We can be in South Africa in a day, if we push it, from wherever we are on the tour if news comes in – even quicker if you decide to fly. In the meantime, there's plenty of Africa to see.'

Anna looked at Peter, who put a hand on her shoulder and gave it a gentle squeeze. 'I'm in no rush to turn around and go back to South Africa yet. I think Hudson's right; let's carry on with the tour and if Linley turns up we'll beetle down to see her. Who knows, once she gets her money, she might come back to Zimbabwe.'

'Or fly overseas somewhere.' Anna looked dejected.

'Shall we continue then?' Brand said, and led them back to the vehicle.

Their route took them through about one hundred and twenty kilometres of the national park, towards Main Camp, where they would leave the park to drive to the lodge they were staying at that night. Despite Zimbabwe's problems its parks and wildlife service had kept its national parks ticking over, and Hwange still had the ability to serve up some world class game viewing.

They stopped at Mandavu Dam and Brand escorted the Cliffs to a thatch-roofed hide overlooking a broad expanse of water. He raised his binoculars to his eyes and pointed out a herd of sable antelope grazing on a distant grassy foreshore.

'Have you ever met Linley Brown?' Brand asked Anna.

'Only once, when she and Kate were about sixteen, I think. I was already living in the UK then, and went home for a holiday when the girls were both home from boarding school. I don't really remember much about her, though. I do recall that Mom was having some problems with Kate at the time, but as far as I could tell it was nothing more than the usual teenage hijinks, some staying out late and drinking and smoking. Mom used to hit the Bols brandy every night, though, and she smoked like a chimney, so it's hardly surprising Kate and Linley followed suit.'

'Did Linley ever visit Kate in the UK?' Brand asked.

'Not that we ever knew of,' Peter replied.

They drove to the next picnic site, at Masuma Dam, where another hide overlooked a waterhole. A South African-registered HiLux with a camper unit on the back was parked above the hide. Masuma, Brand knew, was one of the best wildlife viewing sites in Zimbabwe, if not the whole of southern Africa. In the cool of the hide Brand struck up a conversation with the couple from the campervan. They were Serbs who had left their homeland during the fighting that followed the break-up of Yugoslavia in the 1990s. It was ironic, Brand thought, that he had come to Africa in search of a war and people like these had fled there to escape one. Many South Africans left Johannesburg to escape the crime, but this couple felt safe there. What, he wondered, had Kate Munns been running from or to?

'Three wild dog killed an impala here, by the camp fence this morning,' said the woman, who was short and blonde and still carried the accent of her birthplace.

She pointed out a lioness, sleeping under a tree in the distance, and Brand relayed the sighting to the Cliffs, who followed his directions and eventually picked up the cat in their binoculars. Brand thanked the Serbian woman and they moved on.

Their drive through the long, hot afternoon yielded a sighting of a pride of nine lions just before the main Nyamandlovu viewing platform, but the excitement that usually accompanied such an event was absent. Anna had been born in Zimbabwe and Peter, Brand gathered from some comments the couple had made to each other during the drive, had apparently been to Africa for his honeymoon and at least once more before Kate's funeral. Perhaps the couple were still coming to terms with the new developments, because they were happy to move on from the lions within a few minutes.

Brand never tired of looking at big cats, even if they did spend most of the daylight hours like these ones, sleeping in the shade of a tree. He marvelled at their muscled necks, their golden eyes and massive paws, then started the engine and drove on.

They exited the park at Main Camp and crossed the railway line that led back to Victoria Falls, then turned left towards the small town of Dete. Before they reached it, Brand turned right towards the lodge where they would spend the night. It was called Elephant's Eye, and occupied a concession leased from the Zimbabwean forestry authority, which managed the land on the edge of the national park.

The forests acted as a buffer between the national park and surrounding communities, and while they were outside the park proper, there was no fence between them and the reserve and, as a result, there was plenty of wildlife living and moving through the area.

The lodge was aptly named, with safari tents set on stilts that put their guests at about the height of an elephant's eye. Brand had stayed there before and told the Cliffs they could expect to see herds of the giant pachyderms visiting the waterhole in front of the tents, and possibly munching on the trees between the accommodation units.

Along with a porter he escorted the Cliffs to their tent and told them that he would meet them at the bar and dining area in half an hour. Then he walked over to his own tent, which was next to theirs. The sun was low and red in the band of dust and smoke that sat above the tree line. Brand climbed the stairs, dropped his safari bag on the bed and took out his laptop. He connected to the internet and when his mail program opened he typed a message to Dani: *Cliffs have arrived. Thanks for nothing.*

In his inbox was an email from Captain Sannie van Rensburg of the South African Police Service.

'Shit.' He opened it. She wanted to confirm his whereabouts six months ago, and asked if he had been in Cape Town at that time. It would be about the murder of the second prostitute. He shook his head. Van Rensburg was a smart woman, and good looking, but the service she worked for was siloed, under-resourced and overwhelmed with the day-to-day battle against street crime. It didn't surprise him that she had only just worked out the connection between the murder of the woman whose body had been found near the Kruger Park, at Hazyview, and the woman who had been killed at Sea Point when he was in Cape Town with a party of foreign tourists.

He composed an email to her, confirming he had been in Cape Town for the dates she requested. *But then, I assume you already know that. When do you want to see me?* His finger hovered over the send button. He was not afraid of her, or her questioning, but he did not want to end up in a South African prison because of circumstantial evidence. If he was arrested and charged he wouldn't be able to afford a lawyer capable of getting him off. He didn't even know if he was going to return to Hazyview and the house on the Sabie River, but nor did he want it to appear to her that he was on the run. *Not sure of my return date to RSA, but will advise you when I am back in the Lowveld*, he typed. If she wanted to get hold of him sooner she could get a warrant. In the meantime he had his own investigation, and a safari tour, to run.

'Hello?' called Anna from outside his tent.

Brand sighed as he walked to the deck outside and looked down at her. 'Everything all right?'

'Yes, fine. Peter's tummy's a bit upset. He says he's going to skip dinner. Will you walk me over there? It's getting dark.'

'I was going to take a shower.'

'I promise not to rant,' she said. 'It's just that, well, your news that my sister was planning to commit a crime before her death shook me. God, to tell you the truth, I just need a drink.'

She sounded desperate, both for a drink and company. At some stage he would need to ask her more questions about Kate, and now was as good a time as any. It might be advantageous, he thought, not to have the prickly Peter around when he spoke to her.

'Sure.'

15

I ended the phone call and Lungile walked in from the lounge room, joining me in the kitchen of the modest three-bedroom house we were renting in White River.

'You look worried, sister, who was that?' she asked.

'I was talking to Dr Fleming again. He said that investigator I told you about, Hudson Brand, came to see him.'

'What did the doc tell him?'

'That he identified Kate's body by the pin in her pelvis.'

Lungile shrugged. 'So there's no problem. You'll get your money, yes?'

I didn't know exactly how this would work. 'Brand said before, when he left me some messages, that he needed to see me and for me to sign some stuff. I didn't want to, but now I wonder if I acted too rashly. Everything's in order, Lungile, I just don't think I can handle being grilled about the accident again.'

She put her hand on my arm. 'You'll be fine, don't worry.'

We went back to the lounge. Fortune ignored us, and continued killing virtual people. He was playing *Medal of Honour* on the stolen Xbox and flat-screen TV he'd acquired with some of the proceeds of our recent heists.

Lungile hadn't asked me for any money, but I had already made up my mind to give her twenty thousand pounds when the claim was paid. She had been good to me and had helped me survive after the crash, financially and emotionally, even if her job plan and therapy had involved turning me into more of a criminal than I already was.

An explosion and an expletive signalled the death of Fortune. He got up and stretched. 'Were you two talking about money?'

'None of your business,' I said.

'Now, now, don't be like that. Once this claim of yours comes through it's going to be party time. But let's get it started now.' He went to the kitchen. His bare feet slapped the white tiled floor as he returned to the lounge room with three bottles, a Carling Black Label and two Savannas. As he neared the lounge he trod on something and cursed, only just managing to avoid dropping the drinks. '*Eish*, pick up that empty Doom can.'

I frowned at him. He couldn't talk; he didn't know how to pick up after himself. The house had been full of cockroaches when we moved in and I had 'doomed' the lounge room overnight with a roach bomb. It was lethal stuff and the other can from the two-pack was sitting on the dining table, waiting for tonight's attack on the kitchen. Fortune leaned over me and I took the dewy bottle, which he had already opened. The cold cider tasted sweeter than usual. I felt some of the strain of the past few weeks easing ever so slightly in my chest. Lungile was right; everything would be fine.

'Fortune's right, for once. Let's party,' Lungile said.

'In White River?' We had chosen the town, in the hills above Nelspruit, because it was quiet, and we wanted to fly under the police radar for a while after our first job in Nelspruit.

'We can go to the pub at Casterbridge,' Fortune said. 'I sold some more of the loot this morning. Drinks are on me.'

I was easily swayed; I was hungry and the alcoholic cider was going to my head as we hadn't had lunch. Staying clean and sober while I got over my pill addiction had dramatically lessened my tolerance. 'OK, but I want my cut as well.'

I went to the bathroom and touched up my makeup; I hadn't thought about men since the car crash, and only put my face on when Lungile and I were about to play rich housewives or businesswomen at a house inspection. The person I saw in the mirror was a stranger. Who had I become; had I really done all those terrible things? I missed Kate Munns then, so much that my bottom lip started to tremble and I watched, fixated, as the first tears started to gather in my eyes. I sniffed and turned and reached for the toilet paper roll, but it was just bare cardboard. Bloody Fortune. And the seat was up and the place smelled of pee. I looked back at the mirror and convulsed. The tears cascaded down my cheeks, taking my freshly applied mascara with them in muddy black rivulets.

There was a knock on the bathroom door. 'Are you all right in there, *sisi*?'

I groaned, then sniffed. 'I'm fine.'

The door opened. 'No, you're not.' Through the fog of tears I saw Fortune hovering behind Lungile. 'Go away. Leave us for a minute.'

'All right, I'll get the car out of the garage. Be waiting for you outside.'

'It's all right, baby.' Lungile knelt beside me, put an arm around me and drew me to her prominent bosom. 'Shush, shush, you're going to be *fine*.'

I couldn't stop the crying, and had to gasp to catch my breath. 'I was so scared. I watched her *burn*! It was so terrible.' She rocked me, like a child, and I smelled her perfume and the sickly sweet odour of *dagga* that clung to her hair as I sobbed into her dress.

'There's nothing you could have done; it was an accident. She's at peace now.' Lungile kissed the tears from my cheek. It was kind, the sort of thing a real sister might have done. 'Her life was not good but she is in heaven now and I miss her as well, just as you do.'

I looked up into her eyes, and wiped mine with the back of my hands. 'Where did we all go wrong, Lungile?'

She shrugged. 'My problem was men and my mom's cancer. Yours was men and drugs. Hers was men and life. Our country's a mess; it was so full of promise and then we were all cast aside. I used to think everyone in Zimbabwe was good, but we're not any more. The government turned us into rats, scrambling around a sinking ship.'

'Linley, sister. Are you girls all right in there?' Fortune called.

'I thought you were getting the car ready?' Lungile called back out to her brother.

'I did. It's out front. Are you coming or not?'

She held me away from her body and raised her eyebrows to me in a question.

I nodded. 'Just let me clean myself up.'

Lungile helped me to my feet, ran the taps and moistened a face-cloth. 'It's just the stress leaving your body, *sisi*. You're going to be high and dry soon.'

I wiped my face and quickly started reapplying my makeup. She stood there, arms folded, watching me, as if I was about to break down again. I looked away from my eyeliner, to her. 'I'm going to look after you.'

'I don't need looking after.'

'I want to. She would have wanted me to.'

Lungile looked away, out to the lounge room and the open front door beyond. The noise of Fortune's latest hot BMW being revved hard was her dumb brother's none too subtle hint that he was ready to go. 'OK.' She walked out.

She, and even Fortune in his obnoxious way, had looked after me, and I wanted to give something to Lungile, however at that moment I also wanted to run from the house, from this life. But the reality of the situation was that I wouldn't, couldn't, get far without a car. South Africa wasn't England or Australia; I couldn't just hop on a passing bus or car and get to Johannesburg airport in safety. There were daily shuttle bus services running from White River and Nelspruit, but I didn't even know where they went from and, in any case, I didn't have enough money for a plane ticket anywhere.

The cider had tasted so good that I was craving another. I felt in control enough of my addiction to know I could stick to booze and stay away from the pills. I had survived my old life and survived the car crash. I looked into the mirror and blinked a couple of times.

I put my compact, lipstick and lip gloss in my handbag and went to the front door, which Lungile must have closed behind her on the way out, and was about to open it when I saw the can of Doom on the table out of the corner of my eye. I decided it would be better to set off the insect bomb while we were out; the lingering smell of the insecticide in the lounge room had caused Lungile to cough and splutter when she woke up, such was its potency. When we read the can we realised we shouldn't have even been in the house in our bedrooms when using the stuff, although Lungile had been too stoned to check the label before going to bed.

I snapped the safety seal on the can, set it down on the floor and depressed the plunger. It locked into place and a noxious stream of spray jetted towards the ceiling. I picked up my handbag, grabbed the door handle and turned it, but as I started to pull, it was flung open into my face. Lungile barrelled into me with enough force to knock me backwards. She reached for me, but I fell to the floor. 'What the hell . . .'

'Get up. Come, quickly! Out the back; it's the police.'

'What?'

'They've got Fortune, on the ground, with a gun to his head.'

'Who?'

'The cops.' Lungile grabbed my wrist and dragged me to my feet. I coughed as my head passed through the cloud of bug spray. 'Come on!'

Spluttering, I wiped my stinging eyes. 'Shit, shit, shit!'

'Stop, police!'

Lungile pushed me in the small of my back and bent down. I turned, eyes streaming, and saw her scoop up the can. A policewoman, young and dwarfed by the pistol in her tiny hand, pushed through the door.

Lungile held the can of Doom out at arm's length, and directed the spray straight into the officer's eyes. The cop screamed.

'Run!'

No, I wanted to cry. This could not be happening. *What the fuck*, I thought as we ran through the house and out the back door. Fortunately the owners of the house were too stingy or too confident to erect electric fencing on the top of the brick wall surrounding the house. Lungile cupped her hands and I put my bag around my neck and my foot into her clasped palms and she boosted me up. I straddled the top of the wall and reached down for her.

'Give me your hand.'

Lungile reached up and I grabbed her and started to haul. She was a big girl, however, and I felt my arm being pulled from its socket as I tried to heave her up the wall. Her feet scrabbled for purchase on the cement-covered wall and one of her stilettos felt into the unkempt, weedy garden we'd been neglecting. 'I can't hold you. You'll have to get something to stand on.'

Lungile looked back at the sound of the rear screen door of the house flying open and banging against the back wall. She let go of my hand and fell into the geraniums, dropping to one knee. Then she looked up at me. 'Go!'

'You, on the wall, stop!' yelled the policewoman.

I was going to try to grab Lungile again, but the cop pointed her pistol at us. The pistol kicked in her hand and a bullet drilled into the wall next to my friend, sending a puff of dust and flying masonry into Lungile's hair. She screamed and put her hands over her face. I put both palms on the top of the brickwork and propelled myself off.

Landing badly, I found myself in the backyard of the house behind us. I got up and ran past a kids' swing set. The back door of the house opened and an elderly woman with curlers in her hair put her hand over her mouth, then dropped it to say, '*Wat doen jy?*'

'Sorry, *Tannie*!' I didn't have time to explain what I was doing, and instead palmed her aside as I ran into her house and down the hallway to the front door.

'Stop!'

I ignored her as I fumbled with the two locks on the door and let myself out. I ran down the paved driveway and stopped at the iron gates. I grabbed the upright railings and shook them, like a prisoner in a cell. 'No!'

There were spikes and a three-strand electric fence running along the top of the front fence. The residents probably assumed no one would break into our house, behind them, and then into theirs. I looked back to the house and saw the woman peering at me from behind the half-closed front door. I glared at her, trying to look as crazy as I could. 'Let me out!'

An arm protruded from the crack in the doorway and I saw the remote in her hand. She pushed the button, probably figuring she was in more danger having me on her property than waiting for whoever had fired the gun behind her house to come after me. I stepped back as the gates started to swing open inwards. I turned my body sideways and slipped out as soon as the gap was wide enough for me.

Luckily I was still wearing running shoes, having not changed out of them yet; I sprinted down the street, spurred on by the sound of a police car siren wailing nearby. This was so unfair, I thought as I ran. My money was coming to me and I could give up the crime. But if I had stayed, then I would have been implicated once the cops worked out that Fortune had stolen the car. I prayed the police wouldn't grill Lungile too hard, and that Fortune, the creep, wouldn't give up his sister and me as part of some plea bargain deal.

I barrelled along the road and then cut right into another street that led me up the hill to Danie Joubert Street. I had no idea where I was going or where I could run to. I needed to get away from White River and Nelspruit, but I had no wheels and precious little cash.

Danie Joubert formed a bypass in downtown White River for traffic heading on the R40 to and from Nelspruit in one direction and the Kruger National Park in the other. I came to a robot and waited for it to turn red. I was panting hard as I checked the stream of vehicles coming to a halt and unslung my handbag from around my neck. I put it on my shoulder and reached into it, feeling the weight of the pistol I swore I would never use in the commission of a crime.

Where did I want to go? Nelspruit was a big city by provincial standards, and in theory bigger places were easier to hide in, but it was also where I had committed my most recent crime. I felt like an animal on the run from pursuing predators; the bush might be the best place for me to get lost in for a few days. I had a gun, a few hundred rand, and my looks. I pushed the hair from my face, undid another button on the simple white blouse I was wearing, then crossed the road to the second vehicle in the queue at the stoplight, a green Land Rover game viewer with a canvas canopy on the top. The vehicle was towing an enclosed trailer. The safari guide behind the wheel was late twenties, I guessed, broad shouldered with dark curly hair. He was good looking. I smiled at him and made eye contact as I darted in front of his vehicle, between it and the Audi in front of him. He winked at me.

As I passed him I stopped at the kerb, then, as if it were an afterthought, doubled back to his front passenger-side door. His eyes widened in surprise as I opened the door.

'Hey, what do you think you're doing?'

'I need a lift to the bush.'

'You what?'

The light turned green and the driver behind us started honking his horn as the traffic in front pulled away.

He looked behind him, then at me. 'I can't. My boss won't let me take any non-customer passengers and . . .'

I pulled the revolver from my handbag and, holding it low, pointed it at him. 'Drive, handsome.'

'Shit.'

He put the Land Rover in gear and took off, silencing the several other horns that had joined the chorus behind us. We just made the light before it turned red again, leaving more angry drivers in our wake.

'What's your name?'

He licked his lips. 'Bryce Duffy. *Sheesh*, I can't believe I'm getting hijacked by a chick.'

'Don't be sexist. Just drive.' I looked back to see if there were any police cars behind us. It was all clear. 'Not too fast.'

'In this thing? Where are we going?'

I didn't know. 'Where are you going?'

'I've got to pick up some guests at a hotel in Hazyview and take them into Kruger for three nights. I can't take you with me.'

'Er, Bryce, I think while I have the gun I can tell you what you can and can't do.'

He nodded. 'Right. Do you want the truck? I mean, like, if you do, that's cool. I can just pull over and you can have it. That's what the boss always tells me; no truck is worth a life.'

'I don't want your game viewer, Bryce, I need to disappear for a few days.'

He looked at me; his face was pale and he wiped the beaded sweat from his upper lip. 'You want to come *with*?'

I weighed up my options. I didn't want to steal his Land Rover as I wouldn't get far in it, and if the police came looking for me once I let Bryce go the truck wouldn't outrun a determined officer on a pushbike. I could leave him in Hazyview, the next town he would pass through on his way to the park, but he would report me to the cops and unless I stole or hijacked something faster they would find me soon enough. 'Give me your phone.'

'What phone?'

'Your cell phone, Bryce.'

'I don't have one.'

The traffic had spread out now that we were clear of White River, driving through hills covered with plantations of pine trees. I raised the gun until it was level with Bryce's ear and cocked it. 'Everyone has a cell phone.'

He shook his head, reached into the top left pocket of his safari shirt and pulled out a cheap Nokia.

'Toss it over here.' I caught it and slipped it into my handbag. Keeping the gun on him I leaned closer to him. He flinched away from me. 'Relax.' In the centre of the dashboard, where a stereo would normally have been, was a two-way radio. I grabbed the handset by the cord, near where it was connected to the unit, and wrenched it out. I tossed it over the side of the door into the field beside us.

'Shit, he'll make me pay for that,' Bryce said.

I gave a snort. 'I'll kill you if you try anything funny.'

Bryce looked at me and sneered. He was getting over his initial shock and I could see the alpha male that lives in all safari guides getting his balls back to their correct position between his legs. I had to show Bryce I meant business. There was no one coming towards us and the Volkswagen Golf that had been behind us had taken advantage of the break in the oncoming traffic to overtake us. I took aim and fired a single shot.

The noise and buck of the pistol in my hand startled me, but not as much as it did Bryce. The bullet had cleaved the air no more than a couple of inches in front of the waxed chest I could see through the folds of his shirt.

'Fuck!'

'If you think I'm joking, or I'm not desperate enough to hurt you, Bryce, just try that look on me again.'

'OK, OK. This is hectic. You're crazy.'

'No. I just need somewhere to hide, Bryce. I won't hurt you, but I can't have you calling your bosses or the police. Where are you going on your safari?'

'Balule.'

It was a rustic camp in the Kruger National Park, I recalled from holidays we'd had on the game reserve when I was a kid. Kruger was crowded compared to the national parks from the country of my birth, but success wasn't a bad thing and the variety and number of wildlife kept the locals and the international tourists coming back. It wasn't a bad place for me to hide out, as long as I could keep Bryce quiet. If the police did come into one of those camps there would be nowhere for me to run; I'd be like a cornered animal, and despite the effect the single shot had had on Bryce I didn't relish the idea of firing the pistol ever again. 'Are you staying in chalets?'

He shook his head. 'I've got tents in the trailer. We're camping.'

'Who's cooking?'

'I am.'

I raised my eyebrows.

'I'm a good cook, actually.'

'I don't doubt you are,' I said. 'But you can tell the people you're picking up that I'm the cook. I'm a bad cook, *actually*, but that will be one of our many little secrets. I'll peel the potatoes.'

'If my boss finds out –'

'Bryce, if your boss finds out, I'll shoot your penis off.'

He swallowed and glanced down at the pistol.

*

Bryce turned left off the R538 onto a dirt access road, following a sign that read *Rissington Inn*.

I kept my left hand clamped to the top of the Land Rover's door top as the truck swayed on its coil springs along the rutted road, but I still held the pistol in my right, covering Bryce. 'I'm going to put the gun in my jeans when we get to the hotel, but you're not leaving my sight. If you try anything silly I'll fill this rust bucket and its engine full of holes and you can try explaining that to your boss and your clients.'

'It's a Land Rover. It's made of aluminium so it doesn't rust.'

I liked that he was getting his cool back, but he kept licking his top lip; he was still a little nervous. The hotel came into view. It was a low-rise whitewashed colonial-style affair, overlooking a grassy field that gave way to bush in the distance. The countryside beyond was hilly, picturesque. The paths and access road to the hotel were marked with neat lines of painted rocks that contrasted nicely with the blood-red African soil.

Bryce pulled up in a gravel parking bay at the foot of a flight of stairs which led up to the swimming pool and the restaurant and bar beyond. A young man with red hair and baggy shorts came down to greet us.

'*Howzit*, Bryce.'

'Ben.' The guide nodded.

The other man's idiom was South African but his accent was plummy English. He advanced on me enthusiastically. 'Hello, I'm Benjamin.' I just had time to slip the pistol into the waistband of my jeans, in the small of my back, as he opened my door for me.

'Naomi,' I said, not wanting to use my real name in front of any of them.

Ben shook my hand. 'Pleased to meet you. Are you going on the safari as well?' He looked to Bryce as I tried to formulate an answer.

'Naomi's our new cook. Greg and Tracey will tell you all about her, how talented she is, next time you see them.'

'Right,' said Ben. 'Your guests are in the bar. I'll get Canaan to load their bags in the trailer, shall I?'

'Yes, that's fine.'

I followed Ben up the stairs and caught his elbow. 'Um, Ben?'

'Yes?'

I lowered my voice. 'Ben, Bryce's been a bit careless with the truth. We met at a party and he's taking me on the safari as, well, a bit of a camp helper. His bosses, Greg and Tracey, don't know about me coming along, so we'd both really appreciate it if you didn't say anything to them about seeing me, OK?'

'Sure. Mum's the word.' He touched the side of his nose then bounded up the stairs with the enthusiasm of an English youth abroad amid the intrigue of Africa.

Bryce was just behind me so I reached around, lifted my blouse and showed him the pistol, to remind him. When he drew alongside me I said out of the corner of my mouth, 'Maybe I'll fill you full of holes and take the Land Rover.'

'You won't get far.'

'That was stupid of you.'

'Recklessly brave, I would have said.' Bryce grinned at me.

'No.' I shook my head and stopped on the stone patio, by the pool. He paused beside me as the tourists started bustling out of the bar. 'Just stupid. I don't want to hurt you or your clients, Bryce. I need help.'

He looked down into my eyes and I blinked a couple of times. I was talking tough and pretending I was in control, but I wasn't. I saw his Adam's apple bob as he read my weakness and swallowed. He really was a good-looking guy, although I couldn't ever recall seeing an ugly safari guide in all my years in Africa.

'All right,' he whispered quickly. 'But later, I want you to tell me what's going on.'

He put his hand on my shoulder and I felt myself start to choke up a little as the tears fought to burst from me. He gave me a little squeeze. 'And don't do anything to upset my tourists,' he said, flashing me his goofy grin again.

I wiped my eyes. 'I won't. Promise. I'll just shoot you if you try anything.'

'OK, well, *lekker.* All right then. I have to look after the clients. Please don't shoot any of them.'

'As long as none of them are Americans.'

He chortled, smiling, then walked up the stairs to greet his guests.

A big-bellied, grey-haired man in designer safari gear waddled up to me and stuck out his hand. 'Herb Lipschitz from New York.'

16

When Brand walked downstairs from the deck of his elevated safari tent he noticed Anna had showered; her damp hair was pulled back in a ponytail and she had changed into a sleeveless floral sundress. Her orange sandals had a slight heel.

They walked together through the grey sand that was typical of Hwange's soils to Elephant's Eye's thatch-roofed and canvas-walled bar and dining area.

'What can I get you?'

'Gin and tonic, please, ice and lemon. Double.'

Brand went to the bar and asked the pretty lodge manager for Anna's drink, and a Zambezi Lager for himself. He took the drinks and led Anna to the lodge's library, which overlooked a swimming pool. A floodlight had been switched on, illuminating the waterhole beyond.

They sat down on a lounge and Brand set Anna's drink in front of her.

Brand sipped his beer. She looked good, and as she'd just come from England he guessed the tan on her bare arms and legs was the spray-on kind. Her muscles were toned, no bingo wings as the Brits called flabby arms, and her legs were smooth and nicely sculpted. 'What do you want to know, Mrs Cliff?'

'I thought we were past that. Call me Anna. But then, this is business, not pleasure, isn't it?'

He said nothing.

'Tell me everything you know about Kate. You said you had confirmed my sister's death.'

'Yup.'

'*Yup*? Can I have some more information, please? You said she had *planned* to fake her own death.'

'Mrs Cliff, Anna, I know this can't be easy for you, but your gut reaction was right, in a way. Kate did try to fake her own death. She went as far as buying a phony death certificate from a crooked Cuban doctor. The cause of death was listed as a cerebral haemorrhage. In my experience a sudden medical problem is not uncommon as a fake cause of death in these types of cases, as the police don't need to be involved. However, your sister's plan went awry.'

'Awry.'

He drank some more beer. He noticed that Anna was almost halfway through her G and T already. She looked out at the waterhole, lost in her thoughts for a minute or more, then turned to Brand. 'Why would she do something like that?'

'Well, if I was continuing this investigation I'd most likely be asking you the same question.'

'What do you mean *if* you were continuing with the investigation?'

He shrugged. 'Now we know your sister's passed, there doesn't seem to be much point digging deeper. It's been my experience that some secrets are best taken to the grave. The insurance company will decide whether or not to pay Linley Brown as soon as I file my final report. I've emailed Dani Russo and suggested that she get the company to run through all the contact they've had with Linley Brown. We know she and Kate had obtained the fake certificate, but if there was no indication they did anything with it then that plays into Linley's favour. However, the company will be concerned that there was intent to defraud.'

Anna shook her head and waved to the lodge manager behind the bar. The woman came over to her. 'Could I have another gin and tonic, please? Double.' She looked at Brand and down at his beer. He shook his head; he had barely drunk a third of the green bottle.

'Have another drink with me.'

'I'm still on duty,' he said.

'Consider yourself off duty. Peter's out like a light and you don't have to drive me anywhere tonight, or even tell me anything about the trees of Zimbabwe. You'll be on duty with Peter in the car tomorrow, believe me.'

'Whiskey and Coke,' Brand said to the manager, then raised his beer to his lips and chugged it down. *What the hell*, he thought. 'Double. Bell's.'

Anna brushed an errant strand of hair from her face and leaned towards him, elbows on her bare knees. 'I do want you to continue your investigation.'

'What am I looking for?'

'The friend, Linley. What if this was all some elaborate con job: Linley cried poor to Kate, perhaps played on some insecurities I don't know about, lured her back here to Zimbabwe and killed her?'

Brand had heard of more devious crimes, but it seemed unlikely. 'I interviewed the police officer who attended the car crash. Her report was thorough and I believe she told the truth. Running a car off the road and flipping it is a risky way to try and murder someone if you're the passenger.'

Anna leaned back in her chair. 'But there is something wrong in all of this. I've no idea why my sister would turn to crime. She had a good job, a place of her own . . .' She sniffed.

Brand picked up a cocktail serviette and handed it to her. 'Were you close?'

Anna carefully dabbed her eyes and Brand noticed for the first time the makeup she had applied. He didn't recall her eyes being lined when he'd picked the couple up from the airport. 'We were sisters. You know how families are.'

'My dad was an oil man, in Africa. He married my mom, who was half Angolan and half Portuguese, when he was living in Luanda. When they went back to the States he left her to raise me alone. My family life wasn't great.'

'I'm sorry. What family is perfect? Ours was all right, I thought; Kate and I talked often, but we didn't live in each other's pockets. I wouldn't say she told me every little thing that went wrong in her life, but I'm sure that if she was in trouble she would have come to me. It's ironic, the way she died, as she had a car accident a year ago; quite a serious one in fact.'

'Dr Fleming mentioned Kate had a pin in her pelvis from a prior accident, further proof that the body he examined was hers.'

'Yes. She shattered her pelvis and stayed with Peter and me for a month or so after she got out of hospital.'

'And how did that go? Did you all get on?' Brand asked.

The waiter brought their drinks. Brand savoured the sharpness of the liquor through the Coke. Anna took two big gulps of her gin and tonic before setting it down on the table. 'Yes. And when she got better she moved back to her flat in the city.'

'Boyfriend?'

Anna pursed her lips then looked up as if searching her memory. 'Nothing steady that I knew of. There was a boy, I forget his name, but he had an affair with another woman and they broke up.'

'How did she take that?'

Anna looked at him. 'How do you think?'

Brand nodded. 'But she wasn't still in touch with him?'

'No, not that I know of. As I mentioned to Dani, Kate only had a couple of other shortish relationships. She kept to herself mostly.'

Brand thought of his first reaction when Dani had briefed him about the case. 'Do you think she and Linley were more than just old school friends?'

'I did think about that. I suppose people can be clever at hiding their sexual preferences, but no, I never had any cause to think Kate might be gay. We had an aunt, on my mother's side, who was a lesbian. She was a lecturer at Cambridge and quite out there. She was also our favourite aunt so we never had a history of stigma or shame about that sort of thing in our family. If Kate was in love with another woman she wouldn't have tried to hide it from me.'

'Your parents?'

'Both deceased, but they approved of Aunt Lavinia anyway, so I doubt they would have been shocked if Kate had turned out gay.'

Brand heard a low rumbling noise and raised a hand to his eyes to shield them from the glare of the floodlight.

'What is it?' Anna asked.

There was crack from the tree line beyond the ring around the waterhole where the ground had been denuded of grass and pounded to sand and dust by the constant passage of massive round feet. 'Elephant. Listen. You can hear them communicating with each other – that's the rumbling – and the sound of them breaking branches. They'll be coming just now.'

'*Just now*? You sound like a Zimbabwean. Are you American or African, Hudson?'

He shrugged. 'Both – either when it suits me, and sometimes neither. Did Kate have any history of gambling or substance abuse? You said she was a troublesome teenager.'

'I also said she and Linley apparently got up to the usual teenage stuff. But no, nothing else that I was aware of. Dani might have told you; there was money in her bank account. Not a fortune, but about two thousand pounds and very little credit card debt.'

Brand thought about that for a moment. He knew the cost of living was far higher in the UK than in Africa. 'What about her outgoings; did she spend a lot on clothes, travel, that sort of thing?'

Anna rocked her head from side to side as she mulled the question over. 'No, not really.'

Brand took another drink. A tiny scops owl made its high-pitched chirping call from a tree nearby and somewhere beyond the waterhole another answered. He'd investigated enough cases to be able to read people, and as far as he could tell Anna Cliff was telling the truth. Her British cool was melting and she seemed to be genuinely at a loss to explain her sister's actions. 'No history of mental illness in the family?'

'None.'

Brand had had the feeling when he was interviewing Geoffrey Fleming that the doctor had held something back about Kate and Anna's early family life. Fleming had told him he'd have to ask Anna about it. Now seemed like the right time. 'How would you characterise your childhood, and Kate's?'

She stirred her drink then looked up at him. 'Perfectly happy.'

'Really?'

'Yes, why wouldn't it be? We grew up in a loving family home.' She held his gaze, but there was no warmth in her eyes, no nostalgia. 'This isn't about our *family*, Hudson, it's about my sister and this mysterious friend of hers.'

In Brand's experience there was no such thing as a perfect, loving family, but he sensed Anna would open up no further. 'So, you want me to find Linley for you?'

'That would seem to be our best lead, don't you think?'

He nodded. 'I do. But I have to warn you, when people go to this length to get away from something it's rarely a nice story. Are you sure you want to know what your sister was really up to?'

She finished her drink; Brand was only halfway through his. Anna signalled the lodge manager again. 'To tell you the truth, I don't know, but the unknown is eating away inside of me. I can't sleep, it's affecting . . . well, just let's say it's not making things any better at home.'

Brand didn't want to go there. 'I had a South African mobile phone number for Linley, and I called her before I left South Africa, but she never got back to me. I don't think she wants to be found.'

'You can track animals in the bush, can't you?'

'She's not an animal.'

'No, but humans leave a trail, don't they?'

Brand nodded. 'They do.'

Anna leaned forward again, closing the gap between them. She put a hand on his knee and her touch felt hotter than the sun had all day through his khaki trousers. 'Can you find her for me, Hudson? Can you track her down for me?'

'I'll do my best for you, ma'am.' Even as he agreed he felt he was doing the wrong thing. He felt for Anna, and perhaps that was part of the reason the case troubled him. Most of his work was done remotely – emails from Dani asking him to chase down people he had never met. The last time he'd dealt with the family of someone who had tried to fake their own death it had been the Mbudzi clan, and they had very nearly succeeded in leading him to an unmarked grave in the Harare municipal cemetery. There was much more to Linley Brown than Anna knew, or was letting on, and Brand wasn't sure he wanted to find out what it was. But there was the money to think about.

'I'll pay you, of course,' Anna said. 'We don't want for much, Peter and I. He makes good money and we have no children. You can name your price and we'll pay it; we're hardly likely to find another private detective in Zimbabwe at short notice.'

'I'd charge my normal daily fee, nothing extra,' he said. *Why?* he asked himself, particularly given his reservations.

Anna put her hand back on his thigh and he didn't move to deter her. 'Thank you, Hudson, thank you so much.'

The lodge manager had sent a waiter, who arrived with Anna's drink, forcing her to break the physical contact with him. He saw the longing in her eyes, and perhaps it was not just for answers about her sister. She kept eye contact with him as the man set a fresh gin and tonic down in front of Anna. Her cheeks were already colouring a little. He reached over, took his own glass and finished it. Against his better judgement he said, 'I believe I'll have another of those.'

*

Peter Cliff stirred on the bed and blinked. For a moment he was disoriented, not knowing where he was.

He checked his watch; it was after seven and it was dark. His mouth was dry. He reached for the light switch on his bedside table and saw the khaki canvas walls of the tent. He was in Elephant's Eye lodge. In his dream he'd been in another place, another time. His cock was hard.

Peter had wanted to go to dinner with Anna, to hear what Brand had to say about Kate and Linley Brown, but the fatigue from the journey had overtaken him and, as he'd told Anna, he had passed a loose stool. Peter sat up, stood and went to the writing desk in the room, where he poured himself a glass of water from a jug and drank it. He sniffed under his arms and decided he needed a shower.

In the bathroom, as he stripped off, he saw Anna's makeup bag and smelled the lingering scent of perfume. Her case was open on the luggage rack back in the room, and the clothes she had worn on the aircraft were folded beside her bag. She had gone to meet the American, he assumed, and he felt a twinge of jealousy.

Peter unzipped the flyscreen door that led to an outdoor shower on the timber deck running along the waterhole side of the tent. He turned on the mixer tap and tested the temperature with his hand. He wondered if his wife fancied the safari guide. Their sex life had been non-existent for a long time. She could not, would not, give Peter what he wanted.

His view of the main dining and lounge area of the camp was blocked, but he could see out over the waterhole. A herd of elephant had silently arrived and were wading into the shallows. He watched the thirsty beasts sucking up trunkfuls of water as he stepped under the shower. His mind wandered from the animals to the subject of his dream, a replay of the last time he'd had really good sex. It was not with his wife, but at a medical conference in São Paulo, Brazil. She was coffee coloured, with big brown eyes and a mischievous wink, and she had been sitting at the hotel bar. Peter had been to dinner with some fellow doctors, who decided to turn in as soon as they returned to the hotel. He had gone to the lifts with them, but had stood back to let in a tired-looking family of four, newly arrived off a late flight and pulling wheelie bags. Instead of taking the next lift he had wandered over to the bar; he had glimpsed the girl on the way in.

When he'd asked if he could sit next to her she had said, in accented English, 'Of course, no problem at all. How can I say no to such a handsome man?'

He wasn't an idiot, and had travelled enough to know from the girl's come-on and the bartender's sly smile that she was on the game. He wondered if the man was getting a kickback to let her sit on her drink. He ordered her another of what she was drinking, a Cosmopolitan she claimed, and a Johnny Walker Blue on ice for himself.

She nodded her thanks for the drink. 'You are here on business?'

'Yes. Oil exploration.' The less she knew about his real job, the better. Also, it was impossible to make small talk with people once they found out he was a cosmetic surgeon. He loathed the nip-tuck jokes and had heard them all a thousand times over. When he travelled he liked to be anonymous.

In the outdoor shower, as he soaped himself and the elephants slurped noisily, he remembered her smooth skin and her overly full, red lips. He closed his eyes and saw her kneeling in the hotel room, the red bow parting to take him into her mouth, his hand bunched in her dark, flowing hair.

'How much to do something special for me?' he'd asked as he removed himself from her and tilted her chin so she could see his eyes.

'Depends on what is so special.'

Peter had told her, and she had shrugged and nodded her head and quoted him the figure, a fraction of what it would have cost in a British establishment, and the girl had given him a slow, wide smile, sealing the deal. He was hard at the memory of her and would have done something about his erection when he heard the *whizz* of a zip opening and footsteps on the timber floorboards inside the tent.

'Who is it?' he called, looking over his shoulder.

A maid had entered the tent's en-suite bathroom. She stood there, her hand over her mouth. 'Sorry, sorry,' she gasped, and darted back into the bedroom.

He slammed off the mixer, grabbed a towel, wrapped it around him and strode in off the deck. 'Why didn't you knock?'

'Sorry, sir, I did. I was just turning down the bed.'

He saw the chocolates on the pillows and the neatly folded sheets. 'I'm sorry, you just gave me a start.'

She put her hand over her mouth again, lingering by the door. He was flaccid now, but he could see the smirk in her eyes. It angered him that he had been caught out. He reached into the pocket of his trousers and pulled out the two loose dollar bills he knew were there and handed them to the woman. She thanked him and let herself out of the room.

He debated getting back into the shower, but he was out now, and clean enough. He towelled himself dry and pushed the erotic thoughts from his mind. He really needed to get a grip, he thought, though not in that way. He put on clean underpants and cargo pants, and found a fresh shirt in his bag. He combed his hair, put new socks and his shoes on and let himself out of the tent via the sliding glass doors that had been built into the structure.

It was dark, but Peter called over a security guard who was escorting another guest to dinner; Brand had told them that after dark they would need to be accompanied by a guard because of the possible presence of elephant, buffalo and other dangerous game that could roam through the unfenced lodge at night.

As they approached the main building he spied Anna, sitting next to Brand on a sofa in what looked like a sitting area, or library. She was too close to the guide for his liking. As he left the guard and walked towards them he heard a girlish laugh. He moved slowly, using the canvas wall of the library to mask his approach. He trod lightly on the wooden deck that joined the bar, lounge and dining area. Anna was leaning in closer to the American now, putting a hand on his knee as if to emphasise a point. Or she was simply flirting.

Peter sucked in his cheeks and bit down on the skin until it started to hurt. He breathed in deeply through his nose. The bloody safari guide was coming on to her. They needed the guide; Peter knew he wouldn't be able to track down the mythical Linley by himself and it would take them too long to find a replacement guide and vehicle. Besides, they had paid for him already.

He coughed as he closed on them, no longer muffling the sound of his steps. Anna leaned back into her chair and looked over her shoulder. 'Darling. We were just talking about you.'

'Amusing, was it?'

'Anna was telling me about how you had a mishap falling off a camel in Egypt. They're ornery beasts, and that's the truth. I slipped off one on a beach in Mombasa. Damn near broke my leg.'

'Quite. Well, I'm glad I'm good for a laugh.'

'Don't be churlish, Peter. Join us for a drink,' Anna said.

'I think we should have dinner. You should eat something now, since you've obviously been drinking,' he said.

She frowned at him, but he stared her down before she could answer him back.

'You're feeling better, Peter?' Brand said, hoping to defuse the situation.

'Yes, probably just the change in water, I expect. I've taken some tablets. We doctors do tend to carry a comprehensive first aid kit.'

'Well then, if you're having dinner, perhaps I should get back to my tent and freshen up,' Brand said. 'I'll leave you two to dine alone.'

'Not at all, Hudson,' Anna said. 'You *must* join us. In fact, I'm fairly sure our brochure said the guide would join us at all meals.'

'It said *most*,' Peter said.

'It's optional, in fact,' Brand said. 'We'll all be living in each other's pockets the next couple of weeks and it's perfectly OK if you guys need some quiet time alone. I'll go with the flow.'

'You're dining with us, and that's that.'

Peter heard the grate in her voice. He was in no mood for an argument; he had arrived just in time, though, and the American would be careful from now on. He knew Anna could be flirty after a couple of drinks. They had business to do with this man, and that was all. 'Very well. I don't want to be a spoilsport.'

Brand stood. 'I will go take a shower, though, and get changed. I'll see you back here in about twenty minutes. Will that be OK?'

'Perfectly fine,' Peter said, though he would have preferred it if the man had dined alone. He was annoyed at Anna for insisting that the guide join them. Brand took his leave of them, giving some cash to the bartender on his way out. Peter took the American's seat. 'You two seem to be getting along splendidly.'

'Oh, Peter, drop that tone. For God's sake, every time I have a laugh with a man you think he's trying to get me into bed.'

He crossed his legs and folded his arms. 'I do not. Anyway, what's wrong with a husband being protective of his wife?'

She drained her drink and set it down and looked at him as though she were about to say something, but instead turned away to gaze out over the hotel gardens.

'What were you talking about?'

She looked back at him. 'A man hunt. Or, more specifically, a woman hunt.'

He nodded. 'Good. That's what we're paying him for, Anna. Nothing else.'

17

Sannie van Rensburg and Mavis Sibongile stood back as the uniformed officer unlocked the cell door in the Nelspruit police lockup.

The prisoner, who they now knew as Lungile Phumla, sat at the simple metal desk. She glared at Sannie and Mavis as they entered.

'*Goeie more*,' Sannie said.

Lungile looked at her and shrugged.

'*Verstaan jy Afrikaans?*'

Lungile stared at her.

'You are not Tsonga, are you?' Mavis said, confirming the suspicion she'd shared with Sannie before entering the cell that Lungile was not from one of the local communities.

'We're running a check on your South African ID book, Lungile,' Sannie said, taking a seat opposite her. Mavis leaned against the door that the uniformed officer had just closed. 'But my colleague here, Warrant Officer Sibongile, thinks it's forged, and that you're an illegal. I'm Captain Sannie van Rensburg, Nelspruit serious and violent crime unit, and you are . . .?'

'Lungile Phumla.'

'You can save us some time, if you like, and maybe things will go better for you for cooperating with the police. If you want to mess us around, Lungile, we can mess you around. Believe me.'

The woman shrugged. She was pretty, Sannie thought, and had a vestige of confidence about her despite her predicament.

'I have done nothing wrong,' Lungile said.

Sannie leaned back in her chair and folded her arms. 'You assaulted a police officer.'

'Yeah, with a can of *fly spray*; I was sitting at home innocently and she burst in and pointed a gun at me. I didn't see her uniform.'

'Or hear her identify herself as a policewoman, I suppose?' Mavis said.

'It wouldn't be the first police officer who was committing a crime.'

Sannie shook her head. 'Don't play smart with us, Lungile. I've got enough evidence to put you in prison without you saying another word.'

Again, Lungile shrugged. 'I just heard my brother scream and then this woman with a gun burst in. I acted in self-defence.'

'*Eish*, you were trying to escape police. You were lucky that officer didn't shoot you,' Mavis said.

'My brother and I have done nothing,' Lungile persisted.

Sannie uncrossed her arms, put her elbows on the table and closed the distance between herself and Lungile who, reflexively, leaned back. 'Your brother's being charged with car theft – a random patrol checked the plates on his BMW against the make and model and they didn't match. He's a fool – the patrol was only in the area because there had been complaints about you playing your music too loud too many nights in a row.'

Lungile shook her head. Sannie knew she was cursing her sibling, Fortune, who was not living up to his name right now. 'And I'll be charging you, as well, just as soon as I hear back from the detectives I've sent your mug shot to in Joburg. In order to wrap things up nicely, I'll put you in a line-up for the local real estate agent who showed you and your friend the house in Steiltes, to confirm who you are.'

'I don't know what you're talking about.' Lungile's voice was raised in anger. 'I want a lawyer.'

'Oh, you'll get one soon enough, and I'm sure he or she will do their best for you, but the only chance you have at getting any kind of a reduced sentence, or maybe avoiding prison time, is to cooperate with me. *I'm* the only one who can speak for you when the prosecutors decide what penalty they're going to recommend. Where are you from, Lungile? Your English is *lekker*, better than mine. Zimbabwe? Zambia?'

'I'm South African.'

'Whatever,' Sannie said. 'I'm sure your prisons are much worse than ours, but I can assure you, women's prison in South Africa is still a very, very bad place, especially for a pretty girl like you.'

Lungile swallowed. 'I still don't know what you're talking about.'

'Did your brother tell you he didn't fence all of the stuff you took from the Steiltes house?'

'I stole nothing.'

Sannie smiled and sat back again in her chair. 'Mavis?'

'I checked the serial numbers on a MacBook and an iPhone found in the boot of your brother's car with the owners of the house in Steiltes,' Mavis said. 'They're a match. If he told you he sold them already he was lying; he either couldn't find a buyer for them or he wanted them for himself.'

Lungile sat up straighter and jutted her chin out as she addressed the warrant officer. 'So, maybe my brother bought some stolen goods. I won't lie to you and tell you he's above such a thing. But this has nothing to do with me.'

'You never saw the MacBook or the iPhone?' Sannie asked.

Lungile looked to her now. 'No, I swear I didn't.'

'Then why are your fingerprints on both of them?' Sannie said.

Mavis laughed. 'Criminal mastermind.'

Sannie put her hands, palms up, on the table. 'Look, Lungile, Mavis and I can help you. You hurt no one in your robberies, we know that, and I am sure you will be full of contrition when you go before the judge, and tell them some story of woe from Zimbabwe or wherever you're from. But believe me, things will go a lot easier for you if you help us find your partner, the white lady.'

Lungile said nothing.

'Salt,' Mavis chimed in. 'That's the name *The Citizen* gave you, isn't it? Salt and Pepper. You two had a nice operation going, sister. Shame your dumb brother screwed things up for you. Where is she?'

'When the uniformed officer followed you out the back door,' Sannie said, with the same patient but disapproving tone she used with her children when she was explaining to them what they'd done wrong and how they couldn't fool a mother by lying about it, 'she saw you boosting another woman in jeans and *tekkies* over the wall. She didn't see any more of her than that, but the lady who lives in the house behind you said a white woman came running through her house and out onto the street. Who's your friend, Lungile? Give me a name and I'll do my best to keep you out of prison. Hell, you can sell your story to the *Sunday Times* and make some bucks. If your friend comes peacefully I'll do what I can for her, as well.'

'I don't . . .' Lungile trailed off.

'You *do* know what we're talking about. Tell us her name. Better we find her before she does something desperate. Tell us about her, Lungile. Does she have money, does she have a place to stay? She has no house to go to, no car that we know of. Why did you two steal – are you junkies? What can it be like for a poor young woman on the streets of South Africa with nowhere to go? How will she make money?'

Lungile lifted her head and stared hard at Sannie, and suddenly the detective realised she'd said something wrong. She thought she'd almost convinced Lungile that turning her friend in would help her, but a word – had it been 'money'? – had galvanised the pretty young woman's will.

'Go fuck yourselves, and while you're at it, get my lawyer.'

*

'Fortune, we know you stole the car, in Johannesburg, two weeks ago,' Sannie said to the young man in the next interview room as she took a seat and opened a docket in front of her. Again, Mavis watched on. Sannie wanted to make sure she didn't repeat her previous mistake.

'I bought the car off a guy in Nelspruit. I'm sorry, I didn't know it was stolen.'

She had thought he would be arrogant and aloof, or at least react in some way to being interviewed by two women, but he was playing the nervous innocent. His voice, unlike his sister's, was reedy and needy.

'I'm so sorry, I've never been in trouble with the law before; please, you have to understand me.'

'We know that, Fortune,' Mavis chimed in. 'We checked your record; you're clean as a whistle. Come, brother, don't be too hard on yourself, we all make mistakes.'

Sannie nodded. 'You'll have to help us find the man who sold you the car, of course, but I imagine that will be hard.'

Fortune mimicked her, nodding his head vigorously. 'Yes, he seemed like a bit of a *tsotsi*. I should have known it was too cheap a price he was asking and now I feel like such a fool.'

'You know, of course,' Sannie said in a concerned voice, 'that it's a crime to buy a stolen car, but it's a grey area, because how is a man to know if a car is stolen?'

'Um, perhaps I should have checked.'

'Yes, you should have. There may be a fine for you, Fortune, but at least you didn't assault the arresting police, unlike your silly sister,' Sannie said.

Fortune raised his hands and shrugged his shoulders. 'Ah, what am I to do about her?'

'Well, there was no real harm done to the policewoman she sprayed with Doom.' Sannie smiled and closed her manila folder on the desk and patted it, then pushed her chair back, as though the interview was concluded. She paused and looked at him. 'Sorry, just one more thing. Where did you get the iPhone and the MacBook that we found in the back of the car? I presume they are yours?'

Fortune licked his lips. 'Um, no. They actually belong to my sister.'

Sannie pulled her chair back under the table and opened the folder again. 'Ah, OK. But I'm confused, Fortune. Those items were reported stolen from a house in Steiltes – a house robbed by two women, one white and one black, who posed as buyers. Do you think your sister might be a thief?'

Fortune's eyes widened in mock surprise and he gave a theatrical shrug of his shoulders. 'I don't *think* so. If she is, she never told me.'

Sannie nodded. 'I see. Mavis?'

'*Yebo*.'

'Please won't you charge Fortune here with car theft and possession of stolen goods.' Sannie stood.

He looked up at her. 'Hey, wait a minute. You said you believed I bought the car in good faith, and I didn't know it was stolen.'

Sannie sighed. 'Fortune, you're a criminal and a liar and you make a mockery of the expression "honour among thieves". You sold out your sister in the blink of an eye. I hope you go to prison.'

'No, no . . . wait, mama.'

'I'm not your *mama*, you piece of shit.'

Mavis spoke some rapid Zulu to Fortune and though Sannie normally spoke Tsonga with her partner when she could, to keep up her fluency, she was able to get the gist of the offer Mavis was making. They had orchestrated this, almost to the letter. Mavis was offering to put in a good word for Fortune and admitting that they might find it hard to prove he stole the car, if he helped them out. She also said that Sannie, as the senior officer, was a nasty woman. Sannie fought back a smile.

'Wait, please,' Fortune said to Sannie again. 'Please, I can help you. I *didn't* steal the car, honest.'

Sannie crossed her arms. 'Maybe you did, maybe you didn't, but at the very least you had to know you were buying a stolen vehicle.' She went to the door and started to turn the handle. She paused. 'Who is the white woman who pulled the jobs with your sister?' She looked into his eyes.

'Her name is Linley Brown.'

Back in the detectives' office, Sannie and Mavis set to work discovering what they could about Linley Brown.

'There's a news story online, from the Zimbabwean newspaper the Bulawayo *Chronicle*,' Mavis said, looking over the top of her computer screen.

'Tell me. I'm on hold.' Sannie had called the Department of Home Affairs investigation branch. Her contact there, Jay Suresh, had helped her track down foreign visitors to South Africa in the past by supplying details of when and where they had entered the country, and if they had left.

'It says here Brown was in a car crash; drove off a bridge. Her travelling companion, Kate Munns, who was visiting Zim from the UK, was killed – burned to death. There's a comment in the story by a local cop, Sergeant Goodness Khumalo.'

'Call her, and see if Brown has any family in Zimbabwe we can talk to by phone, or whether this Sergeant Khumalo can help us,' Sannie said. Jay answered the phone then and she asked after him and his family and then got down to business. He told her he would check the immigration records and find out what he could about Linley Brown.

Mavis had found a number for the Bulawayo police station online. 'It took me three tries to get through, and when I was finally connected the person on the desk told me the sergeant was out so I left a message for her. What do we do now?'

Sannie tapped the end of her pen against her teeth. 'We could just sit around here and wait for people to call us back, or we can go and find this woman. Let's go back to the house she shared with those other two. We'll see what we can find there.'

'Must we get a warrant?' Mavis asked.

'Unless she's at home we're not going to arrest anyone. I want to find out more about this Linley Brown.'

While Sannie drove out of Nelspruit and up into the hills towards White River, Mavis tapped the screen of her phone.

'It's Vusi,' she said, smiling. 'He's a terrible flirt.'

'And on police time, too.'

'He's off duty. I'll stop it if you like.'

Sannie shook her head. 'No, I'm only joking. It's fine.' Sannie was happy for the time to think. But her thoughts weren't about Linley Brown. They would either find something in the house Brown rented that would help them identify her better, or track her down, or they would not. It was not a matter of life and death, but the other case occupying her mind was. If it had been the same man who had committed the strikingly similar rapes and murders in Hazyview and in Cape Town, then it was quite likely he had struck before, and would commit his foul crimes again. Brand was still very much a suspect, by virtue of the fact that he had been in both locations at the time of the killings. As a detective, she didn't believe in coincidences.

Sannie turned on her GPS satellite navigation device and Mavis took a break from her texting long enough to enter the address of the house that Linley Brown, and Fortune and Lungile Phumla had rented. Sannie turned left at the NTT Toyota, onto the bypass road that led to Hazyview and the Kruger Park beyond, and then right into a side street that led to the house where the criminals had been living.

They stopped outside the house. It was single storey, whitewashed and nondescript. The grass looked like it hadn't been mowed in a while and the gardens were overgrown with weeds – typical of a place rented by three criminals. 'Good, no security fence or gate,' Sannie noted. They got out of the car and Sannie opened the boot and pulled two pairs of latex surgical gloves from a box, handing one set to Mavis. 'Put these on.' They walked around the house. At the rear she noticed one of the windows was open. The police who had arrested the trio had clearly not been diligent about securing the place, which was a good thing; Sannie didn't want to alert any nosy neighbours by smashing a pane of glass. She opened the window fully and boosted herself up on the sill. She prided herself on her fitness, and her figure. Tom used to compliment her on her body all the time, but since the fights had become more frequent the appreciative comments had fallen away. She thought of him at home on the farm; he would be getting ready to go and pick up the children from school. She felt a moment of shame then, because as much as she loved her family with all her heart she knew she was happier here, with Mavis, illegally entering a house.

Sannie climbed through the window and slid over a kitchen bench top. She unlocked the back door of the house and let Mavis in.

'This is fun,' her partner said.

'No, it's against the law, and I don't want you doing this sort of stuff when you're not with me.'

Mavis laughed. 'A fine mentor you are.'

They checked the kitchen and lounge room together, then split up to search the bedrooms.

'This must be Fortune's, it stinks of sweat and cheap cologne, and much worse stuff,' Mavis called.

'Shush, we don't want the neighbours hearing.'

'OK.'

Sannie had found herself in a woman's room, but the size of the lacy purple bra she found on the floor told her this was probably Lungile's, unless Linley was similarly endowed.

'In here,' Mavis hissed from the next room.

While Fortune and his sister's rooms were strewn with dirty clothing and the beds unmade, Linley's was well ordered and neat. There were throw cushions on the duvet, which had been pulled tight so that not a crease showed.

'I wish my place was this tidy,' Mavis said.

Sannie began searching the drawers in the pine bedside table. Linley's underclothes were folded and sorted into bras and pants. There was nothing fancy or frilly here; it all looked like sensible, affordable, practical stuff from Mr Price.

Mavis had opened the built-in wardrobe and was sliding clothes along the rack. 'Some nice stuff here. Expensive, stylish, conservative.'

'*Ja*, it fits with the image they presented in their previous jobs, of rich housewives out house hunting. Linley must have put her share of the profits into her identity. Interesting.'

'Unlike Fortune; his room stinks of weed and his clothes are all knock-offs. He also has an impressive collection of porn. A real player. What exactly are we looking for?' Mavis asked.

'Passport, ID book maybe. The uniforms said she left in a hurry, so hopefully she didn't have time to take her important documents with her. They couldn't tell if she had a handbag with her when she jumped over the back wall.'

'Three bags in here – Gucci, Prada, Luis Vuitton. All empty though.'

'They're probably props, part of her disguise, and look how they're all oversized. I bet this is what she stuffed the stolen goods in.' Sannie pulled each of the drawers out of the bedside table and sat them on the perfectly made bed. She lifted the contents out of them, placed each item on the duvet then turned the drawers over. 'Here.'

'What have you found?' Mavis asked.

Affixed to the bottom of the middle drawer with sticky tape was an envelope. Sannie peeled off the tape and opened it. 'Cash. A few thousand rand and a passport. Maybe she didn't trust her partners in crime.'

'I wouldn't trust Fortune.' Mavis peered over Sannie's shoulder as she opened the passport. It was Zimbabwean. 'Linley Brown. That's our girl.'

Sannie looked at the picture. The girl was blonde, pretty – very pretty – but her eyes looked tired, sad. The passport was new, issued just three months earlier, and flicking through it Sannie could only find one stamp, when the woman had entered South Africa shortly after the travel document was issued.

It was, Sannie thought, one thing to hide your cash from the other criminals you were sharing a house with, but the fact that Linley had hidden her passport as well told the detective that Linley was smart. She probably knew there was the prospect that the police would come calling one day, and wanted to keep her identity a secret as long as possible. Also, she wouldn't want to carry it with her all the time in case she was caught pulling a job. But Linley hadn't been smart enough to fool her. She would catch this woman, quickly, and then get back to the cold case that was increasingly becoming the focus of her life. Sannie was a good detective, but she felt like she had failed Nandi Mnisi, the woman who had been butchered and dumped near the Kruger Park. She wasn't convinced Hudson Brand was the culprit, but if he was she couldn't bear the thought that he had outsmarted her once before; if he was guilty he would not escape again. The sooner she caught Linley Brown the sooner she could delve into the Cape Town killing.

Sannie's phone vibrated in her bra; she had turned off the ringer. She took it out, unfolded it and said quietly, 'Van Rensburg.'

'Sannie, it's Jay Suresh, how are you?'

'Fine.' She read out the date Linley had entered the country.

'How did you know that?' he asked.

'I've got her passport in my hand. But you can help me with something else, I hope.'

'Name it,' Jay said.

'I think Linley Brown might try and cross back into Zimbabwe. Can you put her name on the watch list, please?'

'Zimbabweans are technically not allowed to hold dual nationality. You can only vote there if you relinquish claims to any other citizenship and you can't get a passport if you're entitled to another country's passport unless you get a letter from that other country's embassy saying you have not been issued a passport.'

'I'm not sure I follow,' Sannie said. 'Are you saying there is no way she can have another passport?'

'Legally, no, but I've got a white Zimbabwean friend who was entitled to South African citizenship as his father was born here. He got a letter from our people saying he didn't have a South African passport, in order to get his Zim passport, but our embassy told him that once he got his Zim document he'd be welcome to simply apply again for a South African one and not tell the Zimbabwean government about it.'

'I see,' Sannie said. 'Linley Brown's passport was issued about three months ago.'

'Hmmm. Well, it's feasible she could have had another passport issued in that time. I'll do a check to see if she's been issued one, and I'll put her name on the watch list in case she's been able to get another one. A lot of Zimbabweans have British heritage and plenty have moved to other countries, such as Australia, New Zealand and Canada.'

'Thanks, Jay.' Sannie ended the call. She explained to Mavis the complexities of Zimbabwean passports.

'So she can't leave the country?' Mavis asked.

Sannie shrugged. 'Maybe, maybe not. If she's entitled to another passport she might be able to get it issued here in South Africa. We need to find out more about this woman. Try that Zimbabwean police officer again from the car.'

'OK. No laptop or iPad in the drawers?'

Sannie shook her head. 'No.'

'And not in the wardrobe either. There was one in Lungile's room, though. We should check it; if Linley didn't have her own she might have been using her friend's. Everyone needs email access.'

'Good thinking, but now it's time for us to get a warrant and do this properly.'

Sannie replaced the packet of cash under the drawer, but pocketed the passport. She put the contents of each drawer back, then slid all three into the side table.

'You're keeping her passport? I thought you wanted to do this properly?' Mavis chided.

'Lungile and Fortune might get bail, and we wouldn't have the manpower to put surveillance on this place in case Linley sneaks back in. But now we know where her stash is, when we get our warrant and come back for the laptop we'll know if she's been here looking for her passport. I don't want her leaving South Africa. Also, we can scan the ID page of her passport and then release her picture to the media once we announce that we've arrested and charged Lungile and Fortune.'

'Ah, so what you're saying is there's "proper" and then there's "clever",' Mavis said.

'Exactly. Let's check outside before we leave, and retrace Linley's steps.'

They went out into the yard and Sannie closed and latched the window she'd entered. There were monkeys and baboons around the suburbs of White River and she knew from personal experience on the farm what a colossal mess these primates could make if they broke into a house. There was no point in making things worse for the owners of the property, who would have to re-let it now the criminal gang who had been their tenants had vacated.

Sannie led Mavis down the path into the backyard. 'There're some creeper vines that have been broken on the fence. That must have been where she climbed over.'

'Well spotted,' Mavis said.

Mavis used the pointed toe of her boot – flat heeled and more sensible these days, unlike those she had worn when she was first partnered with Sannie – to check the uncut grass and weeds at the base of the fence. 'Hey, look.' Mavis knelt down and pulled an iPhone from the overgrown garden bed.

'Bingo,' said Sannie.

'Can we take it with us?' Mavis asked.

Sannie knew that without a warrant she should leave the phone where it was, but it would have Linley Brown's fingerprints on it, and her call log may give them some valuable clues as to the woman's whereabouts or intentions. 'Give it to me.'

Sannie tried to switch on the phone but the battery was flat.

'It's a similar model to mine,' Mavis said, looking over her shoulder. 'I've got a car charger in my handbag.'

'OK, let's get it started.'

The two detectives went back to the car and Mavis plugged the phone into the cigarette lighter. After about a minute there was enough charge in the phone for it to be turned on. Sannie checked the log of incoming and outgoing calls. There were not many. She took out her notebook and wrote them down.

'She was probably changing SIM cards,' Mavis said.

The iPhone beeped; it was the message bank call-back. Sannie dialled the number and listened to the last message.

'*Bliksem*!'

18

'Just wait until you taste Naomi's homemade rolls – they're to die for,' Bryce told the American tourists, then beamed his perfect smile at me as he climbed into the front seat of the game viewer. 'They'll be ready, along with dinner, just as soon as we get back from the afternoon game drive, won't they, Naomi?'

When Bryce had called me Naomi the first time, I'd had to think twice before I remembered that it was the false name I had given to him; my head was a mess. On the cooking front, I could barely boil an egg, so the prospect of making bread on a campfire in a blackened steel pot was as likely as me coming up with a cure for AIDS. I felt like revoking my no-shooting policy and capping him. 'I hope you like cold baked beans,' I said out of the corner of my mouth.

One of the tourists in the back of the Land Rover overheard me and chuckled at my joke, but the others may have detected that it was no laughing matter. Bryce drove out of Balule camp and I contemplated the unlikely prospect of whipping up dinner for eight – the six tourists and Bryce and myself – with no electricity in the middle of the Kruger National Park. I sighed. I had got myself into this mess – well, Fortune had got me into it – so I had to make the most of it.

Maybe Bryce wanted me to make a hash of dinner so that one of his tourists would call Greg and Tracey, Bryce's employers, and report my appalling cookery. Or perhaps he would borrow one of the Americans' phones while he was out on the drive and call them himself, or perhaps he'd just call the cops. I still had Bryce's Nokia, but had promised him I'd let him know of any life or death messages, and agreed that he could use it in my presence.

I was feeling glum as I plonked myself into a camp chair and rested my chin in my palms, elbows on my knees. I stared at the plastic storage boxes of food, pots and utensils, wondering where to start. The thought of stealing a car and leaving the park crossed my mind, but I had seen on the way into Kruger how the security guards also checked people's paperwork on the way out of the national park. Also, Balule was in the east of the reserve, on the Olifants River near the Mozambican border, so a vehicle would be reported missing long before I made it to the nearest exit gate.

'*Wat doen jy?*'

I looked around. There was an elderly lady behind me in a lime-green pants suit and sensible shoes. She was stooped and leaned on a walking stick. 'Sorry, I don't speak Afrikaans,' I said.

'I asked what you are doing.'

I shrugged. 'Nothing. I'm supposed to be the camp cook.'

She smiled. 'Well you better get started if you're going to feed all those big fat tourists.'

I should have laughed, but instead I felt the hot sting of tears welling behind my eyes. I wiped them away with the back of my hand. She hobbled over to me and put a bony hand on my shoulder. 'What's wrong, girl?'

'Nothing,' I lied. Her touch and the concern in her voice made the tears flow. I tried to stem them with the hem of my T-shirt, but they wouldn't stop. I convulsed in her spindly arm as she stood there, drawing me into her as she leaned over me. She smelled of baby powder and an old-fashioned perfume.

'There, there. It will be all right.'

I sniffed and managed to stop the tears. 'I don't know how to cook.'

'That's nothing to cry about. You let *Tannie* Rina help you. You'll be all right. We'll make a *lekker* meal for your people.'

I felt silly, crying in front of this kindly stranger. It had been a long time since I'd wept like that. I had been through so much, been so close to, well, not wanting to be around any more, but I thought I had emerged stronger. I'd stopped crying but I could feel a lava flow of emotion welling up inside me, waiting to burst out. I was off the drugs, but the problems that had led me into dependency had not gone away. Now that the chemical balance in my brain and body was returning to normal there was nothing to dull the pain of the memories and the fears that had driven me away from home and into a life of crime in the first place. If I could just get my money and get on a plane I would be fine, but I didn't have my passport. I'd hidden it carefully in the house in White River, but even if the cops didn't find it under the drawer in my bedroom I couldn't get back there to retrieve it. I'd have to apply for another as soon as I could, but it was Sunday and I knew the high commission's visa section would be closed.

The old lady introduced herself as 'Aunty' Rina du Toït. 'Linley,' I said to her, realising as soon as the word was out of my mouth that I'd forgotten my alias, Naomi. I was juggling too much in my dishonest life and I hated it. Rina's husband, Attie, was asleep in the Jurgens caravan on the other side of the campground, she said. Bryce had explained to the Americans as we were driving that Balule was one of the smallest and quietest of the rest camps in the Kruger Park. It had been a good game drive – we had seen elephant, giraffe, zebra, wildebeest and a magnificent trio of male kudus with impressive spiralling horns, but the tourists, predictably, were chirping about wanting to see cats. Bryce had shown the group how to erect their green canvas bell tents when we'd arrived and I'd hovered uselessly on the edge, impressed by his professionalism and organisational skills, not to mention his bum in his short green shorts. He'd winked at me from behind the back of an overweight man wrestling to clip his tent to its bowed metal poles. Bryce was over the initial shock of being hijacked, and now I think he was curious about what was motivating me; perhaps he wouldn't shop me to the police while he was out on his game drive after all.

Rina shuffled to the camping trailer that Bryce had towed behind the Land Rover. She opened the refrigerators. 'What have we got here? Hmmm, steak, *wors*, *potjiekos*.' She lifted a packet. '*Blou* wildebeest?' She wrinkled her nose. 'Well, I'm sure the tourists will like it. Do you know how to make a *potjie*?'

A *poikie*, as it sounded to me, was, I knew, a slow-cooked stew. There was a black steel pot with three legs in the trailer and I knew that was what it was cooked in, but that was the extent of my knowledge and interest in South African bush cuisine. 'No, *Tannie*,' I said, using one of the few words of Afrikaans I knew.

'Shame. Well, you're never too old to learn. And that cheeky boy, the good-looking one with the curly hair, he said something about rolls. You don't know how to cook bread?'

I shook my head.

She grinned and her watery eyes sparkled. 'My kids are all grown up now. My two daughters live in Australia and my one boy is in *England*.' Her mouth puckered as though she'd just sucked on a lemon. 'My grandkids don't want to learn to cook; they're too busy on the computer and the iPhone. Do you want to learn?'

I did. I wanted to do something other than lie and steal and cause misery to other people. I wanted a sleeping husband and a caravan and for any kids to have the fairy-tale childhood I'd never had.

Rina fossicked in the cargo boxes for condiments and staples and talked me through how to light a fire in the campsite's *braai* stand. 'You know this camp used to be for blacks only?' she asked, lowering her voice.

'No, I didn't.'

'Yes, during the apartheid era, but someone decided maybe we should let them into the Kruger to see some animals, and this camp, Balule, was the only place they could stay. It's only got the six rondavels, the small roundhouses, and none of them even has windows. Can you imagine how hot the people was in the summer? All the other camps in the park have electricity, but not this one, still. The funny thing is that now this is one of the most popular camps in the Kruger.'

People wanted to get away from the trappings of modern life, it seemed, and a place once regarded as Spartan and primitive, second class, was now sought after. South Africa had been turned upside down in the mid-nineties and it had changed. I wondered if I could change, really.

'People said the blacks would rise up and kill us all when Mandela took over, and then when he died, but they didn't. Change happens,' Rina said, reading my mind as she laid out a can of tomatoes, a couple of onions, and opened the packet of wildebeest neck, 'and however bad you think life is now there is always hope.'

I swallowed, feeling the tears welling again, and while I chopped the onions, under Rina's instruction and correction, they did flow, but she rubbed my back and I managed a smile. 'Good girl. You're getting the hang of it. You see, it's not so hard, nothing to cry about.'

I heated oil in the steel pot on the fire and cooked the onions, then added the pieces of neck, which we had coated in flour. Once they had browned I opened the can of tomatoes and poured them in. 'Shit. Sorry, *Tannie*,' I hastily added, seeing her disapproving scowl. My white blouse was splashed with tomato slop and oil, and when I tried to wipe the stain away the dirt and soot on my hands from the pot just made the stain worse. 'Sh . . . sugar,' I said.

'We worry about that later. Now, add some white wine, not red; it helps break down the fat and tenderise the meat.'

I found a bottle already chilling in the camping fridge, unscrewed it, and tipped some in until Rina held up her hand. 'You have to save some for the cook.'

'Would you like a glass?' I asked. She cast a wary eye at the caravan then winked at me.

'Just a small one.'

We sat at the fold-out aluminium table and I poured her half a glass. The sauvignon blanc was cold and crisp, and for a moment I took a look out beyond the low, non-electrified fence and marvelled at the beauty of the African bush for the first time in a long while. Inside the camp were big sausage trees, so named because of their long, heavy fruit. Birds called from the thickets around the camp. It was a lovely place.

'If you don't know how to cook, what are you doing working on a safari? Are you a guide?'

'No, *Tannie*.' I looked at my feet. I wasn't even dressed for the part, in my jeans, trainers and grubby white shirt.

'Are you running away from something?'

I nodded. I did not want to burden her, but I could not lie to this strange, gentle woman either.

'You can't run forever,' she said.

Her advice was so simple, so clichéd, yet so right. I was sorry for the crimes I had committed, but I could not bear the thought of going to prison in South Africa, or any other country for that matter. I needed to disappear, just as Kate Munns had disappeared, though not in the same way. I was past wanting to kill myself – at least, I was pretty sure I was – but I knew there was something more I had to do in life, whatever happened to me. With money, I could do it all. I regretted not calling Hudson Brand back when I first had the chance. All the paperwork for the claim was in order and even if he was an investigator rather than an assessor, I had nothing to hide. I was so used to running and hiding I'd become overly paranoid. But I had lost my phone out of my pocket when on the run from the house in White River and I didn't have his number written anywhere or committed to memory. 'I know, *Tannie*,' I said to Rina, 'believe me, I know.'

She leaned over, put her hand on my knee and squeezed it. 'You will be fine, but first you have to learn how to make bread. Go stir the *potjie*.'

Bread making made even more of a mess of my shirt, and soon my jeans too were covered in flour and sticky dough, even though Rina had tried to stop me from wiping my hands on my thighs. Mixing and kneading the dough was tricky, but in the end, with a couple of retries, I had a dozen little rolls rising in another pot placed on the camping table in the afternoon sun.

'You should change now, before your people get back from their game drive,' Rina said.

I looked down at the mess I'd made of my clothes. 'I don't have any other clothes, *Tannie*.' Annoyingly, I felt the prick of tears again. I had made up my mind long ago not to feel sorry for myself, but here were those emotions, constantly bubbling to the surface. It had been so long since I'd last cried and now I couldn't seem to stop.

'Do you have money?'

I cuffed the back of my eyes, sniffed, and shook my head.

'But you're going to get paid for working on this safari, yes?'

'Yes,' I lied.

'Then that young man can give you an advance on your pay. Better still, his company should be paying for you to have a *lekker* little uniform like his one.' She hobbled back to her *bakkie* and opened the door. I slumped in a camping chair, still feeling sorry for myself. What kind of a thief was I? I could demand some cash, at gunpoint, from Bryce when he got back, I supposed.

Rina returned carrying a blue handbag in her free hand. She put it on the camp table next to me and reached in for her purse. She unsnapped the lock and pulled out a wad of hundred-rand notes. 'Here. Go buy yourself some nice clothes. You can pay me back later.'

I looked up at her, blinking, fighting back the urge to weep again. '*Tannie*, I can't –'

'You can. And you will.'

'Why are you being so kind to me, *Tannie*?'

She folded the notes, put them in my hand and closed it around them. Her dry, papery skin touched my heart. 'I think in this new

South Africa the problem is we forget the simple message that Mr Mandela left us: that people must be nice to each other. Everyone wants, wants, wants, either because they had nothing in the past and their government let them down, or they had so much and now they know what it's like to be discriminated against. You look like a good girl to me, Linley, but one who is in trouble. Believe it or not I remember what that was like, a long time ago.'

She looked the picture of grandmotherly honesty and innocence, but, then, I suppose we never really know the true stories behind the façades we see. 'Thank you, *Tannie*. But, really, you should take this back. Besides, Bryce, the guide, won't be back until dark so I've got no way of getting to a shop.'

Rina pushed my hand away. 'You should look nice for him and his tourists and then maybe he will notice you some more. You can take our *bakkie*. The Olifants camp is not far from here and they have a shop. You can buy some nice clothes there – expensive, but nice.' She fished her keys from her handbag and put them on the table in front of me.

As I reached for them I blushed, remembering how I'd contemplated stealing this very same vehicle from this kind-hearted woman and her sleeping husband. 'Thank you, *Tannie*.'

I looked at the Kruger Park map book in the car and Rina told me that the shortest route to Olifants, across the river of the same name via the low-level bridge close to Balule camp, was closed. The bridge had been damaged in the 2012 floods and was still out of action. She said I would have to drive in a loop back to the main north–south tar road, cross the river on the high-level bridge, then take a right to the camp.

I thanked Rina again, kissed her on both cheeks, and returned the hug she gave me. In the truck I looked at my red-rimmed eyes in the rear-view mirror and tried to ignore the wreckage they spoke of as I drove on a dusty road flanked by thick mopane trees.

On the high-level bridge half a dozen cars were stopped – people were allowed to get out of their cars here, unlike on the roads through the park. I slowed and followed the direction of binoculars and massive camera lenses picking out hippos, elephants and, when I craned my neck, the malevolent form of a giant crocodile just below the water's surface.

On the other side of the river I continued on, golden light flooding the inside of the Toyota, and took the right turn to the Olifants camp. Checking my watch as I pulled up to the shop, I realised I would only have about twenty minutes before I'd need to head back again. This posed no problem as I was used to picking out the best of the best in much shorter periods. The shop sold souvenirs – carved giraffes, decorative cups, postcards and a few books; a selection of food and drinks and a range of clothes in greens and browns for the tourist on safari.

I found a couple of tops, one sleeveless and the other a T-shirt, a pair of green shorts and a khaki skirt. That would use up my loan from Rina. There were some nice beaded sandals, but I didn't have enough for them. The shop was filling with customers, and I guessed this was visitors returning from their afternoon drives and stocking up with supplies for the evening meal, which they would cook in their self-catering chalets. Ducking behind a counter I took off my running shoes and socks and kicked them under a set of shelves. I selected a pair of sandals from a hook and, glancing at the counter to make sure no one was watching, separated them from the plastic tie holding them together and shrugged my feet into them. I took a chance that the size I'd selected would fit me, and made my way quickly, but not at a run, to the checkout.

I made small talk with the cashier as she scanned my purchases, and I handed over Rina's cash. A wave of guilt broke over me as I walked past the security guard at the door – he hadn't spared me a second glance as I'd browsed. I was planning on going straight back to the *bakkie*, but I could see people gathering down a pathway at a stone and thatch hide that looked out over the river below. I walked down to join them.

The view was spectacular, taking in the sweep of the majestic river, studded with granite boulders lit pink in the low afternoon sun. People were oohing and aahing and a man lent me his binoculars and pointed out a solitary lioness on the far bank, sunning herself on a flat rock.

'See the cubs, on the right,' he said, clearly enchanted.

I shifted my focus and saw the tiny babies, still bearing the spots they would lose with maturity, climbing the rock to be with their mother. One nuzzled at her teats. I swallowed. I did not know if I wanted children, but I wanted some semblance of a normal life again. This wild creature's existence was simple – to fight to feed and protect her babies. I wanted to know, again, what it was like to care for someone, and to have someone care for me. Suddenly overwhelmed with emotion, I handed the guy back his binoculars, turned away and ran up the pathway to Rina's car.

*

Bryce Duffy's eyes were wide as he pulled up at the campsite, and I noticed more than one of the men in the back of the truck was similarly slack-jawed.

'Hi all, dinner will be ready in half an hour, just in time for all of you to freshen up.' I brushed my clean hands unnecessarily but theatrically down the front of the checked pinafore Rina had lent me.

I turned and bent to lift the lid on the *potjie*. The men would be able to see my short shorts, bare legs and stunning new beaded sandals. Well, maybe I was more interested in the sandals than they were.

As the tourists dispersed, Bryce sidled up to me. 'What have you been up to?'

I gave him my best domestic goddess smile and come hither glance. 'Just doing as ordered, sir.' I lowered my voice to add: 'If you ever drop me in the shit like that again I really will shoot you.'

Bryce took a step back. 'The *potjie* smells delicious.' He looked around and saw Rina, sitting by her caravan, return her smiling face to her copy of *Sarie* magazine. 'You had help.'

'More than you gave me.'

'You pulled a gun on me and hijacked my truck,' he pointed out, correctly. 'You're lucky I didn't use one of the tourists' phones to call the police.'

I put my hands on my hips. 'Why didn't you?'

'I don't know. I thought I'd get back to find you gone, that you might have hitchhiked out or stolen someone else's truck.'

'The thought crossed my mind.'

'So why did you stay and learn how to bake?'

I smiled. 'I don't know.'

'What kind of trouble are you in?' he asked me.

'Just going to the shower, Bryce, OK?' Herb Lipschitz called.

'Sure, Herb. No rush. We'll wait 'til everyone's ready.'

A handsome older guy who'd been sitting at the back of the game viewer, out of my earshot, wandered over to us. I had little inclination to share my troubles and my crimes with Bryce. 'Hello there,' I said to him, brightly. 'We haven't formally met.'

'Andrew Miles,' he said, extending a hand. 'Most people call me Thousand.'

He was tall with a short crop of still thick grey hair and a neatly trimmed moustache. I don't normally like facial hair on a man, but it seemed to suit him; it gave him an almost military bearing. His khaki shirt and shorts were starched, adding to the image of a man in uniform, but he was, I noticed, barefoot – a relaxed counterweight to the ramrod rest of him. His face and arms were tanned a mellow mahogany and he had piercing blue eyes.

'Most people call me Naomi,' I said. He held my gaze, and my hand, for a little too long for my liking, but a not totally unpleasant chill tinkled through me. 'Why "Thousand", is that in reference to your age?'

He laughed, from deep down. 'No, the speed at which I work.'

Flirt, I thought. Or sleazy, given our age difference, which would be approaching twenty years or more.

'Or worked, I should say. I flew jets for a while and the "thousand" was a reference to a certain penchant I had for being something of a fast mover in the old days. It got me in quite a bit of trouble, but it was usually worth it.'

I didn't know much about aeroplanes, but I didn't think passenger jets flew that fast. 'Were you a fighter pilot?' Now that I thought about it, he looked a bit like the old guy in the movie *Top Gun*, Tom Cruise's boss.

'Yes, I was. Cheetahs, the South African version of the French Mirage, during the border war, then MiGs in Angola for a mercenary mob. Now I do private flights. Herb is one of my clients; I fly him and his friends around Africa on safari in my Beechcraft.'

'That must be expensive?'

'Almost prohibitively,' Andrew said. 'Only people like Herb can afford to fly and there aren't many like him.'

I wondered what he was doing here. 'Shouldn't you and Herb be in some fancy luxury five-star game lodge?'

'Herb wanted to rough it, and I was a friend of Bryce's father, Kim, who was also a merc, ex-infantry. I was happy to give the work to Bryce's employers on the condition that we got him as a guide for the Kruger leg of the trip.'

Bryce coughed. 'Yes, well, Naomi, I'm sure you need to get back to the cooking.'

'Not so fast, my boy,' Andrew said to Bryce. 'I've got a better idea. Since Herb and I are paying, why don't you get us a drink and put one for each of you two on my tab while we're at it?'

Bryce frowned at being treated like a waiter, but he clearly respected his father's old war buddy because he nodded and went to the cooler box in the camping trailer.

'You look like you've got everything under control here, Naomi,' Andrew said, gesturing to the fire and the bubbling pot. 'And your new clothes suit you very well, I might add.'

I was surprised he'd noticed. 'How did you . . .?'

'Price tag, on your collar.' He pointed to it and I blushed as I ripped it off.

'Bryce was right, I'd better see to the meal.'

'Naomi,' he said softly, 'I didn't mean to offend.'

'No problem.'

'My ears are burning.' Bryce walked back over, handed Andrew a can of Windhoek Lager and popped the top on a Castle of his own. He passed me a miniature can of Coke.

'What, no brandy?' I quipped.

'You're working,' said Bryce shortly.

'Hell, Bryce. Get the lady a proper drink, or *I* will,' Andrew said.

I could see the muscles in Bryce's jaw bulge. He might respect this old air force officer, but he clearly had his limits when taking orders from anyone.

Andrew gave one of his belly laughs and clapped Bryce on the arm. 'Come. What would you like, Naomi? I'm being barman. Bryce, sit down by the fire, man. You've earned five minutes off. You gave those Americans the game drive of their life and your only challenge now is to do better over the next two days!'

He'd disarmed the situation immediately and Bryce gave a sheepish grin as he lowered himself into the camp chair. I'd put him through a lot. I followed Andrew 'Thousand' Miles to the camping trailer.

'Cane, if he's got any,' I said, as Andrew rummaged through a cardboard box of spirit bottles.

'Here we go. Haven't had any of this since my days in Rhodesia.' He unscrewed the cap and poured me a double of the white cane spirit. 'Allow me.' He set the bottle down and took the can of cola from my hand. I found myself staring at my sandals. 'They are quite lovely. New as well, by the look of them.'

'What do you care about my shoes?' I looked up at him, trying to hold his gaze longer than he could mine.

'One of my ex-wives told me you should always compliment a woman on her shoes.'

'Really? Does that work as a pick-up line?'

'Well,' he emptied the can into my glass, 'I tried it on her best friend and she became my third wife. However, you're too young for me and out of my league. Forgive me, again.'

I couldn't help but laugh at his caricatured sexism. 'You're forgiven.'

'As the catering manager for this expedition you really should know what's in the drinks cabinet.' He poured me a drink and handed it to me. 'First day on the job?'

He was probing and as much as I was relaxing around him I had to remember to keep my guard up. Whenever possible, it's best to base your lies on truth. 'How did you guess?'

'The clothes were a good indicator. That and the fact that you don't seem to know how to act the part of the camp cook and bottle washer.'

'Who said I was acting?'

He took a swig of beer. Bryce craned his neck to look back at us, and I could see the anxiety in his eyes. 'Bryce told me, when I made the booking, that he'd be doing the cooking. I stirred him up a bit; his father was a terrible cook when we shared digs in Sierra Leone.'

'You didn't mention Sierra Leone before in your CV,' I said.

'You're trying to change the subject.'

'You're assuming I'm interested in talking about me or what I'm doing here, Mr Miles.'

'Thousand.'

I turned and walked back to Bryce and my pot of frankly delicious-smelling *potjie*. Andrew went to his tent and emerged a minute later with a towel over his shoulder. He grinned and waved to me.

Bryce saw me glance at Andrew and smile. 'He's old enough to be your father.'

I shivered involuntarily. 'Don't talk like that,' I said, faster and with more vehemence than I'd wished. I took a breath and exhaled. 'Don't talk like that. He's funny, but I'm not interested in him, or any other man for that matter.'

He looked genuinely hurt. 'Hey, I'm sorry.'

'It's OK.' I didn't want to expose myself or my problems to Bryce any more than I already had. I lifted the lid off the pot and ladled out some sauce. I blew on it and sipped it. God bless Afrikaner grandmothers. 'Jealous of my cooking ability now?'

Bryce relaxed, his eyes turning from sad to excited puppy again with my forced change of mood. 'Yes.'

I corrected myself, mentally. I didn't *want* to be interested in any man in the foreseeable future, but then I'd gone and hijacked Bryce Duffy. Damn it.

19

The next day, Hudson Brand drove the Cliffs from Elephant's Eye lodge towards Binga, on the edge of Lake Kariba, about a two-hour drive from Hwange National Park. The route took them through hilly country to the bridge Kate had accidentally driven off.

'This is it, isn't it?' Anna said as Brand slowed to a stop. They got out.

'It is.' He walked back and forth a few metres, remembering the reference in Sergeant Khumalo's report. 'They've replaced the crash barrier. See here how new the paint is.'

'I didn't get a chance to visit here after the funeral. Everything was so rushed and this place is too far from Bulawayo.'

A fish eagle gave its pining cry and they all looked up to see the majestic bird swoop low over the river and then up into a tree, where it perched near another. 'Probably its mate. They pair for life, you know,' Brand said.

Anna shaded her eyes with her hand to better see the bird. 'The fish eagle was Kate's favourite bird. I wonder if it's a sign.'

'I read that,' Peter said, 'that they mate for life.'

Brand noticed Anna shoot her husband a resentful glance. Dinner the night before, at the lodge, had not gone well. The couple had been bickering about something when Brand had returned from his shower and joined them at the dinner table in the lodge's dining area.

'We were just trying to figure out what was wrong with Kate,' Peter had said over drinks.

'There was nothing *wrong* with my sister. That's the problem with this whole bloody mess.' Anna was already slurring her words.

While they were eating, the herd of elephants that had arrived earlier glided silently towards the waterhole in the *vlei* in front of the lodge. Three big bulls stepped into the cone of light cast by the floodlight, and noisily slurped fresh water that was being pumped into a cement trough. The rest of the herd had to content itself with the muddy water in the waterhole further along the line of elevated tents.

Anna had said over dinner that she had saved some of Kate's ashes and that she wanted to sprinkle them on Lake Kariba, where Kate and Linley had been headed at the time of their crash.

'I remember she loved the lake when we were kids,' Anna had said.

Now, at the bridge, Brand asked Anna if she wanted to scatter some ashes there, where her sister had died.

'No. I don't want to remember her here, although it's a beautiful gorge. I'll do it on the lake.' Anna wiped her eyes.

'Come on, let's get to the boat,' Peter said, putting a hand on his wife's shoulder. Brand saw her look into his eyes. Perhaps there was still tenderness there, but Anna moved away from her husband and walked ahead of him to the Land Cruiser.

The country was harsh in this part of Zimbabwe, with steep-sided rocky hills covered in sparse, leafless trees desiccated by the dry wind and furnace-like temperatures. The people were similarly hardy; the Batonka had been forced from their homes in the lush Zambezi River valley in the late fifties and early sixties when a dam had been built about two hundred and forty kilometres downstream at Kariba, forming the lake of the same name. They passed roadside stall after stall selling axes with shafts made from rough-hewn mopane wood and heads crafted from leaf springs from old car wrecks that had been hammered into heavy, wicked blades. Peter asked Brand to stop and when he pulled over an old lady, bent at the waist and with deeply wrinkled skin, emerged from the dying bush to offer them a handmade marijuana bong for sale.

'What's that all about?' Peter asked, fingering the edge of an axe blade with his thumb.

'The people here are allowed by the government to smoke *dagga* as part of their traditional beliefs.'

'About the only thing that keeps them sane in this kind of country,' Anna observed.

The weather became hotter and more humid as they descended to the lake, near the town of Binga. Brand drove through the gates of a fishing lodge, up over a hill, past thatch-roofed accommodation units and down to the water's edge, where the single-hulled steel *Lady Jacqueline* was moored.

'This is the boat your sister and her friend were booked to travel on. I checked with the owners' booking office in Cape Town; there were no other guests registered. It's a nice boat, and has cabin space for ten people and deck space for another thirteen sleeping outdoors.'

'Quite extravagant for just two people,' Anna said.

Brand nodded. It was similarly extravagant for the Cliffs and him to be taking the boat, but they were only booked for one night. When he'd made the enquiries about Kate Munns's booking Brand had booked the boat for the night, telling the operators that the Cliffs wanted to sprinkle some of Kate's ashes on the lake.

It was Sunday and the sound of singing carried across a small bay from the village beyond, which housed staff and boat crew who worked for the fishing lodges and houseboats in the area. Brand shook hands with the captain, Steven Mpofu, and exchanged greetings.

'I'm taking you not far, to a nice place towards the Sengwe River, and we can stay one night there, then come back tomorrow morning. Is that fine?'

'Fine, thanks, Steven.'

The crew, a cook and deckhand carried Peter and Anna's baggage aboard. Brand hefted his duffel bag and climbed the steel ladder that jutted out from the prow of the boat to the rocks on the shoreline.

On the middle deck was the deckhouse, which doubled as a small kitchen, and an enclosed lounge area with comfy leather couches, a television and a little library. Below that, on the lower deck, were the cabins – a double state room fore and aft, and two cabins with bunk beds amidships. Brand took the rear cabin and showed Anna and Peter to the master cabin.

'It's lovely,' Anna said.

Brand wondered where Linley Brown and Kate Munns would have slept, just the two of them on a boat that could carry twenty-three people. There were smaller boats they could have chartered; why had they chosen this one?

'You said your family had been on the lake before?' he asked Anna.

'Yes, several times, but never on this boat, as far as I can remember.'

Brand's phone beeped. He took it out of his pocket. There was no signal from the Zimbabwean mobile phone providers, but it seemed the boat's mooring was in range of Zambia, across the lake. He got a message telling him he was on roaming, along with numbers to check his messages. The phone beeped again.

He read the message on the screen: *Mr Brand, this is Captain Sannie van Rensburg, Nelspruit Police. Please call me urgently.*

'Anything interesting?' Anna asked him. Peter had left the cabin and was walking up the stairs to the upper decks.

Brand shrugged. 'I don't think so. Nothing about Kate, in any case.'

She leaned against the doorway to her cabin. 'Do you spend a lot of time on tour, on the road with clients?'

He nodded. 'I do.'

'Do you have anyone at home, a wife, a girlfriend, a partner?'

'I'm a fairly private person, Anna.'

'Sorry, I didn't mean to pry. None of my business.'

He put up a hand to signal it was OK, and that he hadn't taken offence. 'But to answer your question, no. No one's been silly enough to put up with my wandering ways for an extended period of time.'

He thought about Hannah. She was the closest thing he'd had to a steady girlfriend in years, since Angola in fact, and it hadn't worked out between them when they had cohabited for a short time. Dani and he were close, but despite them having slept together theirs was more a platonic business relationship these days.

'Gosh, a handsome, single man like you would be off the market in minutes in London.'

'Well, perhaps I like staying on the market.'

Anna lowered her voice. 'Is it wrong for me to say I envy you?'

Brand had a fair idea where the conversation was headed. 'I'll go check with the captain what time lunch is served.'

Anna reached out and put her hand on his forearm. 'Can't you call someone in South Africa, try and get a lead on Linley Brown?'

'It's not that simple.' He wasn't used to looking for people, alive or dead, in South Africa. So far his insurance work had been confined to Zimbabwe and although he didn't want to let on to Anna, he had precious little experience as an investigator. 'If she was still in Zimbabwe we could trace her through places where she'd worked, through the electoral roll, neighbours, that sort of thing. But Linley's in the wind, in another country, so we've got to start from scratch. I'll keep trying her phone number, though, and hope she picks up.'

Anna took a step closer to him. She was perspiring, as was he, but the musty odour of her body didn't turn him off; the opposite, in fact. He needed to get above the confines of the lower deck. 'Excuse me,' he said, and moved past her into the corridor.

They had lunch while cruising to the sheltered bay where they would spend the night and Anna would scatter Kate's ashes. Brand stayed with soft drink, but Anna had three glasses of wine. Peter eyed him coolly over his sparkling mineral water. The conversation was stilted and when they had finished their meal of grilled Kariba bream Brand excused himself. He lingered in the lounge for a few minutes, inspecting the library's offerings. He flicked through the guest book then went to his cabin. He stayed below deck for an hour, lying on his bunk thinking about the case and hoping he might catch forty winks, but sleep wouldn't come. Through the wall he heard the Cliffs talking, arguing at one point over something.

At five Anna knocked on his door. 'We're going to do the ashes now, if you'd like to join us.'

The setting sun was red through the dust layer that hung above a range of purple hills. Anna and Peter stood side by side at the railing and Hudson waited behind them.

Anna cleared her throat. 'We don't know why you wanted to leave us,' she said, looking up, 'but you did, and all I can hope is that you're at peace now.'

She looked to her husband, who just gave a little shake of his head, and looked down at his hands on the railing. Anna lifted the lid on the wooden box and shook the ashes into the lake, which was the colour of molten metal. 'Goodbye, Kate.'

Peter turned from the railing and mumbled an 'excuse me' as he shuffled past Brand and into the lounge. Brand looked over his shoulder and saw the doctor was walking downstairs. He was alone, again, with Anna. A fish eagle cried and they both looked up to see it circling. 'There's her favourite bird again. Eerie.'

Brand knew people looked for signs, and hoped for Anna's sake that the bird's presence did indeed indicate that Kate Munns was at peace now. 'I'm sorry for your loss,' he said.

She looked up into his eyes. 'Would it be wrong if I asked you to hold me now?'

He looked over his shoulder.

'Don't worry about Peter,' Anna said. 'I doubt he'd care. I just need someone to tell me she's in a better place.'

Brand put an arm around her shoulder. 'Whatever was worrying her, she's away from it now.'

Anna nodded and wiped her eyes. 'I'm sorry.' She broke away from him. 'I'm rather tired now, I think I'm going to skip dinner tonight. But thank you, Hudson, just for being here, and for trying to help us sort this mess out.'

He waited for Anna to leave, then went below deck to his cabin. He checked his phone and found he was still picking up a signal from Zambia. He sent an SMS to Dani, asking her to call him. His phone rang a couple of minutes later. 'How are the Cliffs?' she asked.

'How do you think?'

'Terrible business, finding out Kate had faked her death then died for real.'

'You think? That was some move, leaving it up to me to tell them, and . . .'

'Hudson, listen to me,' Dani interrupted. 'We've got more important things to talk about. I was just about to call you so your timing is good. There's been a new development; you were right to suggest the insurance company review their file.'

'What did they find out?' he asked.

'Well, with your confirmation that there was a genuine death certificate and that the police report checked out, they were still inclined to pay up, despite you finding the fake certificate.'

'*Were*?'

'There was a note on the Kate Munns file that said Linley Brown had called the insurance company's UK call centre on the same day as the car crash to report that Kate had died and to ask what she had to do to claim on the policy.'

'A little hard-hearted, calling just after her friend had died,' Hudson said.

'That's the thing, Hudson. She didn't call *after* the accident, she called before.'

Brand digested the information. 'You're telling me that she called to report the fake death on the same day that Kate really died?'

'Yes,' Dani said. 'When the company first reviewed the file, after Anna Cliff raised her concerns, the timing of the call didn't stand out – a call had been received from Linley on the date of death recorded on the legit death certificate. After you suggested they go through the file again, one of their assessors listened to the recorded voice file of the telephone conversation and found the actual time of day it was made. They played the recording to me down the line; you can clearly hear Linley Brown saying that her friend Kate has died. She sounds upset, but it's an act. Given the time difference between the UK and Zimbabwe, we worked out the call was made at 9.12 in the morning, two hours *before* the car crash. Linley didn't call again after the real death.'

'Because she already knew what she had to do to make the claim. Does making a call to the insurer to report a fake death constitute a false claim?' Brand asked. He knew enough about the insurance business to figure that if Linley had made a false claim, or if it had been Kate making the call pretending to be Linley, then such a move would automatically invalidate the policy.

'That's the question we're grappling with at the moment,' Dani admitted. 'And the answer is, I don't know yet. I'm consulting with some of my colleagues and we're meeting with the insurance company's claims department, in-house legal and corporate affairs, in case any of this goes public. Linley hadn't submitted an online claim form using the fake certificate, but we have proof that she and Kate were about to make a false claim.'

'What does this mean for Linley Brown now?' Brand asked.

'I still doubt the company will get the police involved, but worse case, she can kiss her money goodbye. Whatever happens, there won't be a decision for a few days at least.'

'OK,' Brand said. 'At least this buys me some time. If I can manage to make contact with Linley Brown then I can legitimately tell her she's got some explaining to do and that she should meet with me. I've got the Cliffs breathing down my neck and no idea how to find one missing white woman in a country of fifty million people.'

'I'm sure you'll think of something, Hudson. Do the Cliffs have any theories about why Kate would have wanted to fake her own death?' Dani asked.

'We talked a bit today and last night, but Anna seems bereft and Peter is a prickly man. Neither of them can think of any reason why she would have needed to disappear.'

Brand's phone beeped and he looked at the screen. 'I've got another call coming through, Dani. It's from a South African land-line. I'd better take it in case it's Linley.'

'Well, good luck with that. I'll call you on this number if I hear that Linley's been in touch with the insurers.'

'OK.' Brand hung up and answered the incoming call. 'Hudson Brand.'

'Mr Brand, it's Captain Sannie van Rensburg.'

*

Sannie's husband, Tom Furey, was in the kitchen of their farmhouse adding spaghetti to a pot of boiling water. Little Tommy came up to her to show her a picture he'd drawn of her at school. The blonde woman in the drawing was holding a gun.

Tom came to her rescue as Hudson Brand answered the phone, scooping up their son. The older children, Christo and Ilana, were doing their homework in their bedrooms. Sannie stood up from the lounge and walked outside onto the timber deck that overlooked the banana farm and the valley and the town of Hazyview beyond. She felt bad for Tom, bringing her police work home, but all the same her pulse quickened.

'Captain Van Rensburg; my favourite detective. How are you?'

'Fine, and you?' she said, ignoring the sarcasm in his voice.

'Dandy.'

'Where are you, Mr Brand?'

'Zimbabwe.'

'Mr Brand, what's your interest in Linley Brown?'

She could tell by the seconds of silence that followed that Brand was taken aback. 'Why do you ask?'

'I'm a detective, Mr Brand, unlike yourself, who is a safari guide. It's my job to ask questions. What do you want with Linley Brown?'

'What do *you* want with Linley Brown, captain?'

'That's police business. I don't need to share that with you.' Inside the house, Tom called to the older children, telling them dinner was almost ready.

'Well, my business with Linley Brown comes under the realm of client confidentiality.'

'You're a jeep jockey, Mr Brand, not an attorney or a priest. You have no legal right to claim client confidentiality as an excuse not to assist the police. You're looking for Linley Brown, and so am I. This is your opportunity to help me.' Sannie looked inside. Tom was behind the kitchen bench, where she should have been. He looked annoyed. She held up a hand, indicating five minutes. Her fixation with the cold murder case was already driving a wedge between them as it occupied more and more of the time she should have been spending with Tom and her kids. Now Brand was part of her current investigation as well, and here she was talking to him when she should have been sitting down to dinner with her family. It annoyed her, not least of all because she could feel the adrenaline jolting her as she spoke to him. She turned her back to Tom.

'You haven't exactly helped me, captain. You falsely accuse me of rape and murder, and leak my name to the press during an investigation, which resulted in no charges, and now you want me to help you do your job? I don't think we have much to talk about.'

Sannie had not given Brand's name to the media. That had been someone else in her office, though she didn't know whom and she had been annoyed at the leak. She was sure it was not Mavis, but other cops were cosy with journalists and sometimes reporters paid for information, or traded favours. She knew through her investigation that Brand was an outsider in the tight-knit community of safari guides, a loner with few friends among either the white or black guides. He was brash, as most Americans are, and by all accounts – some grudging – an excellent guide, and he had a reputation as a ladies' man. 'You left more than one voice and SMS message on Linley Brown's phone saying she must sign some papers to expedite an insurance claim relating to the death of a woman named Munns. We do need to have a conversation about this.'

Again, the pause on the line. 'How did you access those messages?'

'Linley Brown's phone was taken as evidence earlier today as part of the execution of a search warrant in relation to an ongoing police investigation.'

'I see.'

'Really? I don't see, Mr Brand. This Brown woman is wanted for questioning in relation to several crimes and now you pop up on my radar again, doing some deal with this woman.' Sannie felt she had him now. Tom was serving up the meal and Ilana and Christo were chatting to their stepfather at the dinner table. Her heart hurt and she began to feel not excited but annoyed that she had finally got through to Hudson Brand.

'I'm not doing a *deal* with her, captain, I'm working on a case for an insurance company. Linley Brown is the beneficiary of a policy for two hundred thousand British pounds.'

'Life insurance, like those other cases you investigate?'

'Yes. Kind of. A Zimbabwean-born British woman, Kate Munns, was killed in a car wreck on the way to Lake Kariba and Linley Brown is the beneficiary of her policy.'

'Hmmm,' Sannie said. 'And you were checking to see if Linley Brown is who she says she is, and not Kate Munns faking her own death.'

'Linley Brown's for real, and Kate Munns is dead,' Brand said.

'So it would appear. Do you really need Linley Brown to sign some papers or was that just a pretext for you to meet her and confirm she was who she said she was?'

'Very astute, captain,' Brand said. 'There are no papers for her to sign, but the insurance company is going to want an explanation from Brown if she's going to get her money.'

Brand gave her a run-down on the fake death certificate, the initial call to the insurance company and on the Cliffs and their need to make contact with the last person who had seen Kate alive. Sannie felt for the couple who had travelled from London. Kate Munns's best friend was a criminal who could become rich, by African standards. Linley Brown would need that money to pay for a good lawyer once Sannie got hold of her.

'It's clear we both want to talk to Linley Brown,' Sannie said. 'She's not going to turn herself in to me, but if you try again, nicely, you might get her to come to you, and I could be there to have a word with her.'

'So, you want me to help you run a sting operation?' Brand said.

'You've been watching too much American TV. I want to catch a criminal, but if you help me get to Linley Brown, I'll give your clients half an hour with her before I take her into custody.' There was silence, again, and Sannie wondered if the connection had been broken. 'Mr Brand.'

'I'll put it to them. I have to warn you, though, Linley Brown probably won't fall for it. She obviously checked me out the first time I tried to contact her. She's wary, and now that she's on the run she'll be even more careful.'

'Yes, but she'll also be more desperate. We need each other, Mr Brand,' Sannie said. 'Between us I think we can find her. I'll call you back tomorrow, and don't email or call Linley Brown until we've talked again and worked out how, when and where we will meet her.'

Sannie ended the call and walked inside off the deck. She paused for a moment and took in the scene of her three children and her husband laughing at a shared joke or funny story of someone's day. She felt like an outsider.

'Come, dinner's ready,' Tom said curtly.

On impulse she went to her husband and put her arms around him. He was stiff, but softened to her kiss, put down the ladle and encircled her with his arms.

'*Mom*,' Ilana groaned. She was just entering a difficult age and Sannie knew they were in for a bumpy ride. 'It's so gross seeing old people making out.'

Sannie tousled her daughter's hair as she sat down next to her. It was the little things Tom did, like making dinner and not hassling her, no matter how annoyed he was, that reminded her every day how much she loved him.

'I told the kids to start, before it got cold,' he said.

She didn't mind, but she held out her hands, either side of her. Ilana took her left and Christo her right, and they in turn joined hands with Tom and little Tommy. 'Tommy,' Sannie said, 'in *Engels*.'

Their little son, his face frowning in concentration, nodded his head. '*Dankie* – thank you – God, for the food and our family. Amen.'

'Amen,' she said. Tom wasn't religious, but her family had always said grace when they were growing up. They each kissed the fingers of the hands they were holding, then Sannie wound the spaghetti and sauce onto her fork. Tom was a good cook; his first wife had died of cancer and he had lived as a bachelor before he had come to South Africa, as a police protection officer – bodyguard as they were called in the movies – and met Sannie, who was doing the same job at the time. 'I'm sorry, about being on the phone.'

Tom shook his head. 'No problem, love. I know what it's like, I know what you're like when you get on the scent of someone.' She could tell he felt otherwise, that it *was* a problem, perhaps because it was her and not him who was on a suspect's trail.

She explained how Brand had once more come into her sights.

'Did you ask him about the Cape Town business?' Tom asked.

Tom was being oblique in his questioning so as not to raise the subject of rape and murder in front of the kids. She often talked about her cases with him, as he'd had to qualify as a detective before being selected for protection duty in the London metropolitan police's Special Branch. He had an analytical brain and she wondered, despite his reassurances of how much he loved farming, if part of him missed police work. 'No, I don't want to scare him off. I know he was in Cape Town when the second incident happened, and I want to question him about it, but I need his help, first.'

'I wouldn't want to have you chasing me,' Tom said.

Sannie reached across the table and laid a hand on his. 'I'm always chasing you, baby.'

'*Mom!*' said Ilana. 'Get a room.'

'Kids, take your plates to the sink and you can go watch some TV. Your mum and I have work to do,' Tom said.

Sannie raised her eyebrows. 'What kind of work?'

'I thought that maybe I could have a look at your files on the cold case.'

'Really?' She was surprised. He'd never shown much interest in her work in the past. She had thought, for a moment, he was going to suggest they quickly escape to the bedroom. Part of her felt instantly resentful that he might be insinuating that she had missed something in the files, but then she realised that if the case hadn't been solved because she *had* overlooked some small detail then her detective husband could possibly help out with a fresh set of eyes. Her resentment washed away and she was glad to have someone other than Mavis who she could talk to – really talk to – about this case that had burdened her for so long.

'It's OK, I understand if you don't want to,' he said quickly. 'After all, I'm not a detective any more and it wouldn't be proper.'

'No, no, no. I'll get the case docket.'

20

The next day the captain of the *Lady Jacqueline* took them back to the mooring in Binga and Brand drove the Cliffs to Victoria Falls. It was late afternoon before they got to their hotel, The Kingdom, which was part of a casino complex.

Not long after he'd unpacked, Brand's room phone rang. 'Hudson, we're not going to make it to dinner tonight, sorry,' Anna said. 'I'm not feeling the best and Peter has been, well . . . I think we're both out of sorts. He's gone to play blackjack – he's always been a bit of an amateur gambler. I thought I'd order in room service. You could pop in for a drink, if you like?'

Brand thought about the kind of man he took Peter Cliff to be, and remembered the way Anna had flirted with him downstairs on the houseboat, and how she'd asked him to hold her. He didn't need to get himself stuck in the middle of a marital tiff, or have a client succumb to khaki fever, where tourists swooned over their safari guides. 'Sounds like it's best if you get some rest, Anna. Thanks for the offer of a drink, but I think I'll turn in early.'

Brand hung up and contemplated a night in front of the TV. He got up off the bed and left his room. He walked past the pool bar;

there was a function going on, perhaps a conference of some kind, and the delegates were overwhelming the barman.

He headed into the interior of the hotel's main building, where the casino was located. It was early and there were no more than a score of people there, mostly playing slot machines, but he did see Peter Cliff sitting at a blackjack table with two other men, in front of a pretty croupier.

Cliff was staring intently at the cards coming out of the shoe and didn't notice Brand. Brand didn't want to talk to him just then, and went to another bar, out of sight of the tables. He took a seat and ordered a Zambezi Lager.

He caught a whiff of perfume and turned around. 'Excuse me, do you have a light?'

The woman was attractive, tall, wearing a simple black cocktail dress and heels. She held the cigarette up to him between long, elegant fingers tipped with deadly scarlet nails. Brand reached into his pocket for his Zippo and flicked the wheel. She put her hands on his to steady the flame.

'Thanks.'

'My pleasure.'

'Mind if I join you?' She placed her bag on the counter and climbing onto a bar stool.

It was a casino. He was a guy sitting alone. She was good looking, though her eyes were cold obsidian. He guessed she was a hooker. He didn't have enough to pay for her, even if he'd wanted to, and besides, he needed to think about Van Rensburg's call and how he should play her request, or, rather, order.

'Sister, if you're selling, I've got to tell you, you're out of my league.'

She blew a stream of smoke just past his left ear. 'I should slap your face for that remark.' She reached for her clutch bag and began sliding off the stool.

He felt like a jerk. 'Hey, sorry. I didn't mean to . . .'

She stood, rocking her head from side to side, as if wondering if she should accept his apology. 'I'm not a whore, although I do work in advertising, so you could say I'm not a million miles away from that profession. I lie to sell people things they think they can't live without.'

She returned his smile. 'Hudson Brand.'

'Melanie Afrika.'

Her hand was soft. 'Drink?'

'What are you having?' she asked.

'Bell's on the rocks.'

'Same.' She sat back down on her stool, put her bag on the bar again and crossed her legs. 'I'm with the conference out there.' She gave a disdainful toss of her head. 'Zesa, the electricity company. They can't supply power to the country, but they can afford to waste money on booze and food here.'

'And on advertising.'

Melanie grinned. 'You're full of compliments for a girl. What's that accent? Are you American? You look, I don't know, Latino or Spanish.'

'Half Texan, half Portuguese Angolan.'

'Ah, my father was Scottish. My mother's Ndebele, from Bulawayo, but I live in Harare now, away from my people, whoever my people are. Do you find it hard, not knowing which half is more you, which half you want to be?'

'Sometimes.'

'You want a smoke, Hudson Brand?' She held out the packet.

'I'm trying to quit.'

'Good for you.' She put them back in her bag. 'I wouldn't want to be your undoing.'

He sipped his Scotch. There was a tattoo on her ankle, of a cross. Her cleavage was enticing. He went back to her eyes. Again, they let the rest of her down. But it wasn't unusual in his experience. There was a flinty quality to women in Zimbabwe, a hardness about them that was missing from the pampered *kugels* and black diamonds of South Africa. No one lived in this country any more without having to make sacrifices or compromises. 'Shouldn't you be getting back to your conference, do a little schmoozing?'

'I came in here to escape it. This conference was supposed to be about me having some fun.'

'You don't seem to be enjoying the party.'

'Getting groped by overfed civil servants who can't deliver the service starving people pay for, or drinking with a rich, handsome tourist? What's a girl to do?'

'You got one out of three right. I'm not rich, and I'm not a tourist. I'm a guide.'

'Hence the khaki ensemble. All you need is a pith helmet. Shouldn't you be getting back to your tourists?'

'They're squabbling. One's gambling and the other one's drowning her sorrows with room service Nederburg.'

A portly man in a shiny suit weaved his way to the bar. 'Ah, Melanie, there you are, baby. What's going on, you said I'd see you later?' He put his hand over his mouth to try and cover a burp.

'Um, you will. For sure. I'm just catching up with my, um, cousin here. He's in the Falls on business.'

'Oh,' said the man, looking embarrassed. 'Sorry, maybe later then?'

'*Ja*. We just need to go talk some family business for a while.'

Melanie slid off her stool and grabbed her bag. She started to leave the bar and looked over her shoulder. 'Coming, cousin?'

Brand nodded to the disappointed bureaucrat and followed Melanie out of the casino and into the dusk. Her dress shimmied hypnotically over the pert mounds of her buttocks. 'Where are we going?' he asked when he caught up with her.

Melanie laughed. 'There's a nightclub I know, from previous conferences.'

The deep bass throb announced the club's presence long before they reached it. Inside it was hot, lights strobing, a mixture of colours as backpackers and locals writhed to the beat, the dance floor already crowded despite the early hour. Hudson spotted a river rafting guide, still in shorts and sandals, with a sunburned Nordic blonde grinding against him. 'Let's dance,' Melanie yelled above the noise.

She put her hands on his hips and he mirrored her, ignoring the smarter, newer moves of the younger people around him. Melanie was much younger than he, but she seemed content to stare into his eyes and sway slowly to the rhythm. He drew her to him and she moulded her body into his. She looked up, eyes full of mock horror as she felt his hardness press into her. He would have kissed her, then, if he hadn't turned and seen the man at the bar.

'Shit.' Brand pressed his lips to Melanie's ear. 'I need a drink.'

'What's wrong?' she called as he broke their embrace.

Brand threaded his way through the crush of bodies. The squat, muscled man in shorts and bush shirt turned to say something to the young woman behind him in the queue at the bar, confirming Brand had not been mistaken. Patrick de Villiers laughed at something the girl said.

'Hudson?' Melanie tried again over the noise.

As far as Brand could see Patrick was alone, without his thuggish older brother to back him up. Brand walked up to the bar, where Patrick was being served. 'Excuse me, ma'am,' he said to the girl the guide had been chatting to.

'Hey, no cutting in,' she said.

He ignored her and tapped Patrick on the shoulder.

Patrick looked around and his face showed annoyance mixed with surprise and, Brand hoped, a trace of fear. 'What the fuck do you want?'

'You,' said Brand.

'What are you doing here?' De Villiers said.

'Babysitting tourists on a road trip instead of walking in the bush, thanks to you, you little shit. Outside.'

De Villiers took a shot from the barman and downed it. '*Ja*, right. Time to finish what I started last time.'

'What you and your brother started, you chicken-shit runt.'

'Hudson!' He shrugged off Melanie's hand from his arm.

'Still got a taste for coloured whores, I see. Remind you of mom?'

'Outside,' Brand said through gritted teeth. He started to wend his way back through the crowd when he felt the short, sharp stab of pain in his kidneys. He buckled, then the bottle smashed on his head, sending shards of glass flying into the crowd like shrapnel, and backpackers screaming.

De Villiers had suckered him, but Brand had crouched and rolled as soon as he felt the kidney punch, lessening the impact of the bottle. He skittled a pair of girls in short skirts sitting at a table. As one of the pair toppled backwards Brand grabbed her chair and swung it at Patrick, catching him in the chest and knocking him backwards. However, De Villiers fell into the arms of a couple of Irishmen who started yelling, 'Fight, fight, fight, kill the *fooker.*'

People were jeering and screaming above the constant blare of the music as Patrick was catapulted back into Brand's range. He swung a haymaker that landed squarely on Patrick's jaw, and had the satisfaction of seeing the younger man drop to his knees.

'Get up, you sorry son of a bitch,' Brand said.

Patrick spat blood onto the nightclub floor and shook his head. He raised his hands. 'I'm done.' He coughed.

'Hudson, let's go before the police get here,' Melanie said.

Brand balanced on the balls of his feet, both fists clenched. De Villiers was down, and as much as he wanted to finish him off, Melanie was right – he didn't need trouble with the local cops. Patrick retched.

'Get up, you piece of shit.' Brand reached out a hand to the other guide. Patrick was a useless coward without his brother for backup, and, by the look of it, he had a glass jaw.

Patrick spat more blood. 'Just getting my handkerchief.'

Brand grabbed hold of his shirt by the shoulder and started to heave. Patrick's right hand flashed out of his pocket and arced upwards. Brand caught sight of metal glinting in the strobing nightclub light.

Brand stepped back, but the point of the knife slashed his shirt and scored the skin of his abdomen. 'Crazy fucker.'

De Villiers came at him, slashing the pocketknife from side to side in wide swinging arcs. The crowd surged back in fear as Brand kept out of range. Brand put a hand to his belly and felt the hot, wet blood seep through the fabric of his shirt. He needed a weapon – another chair or something to use to keep Patrick at a distance until he could finish him off. His nostrils flared in anger.

Too late, Brand realised he was standing on an empty beer bottle. His right ankle rolled and he started to fall. Patrick lunged forward, eyes blazing with hatred. Brand tried to reach for the bottle that had tripped him, but his fingertips just brushed it, unable to find purchase.

Above him, Patrick bellowed, but this time not in rage. He straightened and reached around behind him, scrabbling for something. Melanie Afrika darted around Patrick and reached out her hand to Brand. He grabbed it and she helped drag him to his feet. Her hand was wet and sticky and when he looked down he saw blood.

'Fucking bitch!' Patrick bellowed in agony.

Brand saw the cause of De Villiers's outrage as the other man turned his back to them. Melanie had stuck a pocketknife of her own into the muscle just below Patrick's right shoulder.

'Run!' Melanie cried.

Brand needed no further urging. People crowded around Patrick, who was still frantically clawing at his back. Brand and Melanie pushed their way through the mass of screaming bodies, catching a wave of those rushing for the door now that blood had been spilled. The muggy warmth of the Victoria Falls evening felt like crisp alpine air compared to the fug of sweat, perfume and tobacco smoke inside the club. They ran down the street towards The Kingdom, only slowing to a walk when a police Land Rover rushed past them in the opposite direction, blue lights flashing.

Brand felt the sweat drying on him as they walked. Melanie put her hand in his. Back in his room, he pushed her against the wall as soon as he'd opened the door. Her tongue was deep in his mouth, searching as she clawed at the buttons of his bush shirt.

He fumbled with his belt buckle and broke from her to quickly fish one of the free condoms he'd picked up in Bulawayo from his open bag. He unzipped, rolled it on and grabbed her again and lifted her. She was skinny, light, and he hooked a finger under her lacy thong, pulling it aside and feeling her readiness. Melanie bit and kissed his neck as he pushed up into her, steadying her against the wall as he raised up onto his toes, thrusting deeper. She muffled her cries into his skin as she bucked on him, and squeezed him tight with her arms and her body as he came.

They stayed like that, alternately kissing and panting for a while until he recovered his strength and his wits and carried her to the bed. She sat on it.

'Your stomach?' she asked.

He opened his bush shirt. The wound was superficial, though it still oozed blood. 'It can wait.' Melanie stood, smiled and slowly stripped for him in the light of the bedside lamp as he lay on his back, languidly stroking himself back to readiness.

When he was there she took a new condom from her clutch bag, put it onto him and straddled him. Brand played with her dark brown nipples, kneading them and gently tugging on them as she arched her back and closed her eyes. When she sensed from his breathing that he was nearing climax she stopped riding him.

'What's the matter?' he breathed.

She rolled off him. 'Take off the condom.'

'Why?'

'Mark me.'

Her lasciviousness turned him on as he knelt above her. When he had finished he slid down the bed and brought her to climax with his tongue. She screamed his name.

'Do you want a shower?' he asked as she reached for her cigarettes from the bedside table. He wanted one almost as much as he wanted her again. There was blood on the bedsheets, from his wound and her hand where she had stabbed Patrick. *What a night*, he thought.

'Later. Order some food and booze. I'm not finished with you yet.'

Brand thought he might just have a heart attack before the night was through. He picked up the phone and dialled room service; he'd need something to keep his strength up.

*

Anna Cliff switched off the TV. The movie was soppy, a romance with Julia Roberts. A sad fact of life was that everything did not always work out in the end and few stories had a happy ending. Her husband was out gambling and all she'd learned about her sister was that she was dead and had tried to commit fraud before she'd been burned alive.

She finished the last of the bottle of white and contemplated ordering another. She felt dreadfully sad and, at the same time, angry.

Anna had showered and put on her pyjamas to watch the movie, but she didn't feel like going to bed yet. She went to the wardrobe where she'd hung the sundress she was going to wear the next day. She put it on and went to the bathroom, where she brushed her hair and applied fresh makeup. From her suitcase she took the one pair of high heels she'd brought with her.

Walking down the external corridor towards Brand's room, she felt panic flutter in her chest. What if he rejected her? They were of an age, but Brand was a single safari guide. She remembered enough guides and professional hunters from her youth in Zimbabwe, and knew of their legendary prowess with women. Brand would have his pick of single young women; what would he want with a middle-aged married housewife?

Anna felt her resolve begin to crumble. She should turn around, go back to her room, order that second bottle of wine and drink herself into a stupor.

From the walkway she could see over the gardens and the pool bar; men in suits and much younger women in scant nightclub clothes laughed and drank, and a couple of them danced slowly, sensually, to a subdued beat from somewhere in the warm African night. *Screw it*, she thought. Peter was always working late and his new receptionist, Sandy bloody Hann, had gossiped to her about the stripper who had been for four appointments to discuss her boob job. Sandy had been laughing about the patient, but Anna knew Peter cheated on her regularly so she was sure there was more to the dancer's regular visits than her breasts. She thought she might kill the tart if she ever found out who she was.

Hot flushes coursed through her and she could feel the redness that she knew was colouring her cheeks and the skin across her breasts. She was frustrated and angry – at herself, her husband, and her sister, who had tried to fake her own death. She and Brand had shared a moment on the houseboat. He hadn't kissed her, but she was sure he'd been close. Perhaps the tall, dark, handsome guide would give her what her husband no longer would.

The door to Brand's room loomed large in her vision. Anna's heart stopped as the door opened. A tall, thin girl of mixed race came out. She was wearing a black cocktail dress and carrying a handbag in one hand and a pair of matching heels, dangling from their sling-back straps, in the other. The woman closed the door gently, as if not wanting to disturb the man inside. The woman saw Anna there but ignored her and walked past, briskly.

Brand would be smelling of the perfume that still hung, just a trace, in the night air, not yet overpowered by the moist, rich scent of the garden.

She took a deep breath, brushed a stray strand of hair behind her ear and smoothed imaginary wrinkles from her dress as she sucked her tummy in.

Anna knocked on the door. 'Hudson?'

21

I had Bryce Duffy, handsome, young, presumably penniless safari guide on my left, and Andrew Miles, handsome, older, former fighter pilot and rich aviation enthusiast on my right. We – the two boys and me and three of the Americans who hadn't yet gone to bed – sat around a fire in the Balule camping ground.

With both the men fetching me drinks, I was getting increasingly drunk. That wasn't good for my rehab regime, but I felt I'd earned the right to unwind a little. I was worried about Lungile, but there was nothing I could do for her. She wouldn't rat on me, but I was sure Fortune would. My biggest fear was that when I got to civilisation again there would be an identikit picture of me on the front page of every newspaper and Linley Brown would be South Africa's most wanted woman.

OK, perhaps I was being a bit paranoid; South Africa's police should be more focused on catching violent bad guys than a girl who robbed open houses, but I also knew that the media here, as elsewhere in the world, was a fickle beast. Salt and Pepper, as Lungile and I had been dubbed, had captured the media's imagination, and I had a feeling that even if I wasn't front-page news, I'd at least make it to page three or five.

What I needed was to get out of this country, fast. I thought of my passport, in the house in White River. Andrew returned from the cooler box in the trailer with a fresh bottle of sauvignon blanc. He refilled my stainless-steel goblet.

'Do you fly outside South Africa?' I asked him.

'Yes, often. Why, where do you want to go?'

I crossed my legs and leaned in closer to the fire. 'I've always wanted to see Kenya.'

'The great wildebeest migration in the Masai Mara?'

'Yes, and more of east Africa,' I said. It was the truth; Kenya and Tanzania and the mountain gorillas of Rwanda had been on my bucket list for as long as I could remember. I used to dream about running away to Kenya when I was a little girl.

'When do you next get leave? I have to ferry a twin-engine aircraft up to Nairobi. A friend of mine from Kenya flew his plane down to Nelspruit for some specialist work to be done on the avionics then took a commercial flight home. It's ready to go back whenever I'm ready. I've got the time after this safari.'

I was taken aback. Herb was talking to Bryce about leopards, but I could sense Bryce was half paying attention to the client and also straining to eavesdrop on the conversation between Andrew and me. Both discussions stopped when a hyena let out a loud whoop and a cackle of laughter very close to the camp. Bryce excused himself and got up to investigate; the Americans trailed after him, leaving Andrew and me alone by the fire.

'To tell you the truth,' I said to Andrew, 'I don't think I'll be working with Bryce for much longer.'

'Why not?'

'I think I made a mistake taking this job. It's not for me.' I stared at the flames and swallowed hard, trying to hold back my emotions which, annoyingly, were bubbling up again.

'What's wrong, Naomi?'

I wiped away a half-formed tear. 'Nothing.'

'Why do you need to get out of South Africa?'

I sniffed and looked at him, forcing myself to regain my composure. 'I didn't say that.'

He gazed at me. 'You weren't dressed for a safari when we met you and Bryce is an accomplished bush cook. You've hitchhiked into this trip and now you're looking for a way out. Perhaps I should call Bryce's bosses and see if they know anything about their new cook.'

I put a hand on his forearm. 'No need to go worrying people at this time of night, Andrew. Let's just say I'm a bit of a drifter and Bryce was kind enough to give me a lift.'

'I can see why he would have stopped to pick you up off the side of the road.'

If only you knew, I thought. 'What are the immigration formalities like at regional airports in South Africa, if you're taking people out of the country?'

Andrew shrugged. 'Depends on where you are; ditto the destination country. What sort of trouble are you in, Naomi?'

Andrew seemed like a genuinely nice guy, though I was still somewhat suspicious of why he was being so generous to me. In any case, I couldn't tell him the truth. I was going to have to spin him some story he'd believe, but not the whole truth in case he decided to wash his hands of a criminal on the run.

'There's a guy . . .'

'Bryce?'

'No, no. Another guy. I was living with a man in Johannesburg and he became abusive. He hurt me, and threatened to hurt – to kill – people close to me if I ever told the truth about him. I stayed in the relationship for too long, thinking I'd never be able to escape with my life, but I did. I ran away, from him, from my job and my family. I had to disappear, but I'm worried he's out there looking for me.'

Andrew exhaled a long breath. 'Did you go to the police?'

'He *is* a policeman. I took out a restraining order against him, but he stalked me. I called the cops, but he paid them off, I think, to drop the case. I'm scared of him, Andrew, very scared.'

My story was partly made up, but the fear was there, always just below the surface. If I waited in South Africa too long for a replacement passport or emergency travel document I ran the very real risk of the South African police catching me. I needed my money, but I figured that I could get that from anywhere in the world once I had access to a computer and a decent internet connection.

'Why don't you leave the country?' he asked me, his hand still in place.

'I don't have enough money. I have money owing to me, but it's going to take some time. I want to leave, though. I'll only feel safe outside of South Africa.'

'Why did you ask about immigration formalities?'

'Um,' I said, peering into his kind blue eyes, 'I lost my passport. Or, rather, it was stolen. I think by my ex-boyfriend.'

'You really are scared, aren't you?'

I sniffed again and nodded. 'Yes.' It was my turn now. 'Andrew, why are you being so kind to me? You don't even know me.'

He stared into the flames. He didn't look at me as he started to speak a short while later. 'I had a daughter, she'd be about your age now. She had some troubles – a bad boyfriend, like yours – and he got her involved with drugs. But as well as all that she suffered from depression. They broke up and she went off the rails. She . . .' He coughed to cover the choke in his voice. 'She killed herself. The doctors told my wife and I it wasn't our fault, but I've never got over the feeling that I could have done more to help her, that I could have tried harder.'

This continent surrounded us with beauty at every turn, and enshrouded us with sadness with every breath.

'I'm sorry,' I said. It sounded pathetic.

He sat up straight and looked at me again. 'You know that I'd be putting us both at risk if I flew you out of the country without a passport.'

'I know. Forgive me, I had no right to even suggest you do

something like that. It's just that . . .' I felt the helplessness plucking at me again, unravelling me.

'Come stay with me in Cape Town. I'll keep you safe until you can get your new passport. I'll go with you to Pretoria when it's ready and take you to the airport.'

'I couldn't put you through that. And I don't want to put you at risk. He said he'll kill me and anyone – any man – he ever sees me with. I won't do that to you, Andrew.'

He frowned. I knew he wanted to help, but I could see he was also weighing up the risk of confronting a psycho cop. I stood. 'Sorry, Andrew. I need to go check on the dessert, and I need some time to think.'

I moved away from the fire towards the camping trailer which served as our cooking preparation area. I looked back and saw Andrew staring at me.

The chirp of the scops owl and the *good Lord, deliver us* of the nightjar were replaced with a maniacal cackling and whooping noise. 'Over here!' Bryce called, and shone his bright torch beam over to the fire and back to himself. He was standing at the fence.

Andrew's attention diverted from me to Bryce. 'What is it?'

'Hyenas,' Bryce said, directing his light over the fence and into the bush. 'They've caught an impala! Come quick!'

I joined the group. Andrew was beside Bryce already, peering into the gloom. 'There, look, Herb,' Andrew said. 'Sheesh, they're ripping it apart.'

I followed the light and saw two hyenas engaged in an obscene, bloody tug of war with the carcass of an impala doe. The hyenas' tails were sticking up like feather dusters as they jostled back and forth. A third joined in the scrummage and with a sickening tearing of sinew and cracking of bones the impala was suddenly jointed. One hyena whooped with joy as it ran off with the head.

'My God,' said Herb, 'it's sickening, but mesmerising at the same time.'

He'd nailed it. Tourists came to Africa full of expectations of seeing animals killing each other, but the wildlife documentaries on pay-for-view TV painted unrealistic pictures of life in the bush. Most people could go a whole life visiting national parks on holidays without ever seeing a kill take place, but the Animal Planet and National Geographic channels made it seem like something was chasing and catching something every five minutes; it was the same as watching cricket highlights instead of sitting through a test match. Even now, for all the gore, we had missed the actual kill.

'Did they catch that impala?' Herb asked Bryce. 'I thought hyenas were only scavengers.'

'I'm sure they did. They could have stolen it off a leopard, but hyenas are also accomplished, opportunistic hunters.' Three more hyenas loped into view through the thorny bushes, ready to try and score their share of the fast disappearing impala. One of the hyenas stopped and did a one hundred and eighty degree turn and started running. 'Check!'

I followed Bryce's torch beam as it tracked the running hyena, and saw that a second impala had started to run. It had taken refuge in the long golden grass and, thinking the hyenas were occupied, was making its move. Without a call of any kind the hyenas not engaged in eating the first doe also turned as one and split into a flanking attack. The impala was run down within seconds, before our eyes. *Animal Planet, eat your heart out*, I thought to myself.

My own heart was pounding with a mix of fear and adrenaline. On one hand I wanted the beautiful doe to escape, but on the other I was charged with the excitement of seeing this perfectly tuned killing machine in action. The hyenas caught her and brought her to the ground before re-enacting the earlier grisly bout and ripping her to pieces.

'Oh, my Lord,' said one of the Americans.

Bryce turned to me, grinning like a mad man. 'Did you see that?'

'I did. Amazing.'

'Yes, wasn't it! You're good luck for me, Naomi,' he said.

Carnage followed me, it seemed. Still, I took his words as a bushveld compliment; kind of a carnivorous come-on. 'Thanks.'

'I mean, I know hyenas hunt, because I've read about it, but I've never actually *seen* them in action. Wow.'

His boyish excitement was infectious. He stood there grinning at me, but his smiled waned when he saw my lower lip begin to tremble. I felt stupid and weak, as I had with Andrew. I did not want to drag Bryce into my predicament any more than I had already, but I suddenly realised that nor did I want to take off with Andrew in an aeroplane and never see Bryce again. Shit. I was falling for him.

'Hey, what's wrong?'

I went from sad to angry. Bryce looked over his shoulder and saw that Andrew, Herb and the others had moved down the fence line away from us, tracking the back and forth of the hyenas' dual feeding frenzy. Bryce switched off his torch and put his hands on my shoulders. 'Tell me what's wrong.'

I shook my head and felt the tears start to roll down my face. 'I'm not your problem, Bryce. I'll leave as soon as I can.'

He pulled me to him, and I buried my face in the manly, salty smell of his khaki shirt. It felt good to be held by someone I knew wasn't about to hit me or use me. 'I'm in trouble, Bryce, real trouble.' I cursed myself even as the words tumbled out.

'I guessed.'

I prised myself away from him, reluctantly. 'I'm so tired. I think I just need to lie down.'

He ran a hand through his mop of curly black hair. 'Hell, we don't even have a tent for you.'

'I can sleep in the Land Rover.'

'No, no, you can use my tent. I'll sleep outside, by the fire.'

'But what about the animals?'

He waved a hand. 'We're fenced in, and besides, I've slept in the open plenty. You need some rest, and you can tell me what this is all about tomorrow. I'll get dessert, and I'll make breakfast, like I was going to do all along.'

I put a hand out and touched him on his chest. I felt the hard muscle of his pecs. He was gorgeous. I felt bad about asking Andrew to help me get away, but all I wanted to do now was lie down and sleep. It seemed the excitement of the hyena hunt had drained the last of my energy. I had been running too long, even when I'd been thieving, and now I just needed to stop.

'Come.'

I followed him to his tent and he cleared out his gear, which he hadn't yet unpacked. He went to the trailer and retrieved a sleeping bag. 'I always carry a spare. I've had kids wet the bed in these things. Not nice.'

I smiled at his simple generosity. I had pulled a gun on him and now he was just being plain nice. 'Thank you.'

I borrowed a cake of soap and a towel from Bryce and went to the ladies' ablution block to shower by the light of a paraffin lamp. When I was finished I headed back to the campsite via a circuitous route along the perimeter fence, glancing out at the moon-shadowed bush while I thought about what to do next. I weaved my way between tents and caravans full of snoring people and arrived back at our stand with the camping trailer between me and the remains of the fire. All the tourists had gone to bed and only Bryce and Andrew remained, each standing with a drink in his hand, staring into the glowing embers. They hadn't noticed me, but I could hear them, and knew instantly they were talking about me.

'She's not feeling well. I think the hyenas unsettled her a bit,' Bryce said.

'It's more than that, Bryce,' Andrew replied. 'You need to talk to her.'

'I tried, but she won't.'

Andrew lowered his voice, and I strained to listen in. 'Bryce, I want to ask you a question. Are you two . . . well, are you sweet on Naomi?'

I waited quietly. I had been resentful of the way they were discussing me; now I was breathlessly awaiting Bryce's words. Like a silly schoolgirl, I wanted to know if he liked me.

'I've only just met her. I've known you all my life, Thousand; don't hurt her, she's in some kind of trouble.'

'No, you misunderstand, my boy. She's not interested in me in that way, nor me in her. But she's running from something, someone, and there's probably more to it than that.'

'I want to help her,' Bryce said.

'Naomi needs to get out of South Africa, fast,' Andrew said. 'I can help her with that.'

From the pause that followed I knew what Bryce was thinking. No matter what attraction he might be feeling for me there would be a part of him that would be happy for Andrew to take me off his hands. What were his alternatives – call his bosses, call the police? 'Naomi's my problem; you don't need to put yourself out.'

Fuck. I didn't want to be anyone's problem.

'I'm not putting myself out, Bryce,' Andrew said. 'She needs help and I can give it to her.'

'What did she tell you, before, when I was out on the fence investigating that commotion with the hyenas?' Bryce asked.

'She's on the run from a crazy ex-boyfriend, a cop who's threatening to hunt her down and kill her.'

'Hmmm.' I knew the story didn't gel with the way Bryce and I had met. If I was on the run I wouldn't have hijacked him. Bryce already knew I was criminally desperate. 'I'm not sure about that.'

'How did you two meet, anyway?' Andrew asked.

'Funny you should ask . . .' Bryce began.

It was time for me to break up this little party. 'Isn't it past your bedtime, boys?' I said, stepping out of the shadows.

Andrew laughed. 'I'm allowed to stay up late on weekends. As long as I don't tell my geriatrician.'

'My mom doesn't know. Don't tell her,' Bryce added.

'What's a lady have to do to get a drink around here?'

'I thought you were tired,' Bryce said.

'Sheesh man, get her a drink, or I will.'

Bryce stared at Andrew and the pilot gave a snort and walked to the camping trailer.

'Fine safari guide you are,' I said to Bryce. I sat on a camp chair and he took the one next to me.

'I'll have another beer,' he called to Andrew. 'You have to level with me, Naomi.' He looked over his shoulder, towards the trailer, where Andrew was fixing the next round of drinks. 'Andrew says you're running from a jealous boyfriend, but you looked more like a *tsotsi* on the run to me.'

'Yes, well, it's complicated. But we can talk more in the morning, if you like.' I got up. 'I think I'll leave you two to it for now.'

He reached out a hand and grabbed mine. The touch felt electric. 'Naomi, wait.'

'Yes?'

'I . . . I know it's been hectic, but whatever trouble you're in, I'd like to help. I know you've been talking to Andrew, but I'm on your side, too.'

'Thanks.' I didn't want to let go of his hand, ever, but I knew I had to. 'Night, Bryce. Oh, and by the way, I made up the name Naomi. My real name's Linley, Linley Brown.'

He didn't question me, just looked into my eyes. 'That's a beautiful name. Nice to meet you, Linley.'

22

'Hudson? Hudson, can you hear me?'

Brand coughed and blinked. His head was pounding. When he forced his eyes open he saw a beam of daylight shooting through the gap in the curtains, and like a laser it seared his vision, adding to his pain. For a moment he couldn't remember where he was.

'Hudson, it's Anna. Are you awake in there?'

His throat was dry and as he tried to sit up he dry-retched. He blinked again and saw the digital alarm clock on the bedside table. It read 10:13. No, that couldn't be right. He should have been on the road by then, to Chobe National Park across the border in Botswana with the Cliffs, but here he was in bed, in a hotel room. No, this wasn't right.

'Wake up!'

She was angry now. 'Shit, shit, shit,' he said to himself, swinging his legs over the side of the mattress and fighting down another wave of nausea. He was naked. He could smell her, the girl . . . what was her name? 'Coming,' he called out, and coughed again.

He struggled into shorts and zipped them up as he weaved his way to the door. His head spun. Brand gripped the handle for a second to steady himself before opening it. Anna Cliff was standing there, an angry wife look on her face.

Peter Cliff was behind her. He shook his head. 'Hopeless. I'm going back downstairs to the dining room for another cup of coffee.' He turned and walked away.

Anna put her hands on her hips. 'Hudson, we were supposed to have left an hour ago.'

He rubbed his face. 'Sorry, I don't know what happened.'

'I called your room but you didn't pick up. I checked the vehicle and looked all over the hotel for you.'

She sounded pissed off, not concerned. He retched again. 'Sorry, I'll get cleaned up. Give me fifteen minutes.' He stumbled sideways, catching the door frame.

Anna's scowl softened. 'You're a mess. Let me help you.'

'I'm fine.'

She pushed open the door wider. 'Oh my God, you're bleeding!'

Brand looked down, following her eye line. He saw the gash, touched it, then remembered being at a bar. Bloody Patrick de Villiers. The girl, was it Mandy? Mary? No, Melanie, that was it. She had stabbed Patrick. 'It's nothing.'

'It's not,' said Anna. 'Here, let me see.' She touched his stomach and he winced. The action caused the cut to open and she pulled her fingers away, sticky with blood. 'I need to wash my hands, and we need to get you cleaned up.'

Brand relented and stepped aside as she walked into his room. He saw her take in the rumpled sheets, the bloodstains on them. He was surprised by the amount of blood he'd lost. He didn't remember pain, only the sex with Melanie. He was embarrassed that the smell of her lingered in the room. Brand saw Anna sniff.

She shook her head disapprovingly. 'Have you got any antiseptic?'

'I've got a first aid kit in my pack. I'll get it.' He winced again, feeling the cut now he'd remembered it was there. He shook his hand; his knuckles were sore and red where he'd hit Patrick. He rummaged in his bag and found the kit, and Anna took it from him.

'Come to the bathroom.' She walked ahead of him, not looking back to see his eyes as she said, 'I saw the girl leave, last night.'

'I thought you were staying in your room, ordering room service.' He turned it back on her. What he did on his own time was his business. He had no idea why he'd slept so late – he almost never did, and was always awake with the dawn no matter how much he'd had to drink the night before. It was a safari guide's force of habit. Hell, he hadn't even had *that* much liquor.

'I was thinking about Kate, if you must know. I thought of some things I wanted to share with you, information that might help you track down Linley Brown.'

He was facing her now as she ran the water in the sink, but she couldn't hold his stare. She was lying. Anna washed her hands and took out a sterile swab from its packet, then doused it with Dettol. She looked up at him and started to blush. 'Partying with that girl made you sleep in. Peter is furious; he wanted to call the agent back in London and report you.'

Brand shrugged. 'I'm sorry I overslept. That's never happened to me on a tour before.' Anna reached out and wiped the knife wound with the gauze. It was cold and it stung. He felt he deserved a little pain. 'I can find Peter a replacement guide, or get him a refund. To tell you the truth I'd be happy to go back to South Africa right now.'

'Sit down.' He closed the lid on the toilet and did as she ordered. 'We need you, Hudson. You know that. We can't find Linley without you, or with some other safari guide.' She finished cleaning the wound and the skin around it, then sorted through the first aid kit until she found some steri-strips. 'What happened to you, anyway?'

'I cut myself shaving my stomach hair.'

'Very funny. Was it something to do with the girl?'

'Why are you so interested in her, Anna?'

She shrugged. 'I don't know. She was very pretty. Was she a prostitute?'

'Not that it's any of your business, but no, she wasn't. She was with that conference group that's staying here.'

'I didn't see her at breakfast this morning; all the rest of them were there.'

'Perhaps her head feels something like mine. I don't know what I ate or drank last night to make me feel like this.'

Anna peeled the backing paper off a strip and pinched the sliced skin together as she placed it on. It hurt a little, but her fingers were cool, soft, soothing as she smoothed the dressing down. As she stayed bent over him he caught the scent of perfume, something floral and more understated, more expensive than Melanie's. Thanks to the open top two buttons of her sundress he saw red lace. She was an attractive woman, like the sister whose face he'd seen in the scanned photo he'd been emailed. He recognised the danger signals – her jealousy, her touch, her tone. She took up a second strip.

'What did you want to tell me, about your sister? You said you'd remembered something else?'

'Lean back more,' she said. Brand rested his spine against the cool tiled wall. Anna took the next strip and got down on her knees this time to apply it. Her hair brushed his chest as she moved her face closer to his wound and he felt her fingers again. 'Kate had a serious car accident about eighteen months ago; I think I told you about that?'

'Yes.'

'She was in hospital for four months – broken pelvis and a shattered right leg. We had her mail redirected from her flat to our place and I remember I got a get well card from Zimbabwe, just the one, from a girl named Lungile Phumla. I remembered her, from Kate's time at school. I never had any black friends when I was young and I think for all their tolerance – about my lesbian aunt and all – my parents were probably uncomfortable with Kate having Lungile as a friend. Kate brought her to stay at Mom and Dad's place once – I was already in England – and I remember telling my mom not to be so racist because she didn't like having Lungile sleeping in my bed.'

'That could have waited until this morning,' he said.

She stayed on her knees, looking directly into his eyes now, her hand still covering the knife wound on his belly. 'Peter says you're a disgrace as a guide.'

'He's probably right.'

'Are you a better private investigator?'

'Jury's out on that one, as well. I was going to tell you today, but the South African police called me yesterday. Linley Brown's wanted for questioning in relation to some crime or other. They know I'm on the case, trying to find her, and they want me to help set up a sting to catch her.'

Anna's eyes widened. 'Gosh. Are you going to? I mean, with the police involved we'll have a much better chance of tracking her down.'

Brand nodded. 'But if they catch her you may not get a chance to talk to her. I'm trying to get a commitment from the cop in charge to give you some time with Linley, but the detective's a hard woman. She may renege. Plus, do you want to play a part in having your sister's best friend arrested?'

'I want to know what was going through my sister's head, what was happening in her life to make her attempt fraud and turn her back on her family. I don't care what happens to Linley Brown. She's probably the brains behind this whole terrible mess.'

'You can be tough when you have to be,' Brand said.

'I've spent the last twenty years doing what I was told and what society and my husband expected of me. Somewhere along the way I lost my sister, maybe because I wasn't trying hard enough or caring enough about her. My husband has lost interest in me and I have no job or professional qualifications. You don't know how lucky you are not to have any family ties. How I envy you, Hudson.' She placed her other hand on his knee. 'I wish I was free to do what I wanted.'

'Anna . . .'

She leaned closer to him and he could feel the heat of her breath on him. Brand closed his eyes, another wave of nausea rising up. What the *hell* had he eaten or drunk to make him feel like this? He had let down his clients and he should be feeling bad about that, no matter how much he disliked Peter Cliff, but here he was thinking of nothing other than how easy it would be to screw the man's wife. Hell, it even sounded like the man deserved it.

'I want you.'

'No.' He put his hands on her shoulders, keeping her at arm's length.

Anna smiled and moved one of her hands to her chest. She began undoing the buttons of her sundress. 'I can smell that woman on you, Hudson. It should repulse me, but it doesn't. It turns me on. Is that wrong?'

He could *not* do this, perhaps literally after the workout Melanie had given him. His stomach churned. The last thing he remembered was her pouring them both a drink from the minibar. Her back had been to him – he recalled how superb her ass was. She had slipped him something, he was sure of it. He expected he'd find his wallet empty of what little cash he had, if he could get past Anna to check it. There was a thumping on his hotel room door, just as Anna started to play with one of her nipples.

'Anna? Brand? Are you in there?' Peter called from outside.

Annoyance clouded Anna's face. 'Shit.'

She sighed, stood up and started buttoning her dress. 'I feel a complete idiot.'

He paused to put a hand on her forearm. 'Don't. You're a beautiful woman, Anna.' He walked past her out of the bathroom and opened the door.

Peter glared at him, then past Brand to where his wife was emerging from the bathroom. 'What's going on in here?'

Brand looked down at his bare midriff. 'Anna was just patching me up. I had an accident last night.'

'Bloody hell. I can smell the booze on you. What kind of a tour operator *are* you? Getting drunk, sleeping in, getting in knife fights. Are you even fit to drive?'

'I can drive.'

'Leave him alone, Peter. We all make mistakes, and Hudson has a firm lead on Linley. The South African police want her for questioning in relation to a crime, and they want Hudson to set her up so they can arrest her. He's brokering a deal that would allow us to talk to her.'

'*What?* You want us to become part of a criminal investigation?'

'We are already part of an investigation,' Anna said.

Brand picked up his safari shirt off the floor and sat on the bed, putting on his Rocky sandals and packing his bag while Anna and Peter bickered to and fro about the merits of continuing with their quest. His head was throbbing and right then he didn't give a damn what they decided, whether to try and find Linley Brown or leave her blowing in the wind.

He checked his wallet. 'Shit.'

'What is it?' Anna asked, breaking off from her heated discussion with Peter.

'My cash and credit cards are gone. I might need a temporary loan.'

'You are *un*believable,' Peter said.

Brand stood up and closed the gap between him and the doctor, who was a foot shorter than he. 'You know what, Peter? You're right. I am a failure as a safari guide. I'm unprofessional, hungover, and now I'm broke. Why don't you and your wife just get on a plane back to England? I'll make sure you get a full refund from Wayne Hamilton.'

Peter balled his hands into fists and his face began colouring. 'No. We've come this far and you *are* going to find Linley Brown for us and we *will* find out about Kate's last days, and why she wanted to fake her own death.'

Brand was sick of the little man's attitude, but he didn't have any money to fill the tank of his borrowed Land Cruiser. He didn't want to guess how long it would take to get a replacement credit card sent to Zimbabwe or for Dani to wire him some more cash – not that she would send him any more money if he broke his deal with the Cliffs. They were all stuck with each other.

Brand shouldered his backpack. 'All right, then, let's go.'

They went to reception and while Peter, still fuming, checked the bill meticulously and paid with a credit card, Brand opened his laptop, which he'd had the sense to put in the hotel room safe, unlike his wallet, and composed an email to Linley Brown.

Ms Brown, in light of new information that has come to my attention about a plan by Ms Kate Munns to fake her death, prior to her actual demise, there are certain questions that the insurance company requires you to answer before you can receive your payment. Specifically, I have been tasked to ask you about a phone call made to the insurance company on the morning of Ms Munns's death, prior to her actual demise.

He thought about his approach; he didn't want her to think the claim was dead in the water or she might just keep on running.

Perhaps it's as simple as the time on the police accident report being incorrect. The fact that you did not submit a false written claim or a false death certificate will, I am sure, be in your favour. Nonetheless, some explanation of your actions will be required for the claim to be processed. I am currently travelling in Zimbabwe, but will soon cross into South Africa. Can you please advise your whereabouts so that we might meet and finalise this matter once and for all?

Brand was counting on her being desperate now that she was on the run from the police. He thought of something else:

I can also assure you that I appreciate this matter is a sensitive one. I have no idea why Ms Munns would have sought to defraud anyone, but if we can meet soon I will do my best to ensure that the matter remains private and confidential and is not drawn to the attention of any law enforcement officers in Africa or the United Kingdom.

He looked at Peter Cliff. Sometimes he really hated this job.

23

Sergeant Goodness Khumalo held her police issue hat between her knees to stop it blowing away as she sat in the uncovered back of the white police Land Rover *bakkie*.

Six other officers were sitting in the rear of the vehicle. They had all been dragooned off other duties in Bulawayo to provide extra security for a big party conference to be held in Victoria Falls in three days' time. They would boost the local station's numbers, setting up additional roadblocks on the way into town and searching the route of the president's convoy, checking for bombs under bridges and culverts, and possible sniper positions.

Goodness was not happy about the duty. It would be boring and, besides that, she resented the police being used to provide a visible show of the party's influence. She knew their presence in the tourist town was as much about political muscle flexing as it was security. In her heart she supported the opposition, the Movement for Democratic Change, not ZANU-PF, the old president's party. She suspected that many of her colleagues, particularly the younger ones like her, shared her view that it was time for real political change in their country, but there was no way they could voice or demonstrate their allegiances. The police were seen as a tool of the ruling party, not as servants to the people. She tried where she could, quietly, to do the right thing; just last week she had driven past a known MDC political organiser who was wanted for 'acts of subversion'. Goodness knew that if the man was taken into custody the hardline ZANU-PF guys at the station would beat the man to a pulp because he had dared to distribute pamphlets pointing out the government's shortfalls. The man's picture was on a wanted poster at the station and she had seen the flash of panic in his eyes as she had rounded the corner in a Mercedes. Her partner had not noticed the man. Goodness eyeballed the activist, but said nothing – she could see his relief and thanks in the slight nod of his head.

What she really wanted was a place on the next detectives' course. To get there she had to toe the party line for a while longer, and keep her political opinions to herself. When she returned to Bulawayo she would take up the task she had begun, of reviewing the death certificates issued by the Cuban doctor over the past two years. It was an enormous job, but she had already found thirteen issued by Dr Elena Rodriguez; she wanted to check all of those out. Her supervisor knew how keen she was to get on the course, but when she told him of the lead she had been given on the fake deaths he reminded her that she was a traffic policewoman, not a detective. However, he had told her that if she wanted to pursue the case in her spare time he would not object. He could have told her to hand over all her information to the Bulawayo detectives, but he had given her this chance to prove herself. She had spent her last day off going through the records, from eight in the morning to four in the afternoon.

The leaves on the mopane trees on either side of the road were red gold, dried to a crisp by the long dry winter. The summer rains, which promised renewal and new life, could not come fast enough. The movement of the *bakkie* produced a stiff breeze, but the sky was clear and the sun beat down on Goodness and her comrades. She could feel her skin drying to parchment. The truck slowed. One of the other officers sat up on the side wall of the *bakkie*'s load area to look ahead.

'What is it?' Goodness asked him.

'*Maningi* police and onlookers; some sort of commotion.'

Goodness stood up in the back, bracing herself with her hands on the roof of the cab. As the officer had said there were indeed many people clustered in a vacant block of land by the whitewashed wall of the Sprayview Hotel, on the left-hand side of the road at the edge of the town of Victoria Falls. A uniformed officer flagged them down and exchanged greetings with the driver.

'Can you spare some guys to help with crowd control?' the officer on the ground asked.

'We were on our way to see the member in charge,' the sergeant driving said, 'but I can give you three for now. I may need to come back for them.'

'Sure. Thanks,' said the other officer, looking back at the milling crowd.

'Khumalo, Moyo, Shumba, get out and help these guys.'

Goodness didn't mind leaving the truck. She was curious about what had caused all the fuss in the vacant lot, and her bottom was sore from sitting on the bare metal of the Land Rover's floor for the past four hours.

She climbed down from the vehicle, put her cap on and adjusted it tidily. As the *bakkie* drove off, heading for the main police station, she asked the sergeant who had stopped them what was going on.

'A street vendor found a body this morning.'

'Serious? Male or female?' she asked.

'What does it matter to you? Come, help me keep these vultures away from her. There must be a hundred people already gathered.'

Goodness and the other officers followed the sergeant, pressing their way through the crowd. 'Move aside, move aside,' she said, 'step back and let the police do their work.'

Men, women and children were all jostling to see what was going on. The new officers joined the two uniforms on the scene, linked arms with them, and started forcing the crowd back. Goodness looked over her shoulder and saw a detective pull back a plastic sheet that had been placed over the body. She glimpsed the face of a coloured woman, young, pretty.

The detective looked across at the crowd and caught Goodness's eye. He smiled and winked at her. 'Good to see we've got some reinforcements.'

'Happy to help, sir,' she said. He was a handsome man and she knew a smile of her own could occasionally help her along in the male-dominated world she worked in. 'What happened to her?'

'Keep those people back,' the detective said to her, businesslike now.

'Yes, sir.' Goodness returned her focus to the crowd. A young man in front of her, two back, had his mobile phone raised high; he was trying to take a picture of the body. 'Hey, you can't do that.'

The phone's camera shutter noise sounded and the flash went off. 'I just did.'

Goodness thrust herself into the melee and grabbed the young man's hand. He tried to pull himself away from her, so she twisted his arm behind his back, as she'd been taught some years earlier in unarmed combat training. He winced and yelped in pain.

'Hey, don't hurt him,' another man said.

Goodness found herself mobbed by people. Someone shoved her in her back. Her male counterparts were trying to get to her. 'Get off me!' she yelled, but she held on to the man with the phone, even as she was pushed to her knees.

'You heard the sergeant, get off her!' The handsome detective had weighed into the crowd now and was punching and shoving people out of the way. Goodness got to her feet.

'Sorry, sir, thank you,' she said, panting, as the onlookers backed away and the police regained control.

The detective grabbed the yelping man's other hand. 'You did well to hang on to this one.' He snatched the phone from the man and put it in his pocket. 'You, get away from my crime scene. You can come by the station later for your phone once I've deleted the pictures and recorded all the numbers in your memory. If I find out you're a subversive, you'll be in trouble.'

The young man scurried away, nursing his sore wrist, as soon as Goodness freed him. The others in the crowd who had seen the exchange were backing away even further.

'Thanks again,' Goodness said.

'Always happy to help a beautiful lady,' the detective said, 'and you did well to keep hold of him even when the crowd was on you.'

Goodness didn't like his sleazy tone, but she played along. 'Thank you, sir. We don't want the anti-government media getting hold of pictures of a murder victim in Victoria Falls when the president is due to visit.'

'Exactly. But as much as I'd love to chat to you, sister, I have an investigation to conduct.'

'I've applied for the next detectives' course. I know it's against procedure, but do you think I might watch? I'd love to pick up some tips from an expert.'

The detective rubbed his jaw and looked across to his partner, who smiled and nodded, seeing the interaction between the two. 'But tell her to keep those people away while we work,' the other man said.

'OK. I'm Isaac. My partner is Takeshaw.'

Goodness introduced herself, saying she was from Bulawayo. 'What happened to her?'

Isaac knelt and pulled back more of the plastic sheet. He looked up at Goodness, perhaps thinking she might be shocked by the blood that saturated the woman's skin and the cocktail dress that had been pushed high up her thighs. Goodness had worked too many traffic accidents to be shocked any more by death or gore. 'Was she stabbed down there, between her legs? That's a lot of blood, even for a brutal rape.'

'Looks like it,' Takeshaw said.

'What kind of a monster does something like that?' Goodness asked. Random, accidental death was part of her working life, but someone who hated this woman, or women in general, had taken this woman's soul.

'They say she was seen at The Kingdom last night with an American. Another *goffel*, if we are to believe the witness.' Isaac nodded to a woman of a similar age to the dead person, who sat on a rock with a uniformed constable watching over her.

Goodness ignored the detective's use of the slang term for a Zimbabwean person of mixed race. She herself never used racially derogative terms.

'A coloured American man?' Her heart started beating faster.

'Perhaps the American president has come to our town to view the Falls?' Isaac laughed at his own joke, but Goodness did not join in.

'There can't be many of those in Zimbabwe at the moment. What else does the woman know about him?'

Isaac regarded her with mild annoyance, but when she smiled at him and tucked a stray lock of hair under her hat, he gave a snort of indulgence. 'If you *must* know, sergeant, the woman said he was dressed in safari clothes, not so much like a tourist, but maybe a guide.'

'*Ah*, I think I might know who he is,' Goodness said, unable to stifle the rush of excitement she felt. 'Can I talk to her?'

'Now you want to question my witness? You should go back to crowd control, Sergeant Khumalo,' Isaac said. Takeshaw shook his head and knelt by the body, to continue his examination of it and the ground around her. 'But you say you know an American?'

'The crowd is dispersing,' she said, waving to the thinning ranks. The additional officers and the commotion with the man who had tried to take the pictures with his phone had dampened the onlookers' interest. Unauthorised public gatherings were illegal in Zimbabwe and no one wanted to provoke the police any further, particularly with an army of party bigwigs due to arrive any day. 'I suppose I must get back to the station now and then go spend the rest of the day standing by a boring roadblock.'

'That is your job, sister,' Isaac said. However, he opened his police notebook and took out a pen. 'Who do you think this American coloured man is?'

'Like you said, I must go do my job, stopping cars and checking tourists' driver's licences.'

'Don't be coy with me. If you have information that can help me investigate a murder, then you know you must share it with me. To withhold evidence is a crime, as I'm sure you're aware.'

Goodness knew he was right, but this was also her chance to take part in a proper investigation. 'Let me talk to the witness, find out if it's the same man I'm thinking of.'

'No. Tell me what you know or I'll have you charged,' Isaac said.

'The coroner is here, Isaac,' Takeshaw said, standing and snapping off his rubber gloves. 'Stop wasting time with this woman, we have work to do.'

Isaac looked to the seated woman and back to Goodness, still undecided. 'Two minutes with the witness, and I'll have dinner with you tonight,' she said to Isaac. 'You're paying, though.'

Isaac put his hands on his hips and regarded her with a look of surprise. 'My, you are the feisty one, aren't you? How do you know I'm not married?'

'No wedding ring, and you look like a player.'

Takeshaw couldn't help but laugh from the sidelines. 'Who's playing who here?'

'All right,' Isaac said. 'One minute. Now, I must go meet the coroner. Find me this American murderer and I'll buy you dinner at the Victoria Falls Hotel.'

'Yes, sir,' Goodness said, lacing the title with honey. The Victoria Falls Hotel? She looked at his shoes; they looked new, like his watch. No one in the police force made enough money for such an extravagance as dinner at the hotel they called the grand old lady of the Falls. Isaac was probably crooked, like half the cops she served with, but that didn't mean he would shirk his duty to catch a murderer.

Goodness hurried across to where the woman was sitting, still under the watchful eye of a uniformed officer with an FN rifle. The man looked her up and down, disdain clear in his bloodshot eyes. 'The detectives want me to talk to this woman. Give us some privacy, please.'

The officer looked across to Isaac, who nodded and waved him away.

'My name is Sergeant Goodness Khumalo. I am a police officer.'

'I can see that by your dress sense.'

The woman was young, pretty, but too thin for Goodness's liking. Her wrists looked like they might snap if you shook her hand too hard. She smelled of cigarette smoke, last night's booze, and something else from her previous evening's revelry. Goodness knew a prostitute when she saw one. She was not judgemental though, and ignored the woman's jibe. 'Was the deceased woman a friend of yours?'

The thin woman shrugged. 'We worked together.'

'Where was that?'

'Hotels, mostly.'

'Let me guess, you're in the . . . *hospitality* business?'

'Something like that. Have you got a cigarette?'

'I don't smoke,' Goodness said. 'It's bad for you.'

The woman gave a small laugh that turned into a hacking cough. 'Life is bad for you.' She looked to where the coroner's men were lifting the body and carrying it, wrapped in a cheap plastic tarpaulin, to a van. 'Just ask Melanie.'

'That was her name?'

'You said you were a cop. I told the guys all this; her name is – was – Melanie Afrika.'

Goodness had never interviewed a witness in a murder case before. She chided herself for not knowing all the facts, but then Isaac and Takeshaw were not about to take the time to fill her in. 'You saw her with a man last night. The description is of a coloured man, believed to be American, wearing safari clothes. Is that right?'

The woman wrapped her spindly arms around herself. 'So you do know something.'

'I want to help catch the man who did this. He's still out there and he could be a danger to you . . . to other girls in your business.'

'A serial killer? You think? In Vic Falls?'

'I don't know,' Goodness said. 'The man you saw your friend with; you're sure he was American?'

She shrugged. 'Maybe, though the accent wasn't strong, not like other tourists I've . . . met.'

'Perhaps American with a bit of South African mixed in? Portuguese maybe?' Goodness suggested. She was leading the witness, but her excitement level was rising at the same time.

'Yes, perhaps. I saw them together twice. First time was in the bar in The Kingdom – Melanie was a regular there.'

'A regular customer?' The woman looked at Goodness as though the sergeant was a child. 'Oh, I see. She *worked* there.'

'Yes. I remember, I was annoyed. I'd seen him first and he was good looking. When I walked past them, she ignored me, but I heard him speaking and I thought, oh my, that Melanie has landed a handsome brown American. He must be loaded.'

Indeed, Goodness thought. Hudson Brand could easily be seen as a working girl's jackpot, but she was mildly surprised he was keeping company with prostitutes. She hardly knew him at all, but with his good looks Goodness thought he would have no problem meeting any woman he fancied. She herself had found him attractive; his foreignness added to his mystique, but she shuddered at the direction this interview was taking. *Wait a minute*, she admonished herself. She must not jump to conclusions.

'And you saw them again?'

The woman nodded. 'At a nightclub in town. They were dancing, then there was trouble. The coloured man fought with a white man, who was definitely South African, and there was blood. People were screaming something like, "Hey, he's got a knife". I saw Melanie getting involved and then I ran outside, like nearly everyone else.

Some other tourists were crowding around them, watching the fight. Ai, we don't need trouble like this in the Falls, not with party coming to town. I went home after that.'

'No more business?'

The woman frowned. 'You want to know how bad business is in this town? All the foreign tourists go to Livingstone, on the Zambia side, because they think it's safer there. Ha!'

Goodness tutted in sympathy, for it was well known that all Zambians were criminals. Despite its poor reputation internationally due to its political and economic woes, her Zimbabwe remained one of the safest countries to visit in Africa, in terms of the low level of street crime and violent crime, but the body being loaded into the van behind them belied those statistics. Within the space of a single night this small town had seen a knife fight in a bar and a woman who had been raped and tortured to death.

'You didn't hear the man's name?' Goodness asked.

The woman shook her head. 'All I remember was the accent, and that he was good looking with short hair and about 1.9 metres tall. Khaki shorts and bush shirt, and nicely muscled.'

'I have one more question. Did he have any distinguishing marks, on his face or his arms or legs? Think carefully.'

'Umm, I don't think so. His face was very smooth. He had nice legs and, like I said, good biceps. Hey, wait a minute . . . there is something I forgot to tell the other cop. He had a tattoo.'

Bingo, thought Goodness. 'Of?'

'Of a buffalo's head, inside his right forearm. I remember now seeing it as he raised his hand to drink his beer, when I walked past him and Melanie.'

It was Hudson Brand, without a doubt.

24

Brand sat in the driver's seat of the borrowed Land Cruiser in the Shell service station in Victoria Falls near the Shoprite. The Cliffs were in the small shop picking up some snacks for the road. He felt like he'd been pulled through a wringer backwards; he was sicker and more hungover than he'd ever been in his life.

His phone rang and he saw from the screen it was a Zimbabwean mobile phone number.

'Brand.'

'Mr Brand, it's Sergeant Goodness Khumalo from Bulawayo police, how are you?'

'Terrible, and you?'

'Mr Brand, I'm not in the mood for jokes.'

'If this is about Dr Rodriguez, I'm sorry, I don't know where she is and had no idea she would be leaving town too soon.'

'It's not about her, it's about you.'

Brand swallowed back bile. 'What have I done?'

'Mr Brand, I'm not in Bulawayo, I'm in Victoria Falls on special duties. Do you know a woman by the name of Melanie Afrika?'

'Why?'

'I believe at this point I am supposed to say, "I will ask the questions", Mr Brand. Yes or no, do you know her? She works as a prostitute, and frequents The Kingdom Hotel. That's where you told me you would be staying, didn't you?'

Brand started to sober up, quickly. 'I met a woman called Melanie last night, but she was no prostitute.'

'Well, be that as it may, I need to meet with you. I have colleagues who need to ask you some questions about Melanie Afrika.'

'Why? I paid her nothing.'

'But you had sex with her.'

It was said as a statement, not a question. 'Sergeant Khumalo, I have two very impatient tourists waiting for me to take them on safari to Chobe National Park.'

'You need to report to the Victoria Falls criminal investigation department office. Now, Mr Brand.'

'Why would I want to do that? Has the woman you're talking about been involved in a crime?' She had rolled him and probably drugged him but he didn't need to tell Goodness that yet.

'She's dead, Mr Brand.'

He swore under his breath. Peter Cliff was holding his wrist up to the window, tapping his watch. The petrol attendant had finished filling the tank and was hovering expectantly. Brand turned his back to the window and lowered his voice. 'What happened?'

'I think you might have some information that will shed light on Miss Afrika's death, and the Victoria Falls detectives think the same. Come to the station and we can talk.'

'So, you're a detective now?' He felt the dread rising up inside him, remembering what Melanie had asked him to do to her. His DNA was on her, and there would have been people who remembered the ruckus in the nightclub.

'You helped me, with the lead about Dr Rodriguez,' Goodness said, filling the void his silence had left. 'I want to help you, too, Mr Brand. Meet me and we can go to the detectives together.'

She was in this for herself, he realised. She was pretty and ambitious and he guessed it was hard for a woman to get ahead in an

African police force. He needed to play on that. 'All right. I'll meet you, but I need more information. Tell me, was she stabbed?'

There was a pause as Goodness debated how much she should tell him. 'Yes.'

'In her private parts, yes?'

There was no reply.

'I'm right, aren't I? Raped and stabbed, down there, strangled to death and her pants removed from under her dress. Yes?'

'Mr Brand, Hudson, please, you must come and talk to the police. I can help you, believe me.'

His mind, still dulled, processed the events of the night before. 'Patrick.'

'Hello, Mr Brand, are you still there?' Goodness said. 'Who is Patrick?'

'I'll call you back, Sergeant Khumalo.'

Brand ended the call and wound down his window, signalling to Peter Cliff. 'Can you please pay the attendant?'

With the fuel paid for and the Cliffs back in the car, Brand started the truck and pulled out of the garage, ramming his way through the gears. The sun glared through the Land Cruiser's windows, topping up his headache. What the hell had happened to him last night? Just past the Sprayview Hotel was the turnoff to the Kazungulu border post, the road to Chobe National Park in Botswana where they were supposed to be going. Brand drove past it.

Peter Cliff leaned forward in his seat. 'Are you, at some point, going to tell us what is going on with you today? Our itinerary said we were going into Botswana via that road you just drove past.'

Brand took a breath. He was about to fabricate a story for the tourists when he saw the flash of high-visibility fluorescent yellow. A policeman manning a roadblock up ahead was waving to him to stop. 'Peter, your UK driver's licence – does it have a photo on it?'

'What? My licence? Well, in fact, no it doesn't. I've still got one of the old paper licences, never got around to getting a photo one. Why?'

'I need it, now. Quickly.'

'What the devil . . .?'

'Do it, Peter,' Anna ordered.

Brand glanced back at the couple. Peter had come across initially as a domineering pedant, but right now Brand saw a strength in Anna that he hadn't picked up on; plus, it was good to see the husband buckling a little.

'Very well,' said Peter, reaching for his wallet. He passed the licence to Brand down low, between the two front seats, and Brand tucked it in his shirt pocket.

'Good morning, how are you?' asked the policeman.

'Fine, and you?' Brand replied, affecting an English accent to match the licence.

'Ah, but it is too hot. And I am hungry and thirsty. May I see your driver's licence?'

Brand pulled the piece of paper from his pocket and handed it to the cop, who unfolded it carefully and slowly. Brand's heart pounded as the policeman studied the document, for what seemed like an eternity. 'Ah, you are from England. Sure?'

'For sure.'

'How is the weather there now?'

'Cold and miserable.'

'Myself, I would like to go to England. Perhaps you can give me a job there?' the policeman said.

'You wouldn't like it. It rains all the time.'

The policeman laughed.

'But maybe I can help your thirst. Anna, can you please get a Coke for the good officer, from the fridge in the back of the truck?'

'Gladly,' she said.

The policeman accepted the drink with a polite clap of his hands, signalling his thanks as Brand handed it over.

'Phew!' Anna said as Brand put the truck in gear and drove off. 'Am I the only one here who found that exciting?'

'Terrifying, more like it,' Peter said. 'What have you done, Brand? Why are you hiding your identity from the police? And, more to the point, why should we help you if you're wanted for something?'

Brand watched the roadblock recede in his rear-view mirror and breathed a little easier. The trouble was there would be more roadblocks if he carried on through Zimbabwe. 'I've done nothing wrong, but the police want to question me about a crime committed last night.'

'What sort of crime?' Peter asked.

Brand sighed. They needed to know the gravity of the situation, so that they could decide whether to abandon him or help him. 'Murder. A woman was killed and the police want to question me.'

'My God, Hudson. Why not go to the police if you're innocent?' Anna asked.

'This isn't England, it's Zimbabwe. I could be locked up indefinitely while the investigation proceeds. Also, because of the work I do, I've made some enemies in the government. Once word gets out that I've been taken in for questioning I might never get out again. I'll take you both to the airport, now. If you can't get a flight out straight away, then you'll be able to find a driver to take you back to Victoria Falls and across to Chobe if you still want to go there.'

'No,' said Peter.

Brand was surprised, again, by the man. He thought he would have been ready to get the first plane out of Zimbabwe, and away from Africa.

'You've broken one law already,' Brand said, taking out the driver's licence and handing it back over his shoulder, 'I can't ask you to do it again.'

Peter brushed his hand back. 'Keep the licence. I don't like you, Brand, or the way you conduct yourself – getting drunk and sleeping in – but I'm trusting you're a better investigator than you are a safari guide. Without you we'll never find Linley Brown. I don't care whether the South African police arrest her or not, but

Anna and I need to see her, to put the matter of Kate's death to rest once and for all.'

Brand nodded. Seemed old Peter had grown half a ball, and he really couldn't argue with the man's critique of him as a tour leader on this trip. 'Anna?'

'I'm with Peter. We've come too far to run away now. I still think you should go to the police, but you're our only hope, Hudson.'

'All right. If we continue south, through Bulawayo to Beitbridge, then the police will finally get themselves organised and stop us. There's a very quiet border post not far from here, at a place called Pandamatenga. We can cross into Botswana through the bush; it's a big game hunting area, with few people and only a single cop on duty at the crossing. From there it's a straight run south through Botswana into South Africa.'

As they passed the turnoff to the Victoria Falls airport Brand asked them each again if they were sure they wanted to continue with him; both husband and wife agreed to stay with him. Brand pulled over and took out his phone. 'I just have to send a quick message.'

'Righto. I'm going for a leak,' Peter said, and let himself out.

Brand selected Goodness Khumalo from his list of contacts and typed a brief SMS to her. *Look for a South African tour guide, Patrick de Villiers. He's probably driving an overland truck, maybe staying in the municipal camping ground. Melanie Afrika stabbed De Villiers in a nightclub last night. There will be witnesses.*

That, Brand thought, would give the sergeant and her comrades something to go on with while they looked for him. To be on the safe side he took the SIM card out of his phone once the SMS had been sent.

'The woman who was killed,' Anna said from the seat behind, leaning forward, 'she was the one I saw coming out of your room last night, wasn't she?'

Brand turned to look her in the eye. Peter was still out in the golden grass by the side of the road, though he was zipping his flies. 'You didn't come to my room to tell me more about Kate, did you,

Anna?' Her cheeks were turning pink and she looked away, unable to hold his gaze. He *did* find her attractive, very attractive, and her girlish embarrassment was endearing. 'I didn't kill that woman.'

'I knocked on your door, after I saw her go, and called your name, but you didn't answer.'

'I don't remember that at all,' he said honestly. 'I think she drugged me.'

'I thought you were avoiding me, or ashamed, or whatever . . .'

He shook his head. 'No. I wouldn't have ignored you if I was awake.' The truth tumbled out before he could disguise it.

'You had sex with her.'

'That's none of your business, Anna.'

'No, it's police business, now.' Anna took a deep breath and looked furtively at her husband, who was coming towards them, then straight into Brand's eyes. 'I wasn't just coming to talk to you about Kate. It might sound silly, but I'm attracted to you.'

'Your husband,' Brand said, looking out the window.

'Doesn't love me. Don't worry; I'm over it. We haven't had sex for ages. He doesn't find me attractive and last night, when you didn't answer, I felt like going back to my room and drinking myself into a stupor, which I did.'

'Anna, I didn't ignore you. I don't know that I would have slept with you, or if that would have helped either of us, but I'm not the kind to cower under my blankets.'

'I feel stupid. You must get women throwing themselves at you all the time. Khaki fever, it's called, isn't it?'

'It doesn't happen that often,' he lied, 'but I'm flattered when it does. I think our main priority here should be finding Linley, don't you? I don't want to come between you and your husband and I make it a rule to never sleep with married women.'

Peter opened the door of the Land Cruiser. 'What are you two conspiring about?'

'Nothing at all,' Anna said.

*

Brand turned right off the main tar road about fifty kilometres from Victoria Falls, following a sign to Robins Camp, Hwange National Park.

Once prosperous cattle farms, now populated by subsistence farmers living in mud huts, gave way to thorny bush and acacias, airbrushed uniform grey and khaki by the dry season's heat, dust and wind. They passed a red-rimmed triangular warning sign with a picture of a rampant elephant on it. 'Are we in the national park now?' Anna asked.

'We're in the Matetsi Safari Area that borders Hwange National Park and stretches to the Botswana border, where we're headed. This is a hunting area, policed, after a fashion, by the national parks department.'

'A good place to get lost in, or to hide,' Anna said.

Brand nodded. The situation was still messy, but already he was feeling slightly more at ease being surrounded by the bush rather than people. A plume of dust trailed them. Brand slowed when a herd of eight kudu bounded across the road.

'I'm surprised to see animals here – I would have thought they would be scared of being shot,' Anna said.

'There's not a hell of a lot of hunting going on thanks to the state of Zimbabwe and its economy. Ironically, you can sometimes see more game here in the hunting safari area than in the national park.'

To prove him right they drove past a herd of twenty or more sable, beautiful russet-coloured females and babies shepherded along from the rear by a striking male with a glossy black coat and white underbelly. He held his head high, showing off massive curved horns as Brand geared down so that they could get a better view of the beasts. 'Sable are rare across southern Africa but quite common in this part of Zimbabwe.'

'Seems they got one thing right,' Peter said.

Brand thought about Melanie Afrika as he drove. The smell of her was still on him and he felt a weight of sorrow at the way she had died, no matter what she had done to him. He wondered if Goodness

Khumalo had acted on his tip about Patrick de Villiers. When he called Captain Van Rensburg he'd ask her to check if Patrick had been in Cape Town in February, when the prostitute there had been raped and killed. Brand knew Patrick had been in Nelspruit in 2010 on the night of the Australia–Serbia game – half the goddamned province had been there – and he lived in Hazyview, close to where the girl from the nightclub had been dumped outside Phabeni Gate. If he could place De Villiers near the Cape Town murder then it might take some of the police heat off him; as it was he was now wanted in two countries.

Brand looked in the rear-view mirror to check on his passengers. Peter had his head back, mouth half open, and was dozing. Anna's eyes stared back at his. He thought of what she'd said to him, about last night.

'Elephant,' he said, quietly so as not to wake Peter, and pointed to a trio of bulls resting in the shade of a tree.

'Where?' Her voice was a whisper, her mouth close to his ear as she leaned forward.

'Over on the right.' Brand glanced at Peter again in the mirror; he was still asleep.

Anna shifted and moved her left hand between the front seats. Her right gripped the back of Brand's seat, to steady herself. 'I see them. Look at that one, he's very big.' Her fingers moved to his lap and caressed the bulge, making it harder. 'Mmm, very big.'

He glared at her, but she just smiled. He didn't want to tell her to stop in case it woke her husband. He hadn't thought this day could get any worse, but there was always potential. This was crazy, but her movements were having an effect. 'Anna,' he whispered.

'Shush.'

'Dangerous,' he persisted.

She pressed her lips to his ear now. 'I know. I'm getting off on the danger and I want you to, as well.'

She slid her hand down inside the waistband of his shorts and he could feel those red-painted fingernails deliciously grazing the sensitive skin on the underside of him, dragging their way up to the crown. Her hand was slick with him and she slid it up and down along the shaft. He breathed in, sucking in his taut belly a little to give her more room. This was insanity.

Peter snorted in the back, half snoring. Anna withdrew her hand and sat back in her seat. Peter opened his eyes, then rubbed them and looked out the window. 'I must have dozed off. How far to the border?'

Brand saw the turnoff coming up on the right and took it. The sign to Pandamatenga was so faded he could barely read it, but he knew the road. 'Twenty-seven kilometres from here.'

He glanced at the Cliffs in the rear-view mirror. Peter was looking out at the bush but Anna gave him a wicked smile.

'The border between Zimbabwe and Botswana, is it fenced?' Peter asked.

Brand cleared his throat. 'No, it's just bush, national park and safari areas on this side and forestry reservations on the Botswana side. Elephants and other game migrate between the countries freely, depending on the season and the availability of water.'

'So a man could walk across, unseen, quite easily,' Peter said.

'Yes, why do you ask?' He checked the mirror again. Anna was slumped back in her seat, pointedly looking away from him now that her husband was speaking.

'We could drive the car through the border and you could walk.'

Brand shook his head. 'I can't ask you to do that, Peter.'

'I don't want you to get arrested.'

Brand's eyes flicked from husband to wife. Anna was sitting up again, looking at her husband, perhaps in a new light. His offer certainly surprised Brand. 'Why?'

'You're our only conduit to Linley Brown. I don't like the way this is heading, but if you're in prison in Zimbabwe then we don't get to meet her and, presumably, she slips away from the South African police. If this woman dragged my sister-in-law, Anna's only sister, into a life of crime then to tell you the truth, Brand, I want to her to pay. I want her to pay for her crimes and for the sorrow she has put this family through. Kate could very well be alive today if she hadn't – for whatever reason, good or bad – got involved in a scam that stood to benefit this Linley Brown, at least in part.'

Well, well, Brand thought.

'It's too dangerous – are there lions in the bush here?' Anna said.

That was the least of his problems. 'I'm not worried about animals, particularly as it's daylight. I walk with dangerous game for a living. I don't want to sound macho, but you'll be at more risk than I will.'

'What risk?' Peter said. 'Write me a letter saying you authorise me to drive this Land Cruiser and to take it across international borders. If the cops get suspicious, or have your name on a watch list, I'll tell them the truth, that you gave me a letter authorising me to drive the car and that we parted company. We can arrange to meet up somewhere, later today, and set up some sort of signal system so I can let you know if the police are looking for you, or if the coast is clear.'

Brand had to admit it was an audacious plan, but a good one. He geared down and pulled over underneath a fig tree. A herd of waterbuck, grazing on still-green grass in a boggy area watered by a perennial spring, took flight when he opened the car door. He took out his travel folder and notebook. 'There's a four-by-four track called the Hunter's Road, just across the border. We can meet there.'

25

I slept well in Bryce's tent. It was my first good night's rest in a long time. I'd lain awake for a little while after everyone else went to bed, though, wondering if Bryce might creep back in.

I was half relieved, half disappointed he hadn't. I felt my attraction to him growing, but at the same time I didn't know if I was ready to allow a man back into my life after what I'd been through. I was conflicted; I wanted to trust him, but didn't want to involve him. I wanted him, but didn't want to need him. Andrew, who would only ever be a platonic friend, was a safer bet.

It was still early when I woke, just going on six, but already the sun was warming the tent, eliciting the musky scent of dew-damp canvas cooking. I rolled over and unzipped the tent's flap. Lying on my side I could see Bryce kneeling by the fire, cracking eggs one-handed and dropping them into a heavy, blackened steel frying pan. The smell of bacon sizzling made my tummy grumble. Even his back was gorgeous. I sighed; I could not let my feelings for him get the better of me, nor let him in.

Herb was walking from the ablution block, silhouetted against a gloriously pink sky. I shifted my gaze to another of the tents and saw Andrew stepping from it. He reached for the sky, stretching. 'Morning,' he said.

Herb replied to the greeting. Bryce looked up from the fire and said, 'Breakfast in ten.' Andrew nodded and Herb okey-dokeyed in reply.

I pulled on my new shorts, buttoned my sleeveless bush shirt and pulled my hair back into a ponytail and tied it with a scrunchie. I slid out of the tent and went to the fire. I would have to ask Bryce for his towel again if I was going to have another shower. It was hanging over the wing mirror of his Land Rover.

'Hi,' I said to his back. 'Need a hand?'

'Nope.'

'Hey, I'm the cook, right?'

'Are you going to tell me now, Linley, if that's your actual name, what sort of trouble you're in? I shouldn't have to hear stuff about you from Andrew.'

He was being a bit petulant and I was annoyed, but last night I had promised to tell Bryce about my troubles – well, some of them. 'And Andrew shouldn't have told you anything. Did he tell you about my boyfriend?'

I wanted to never rely on anyone again, and when I looked into those eyes of his I knew, too, that my heart wanted what other people had, to rely on one reliable man for the rest of my life, and to have him need me just as much. I had never had that. Instead I'd been a toy and a pawn and I had learned to please, regardless of my own desire and pleasure.

'Yes. But there must be more – like why did you have to hijack me? If you'd told me you were on the run from a guy I would have been happy to give you a lift.'

I turned away. 'I'm sorry, Bryce, about all of this,' I said quietly. Part of me wanted to tell him everything, but I also wanted to shield him from my problems. Also, because I knew I was falling for him I didn't want him thinking badly of me if I told him of my life of crime.

He turned the eggs and used a breadknife to cut open fresh rolls. I saw how his knuckles whitened around the handle and my spinal fluid was frozen for a second as I remembered the glint of the sharpened blade that reflected the candlelight. 'You've nothing to be sorry for. I can't . . . I mean, I shouldn't judge.'

'I'm sorry,' I said again.

His whole body sighed. 'Then *tell* me, Linley. Tell me.'

I wanted to, right then and there, but I couldn't bring myself to tell him the whole story. Besides, Andrew had extricated himself from whatever boring conversation he was having with Herb and was heading our way. The morning sun already had a sting in it that added to the pain of my hangover. I felt queasy and the *go away* cry of the eponymous grey bird mocked me. I wanted to be gone.

'Morning, Naomi, Bryce,' Andrew said.

'She's Linley, not Naomi,' Bryce said, with a note of triumph that there was something he was privy to over Andrew.

'*Howzit*,' I replied.

Andrew raised his eyebrows. 'Nice name.'

Bryce half placed, half dropped a plate with a roll in front of each of us. 'Breakfast is served.' He wiped his hands on his shorts and walked to his Land Rover.

Andrew lowered his voice. 'Can we talk?'

'Not here.'

'OK. Then how about in Kenya?'

'What do you mean?' I asked him.

'You said last night you've always wanted to see the wildebeest migration in the Masai Mara, so let's go there. I'll be finished with Herb's group in a couple of days and we can leave then. I'll ferry my friend's aircraft back to Nairobi and you're coming with me.'

I glanced at Bryce, who was ignoring us, foraging for something in the truck.

'I want to help you. What you do once you get to East Africa is up to you.'

Here was my ticket out of South Africa and into a new life. I'd never been to Kenya but everyone who knew me had heard me say that seeing the migration was the one thing I wanted to do before I died. Here was a kind stranger offering to take me to see it in a private plane. It should have been a perfect escape for me.

I looked at Bryce.

'Linley?'

I returned my attention to Andrew. 'Where would we fly from?'

'KMIA, Skukuza, the Sabi Sand, wherever you want. I can arrange for someone else to take us if you don't want any tearful farewells.'

I looked to Bryce again, but he continued to ignore me. He must have known Andrew and I were plotting and that he was being deliberately kept out. My heart hurt for him. 'I'll come with you, but I need to get a new passport, or a temporary travel document.'

He nodded. 'All right. You can get it couriered to KMIA, the local Kruger Mpumalanga International Airport, and I can collect it for you from there. I'll fly there from Nelspruit's airfield and lodge my flight plan there.

'I'll take good care of you, Naomi – I mean, Linley,' he said, trying to assuage the concern he no doubt saw on my face. He put a proprietary hand on my shoulder. 'I won't let anyone hurt you. I take it your name change was part of trying to get away from your crazy boyfriend.'

I nodded, and just then Bryce looked back at me and I saw the pain in his eyes and thought I might cry. 'OK,' I said to Andrew.

I don't know what I wanted right then – maybe for Bryce to get up and get away from his goddamned cooking fire and breakfast and come and tell me he'd take me away somewhere to help me sort out my life. Maybe I wanted him to grab me by the arm and drag me to the Land Rover and drive off, leaving Andrew and Herb and the other Americans.

Instead, Bryce said, 'Game drive in half an hour.'

Andrew insisted I come on the drive. Bryce shrugged his shoulders. 'I'd suggest she stay and get lunch ready, but you know she can't really cook,' Bryce said, out of earshot of the guests. I hated him right then.

We took the dirt road south towards Satara, parallel to the Lebombo hills and the Mozambican border. I could get out and walk, I thought at one point, simply disappear into the bush the same way the Mozambican illegals did from the other direction when they were walking these hills to get to a better life in South Africa, or to hunt the country's rhinos. Either way they were trying to get rich and were prepared to die, perhaps from thirst or starvation or being killed by a man-eating lion, to follow their dream. Or were they trying to escape their nightmare? The similarities with my situation were everywhere, and I didn't really care if I died trying. After a couple of hours, in which we saw zebra, giraffe, kudu and jackal, Bryce turned left on to an access road that brought us to a dam.

'This is Gudzani Dam,' Bryce said to his clients. Bryce took out his binoculars and scanned the wall and the far bank. 'I often see a leopard here at this time of day, sunning herself before she goes hunting. She's got a couple of cubs.'

'Hippo,' said Andrew, who was also scanning. He lowered his binoculars and said quietly to me, 'I have a phone and an iPad you can use at Satara. There's a signal there and you can call and email your embassy.'

We left the dam and headed west on a road called the S100 that Bryce said was well known for its cats. We didn't see any on that road, but when we re-joined the tar, just south of Satara, Bryce had to stop for a traffic jam. About fifty metres from us, just visible through the maze of parked cars, were a pair of lions, a male and a female, resting in the shade of a tree. 'They'll have left the pride to mate,' he told the tourists. 'They'll be together for twenty-four hours, having sex every fifteen minutes to half an hour.'

'Impressive,' Herb said.

'Painful,' I chimed in from the back. Herb laughed and Bryce ignored me. Andrew looked at the lions through his binoculars.

The lioness got to her feet, stretched and walked in front of the male. She raised her tail, flicking it, exposing herself to the magnificent black-maned creature. It must have been near the end of the twenty-four-hour session, though, because he looked as though he could barely keep his eyes open. She bared her teeth and snarled.

Behind us I heard a metallic *thunk* and looked around to see a man getting out of a HiLux fitted with roof tents and sporting the stickers of a four-by-four rental company on its sides. 'Bryce!'

Before Bryce could see what the matter was the lion was on his paws, instantly roused from his post-coital snooze. He emitted a throaty growl and took a few steps towards us. I wanted to scream, but Bryce held a hand up then started the engine. He put the Land Rover in reverse and put us between the poised lion and the idiot who had opened his door.

'Get back in your car!'

The lion turned on the spot and ran off into the long dry grass, followed, after a pause and a snarl, by his mate. Around us people were hissing their disapproval at the man, who had got back into his car.

'What were you thinking?' Bryce said to him.

'My car, she will no start,' said the man in an Italian accent.

Bryce shook his head in annoyance. 'I'll give you a push start. Get back in.'

Bryce manoeuvred the Land Rover as the traffic jam began to break up, and pulled up behind the rented Toyota. As he eased his front bumper up to the spare wheels on the back of the other vehicle I said to Andrew: 'Thank you. For everything.'

In Satara we climbed down from the game-viewing vehicle and Bryce told everyone we had half an hour.

'There's a day visitors' picnic site over there, behind the car park,' Andrew said. He pointed to a spot I'd seen near the camp entry gate. 'Most people just go to the shop or the cafe. We can find a quiet spot there.'

Bryce headed to the bathroom and the American tourists went into the camp's curio shop, across from reception. Andrew and I walked across the car park to the picnic site, a complex of timber pergolas and tables and seats set in the bush at the perimeter of the camp. We sat down and, as Andrew powered up his iPad, started planning my escape.

26

Brand walked through the dry bush, his feet crunching on parched golden grass and desiccated twigs. Every now and then something slithered away from him through the dehydrated mulch.

He smelled elephant on the wind, their sour, musty odour as familiar to him now as the scent of the hotdog vendor's stand on his street corner had been to him as a boy. War had brought him to Africa as a hunter of men, but the serenity and harmony of the continent's bush and its wild inhabitants had kept him here.

The elephant would be a herd on the move from Hwange National Park in Zimbabwe, behind him, towards the Chobe River in Botswana, to the northwest. Every year during the dry season tens of thousands of the giant animals did what he was doing now, ignoring the border with Botswana and crossing in search of survival. Drought was not their only worry; despite its reputation as a peace-loving wildlife haven Botswana still held peril aplenty for the elephant, buffalo and other creatures that gravitated to the glittering waters of the Chobe. More and more land was being cultivated for farming along the river, closing off traditional access for migratory animals. Bananas, maize and other tempting goodies lured hungry, thirsty elephants, and farmers were not slow to pull a trigger to protect their crops and, at the same time, bag a mountain of elephant meat for their families and friends.

From far away he heard a shrill trumpet blast, echoed by more frantic calls from the rest of the herd. Perhaps they'd stumbled across a lion or a leopard; Brand had seen elephant chasing predators, even puny cheetahs, many times. The king of the bush was a scaredy-cat when being pursued by several tonnes of angry pachyderm.

This was forestry land, a transition zone between national park and the big wide world where man ruled. An eddy of wind blew a dust devil that danced in the distance then turned towards him. The trees absorbed most of the gust, but a curtain of dust was left. Brand licked his lips; his throat was dry from the booze last night and the heat of the day. A movement made him stop.

He had almost missed them, great, grey legs looking more like tree trunks, but the flap of a giant ear and the swish of a hairy tail had given one of them away. Now that he had stopped and focused he could see it was a whole herd. They moved slowly, conserving their strength, and their big, spongy feet made not a sound. Brand crouched behind a leadwood tree and watched them move, from the left to right, not a hundred metres away from him. If they detected him they made no sign of it. The elephants moved on, continuing their quest for water, for life.

Soon, the Hunter's Road appeared through the dry-roasted foliage ahead, just as he knew it would. The road, corrugated dirt, ran north–south along the border, just inside Botswana. So named because it had transported ivory hunters in days gone by, today it was popular with a small number of hardy four-by-four drivers, and modern-day hunters, now called poachers, in search of meat and ivory.

Brand sat down in the meagre shade of a leafless acacia and wondered if and when Peter and Anna would show up.

He'd been pleasantly surprised by the way Peter Cliff had stepped up and offered to help him get out of Zimbabwe. The man hadn't had to do that. His mind turned to his conversation with Anna while Peter had slept, and he felt bad, for Anna's sake, that he might have unwittingly given her a signal that he was open to her desire for an affair.

Brand was troubled by Anna. The fact was that he did find her attractive. That wasn't unusual – he'd slept with his fair share of clients in the past – but they had always been single. He wondered if Peter's initial prickliness had made it subconsciously easier for him to give Anna the wrong impression. He'd felt sorry for her, and believed her when she said she was trapped in a loveless relationship, but Peter had risked arrest and possible imprisonment by lying on his behalf. Brand sincerely hoped the couple hadn't fallen foul of the law at the Pandamatenga border crossing.

Brand needed a break. The police in two African countries were on his tail for rape and murder and the person he was searching for didn't want to be found. At times like this he wished he'd stuck with simply being a safari guide, but he knew he'd never be happy just driving people around looking for animals. The hunter's spirit lived in him, even though he didn't kill animals for sport.

Looking up the long, straight road he saw the cloud of dust before he heard the diesel engine. Brand stood, brushed the dirt off the back of his shorts and walked out to the middle of the track. The truck slowed and Anna beamed as she wound down the window. 'Fancy meeting you here,' she said.

'Did you have any problems?'

Peter gave a thumbs-up from behind the steering wheel. 'Smooth as silk. No one asked any questions at all. The policeman on duty on the Zimbabwean side made a half-hearted search of the vehicle. He asked if we had any *dagga* on board.'

'Marijuana,' Brand said.

Peter nodded. 'So I gathered. I assured him we had no drugs or even cigarettes on board, to which he said, 'I don't smoke cigarettes, only *dagga*!' Both Anna and Peter laughed at the recounting and Brand thought it was good to see them sharing a joke.

'I'll drive,' Brand said.

Peter jumped down from the front seat, leaving the engine running. 'You're welcome to it. These corrugations are murder.'

Brand got in and put the truck in gear. He accelerated rapidly, getting to seventy kilometres as fast as possible so that the Cruiser's tyres would skip across the tops of the corrugated humps rather than bouncing in and out of the grooves.

They re-joined the main tar road and Brand carried on south. The small town of Nata revealed itself through the heat haze, a donkey in the middle of the road their welcoming committee.

Brand pulled into the Shell garage for fuel. 'The road off to the right leads to Moremi – the Okavango Delta,' he explained to Anna and Peter. 'There's not much here except for fuel, goats and dust.'

A young man came up to Anna's window, holding up jewellery made of beads. 'I am from Zimbabwe, madam. I am hungry, my family is hungry, please buy something from me.'

Brand stood by the service station attendant. He expected Peter would tell the tout to go away.

'Here, give him a hundred rand,' Peter said, and passed Anna the cash. The salesman looked like he'd won the lottery as he handed Anna a bracelet made of lacquered seed pods.

Peter paid the attendant and they set off again. Ten kilometres further on he turned left on a grey sand road to Nata Lodge. After parking the car out the front, Brand took his laptop out of his daypack and they got out and walked through a thatch-roofed reception area to a courtyard with a small pool, bar and restaurant. It was a mini oasis in the dry flatlands of Botswana, and tourists were thronging the sunbeds around the water.

'Gosh, that pool looks inviting. Have we got time for a swim?' Anna asked.

'Sure,' said Brand. 'I'm going to try the wi-fi and check emails, see if there's anything from Linley Brown or the South African cops.'

'I need a beer,' Peter said. 'Want one?'

Brand shook his head. 'Coke, please. I've still got a long way to drive. Could you lend me a few bucks so I can use the internet here?'

Peter rolled his eyes, but smiled as he fished out some bills from his wallet. Brand was liking the man more by the minute. He went back to reception and bought a wi-fi voucher, then sat down in a corner of the bar by himself, away from the flat-screen TV hanging from the timber rafters. A replay of the last Springboks game was playing.

He fired up his laptop and waited for the connection before calling up his webmail account. His pulse quickened when he saw a message from Linley Brown in his inbox.

OK, Mr Brand, I'll meet you. I need my money and want to put this to rest. Meet me at the following location at 10h00, this Thursday. Just you, no one else. If I see you with other people – any other people – you won't find me. I'll sign whatever you need and tell you about Kate. LB.

This Thursday. That was the day after tomorrow. Below the message was a set of GPS coordinates, giving latitude and longitude. Brand called up Google Earth and entered the numbers. The connection was slow, but eventually it came up. He knew the location – it was the access road to Shaw's Gate, one of the entryways into the Sabi Sand Game Reserve on the western edge of the Kruger National Park. Ironically, it was almost back where he'd started this journey, very near to where he'd been living at Hippo Rock.

A barman brought him his Coke and he toasted Peter, who was sitting on the other side of the room, keeping one eye on the rugby game and the other on Brand. Brand rubbed his stubbled chin as he re-read Linley's message. She warned him not to bring *any other people*. Did she think that he knew she was wanted by the police? It was very unlikely Linley could know he had Kate Munns's sister and brother-in-law in tow. This woman could be like a wounded lioness, dangerous and cautious.

Brand looked out at the pool. Anna had changed into her bikini. She was full figured but toned, and carried her years well. Her skin was creamy and pale from her time in the UK, but she dived in and struck out with the skill and confidence of a child of the sun. She did a tumble turn at the far end of the pool and swam back, and when she broke the surface she was grinning at him. He returned her smile, unsure of how he would handle the meeting with Linley Brown. She winked at him and began a lap of backstroke, watching him the whole way. Brand shot a glance at Peter and saw he was now engrossed in the television.

Brand shut down the computer and walked over to Peter. 'We have to leave. I've got a message from Linley Brown. She wants to see me the day after tomorrow and we've got a long way to go to where she is.'

'All right. I'll get Anna.'

Brand didn't look back at the pool; instead he walked out to the Land Cruiser.

They crossed the border from Botswana into South Africa at Pont Drift on the Limpopo River, driving through the dry sandy riverbed.

The route from the border took them parallel to the Limpopo, past the high electrified fences of game farms, many of which hosted hunts. Signs warned of the presence of dangerous animals and even more dangerous owners, armed with automatic rifles. Brand caught a fleeting glance of a black rhinoceros, which turned its rump to them and fled into the thornbushes before Peter or Anna could see it. The dying light turned towering rock formations along the river the colour of blood. This was wild, hard country, the temperature outside the Land Cruiser barely dropping with the setting sun. They passed Mapungubwe National Park on their left, and came to the lodge a few kilometres before the turnoff to Musina.

The place was a clean, quiet self-catering stopover for people crossing to or from Zimbabwe via the Beitbridge border post. Brand checked them in and the woman on duty showed Peter and Anna to one chalet and him to another.

Brand took cans of tuna and tomatoes, a packet of instant three-cheese sauce and a bag of pasta from the food box in the back of the Land Cruiser and cooked them a tuna pasta bake. 'It's nothing fancy, but it's food.'

'It's delicious,' Anna said. She had opened a bottle of duty-free gin and had been able to source some tonic water and ice from reception.

'I'm going to turn in early,' Peter said. 'It's been quite a day.'

'I'll be close behind you,' Brand said, picking up the plates from the table outside the Cliffs' chalet. As Peter disappeared into the chalet and Brand began to head towards his own, Anna interrupted him.

'Hudson,' she began.

He turned at the door to his hut. 'Yes?'

'Can we talk?'

'I've got to clean up, take a shower and shave. We've still got a long drive ahead of us tomorrow.'

A bat squeaked somewhere nearby and a frog croaked from the refuge of a birdbath. Overhead the stars were revealing themselves. Anna took a step closer and lowered her voice. 'I want to talk to you about Peter.'

'Anna . . .'

'No, wait. Let me inside, just for a minute.'

'Your husband's right next door.'

'He's in the shower, he'll be twenty minutes. He's fastidious.'

Brand sighed and kicked open the door to his chalet. Anna followed him inside. He laid the dirty plates on the sideboard, next to the sink. A maid would clean them the next day. 'I'd offer you coffee, but I'm trying to stay away from corny one-liners.'

She leaned against the edge of the bench in the small kitchenette. 'He's been good today, with all that stuff at the border. I think he likes a little excitement in his life, we all do. But he still doesn't care for me, Hudson. Not in *that* way.' She sniffed and wiped her eyes.

Brand didn't know what to make of her, or this relationship. His head told him to tell her to get out of the chalet right now, but her eyes looked genuinely sad. 'I'm not the solution to your marital problems, Anna.'

She exhaled. Her breasts seemed accentuated, the way she stood with her arms back and palms on the bench top either side of her. She'd showered before dinner and her hair was still damp, shiny, held back in a ponytail. She smelled sweet and clean and her nipples strained against the fabric of her simple white T-shirt. 'No, I know that. But I wonder if I even have a marriage any more. I'm thinking of asking him for a divorce.'

'Is it that bad?'

She shrugged. 'I don't really know. What I do know is my husband is a stranger to me these days. Kate dying . . . that wasn't the cause of it, but things certainly haven't got any better between us since then.'

'You don't think finding Linley Brown will help, perhaps get you two back on an even keel?' he asked.

Anna pondered the question for a couple of seconds. 'I thought it might, but I'm not so sure now. I think Peter *is* doing this for me, helping you across the border and trying to be upbeat, but it's like all this is just a distraction for him. It doesn't help me, Hudson. I'm a woman and I have needs.'

He wanted to steer the conversation away from sex. 'I haven't told you yet, but Linley's email specifically requested that I meet her alone, with no one else around. She's threatened to call off the meeting if she sees me with anyone in tow.'

Anna seemed not to hear or register his words as she pushed herself forward from the bench, closing the gap between them. Brand knew he should step back, turn away, but his feet felt rooted to the floor. The accommodation units were close enough for him to hear the water running in the shower next door. Anna was just a few centimetres from him now.

'I'd like to come back to Africa.' Anna blinked a couple of times and he saw the wetness glistening in her eyes. 'England's so cold. I miss the heat and I miss the bush.'

'I'm not your ticket home.' He clenched his fists by his side, trying to stay strong.

'Sometimes I just want to run away, to disappear, like my sister tried to, before . . .' Her body started to shake as the sobs took hold of her.

It was instinctive for him to put his hands on her arms, to draw her to him and try to comfort her. He felt her tears soaking into the dusty fabric of his bush shirt as he breathed in the scent of her shampoo. He could feel her heart beating against his chest and while he told himself he was simply comforting a lost and lonely soul his body betrayed his baser feelings and instincts. Next door the hiss of the shower stopped and he heard coughing.

'Hold me.'

He drew her to him and kissed the wet hair on the top of her head. She looked up at him, silently beseeching him. Brand felt his heart turn to jelly. He was a sucker for a pretty girl, always had been, and the tears melted his resolve.

Brand held her at arm's length. 'You've got to go back to him now.' She shook her head and lowered her eyes. 'Yes.' He crooked a finger under her chin and tilted her face up. 'He doesn't hurt you, does he, Anna?'

'He doesn't show rage, or happiness, or love, or laughter. Nothing. It's like living with a robot. I can't take it any more. He'd rather sleep with whores and strangers than me.'

This was messed up, Brand thought. He'd had clients' wives proposition him in the past, but he'd always been able to bat away their advances; he'd certainly never ended up embracing one and kissing one, nor allowed one to get as close to him as Anna had in the truck. He'd let her draw him in to her risk-taking behaviour and it was dangerous. He still didn't particularly like Peter Cliff, though the man had possibly saved his bacon today, and he didn't want to be a party to breaking up his marriage. He tried to look away from her eyes, but he couldn't.

'Goddamit.'

'It's not your fault, Hudson,' she sniffed. 'I'm irresistible.'

He laughed, and she smiled. Brand released his grip on her and she walked to the door and let herself out.

27

Sannie van Rensburg ended the call to Zimbabwe and swivelled in her chair to face Mavis.

'What did Sergeant Goodness have to say for herself?'

Sannie put her hands together, as if in prayer, and touched her fingers to her chin. 'Very interesting. Our Hudson Brand's now wanted for murder in Victoria Falls. He seems to have escaped the country; some tourists he was escorting crossed into Botswana at a small border crossing, Pandamatenga, but there was no record of Brand leaving Zimbabwe. He's either in hiding or he slipped across the border undetected.'

'The actions of a guilty man?'

Sannie rocked her head from side to side. 'Or an innocent one. If I was wrongly accused of a crime I wouldn't like to spend time in a Zimbabwean prison hoping to clear my name. But the worrying thing is that the MO is exactly the same as in the two murders we're looking at him for in South Africa.'

'Strangled prostitute, with those terrible stab wounds?' Mavis said.

'Exactly. The Zimbabweans do have someone else they're questioning – another of our locals, Patrick de Villiers.'

'The same guy we questioned about the incident with the poachers in Kruger?' Mavis asked.

'The very same man. He and his brother, who's a farmer, have both seen the inside of the Hazyview cells a few times,' Sannie said.

'We need to check if he was in Nelspruit and Cape Town at the same time as the other murders,' Mavis said.

'That's going to be our next job. It seems De Villiers got into a punch-up with Brand and the prostitute the night she was killed.'

'Convenient for Brand,' Mavis said.

Sannie nodded. 'My thoughts exactly. I don't know what was going on between Goodness Khumalo and Brand, but he SMSed her the tip-off on De Villiers. It's quite possible he was looking to set up the other man as a scapegoat.'

'And we still need Brand to help us find . . .' Sannie's mobile phone began to ring and she answered it. 'Hello? Hudson Brand; we were just talking about you.' Sannie smiled at Mavis as she listened.

'Thursday, Mr Brand? Yes, I'll check those coordinates, but I know the area you mean, on the R536 on the road to the Paul Kruger Gate, just by the turnoff to Shaw's Gate in the Sabi Sand Game Reserve. Are you in Zimbabwe, Mr Brand?' She winked at Mavis.

'Why wouldn't you want to tell me where you are?'

Mavis wrote a note on a piece of paper and slid it in front of Sannie. *Because he's guilty?* Sannie shrugged. 'All right, Mr Brand, we'll see you by the entrance to the Sabiepark Private Nature Reserve, near the Paul Kruger Gate, at ten o'clock tomorrow morning.'

*

Tom Furey dropped his three children at their school on the outskirts of Hazyview the following morning. Open game-viewing vehicles were common on the streets of the small town, which made its living largely out of the safari industry, but nonetheless the fact that Tom was driving one drew a crowd of admiring kids at the school gate.

His own three had been chatting excitedly through the drive from the farm to the school and Tom enjoyed the feel of the wind in his hair on the warm spring morning. He kissed little Tommy and Ilana goodbye and ruffled Christo's hair. His oldest, who was Sannie's son by her first husband, had made it clear he was getting too old to be kissed by his parents in public. He was growing into a fine young man, and his birth father would have been proud of him, Tom thought as he watched the kids join their friends in the playground. Tom waved to the principal.

Tom wore a khaki baseball cap, green shorts and a shirt embroidered with the logo of a local tour company above his left breast pocket, but he was no safari guide. He often wondered if he might have become a guide if he'd been born in South Africa instead of England; or perhaps he would have been drawn into the police service here as he had in his home country. He'd met Sannie six years earlier when they were both working as protection officers for politicians from the UK and South Africa. He told himself almost on a daily basis how much he didn't miss the English winters or his job as a policeman, but there was no denying he felt a small thrill to be helping his wife out today, by going undercover.

In truth he wasn't actually going undercover, but rather transporting a plain clothes surveillance team. He'd borrowed the green Land Rover game viewer from Greg Mahoney, who'd had no bookings that day. Sannie was short of manpower but rather than using a real guide and his vehicle she'd told Tom she wanted someone who could drive defensively in the event that their suspect tried to escape in a vehicle, or, worst case scenario, the bullets started flying.

Tom worried about Sannie every single day that she went to work. He worried about her weaving her way in and out among the interminable convoys of mining trucks on the R40, through the hills on her way to and from her work at Nelspruit, and he worried about the number of police officers killed – about one a day on average – in the line of duty in South Africa. Sannie's first husband, Christo and Ilana's father, had been shot by a hijacker in a crime related to his job, and Tom breathed a silent, secret sigh of relief every day when he saw Sannie's car drive up the red dirt access road to their house on the banana farm.

If anyone in town, or his old colleagues back in the UK ever asked, he told them he loved the farming life. The truth was that it was hard work and the returns were diminishing as other suppliers in South Africa and around the world worked hard to undercut each other. Also, there was a fresh land claim on the farm and their lawyer could not assure them that it would be safe this time around. They were already talking about where they might buy a house if the government purchased the farm from them and gave it to some African people. Sannie was resigned to, though bitter about, their likely fate. Her parents had bought the farm from another family back in the sixties and had stolen it from no one. They had put their life's work into it, and while Sannie had been keen to leave it in her teens and had lived in Johannesburg while working for the Police Protection Unit in Pretoria, she had been happy to get back to the farm after she'd married Tom.

And then Sannie had drifted back to police work. As much as he worried, Tom was proud of his wife; proud that she was giving her expertise back to her country and to the service she still loved.

And Tom realised, despite his protestations to the contrary, that he was secretly jealous of her. He loved his kids – Sannie's two and their own son, little Tommy – and knew that he was far more fortunate than most fathers to see so much of them and to be involved so closely in their schooling. He knew all their teachers' names and sometimes helped out around the school, doing handyman projects or sitting in as a teacher's aide when he wasn't busy with planting or harvesting. But this morning, as he'd looped the pancake holster onto his buffalo-hide belt for the first time in a very long time, and checked the action of his SIG Sauer nine-millimetre pistol before sliding in a magazine of freshly loaded bullets, he'd felt the short, sharp burst of adrenaline that had been missing from his life for as long as he'd been unarmed. When Sannie had let him see the case dockets on the murder cases it had taken him back to his days as a police officer and, despite the shocking nature of the crimes his wife was investigating, it had brought them closer again.

'You won't need that,' Sannie had told him as they dressed in the pre-dawn darkness. She had left early to go to Nelspruit to rendezvous with her partner Mavis and the rest of their team.

'No,' he said, 'I'm sure you're right, but you think this Brown woman might be armed, and if Brand's guilty of the murders you're looking at him for then he might try and run. I'm a civilian but I'm licensed to carry, and if I see you're in trouble then I want to be armed.'

'*Liefie*, I'm not asking you to help us because I need your protection. I need a good driver and, just between us, you're better trained and more experienced than anyone the station will give me.'

'Why else?' he'd asked her as he loaded the pistol.

'What do you mean?'

'I'm just the driver, moving the surveillance team. We both know that the likelihood of me even getting close to either suspect is very remote.'

She put a hand on his arm. 'I know, baby. I also thought, well, maybe you might need something like this.'

'Need?'

He thought about her statement and his question now as he drove past Perry's Bridge and the Simunye Centre, and waited at the robot to turn left into the R536, towards the Paul Kruger Gate entrance to the national park, and Sabiepark, where he'd meet his wife again. *Need.*

She'd brushed it off, saying she thought every man, every person, needed a bit of excitement in their life. That implied she thought he was bored, and he'd told her he was happy with their life on the farm. He waited for the coal truck in front of him to creep forward slowly as the light changed, and ignored the minibus taxi that shot up the gravel verge beside him on his left.

'Have you seen it in me? Have I acted like I'm bored?'

'No, no, no,' she'd assured him. 'But I wondered if you missed it, the job. The excitement.'

'Did you show me the case docket because you felt sorry for me?' he'd asked her.

'No, because I needed a fresh set of eyes on them, and I value your opinion and experience. Do you miss the job?'

'No,' he'd lied to his wife, 'but I'll do this to help you.'

'Then thank you.' She'd kissed him. For some reason he had been annoyed, but now he knew she was right, and that she'd read him better than he had himself. He looked forward to seeing her, even more than he usually did when she arrived home and kissed the kids; now he looked forward to seeing her as an equal rather than as a stay-at-home house husband. She knew him so well and that was one of the many reasons he loved her so much.

Tom slowed for a herd of cows crossing the road in the middle of the sprawling township of Mkhulu, then again for the police speed trap he knew would be around the bend ahead. The last thing he needed was to be delayed by a bribe-seeking traffic cop when he was on his way to help with a police investigation. He waved to the traffic officer as he passed the speed camera, and accelerated to eighty kilometres per hour as he left the houses and roadside stalls behind and started seeing bush again.

He passed Elephant Point and Hippo Rock, other estates similar to Sabiepark, where locals and foreigners kept holiday homes in the bush on the verge of the Kruger Park. He thought it might be nice for he and Sannie to buy a house in one of these places, maybe, if they lost the farm. On some of these bushveld estates owners were limited to spending six months or less in their houses, so that the estates could be kept as peaceful bushveld retreats. Maybe they could spend the balance of the year in a townhouse in one of the newer developments in White River or, once the kids were older, travelling the world.

He remembered Sannie in a bikini on their honeymoon, on the beach in Pomene in Mozambique, the kids staying at her mother's house in Johannesburg. He pictured them on a Greek island, just the two of them. It had been a few weeks since they'd had sex; he wondered if it was the stress of the parallel investigations Sannie had been working, the unsolved murder and the women who had been robbing houses. He hadn't pushed the issue or tried to initiate it, but maybe she'd been waiting for him to make the first move? When they'd married they hadn't been able to keep their hands off each other, both starved for physical intimacy since their respective partners had died. Tom's wife had passed away from cancer about a year before he'd met Sannie. Well, he was dressed as a safari guide and had his own open Land Rover – if he couldn't get himself a hot chick tonight then he was a disgrace to the khaki-clad species. He smiled, his mood lightening again. The sky was a perfect, clear blue, and the dry bush was thin enough for him to see the Sabie River and the Kruger Park beyond, off to his right.

Tom approached the access road turnoff on the left that led to the Shaw's Gate entrance to the Sabi Sand Game Reserve. He searched the bush; there was no one loitering in the area and no parked vehicles that he could see. It was still half an hour until the agreed rendezvous between Hudson Brand and Linley Brown, which would take place on the corner he had just glimpsed.

Other than a harem of a dozen or more female impala and their chaperoning ram there were no animals to be seen in the game reserve. On Tom's right he could see the thatch-roofed houses of Sabiepark. Two kilometres on he turned right into the driveway of the estate. Sannie was standing by the reception buildings, her white Mercedes sedan and a police *bakkie* parked to one side.

As Tom turned into the estate he saw in his rear-view mirror a tan Land Cruiser with Zimbabwean plates pulling up behind him. Sannie was surrounded by a semicircle of people, including Mavis, a white couple dressed in khaki and green safari wear, and two police officers in blue-grey uniforms. A couple of security officers in green looked on from the estate's boom gate.

Sannie looked over at the sound of his arrival. Tom switched off the engine and climbed down. She smiled at him. She was wearing jeans, flat-soled brown leather boots that came to her knees and a long-sleeved T-shirt. It had to be pushing twenty-eight degrees Celsius, but Tom knew that Lowveld people considered anything under thirty to be the dead of winter. Despite the heat she looked cool and sexy.

'Everyone, for those who don't know him, this is my husband, Tom Furey. Tom worked as a detective in the UK and he's going to be driving Jaapie and Elmarie today.' Tom shook hands with Sergeant Jaapie de Beer, and said hi to Warrant Officer Elmarie de Bruin, who he'd met a couple of times before socially. Sannie introduced him to sergeants Ngwenya and Valoyi from Skukuza police station, who had been brought in to transport the suspects to Nelspruit in their *bakkie* once the arrests were made.

A tall, dark man dressed similarly to Tom in shorts and bush shirt came up to them from the parked Land Cruiser behind.

'Everyone, this is Mr Hudson Brand. He's our point of contact with Linley Brown, and he's kindly agreed to help us.'

Brand tipped the brim of his cap and said, 'Howdy.'

Tom wasn't sure what to make of the man. He knew Sannie had questioned him twice over the murder of the prostitute whose body had been found near the Phabeni Gate entrance to Kruger. Sannie had nightmares sometimes and Tom thought they were to do with that case – she hadn't experienced them before. It had been her first murder case after going back on the job fulltime and while she'd dealt with other similarly horrific crimes he knew she hated that her first remained unsolved. Brand was wanted for questioning by the Zimbabweans about another murder in Victoria Falls, and Tom knew Sannie also wanted to talk to him about a third killing, in Cape Town. Brand was tall and handsome, in a craggy, rugged sort of way.

'Ma'am,' Brand said by way of greeting to Tom's wife.

Sannie said, 'Your clients, they're safely locked away somewhere?'

Brand nodded. 'In the Protea Hotel just down the road a ways. I told them I was going to meet you before seeing Linley Brown. I neglected to mention I'd be seeing Linley in half an hour. You agree that they can talk to Miss Brown once she's in custody?'

'As we discussed on the phone, when Linley Brown is due to receive visitors she can elect to see Mr and Mrs Cliff if she chooses. It's still up to Miss Brown.'

'They'll have to live with that,' Brand said.

Sannie introduced the rest of the team to Brand and explained the plan, referring to a mud map she had sketched in the dirt at her feet with a stick. Five minutes before Hudson Brand was due to rendezvous with Linley Brown Tom would drive his game viewer along the access road to Shaw's Gate, with Elmarie and Jaapie in the back posing as tourists. They would look for Linley Brown and, if they saw her, try and arrest her on the spot. It was more likely, however, that Linley would be hiding somewhere, perhaps in the bush in the communal grazing land that bordered the Sabi Sand reserve. The access road ran parallel to some eight kilometres of fence line before it actually met the Shaw's Gate entrance to the reserve.

'If Linley stays in hiding until Mr Brand shows up then Tom, Elmarie and Jaapie will drive to the gate and wait there. The only roads away from the rendezvous point lead to Shaw's Gate,' Sannie tapped a stone marking the gate to the north of the map, 'the Paul Kruger Gate entrance to the national park here, to the east; and the R536 heading to Hazyview to the west.'

She explained that the two uniformed officers would set up a mock speed trap five kilometres to the west, towards Hazyview, and act as a blocking force in case Linley Brown had a getaway vehicle ready to spirit her away after her meeting with Brand. 'To get to the Kruger Gate and disappear into the national park she has to get past me, here at base at Sabiepark, and past the security officers on the gate itself, who have been alerted to our operation. If she tries to disappear into the Sabi Sand reserve then Tom, Jaapie and Elmarie will stop her or, if she heads into the bush, they can give chase off road. Any questions?'

'Do we know if she's got any friends or associates?' Tom asked.

Sannie shook her head. 'No, but she had to get from White River, where the police last saw her, to this area. Unless she negotiated the local taxi system she might have stolen a car or hitchhiked or even paid a local safari operator to bring her here. She's a Zimbabwean who was living a fairly transient lifestyle here in South Africa while robbing homes for a living. We expect her support network to be limited, but she's clever, pretty, and she's evaded police several times before, so it's possible she's conned someone into helping her.'

Sannie distributed colour copies of the portrait photograph from the passport they had found in the White River house. 'This passport was issued recently, but as Linley is on the run it's possible she's altered her appearance. She may have cut her hair and probably dyed it. She's about 1.6 metres tall.'

While everyone on the team studied the picture Sannie asked Brand if she could have a word in private, and she beckoned Tom over as well as she moved to a euphorbia tree a few metres away. 'You've agreed to come to Nelspruit police station after this operation is over, and I appreciate that,' Sannie said.

'And you've agreed to take a statement from me for the Zimbabwean police.'

'Reluctantly, yes, Mr Brand. They haven't got around to issuing a warrant for your arrest so I can't take you into custody for something they want to question you about but, as you can imagine, I'm interested in hearing your version of events.'

'I understand. I saw Patrick de Villiers today.'

Sannie raised her eyebrows. 'Really.'

Brand explained that he had been in the lobby of the Protea Hotel Kruger Gate, just down the road, when a Toyota Quantum minibus had pulled up. It was De Villiers, who was running a transfer for some guests from the hotel into a lodge in the Sabi Sand.

'He told me the Zimbabwean police had let him go – something about a cast-iron alibi involving a Swedish backpacker. I don't think he was very happy that I gave his name to Sergeant Goodness Khumalo. He threatened to kill me and probably would have if the concierge wasn't there.'

'I see,' Sannie said. 'I spoke to the good sergeant today and she told me the same story, that you had tipped her off about Patrick and that she had interviewed him. She's not a detective and she's fighting an internal battle with her colleagues to try to stay on the case. The detective in charge hasn't returned my calls since I spoke to Khumalo. They let De Villiers go and he flew back yesterday – he had been driving a one-way overland trip from Johannesburg to Victoria Falls.'

'Are you going to question him?' Brand asked.

She stared into his eyes. 'That's my business.'

'He was in all the same places I was, and I know I didn't rape and kill those women,' Brand said. 'If I were you I'd take a closer look at him; we both know alibis can be faked.'

'We can discuss all of this later,' Sannie said. 'My first priority is to arrest Linley Brown, and then your clients can talk to her in the cells after I've charged her, assuming Brown wants to see them. We can discuss your theory about De Villiers then. Now, one other thing, I want you to wear a wire today, so that we can gather some evidence about Brown before she's arrested.'

Brand shook his head. 'No dice. The first thing Linley will do is check me for a listening device. She's smart, like you say, and she already half suspects a setup. I bought a spare mobile phone and last night I dropped it in the grass under a prominent tree near the RV point. I'm expecting her to search me and get me to hand over my phone, and then if her plan is to abandon me by the side of the road and hijack my truck I'll call you as soon as she's gone.'

'And if she takes you hostage?' Tom asked.

'Then she's only got three ways to go by road, and you've got them all covered. You know she won't get far if she pulls a stunt like that,' Brand said. 'My guess is that she's put her trust in me because she thinks she has no choice if she wants to get her money. She has no reason to suspect I know about her criminal past or that I'm working with you.'

Cars whizzed by, mostly holiday-makers on their way to the Kruger National Park. There was plenty of wilderness around here into which a person could disappear, Tom thought, but if Linley tried something stupid, like hijacking a car, then Sannie could call on police and national parks helicopters to track her. He reminded himself they were on the trail of a young woman who stole mobile phones and laptops from homes, not a murderess.

'OK, it's time we were in position.'

'Yes, ma'am,' said Brand.

Tom held back as Brand went to his Land Cruiser and Jaapie and Elmarie climbed up into the back of Tom's borrowed game viewer. 'You think Brand will stick to his end of the bargain and voluntarily come to the station? He might decide it's better to run off with Linley Brown.'

Sannie stood with her hands on her hips and watched Brand turn his vehicle around in the estate's driveway. 'The thought had crossed my mind. If he *is* guilty then I agree he might try and slip through our fingers. I guess we'll just have to cross that bridge when we come to it.'

Tom smiled. 'You've thought of everything, haven't you? There's no way either of them is going to escape today, is there?'

'There's one more way out of here, and neither Hudson Brand nor Linley Brown is taking it.'

'Let me buy you dinner tonight,' Tom said on impulse.

'Why do you think I invited you to take part in this operation?'

'Why do you think I asked the Oberholzers to pick up the kids this afternoon and keep them until tomorrow midday?'

It was her turn to smile. She leaned close to him and whispered: 'Let's book into a hotel.'

'OK, but only if I get to wear my safari outfit.'

*

Brand checked the Garmin sat nav on the dashboard of the Land Cruiser and ascertained he was in the right spot, on a sharp bend in the dirt access road to Shaw's Gate, just off and out of sight of the R536. He switched off the engine and opened the driver's door to let in what little warm breeze was ruffling the dry grass.

A few minutes later, on schedule, Tom Furey slowed his Land Rover game viewer and waved to Brand. By pre-arranged signal Brand gave Tom an overt thumbs up, as if to say that he wasn't broken down and didn't need assistance. Jaapie had his arm around his detective colleague, Elmarie, and they ignored the two drivers just as two tourists would. Brand wondered idly if it was all an act or if there was something going on between the two officers. Tom's vehicle accelerated and left a lingering dust cloud to settle over Brand's truck.

He got out of the vehicle and looked around him. The tinderbox dry bush seemed deserted. He walked to the tall fence that marked the border of the Sabi Sand Game Reserve and the greater Kruger National Park. It was made of strands of barbed and electrified wire. Brand heard voices and engines.

He walked around the bend and could instantly see that a traffic jam had formed about two hundred metres along the fence line. He went back to the Land Cruiser and got his binoculars. Tom Furey was stuck behind half a dozen other vehicles, *bakkies* and minivans and a couple of cars. On the other side of the fence Brand saw what the commotion was about – lions jockeyed for position around the carcass of a freshly killed buffalo. In contrast with the dull tones of the rest of the reserve a neat swathe of bright green short grass ran along the fence, indicating where a controlled burn had taken place. The fresh shoots, nourished by underground water, had attracted the buffalo and the lions had probably run the hapless creature into the fence, trapping it there.

The plan risked becoming unstuck already. Linley Brown might panic at the sight of so many people near her chosen rendezvous spot. She might reason, correctly, that a couple of undercover police officers might easily hide themselves in the gaggle of tradesmen and tourists in transit who had come to feast on the spectacle.

On the other hand, Linley was a child of Africa and she would know that stuff like this happened in the bush. No one could predict where lions would make a kill. Perhaps Linley was at this moment in the throng watching the lions from this side of the fence. He saw several young females who might fit her general description, but couldn't positively identify her from this distance.

On the other side of the fence were three green-painted Land Rovers from lodges within the Sabi Sand arrayed side-on in a half circle around the pride, each about five metres from the nearest lion in order to give the tourists on board the best possible viewing. One of the guides was waving and calling something to the people on the outside, probably telling them to move along. However, the access road was public and the gawkers showed no sign of leaving any time soon. Brand swung his binoculars again and saw Tom Furey talking on a cell phone, presumably to his wife.

'Hey!' a voice called. 'Hudson?'

Brand lowered the binoculars and turned to face the direction the man's voice had come from. A young man in khaki shorts and shirt with a pair of binoculars slung across his body stepped from behind a grey termite mound about twenty metres inside the reserve, on the other side of the fence, and waved to him, a walkie-talkie in one hand.

'Over here, come to the fence.'

"You do know there's a pride of lions just up the perimeter road a ways?' Brand said. As he came closer to the fence he recognised the man. 'Bryce Duffy? How the hell did you get mixed up in this?'

Bryce flattened himself on the side of the mound furthest from the lions. 'Yes, Hudson, I had noticed the lions. It's a long story.'

Brand stopped by the fence and kept an eye on the action further away. So, Linley Brown had hitched herself to young Duffy. He could see why they might find each other attractive, however he'd always thought of Bryce as a straight shooter; it surprised him that Duffy would get involved with a criminal. 'You do know what Linley's been up to, and why I'm here?'

He nodded. 'She's on the run from a crazy boyfriend, a cop who framed her for a series of crimes she didn't commit. She needs to see you and sign some papers about an insurance claim relating to her dead friend, but she's worried that you might be working with the police.'

Brand exhaled. He wondered what other lies she'd been telling. 'Bryce, buddy, you're being played. The cops are after her because she's a thief, but I've come alone, and I don't know anything about a crazy boyfriend. Where is she?'

'Around.' Bryce looked like he was wrestling with the new information.

'That's not good enough for me, or the insurance company. I have to visually identify her and get her to sign an affidavit before they'll approve her claim. Call her on your radio or go get her, Bryce. You've done your job, the coast is clear.'

'Not so fast.' Bryce peered around the mound to make sure the lions weren't watching, then moved slowly to the fence. 'You can talk to her on my walkie-talkie.'

'That won't do, Bryce,' Brand said. 'She probably hasn't told you, but Linley's friend, Kate, who died in the car crash they were both involved in, tried to fake her death a few days before she died for real. Linley was party to insurance fraud, even though her subsequent claim appears to be legitimate. I've got to interview her and get some answers for the record before the insurers will pay.'

Brand saw the confusion on the young man's face. Clearly Linley Brown had only told him as much of her story as she needed to get him to work for her.

'Why didn't Linley come herself?' Brand pushed.

Bryce shrugged. He wasn't a good criminal, or a good deceiver. 'You said yourself, you suspect her and her friend of trying to defraud someone.' He unslung his binoculars and looked at the vehicles outside the reserve, still parked and watching the lion kill. 'Odd, don't you think, that the woman in that last game viewer is watching you through a pair of binoculars?'

'I don't know what you're talking about,' Brand said, silently cursing to himself.

'You and I both know that's Greg Mahoney's Land Rover up there, but it's not him driving. I called Greg a little while ago and made up a story that I'd had a breakdown and wanted to borrow his Landy; he told me it was in the garage in Nelspruit.'

'Maybe he didn't want to hurt your feelings.'

Bryce shook his head. 'You get on the phone or the radio to your undercover police friends up there in Greg's game viewer and you tell them Linley's gone. If you want to do the right thing, then give me her papers to sign.'

'She's on the run from the law, son. Her partner in crime assaulted a police officer while Linley was trying to get away. She was going to help her friend fake her own death and that friend died. Maybe you should ask her, and yourself while you're at it, what the *right thing* is.'

Brand brought his own binoculars up and focused on the game viewer while Bryce stood there, thinking. Elmarie, the detective, perhaps realising her blunder, was staring resolutely at the lions. The traffic jam was breaking up and he could see why. Three of the lionesses, perhaps sated on their share of the buffalo, had left the kill and were walking up a slight rise to where the trees started again, away from the cleared area along the fence. He swung the binoculars to the right, to take in the game-viewing vehicles within the reserve. Two of the vehicles were shifting to follow the walking lionesses, but the third was still stationary. Oddly it had only one occupant, a female ranger, who was looking his way. Although she wasn't blonde she looked a lot like the woman in the emailed photo he'd received from Dani, and the passport photo that Van Rensburg had distributed.

'Why don't you call Linley on the radio and have her drive that vehicle over here and we'll talk.'

'What vehicle?'

'Don't try and bluff me, Bryce. I saw the brunette driving the game viewer by herself. It doesn't make sense that a guide would be out on her own in the middle of the peak game-driving time. You and I both know that the lodges might send rangers out as spotters, to find game, or let them go have a look at interesting sightings in their own time, but that would be in the middle of the day. Call her on that radio of yours and get her to take that wig off and come see me.'

'Give me the papers. Let me sign for her.' Bryce was quickly losing his cool. He looked towards the vehicle that Brand was now sure was being driven by Linley Brown.

'No. Let's see what sort of a guide *you* are, Bryce.' Brand lowered the binoculars and started running.

28

'Crazy fuck,' I said to myself. Hudson Brand, if that was who I thought it was, started to run along the fence line, waving his arms in the air and screaming something indecipherable at the top of his voice. It almost sounded like he was saying, 'Here, kitty, kitty, kitty', but that would have been insane.

The other guides and the people watching the lions from outside the reserve were livid and most of them started yelling at Brand to stop, and calling him some foul names in the process.

My first thought was for Bryce. Brand had run fifty metres in our direction and was now turning to run back along the fence towards the termite mound where Bryce had been hiding. At the sound of the mad man's ranting the lion pride had instantly focused their attention on him. The two lionesses and four cubs still on the kill got off their fat bellies and stared fixedly at Brand. With a silent signal the females moved away from the commotion, the cubs trotting after them on their stubby little legs. The three that had been walking away from the kill towards the waterhole at the airstrip, less than a kilometre away over the rise, went to ground in the long yellow grass.

'Shit.' I put the Landy in gear and drove towards Bryce. Brand was slowing to a jog and I noticed the black backs of three sets of ears as the lionesses raised their heads to follow his progress. The number one rule of the bush is not to run, and Brand was giving a lesson on why this was so. The killing team began to stalk him, tails extended, fluffy tips twitching. Brand was safe on the outside of the fence, but Bryce was on the same side as the lions. The bastard was setting him up to be eaten. I floored the accelerator.

'I'm coming,' I said into the radio mounted in the Land Rover's dashboard.

'This maniac's trying to get me killed,' Bryce replied.

I saw Bryce just then. He was on top of the termite mound, climbing a tree that was growing out of it. He hoisted himself into the lower branches as Brand stopped near him, across the fence. The lionesses paused. In a few bounds they would be on the rise, clawing at his feet; the tree was not a big one and Bryce didn't have much more room to climb.

'Hah!' I yelled, waving with one hand as I drove at the lions. The trio looked at me and moved away, but not far. They were irked by the noise, but hadn't run off. I knew that we humans, Brand, Bryce and I, were inside their 'fight' zone now, as they hadn't taken the 'flight' option. 'Go away!'

I drove up onto the lower slope of the mound and stopped.

'*Go away?* Did you learn that in Zimbabwe as a child, Linley?' said an exasperated Bryce.

He clambered down out of the tree and jumped into the front seat of the game viewer beside me. A lioness snarled at the vehicle and took three steps towards us. 'I think a thank you is in order,' I said.

'We've got to get out of here. I spotted some undercover cops in a game viewer. They're heading for Shaw's Gate,' he said.

'Shit,' I said. The cops would know that we couldn't get out of the Sabi Sand Game Reserve without using one of the gates, or driving our Land Rover through a highly electrified fence. The vehicle was tough, but I doubted it – or we – would survive a brush with razor wire and several thousand volts without serious damage. The Shaw's Gate Entrance was still about eight kilometres up the road and the police would then have to double back almost as far again to get to the airstrip once they entered; we had about twenty minutes at the most, assuming they guessed where we were heading.

'Linley, how bad is it, what you've done?' Bryce asked me as we jolted our way back to the game-viewing road. 'Brand says you're a thief.'

'Left or right?' I said as we came to a T-junction.

He sighed. 'Right. Answer me.'

'Pretty bad.'

'We can get a good lawyer. My parents have got money, and –'

'Bryce, I'm a criminal, OK? My friend and I robbed innocent people's homes. She's been locked up by the police. I'm a barely reformed drug addict; I still crave it all the time. Fuck – I'll probably end up back on prescription painkillers the way my life is going. The short version is that I need to get out of this country and I need to disappear.' An impala started to cross the road in front of me and I swerved hard to miss it. I was driving way faster than the reserve's speed limit.

'That man who's after you, Brand, he said you and your friend – Kate I think he said her name was – were setting up some kind of insurance scam. Is that true, Linley? Is that another reason the police want you?'

Brand had not wasted his limited time with Bryce. 'Yes, that's true. Kate wanted to fake her own death and name me as the beneficiary. We were going to split the proceeds and she was going to disappear. She had some shit of her own she wanted to get away from. Unfortunately, Kate died for real. Brand's an investigator for the insurance company, that's why he's following . . .'

I started to sniff. The tears came to my eyes despite me rubbing them with the back of my hand and taking a deep breath. I felt so goddamned tired. The littlest thing could set me off. I thought I was getting over the accident, but there it was again, the flames engulfing the car, my hands burning on the glass of the window. The terrible smell came back to me and I gagged.

Bryce leaned over and put a hand on my shoulder. 'I want to help you.'

I coughed and spat, and sniffed up my tears. I had to focus and I had to drive. 'No you don't, Bryce, you need to find a nice South African girl or a pretty tourist and go manage a luxury lodge in the bush somewhere.'

The Land Rover bounced through a rut and Bryce gripped the dashboard. 'No, I don't want a tourist, I want you.'

I forced a laugh and felt bad when I saw the hurt look on his face. He wasn't joking. He was like a puppy with those dark eyes and I would never feel like I was good enough to deserve his love, or to repay the kindness he had shown me, not if we lived together for the rest of our lives and had beautiful babies. 'I'm sorry. You're sweet, Bryce, but as they say in the classics, I'm no good for you.'

I checked my watch. Ahead of us was the long strip of black tarmac that marked the airstrip where light aircraft and regular charter flights dropped and collected guests for the luxury safari lodges in this part of the Sabi Sand Game Reserve. A sign indicated no driving on the airstrip, but I turned onto it and straddled the centre line as I geared down and floored the accelerator.

We whizzed past the terminal building, which was little more than a shady shell for people to wait in, though no one was visible within. I raced to the far end of the airstrip to wait. I didn't want to risk a lodge vehicle arriving at the building and Bryce bumping into someone else he knew, and having to deal with awkward questions about who I was and what we were doing there. Also, I guessed the police were probably all over the reserve's local radio network telling any ranger who heard them to be on the lookout for us.

I checked my watch and scanned the empty blue sky.

'I don't have my passport with me, so I can't force myself onto Andrew's aircraft and come with you, Linley. At least tell me where you're going, so that maybe I can come looking for you sometime.'

He really was in love. 'Mozambique.'

'I won't tell the police, honest.'

'I know you won't.' I leaned over and kissed him, on the lips, but when he opened his mouth and tried to embrace me I pulled back. I was not out of this, or out of South Africa yet, not by a long shot. I touched his cheek. 'I know you won't tell, Bryce, but don't get yourself locked up on my account.'

He shrugged and forced a smile. 'I'll tell the truth, that you carjacked me at gunpoint and I was helpless to do anything other than what you told me to do.'

'Good boy.'

'Please don't patronise me, Linley.'

'I'm sorry.' And I was. 'I'm so sorry, Bryce.' I felt the pain, as real as any heart attack. 'I . . .'

I heard the drone of a plane engine from far off and took the guide's binoculars from the centre console box between us. I scanned the sky and saw the speck coming towards us.

'What?' Bryce asked.

'Nothing. Here comes the plane.'

Bryce slumped back in his seat. He was finally growing tired of the way I was playing him. He would tell the police where I was going, probably because he thought it was the right thing to do and that I would be safer in custody than on the run. He might have been right, but I wasn't going to take the chance. I put my palm on his chest and felt his warm heart beating. 'OK. I'm going to Vilanculos, then catching a boat to the *Ilha dos Sonhos*, the Island of Dreams. Do you know it?'

His puppy eyes brightened again. 'I do. They've fixed up the old hotel there and reopened it. I'll come find you there, once things settle down here.'

'That would be good.' Despite all the degrading things I had done, and those that had been done to me, I don't think I ever felt as disgusted in myself as I did right then, lying to him.

He reached over and took my hand. 'Linley, this may sound crazy. I've only known you a short time and, well, it was pretty hectic how we met. But, I think . . . I mean, I really care for you. I think I . . .'

I lifted my other hand and put my forefinger to his lips. 'Shush.' I couldn't bear to hear what I thought he was about to say. This would have to be the last time I ever saw this good, gorgeous, sensitive man. I needed him not to follow me. 'Thank you, Bryce, for all you've done for me. I'm grateful, but I don't love you. I'm sorry.'

He looked away from me, out at the bush.

29

Sannie sat in the driver's seat of her car with the door open, at the entrance to Sabiepark, listening to the radio traffic.

'Sannie, this is Mavis, over.'

Sannie keyed the microphone. 'Go, Mavis.'

'I'm in the terminal building. Linley Brown and an unidentified white male just drove past me in a Land Rover game viewer. They're parked at the end of the runway. Do you want me to try and arrest them?'

Sannie thought about Mavis's request. She had already told Tom and the undercover detectives to head for the airstrip as quickly as they could; they had a circuitous route to get to the reserve gate and would then have to double back to the airstrip. When she and Tom had pored over the maps of the Sabi Sand Game Reserve the private airstrip had leapt out at her. It would be the perfect way for Linley to get away, which was why Sannie had posted Mavis there. 'The others are on their way to you, Mavis. They shouldn't be more than twenty minutes. Keep Brown and the man under surveillance. If you try and walk or drive to them that might spook them and they might drive off into the bush. They're waiting for an aircraft, for sure. If that aeroplane arrives do not let it take off. Do you copy, Mavis?'

'Affirmative. And for the record, I'm not walking anywhere, not with all these lions roaming around here.'

Sannie smiled. Mavis had confided to her that she had only ever been to the Kruger Park once in her life, on a church outing when she was younger. She had never been into the Sabi Sand Game Reserve and made no secret of the fact that she was terrified of wild animals.

Sannie radioed Tom and gave him an update, confirming that Linley and the man were waiting at the airstrip. 'Hurry, Tom,' she added. 'Mavis is worried she's going to get eaten before you get there.'

'*Roger*,' said Tom.

'*Sannie, this is Mavis, over.*'

Sannie acknowledged the call.

'*Sannie, a van has just pulled up outside the terminal. It looks like a tour guide. I thought there were no flights scheduled for the next couple of hours.*'

'That's affirmative,' Sannie said. She had checked with the Sabi Sand's warden's office. The regular Federal Air flight from Johannesburg was not due for a couple of hours and there were no notifications of private flights coming into the reserve for this time. The last thing she needed was civilians getting caught up in an arrest, especially if Mavis or Tom had to try to forcibly stop an aircraft from taking off. This could get messy. 'Find out who they are, Mavis, and I'll double-check with the warden's office. It might just be some tour guide or travel agent doing a recce. Try to send them away. We also don't want to spook Linley Brown.'

'*Affirmative*,' Mavis replied. '*Leave it with me.*'

Sannie called the warden's office on her mobile phone and relayed the news from Mavis. The assistant warden on duty confirmed there were no scheduled arrivals. Sannie wondered if the van was, in fact, part of Linley Brown's escape plan. She picked up the radio microphone and keyed it. 'Mavis, this is Sannie, over.'

She waited, but there was no reply. 'Mavis, this is Sannie, over.'

Sannie tried a third time and there was still no reply. Perhaps Mavis had inadvertently left her walkie-talkie in the terminal building while she spoke to the driver of the tour van.

They were still a step ahead of Linley Brown, though she wondered where Hudson Brand had ended up after he found himself on the wrong side of the fence. Sannie was about to call him on his cell phone when she heard the low drone of aero engines. Stepping out of her car she saw a twin-engine light aircraft fly low over her head.

'Mavis, this is Sannie, come in, please. There is an aircraft coming in to land, over.'

Again, there was no reply. She called Tom and asked where he was.

'In the reserve, but still about fifteen minutes out, I reckon,' Tom said. *'I heard you trying to call Mavis. I tried her as well, in case there was a problem with her radio, but I got no answer.'*

'I'm getting worried, Tom. Go as fast as you dare. There's an aircraft about to land and we can't let it take off.'

'Roger.'

She heard the rev of his engine over the radio, and the rush of wind around the open vehicle. She regretted telling him to hurry; if he hit a kudu or an impala and crashed she would never forgive herself. Game reserves were no places to speed. Sannie felt a rising tide of helplessness. She got back in the driver's seat, closed the door and started her engine. She put on the flashing light. There was no more she could do from outside the reserve and she needed to get to where the action was.

*

'Hudson Brand,' Bryce said to me, breaking the silence for the first time since I'd said I didn't love him. 'Look, he's coming out of the terminal building. Crazy fool must have got over the fence and followed us here on foot.'

I took the binoculars from Bryce. He was so damned handsome, I thought, and good, and considerate, and I hated having to force myself to be so callous and cruel to him. And now I was about to leave him for good. It had been torture waiting for Andrew Miles's aeroplane, but he had landed and was at the far end of the runway and turning around. Once the aircraft was facing us it stopped, engines still running, and Andrew turned his landing lights on and then off, flashing us a signal; he clearly wanted us to come to his end of the strip.

'Shit, I'll have to drive past Brand,' I said.

I put the Land Rover into gear and accelerated hard and fast, picking up speed as I crashed my way to fourth. Hudson Brand stood in the middle of the runway and raised his hand.

'He's got a gun!' Bryce said.

'He won't shoot.'

'For God's sake, Linley, stop!'

'It's a setup. Brand's working with the cops. This was never about getting me my money. I've got to get out of here.'

Brand's hand bucked twice from the pistol's kicks, and I heard the crack of the shots. The steering wheel twisted in my hands as the Land Rover slewed crazily down the runway. 'He's shot out a bloody tyre.'

I regained control and could hear the flattened tyre slapping the tarmac. Brand fired again and the other front tyre burst. Bryce knocked my hand away from the gear stick and reached over and pulled on the handbrake. 'You're going to kill us.'

Brand ran to us and Bryce got out of the truck, putting himself between the American and me. 'You're not taking her.'

'I'm the one with the gun, Bryce,' Brand said. 'I'll do the talking.'

Frustrated, I pulled off the black wig I'd borrowed from one of the lodge's maids. I glared at Brand. 'Who do you think you are, some kind of cowboy? All I want is the money I'm entitled to.'

In the distance, over the sound of the aircraft, I heard another engine approaching.

Bryce heard it too. 'We don't have time to waste.'

'There's a policewoman dead over there,' Brand said. 'She's got a broken neck, and Patrick de Villiers is in there with her, shot to death.'

'Who?' I asked.

'A local thug,' Bryce explained. 'Not a nice guy. But who killed them?'

The news shocked me. 'My God. How? Why?'

'I'm not sure, but you're going to help me answer those questions, and others.' Brand lowered his pistol.

'But the cops will be here any minute,' Bryce said.

I swallowed hard, trying not to let the instant flush of fear paralyse me. I thought I knew who might have been behind the killings. I looked from Bryce back to the private investigator. 'I don't care about the money now, but I'm not handing myself in to the police. This isn't just about a few burglaries.'

'I know it's not,' Brand replied. 'That's why you and I are going to talk. On the plane.'

'What?' said Bryce. 'You're going to help her get away? I thought you were working for the cops?'

Brand stuck his pistol in the belt of his shorts. 'I'm going to help myself get away too, for now. When the police arrive they're going to try to pin one or both of those killings on me. Let's go, Linley.'

Andrew Miles, tired of waiting, had released the brakes on his aircraft and was moving slowly down the runway towards us. The three of us started running towards the machine. I thought about Bryce, being left at the scene of a double killing. He had committed no felony, and he could tell the police the truth, that I had hijacked him and forced him to help me. Andrew stopped beside us and left the pilot's seat. A side door opened a few seconds later.

'What the hell's going on?' he asked.

'No time for explanations, Andrew,' I said. 'And we've got a new passenger. Meet Hudson Brand.'

Bryce still had his binoculars around his neck. He raised them, tracking a cloud of dust. 'It's a game viewer. Probably those undercover police.'

'Police?' Andrew said.

'I'd get back in the pilot's seat, if I were you,' Brand said. He lifted his shirt to show the butt of his pistol.

'No need for that kind of thing.' Andrew leaned out of the door, took my hand and helped me up the steps. Once I was aboard Andrew clambered back up front into the pilot's seat.

'Bryce . . .' I said, looking down at him as Hudson Brand climbed into the aircraft. I had an enormous desire to jump out of the plane and rush into his arms, but I couldn't. I'd be sent to prison and that would help neither of us.

'Goodbye, Linley,' he said.

Brand reached behind me and started hauling on the hatch. 'OK, boarding's now closed.'

Brand locked the door and I slumped into a seat. Andrew brought the engines up to full pitch and released the brakes. The nimble aircraft leapt away like a cheetah pursuing an impala. I looked out the small perspex window and saw the game viewer with the three people on board bounce off the dirt and onto the tarmac runway.

The Beechcraft left the ground and Andrew banked hard and low over Sabiepark, across the road. I could see Bryce, still watching us disappear as the game viewer made a U-turn and headed back to him.

*

Sannie drove with her blue light flashing along the R536 and then onto the dirt access road to Shaw's Gate. A couple of senior guys from the Sabi Sand's security company were at the gate to let her through quickly. She drove as fast as she dared through the reserve, doubling back along the perimeter road to the airstrip. All plans could be improved with hindsight and she wished now she had set up her command post inside the Sabi Sand Game Reserve, closer to the airstrip, but it had only been a suspicion that Linley would try to escape by air; if her quarry had met Hudson Brand outside the reserve then Sannie would have been trapped inside.

She had tried calling Mavis repeatedly, and while the lack of comms could have been something as simple as a flat battery or faulty police radio, in her heart of hearts she knew something terrible had happened even before Elmarie radioed. Sannie's last fulltime stint in the police had almost ended in the deaths of two of her children, and she had harboured a secret fear that her return to the force would be similarly traumatic.

Tom was outside the terminal building and walked over to the car as she pulled up. He was the one good thing that had come out of her former life as a policewoman. She could see that he wanted to hug her now, to comfort her, but he knew, as did she, that her duty was to see Mavis. She opened the boot of the car, took a pair of latex gloves from the box and put them on. Sannie remembered how Mavis had been sick when she'd seen her first body, that of the dead prostitute. Had that woman's killer been responsible for Mavis's death? Sannie forced herself not to jump to conclusions.

She took a deep breath and walked to the terminal, but had to put a hand on the door frame to steady herself as she let her eyes become accustomed to the cool gloom inside. She forced herself not to rush to her partner's side; this was a crime scene and she needed to respect it. Tom, Elmarie and Jaapie were waiting outside.

Patrick de Villiers lay on his back in a pool of sticky, drying blood, his eyes wide. A wicked-looking folding knife with a bone handle lay on the screed concrete floor by his right hand. There appeared to be two gunshot wounds, one in his belly and one in his heart. *Good shooting, Mavis.*

She knelt beside the body of her partner. Such a smart, promising young woman. Sannie ran her fingers lightly over the ligature marks on Mavis's neck, avoiding the gaze of her lifeless eyes. It was too early to tell, but she wondered if forensics would find traces of the same rope fibres as those found on the other victims. *Did he pack the rope especially?*

Unless Patrick had dropped the knife on the floor earlier, exactly where his dead hand would fall, there was no way he could have strangled Mavis with a piece of rope from behind. And if he had been behind her, there was no way Mavis could have drawn her gun and reached back to shoot him in the heart. Had she perhaps fought him off after he'd crept up behind her and begun to strangle her, and then got the drop on him? Perhaps then De Villiers had pulled his knife and come at her, and she'd shot him.

Sannie shook her head. None of those scenarios made sense. Patrick was maybe twice Mavis's weight and had the physique of a bodybuilder; she was slight and slender. If he'd got a rope around her neck there was no way she could have fought him off. If she'd been able to draw her gun she might have been able to shoot him in the foot, or back up into his head, but there were only the two bullet casings on the concrete floor. There was no rope visible at the scene; someone had taken it, she realised.

'Someone else was here.' Sannie looked around for the source of the voice and saw her husband silhouetted in the doorway. 'Sorry,' he added. 'Didn't want to disturb you.'

'It's OK,' she said. 'I'd just come to the same conclusion. Patrick de Villiers was present in all three locations where the prostitutes were killed – Nelspruit and Cape Town, and then again in Victoria Falls last week.'

'And so was Hudson Brand,' Tom said.

'Yes.' She looked down at Mavis again, this time unable to avoid those once beautiful dark eyes, now locked in a gaze of eternal terror. 'I never thought that there might be two killers.'

'You said there was bad blood between them,' Tom reminded her, 'that they'd been in a fight after Brand shot the poacher in the park.'

'They wouldn't be the first partnership to fight.'

'True,' Tom said. 'But Brand shopped De Villiers to the Zimbabwean police. Does that make sense?'

Sannie shrugged. They were dealing with a psychopath or two, not a 'mastermind' as the press liked to call repeat offenders. 'Brand might have just wanted Patrick locked up; he might have enough contacts in Zimbabwe to get a hit put on Patrick in prison.

As it was, Patrick got away thanks to a possibly fabricated alibi, and Brand killed him the first chance he got. Patrick wasn't to know there was a police operation going down here.'

'Maybe, but we're not in the business of believing in coincidences. Whatever the case, Brand certainly didn't do himself any favours by jumping on that aircraft with a wanted woman. We saw him climb aboard just as we got here.'

'No, he didn't do himself any favours.' Sannie placed the backs of her fingers against Mavis's cold cheek. *I let you down, my friend. I should have seen this coming. There is more to this than Tom and I can see right now, but we will find who did this to you.* '*Hamba kahle*, Mavis.'

'What will you do now?' Tom asked his wife.

'We go to work and we find out who did this, and why.'

'*We?*' Tom asked.

'Mavis is dead, Tom. I need help. I need my partner.'

30

The aircraft droned over the Lebombo hills and into Mozambican airspace. Andrew turned to port, heading north. Brand opened his email program on his phone and scrolled back to the emails he had received from Dani at the start of the case. It seemed a lot longer ago than it was. He found the message that Dani had forwarded from Peter Cliff, with the photo of Linley Brown and Kate Munns attached.

The picture, which he hadn't looked at since he'd sat by the Sabie River in Skukuza, showed two young women, both blonde, smiling. The email from Peter Cliff had identified Linley Brown as the woman on the left and Kate Munns as on the right.

He looked from the image to the woman sitting next to him in the aircraft. He held up the phone so she could see what he had been looking at. 'You really are Linley Brown,' he said. The passport picture Sannie van Rensburg had handed out also showed a true image.

While Linley and Kate did look somewhat alike, there was no doubt he was looking at the woman on the left. 'You were expecting Kate?'

Brand used his thumb and index finger on the touch screen

to enlarge the image. He wanted to look into the eyes of the two women, and the one sitting opposite him. He had trouble using such features on the phone – his fingers were too big – and before he could zoom in on the two faces, the image froze, zoomed in further down, over Linley's hands, clasped in front of her. Brand looked from the phone to the woman, and back again. He searched her real eyes. 'I don't know what to expect in this case. I do know that Kate did try to fake her own death, before she died for real. I found Dr Rodriguez.'

She nodded. 'Ah yes, her. I'm not surprised she rolled over on us. She didn't seem very trustworthy.'

Brand returned his phone to his pocket. 'Why did Kate want to fake her own death? What was she running away from?' Brand asked over the noise of the engine.

'Get me my money and I'll tell you.'

'That seems very mercenary of you, Linley. What about your late friend?'

'She wanted me to have it; at least, she wanted me to have my share.'

'What was she going to do with hers?' Brand glanced out the window of the aircraft. Way off to their right was the blue haze of the Indian Ocean. Andrew had told them they would follow the coast north, to Pemba, and refuel there. The trip to Kenya would take eight hours. He had plenty of time to learn the truth.

'She had issues, OK? Kate presented as Miss Goody-Two-Shoes to the outside world, but she'd done stuff she was ashamed of, stuff that would have hurt her family if they'd known about it. She wanted out, and she wanted to start with a clean slate somewhere. Now, give me whatever papers you need me to sign.'

Brand looked into those eyes and saw the truth. 'There are no papers; that was a white lie. But the insurance company is concerned about the call you or Kate made to them on the day Kate really died.'

She nodded. 'That bloody call. We put off making it; Elena had forward-dated the death certificate at our request but we couldn't put off making the call any more. We were trying to work out what I would say to Anna, to break the news, but we also needed to know how the claim process would work – neither of us had ever done such a thing, of course. But I didn't sign anything and, besides, the company *knows* we planned to defraud them. I'm sunk, aren't I? This was all just a lie to hand me over to the police.'

Brand shrugged. 'I honestly don't know if you'll get the money or not. Yes, you intended to commit a crime, but the company's unlikely to prosecute you. The lawyers and management are discussing it in London, trying to decide if your phone call constitutes making a fraudulent claim.'

'Call them, tell them I confessed to you that I was making a sick practical joke.'

He shook his head. 'No, I want more from you before I make any calls on your behalf.'

'You're double dipping, aren't you? You're working for the Cliffs as well as the insurance people.'

Brand said nothing.

She put a hand to her mouth, as if something suddenly dawned on her. 'Peter and Anna – they're here in Africa, aren't they? He's here . . .'

Brand nodded.

'What were you going to do, let them come see me in prison after the South African police had arrested me in your lame-arse little sting operation?'

'Yes.'

'I wouldn't have seen them. I've got nothing to say to them, especially her.'

'Anna? What's she done wrong?'

'Make the call.'

'Help me understand all this, Linley. I want out of this mess just as much as you do, but the Cliffs need closure.'

She scoffed. '*Closure?* That's such a ridiculous American word. How can you close an open wound that you know is going to be infected for life? How can finding out something that ruins two people's marriage bring "closure", if it means ending that relationship?'

Brand didn't know what she was talking about, but he didn't want to push her. He remained silent, hoping she would fill the void. She stared out the window of the aeroplane for a while, but eventually turned back to him. 'Kate's problems started a long time ago, back when she was a young girl.'

Brand waited and, eventually, Linley sighed and carried on. 'She and her sister were both abused by their father. He threatened to kill them if either of them said anything. Kate wanted to tell their mother, but Anna wouldn't let her; she was too scared of their old man. He would beat them, as well as . . . well, as well as the worse stuff. One time Kate had to go to Dr Fleming as she had bad tonsillitis. Dr Fleming saw the bruises on her arms and asked her what was wrong. Kate didn't say anything, but Dr Fleming, who was a good man, came to their house and started asking questions. The girls' parents sent him away, but Kate caught his eye and she knew that he cared, even if he couldn't do anything.

'The girls' mother was adamant they be sent to boarding school, despite their father's arguments that they should live at home. Their father had a temper; he would sometimes get drunk and beat their mother. Kate and Anna weren't sure how much their mother knew about what he was doing, but she stood up for them and forced the issue of them going away to boarding school. Kate heard her mother once say she would call the police if he didn't allow them to go away, and Kate wasn't sure if her mother was threatening to report him for beating her, or for hurting the girls.

'With Lungile and me coming to visit during the holidays it was harder for Kate's father to get to her, and she moved out of home as soon as she could. A couple of years later the girls' father was killed – murdered in his home. The killer was never caught. Their mother committed suicide soon after; gassed herself in the family car. Kate suffered, of course, from what happened to her as a kid.

It was hard for her to form lasting relationships. When she tried to talk about what happened during their childhood with her sister, Anna refused. It was as if she was in denial.'

That tallied, Brand thought, with Anna's reaction when he had asked about her family life. He simply nodded and let Linley continue.

'Kate did eventually find a nice boyfriend, a couple of years ago. His name was George and she thought he was the love of her life, in fact. Anna and her husband Peter had been drifting apart, their marriage stagnating. Anna was lonely and all of a sudden her little sister, who had always devoted herself to her work and hardly ever went out for drinks, had met this fabulous, funny, intelligent lawyer. True, he was quite a few years older than her, but Kate was deliriously happy.'

Brand waited to find out what happened.

'They all went out to a dinner one night, Kate and gorgeous George, as she called the lawyer, and Anna and Peter. Kate and Peter were the designated drivers, so stayed sober, but Anna and George were having a grand old time, getting drunk. Kate didn't know it at the time, but that night Anna came on to George while they were both outside sharing a sneaky cigarette, and later in the evening George fucked Anna in the restaurant toilet.'

Brand thought of Anna's promiscuous come-ons to him, how genuinely lonely she had seemed, and how he had almost succumbed to her. She was a good-looking woman with a high and unfulfilled sex drive. He could picture the scene at the restaurant. One thing he'd learned as a private investigator was that people cheated on each other for the stupidest reasons, not caring how much they hurt those close to them in the process.

'Gorgeous George broke it off, between him and Kate, and she was distraught. At first he wouldn't tell her why, just the usual "you're too good for me" bullshit, but in their case it was true. Kate hounded him, sitting on his doorstep in the rain, showing up at his work, but he got angry and told her what had happened. He was ashamed and never saw Anna again. Kate spiralled out of control for a while, but then she saw a chance to get even.'

Brand couldn't hold back. 'What was that?'

'Not what – who. Her brother-in-law, whom she'd always felt was cold and aloof.'

Andrew had been flying the aircraft with his headset on, talking to air traffic controllers. He removed the headphones from his right ear and turned back to face his passengers. 'Here's your new passport, Linley. I picked it up from the FedEx office in Nelspruit this morning. I hope you've got a passport, Mr Brand, otherwise the Mozambicans will probably lock you up and the Kenyans won't let you into their country.'

'I brought it with me. I'm not going back to South Africa.'

Andrew looked to Linley. 'He's coming with us?'

'Maybe. I still need my money and he needs to organise it.'

Andrew waved a hand in the air and replaced his headphones.

'What happened between Peter and Kate?' Brand asked.

'The good doctor came on to his sister-in-law, in his surgery, in her hour of distress. Suddenly Kate worked out the perfect way to get back at Anna.'

Brand nodded. 'OK, so Kate got back at her sister by having an affair with Peter, but I still don't get it, why did she try and fake her death?'

Linley drew a breath. 'Peter was not just a cheater, he was kinky. He and Anna hadn't had sex for years because she wouldn't do the things he wanted to do. Anna had wanted Peter to be some sort of saviour – a father figure in a good way, not like her real father. She mistook his dominance and arrogance for strength of character. Instead he turned out to be a pervert who wanted to sleep around, and more. Anna couldn't handle the fact that Peter wanted to sleep with other women. Peter, however, took Kate to swingers' parties, to bondage and discipline parlours, and made her sleep with other guys – even girls. Hookers mostly.'

'She was a mature, self-assured woman by all accounts,' Brand said. 'Was it consensual?'

Instead of answering, Linley said, 'Kate had a car crash a couple of years ago.'

Brand nodded; he remembered Anna telling him.

'Well, as a doctor, Peter prescribed OxyContin for her, painkillers, and kept her on them for way too long. The specialist who treated her after the accident was trying to get her off the drugs, but she developed an addiction and Peter was feeding it at the time he came on to her. Half the time she said she was stoned when he used her, when he lent her out to others.' Linley looked out the window.

Brand hadn't liked Peter Cliff from the start, but he forced himself to think objectively about what Linley was saying. She was telling him a story, but he wasn't sure if it was the truth or just her version of the truth, an exercise in self-justification.

He wasn't buying it, though, as a reason for Kate to drop out. 'She flew to Zimbabwe ostensibly on a holiday. Presumably she told you all this then.'

'We'd been talking on email,' Linley said, 'but yes, it wasn't until she came to Zimbabwe that I realised the full extent of what Peter was up to, how he was manipulating her.'

'So why not just put her into rehab in South Africa?'

Linley licked her lips, as if hesitating about whether or not to go on. 'She was scared of Peter. Very scared.'

'Why? Did he hurt her? Physically?'

'It wasn't just the physical. Kate could take a certain amount of pain during some of their rough play, and the drugs kept her zonked out most of the time. No, it wasn't what he did to her, more what she thought he was capable of.'

Brand looked down at the photo again. Some things were not adding up, but others were falling into place. At least this woman was talking, even if it was in riddles. 'Such as?'

'He had this thing he used to do with a knife. It's called "edge play", I've come to learn. He would take a sharp carving knife, sometimes a scalpel, and run it over her skin, dragging the point over her . . . well her intimate places. He didn't draw blood, but occasionally he'd scratch her. He was fascinated with knives, possibly part of being a trained surgeon, I suppose. She was scared that one day he was going to go too far, or that perhaps he already had.'

'Already had?'

'He would pretend, sometimes, when she was tied up, that he was going to stab her, down there, inside her.'

Brand thought of the murdered prostitute by the Phabeni Gate, of Melanie Afrika in Victoria Falls. It was his turn to shiver. 'Peter has been to Africa before, hasn't he?'

Linley nodded. 'Yes, twice that Kate told me about. Once during the soccer World Cup, in 2010, and then again earlier this year, for an international medical conference in Cape Town.'

Brand felt the jolt of adrenaline spread out from his heart to his fingertips. 'In February.'

Linley pursed her lips, thinking. 'Um, not sure. Yes, wait a minute. That's right. Kate's birthday was in February, the fourteenth, and I remember her emailing me telling me that she was glad he was out of the country, that she could be alone. It was around then, while he was away, that she started sounding me out about dropping out, about faking her own death.'

'She was scared enough of him to think she would have to disappear completely?' Brand said.

'Yes. She couldn't go to the police, she didn't have anything on him other than suspicions of what he might have been capable of. He threatened her, on many occasions, saying he would kill her if she tried to speak to Anna about it, or if she left him. He was in love with her, I think, in his own twisted way, and he couldn't bear to be without her.'

Brand thought about the new information. It was still an extreme move, for Kate to fake her own death, but he had a feeling Kate had been right to worry about Peter. Brand checked his phone. He had picked up a roaming signal in Mozambique. He dialled Tracey Mahoney at her home office.

'*Howzit*, where are you?' she said without preamble when she answered.

'You don't want to know. This line's bad, I'm in an aeroplane. I need you to check something for me: you sent Patrick de Villiers to Cape Town in February, same time as I was there, right?'

'You sound like Sannie van Rensburg. She was just asking about him as well. Why all the interest in Patrick?'

Brand decided not to break the news that Patrick was dead, as Van Rensburg clearly hadn't. 'It's important, Tracey.'

'All right, all right. No need to get your knickers in a twist. I'll tell you what I told Van Rensburg; yes, Patrick was in Cape Town at the same time as you, and he was escorting a foreigner, name of Cliff, from England.'

'And during the soccer World Cup, was he . . .'

'Yes, yes, yes. Same answer. Patrick was looking after the same Mr or whatever Cliff during the World Cup as well, I've still got the name written in my bookings diary. What's all this about, anyway?'

'I'm losing you,' Brand lied. 'Bye, Tracey, thanks.' He ended the call.

Linley looked at him. 'What was that all about?'

'I think Kate was right to be scared about Peter Cliff. I've got a feeling he and Patrick de Villiers – the guy killed along with the policewoman back at the airstrip – have been murdering prostitutes.'

She drew a sharp breath and put her hand to her mouth. 'Oh my God.' Linley was quiet for a few seconds, processing the information. 'I think Peter is still looking for Kate,' she said. 'He won't believe she's really dead until he finds me. I'm worried he'll have guessed that Kate told me everything about him when she was planning to disappear. He needed you to help him find me and if what you say is right I could be next on his list. I'm scared, Hudson, very scared.'

He regarded her. The morning sunlight streaming in through the aircraft's window made it look like she was wearing a halo, but he knew this girl was anything but a saint. 'So you should be, Kate.'

31

Part of me was relieved, in a funny way, that someone else knew my secret. 'How did you guess?'

'Too much didn't add up,' Brand said.

The Indian Ocean was bright turquoise below us and as much as I wanted to feel like I was running away, I knew my past was hot on my heels. 'Like what? I thought I covered my tracks pretty well.'

'For a start,' he said, 'the police report said you were in the back of Linley's car fetching a drink when the vehicle went off the bridge. You'd had a bad accident not long before and you'd been living in the UK – folks outside of Africa all wear seatbelts and I think you were so scared of getting hurt in an accident again that you rode in the backseat. An Austin A40 is tiny by today's standards – you could reach anywhere in the back from the front passenger seat. Where is Linley?'

'Dead,' I said. 'They cremated her as me.'

'And you went to Dr Geoffrey Fleming to get your second death certificate because you knew the insurance company would find out about the accident and that your original certificate, from Elena Rodriguez, wouldn't tally.'

I nodded. 'Doc Fleming really did care for Anna and me, but he was reluctant at first to sign. In the end, I confess I played on his guilt. He knew there was something wrong in our family, but he didn't push the issue. He's a good man, Hudson, and I wouldn't want to see him suffer. He got me into rehab in South Africa. Linley never had a drug problem; she was just dirt poor, like so many people in Zimbabwe. In return for helping me get away from my toxic life I was going to give her half the insurance money. She actually suggested the whole death-faking idea to me while I was chatting to her online one time. My life was spiralling out of control and I was becoming more and more suspicious and fearful of Peter. In my stoned state I thought everything would be better if I could just disappear off the face of the earth for a while. Linley pretended to lose her passport and got a new one, using my photograph. The plan was that I would leave Zimbabwe as her, so there would be no trail leading to Kate Munns, and get myself clean in South Africa. I told Doc Fleming about the pin in my pelvis and he agreed he would tell anyone who asked – Peter, Anna or an investigator like you – that he confirmed my identity that way after an autopsy.'

'So there were always going to be two Linley Browns,' Brand said.

'Yes. For a couple of years, at least.'

He nodded. 'The only thing that let down my theory, that you were really Kate, was the photograph.'

I swallowed. This was the one piece of evidence that confirmed to me that I was still in danger, and that this was far from over. I thought he was on to me straight away. However, my blood had run cold when I'd realised what had gone on.

'It was sent from Peter, wasn't it?'

Brand nodded. 'He reversed the picture, easy enough to do in any digital photo program. I only had a casual look at it when I first checked it on my laptop, but I checked it more closely on my phone just now. My gut instincts were telling me you were really Kate, but the photo seemed to be proof that you weren't.'

I nodded. 'My heart nearly stopped when you showed it to me.'

'You're a good bluffer,' he said. 'You might have still had me fooled, but I zoomed in on the pic and as I was using the touch-screen to get to a close-up of your face I got stuck on a close-up of your hand. It was then that I saw that the face of your watch was was back to front.'

'Peter must have been confident that you would meet me at some stage, and that you'd report back that you'd met Linley Brown. That would be his private signal that I, Kate, was really alive. If you'd got back to him and said, "Hey, wow, I found Kate", then he'd know I was really dead.'

'What would he tell Anna?'

I shrugged. 'Nothing. He's a control freak.'

'How would he keep the news secret from her, regardless of whether he thought you were Linley or Kate?' Brand asked.

'I think you know the answer to that.'

'He'd kill you.'

I nodded my head. I had hoped I was smarter than Peter, but deep in my heart I knew that he would follow me to Africa and that he would probably see through me. He always did, and always would.

'The stuff you told me,' Brand said, 'about how Peter treated you, Kate . . . was it all true?'

'All that and more.' I looked out the window for a little while, then down at my hands twisted together between my knees. I found it hard to meet his eyes.

'What are you going to do?' he asked me.

How the hell did I know what to do? 'I had suspicions about the women who were killed in Cape Town and near the Kruger Park. He had an apartment, in London, where we used to meet, and one day I found some printouts from the internet about the murder of those women. I knew the killings had happened when he was in Africa, and the little of what was revealed in the stories about how they were killed matched some of the stuff Peter liked to do – and pretend to do – to me in the bedroom.'

'Did Anna go with him on those trips?' Brand asked.

'No, though she used them as excuses to go abroad by herself. She sent me postcards – she was old-fashioned like that – from Singapore on one trip, Thailand on another.' I thought about her reaching out to me like that, as though we lived in a different time. I had been avoiding her as much as I could, not returning phone calls and ignoring most of her emails, such was my guilt over what Peter and I had been doing, and my fear that I might confess all to her, or inadvertently let something slip.

'Why didn't you contact the police in South Africa, if you had suspicions about Peter and those murdered women?'

'I was afraid of him. I didn't know how it could be proved, or how an investigation could happen without Anna finding out. I felt so bad about her, I was terrified that she'd find out what I'd done with Peter.' My guilt ran not only deep but in many directions, like blood flowing through an endless web of veins.

'Even after she'd slept with your boyfriend?'

I shrugged. 'I got over that. Part of what happened between me and Peter might have begun as revenge, but I kept it going because I was in thrall to a man who used drugs to keep me with him. What I was doing to Anna was far worse than what she'd done to me. Also, I was scared Peter might hurt her, too. I got especially worried after the girl was killed in Cape Town. Then I got talking to Linley online and she suggested the scam. By the way, I googled you after you first called me and saw that you had a connection with the murder of the girl during the World Cup.'

He looked at me, and for a terrible moment I wondered if Peter was actually innocent – of murder if not of being a philanderer and sadist – and this Hudson Brand really was a serial killer. 'There's something else you should know; two things, in fact,' he said.

This couldn't be good, I thought. 'What?'

'Another woman, also a prostitute, was murdered in Victoria Falls. Whoever did it – Peter, Patrick de Villiers, or both of them – tried to frame me for it. But the funny thing is, Peter helped me escape over the border into Botswana.'

I gave his revelation some thought. 'He's clever. He might have killed her, but thought of a way to tie you to the case so that he could shop you later, after you'd found me.'

Brand nodded. 'That figures. He must have paid Melanie, the girl, to do some specific things with me that would ensure there'd be evidence against me.'

Too much information, but I was right. Peter was brilliant as well as evil. He would have strung Brand along by pretending to help him, all the while using him to track me down. Brand had already told me about the dead policewoman at the Sabi Sand airstrip, and the dead safari guide, Patrick de Villiers. 'You think Peter killed the policewoman, and Patrick, to stop him talking?'

'That would fit. Peter may be feeling on the ropes, and killing his partner protects him. One thing concerns me, though, and it may affect you.'

'What's that?' I asked.

'When I was in the terminal at the Sabi Sand airstrip I made a quick SMS report to the woman in England who hired me, telling her about the dead bodies, and confirming that I'd had visual confirmation of you, albeit from a distance and with your wig on, as Linley Brown. My contact's had to save my butt on previous cases and she's also a friend of your sister's.'

I could see his concern. 'So if Anna called her friend she'd pass on the news to Peter that you'd seen Linley and Peter would know immediately that I was alive. He's definitely coming to find me.'

'How will he know where we went?' Brand asked.

I thought about it. 'He'll get Andrew's flight plan – bribe someone if he has too. Also, he knows the one place in Africa I always wanted to visit was in Kenya, the Masai Mara. Everyone who knows me knows this place is top of my bucket list.'

Brand looked dubious. 'Peter might cut his losses and go back to England.'

'No way,' I said. 'Not once your employer inadvertently confirms I'm alive. He's obsessive. He'll find me and I'm more worried than ever before for Anna's safety.' I took a deep breath. 'I want him to come find me, now.'

'But *why*?' he asked.

'So I can kill him.'

32

They stopped to refuel at the Mozambican island of Pemba near the Tanzanian border, and from there they flew to Wilson Airport, Nairobi's general aviation hub.

The customs search was perfunctory, and the officer didn't find Brand's or Kate's pistols or Andrew's nine-millimetre Glock, all of which the pilot had secreted behind a false panel.

After they had disembarked, Brand made Kate tell Andrew everything she'd told him on the flight while he walked outside to make some calls.

'Who were you talking to?' Kate asked him when he got back to the lounge, where they were all waiting for a minibus Brand had organised from mid-air to take them into Nairobi. A friend of his, Minaz, ran a safari outfit in Nairobi and was sending the bus and booking them accommodation in the Masai Mara.

'Some people who I hope will help sort out this mess. I spoke to Van Rensburg, a detective in Nelspruit who's investigating the murders, as well as you.'

'She's already got my best friend in the cells and she wants me,' Kate said.

'Well, you *are* a criminal,' Brand reminded her.

She pouted. 'Tell me, what about my insurance policy? I had every intention of sending money to all the people we robbed, if I received my payout. I'm assuming that's out of the question now?'

Brand stared at her. 'What do you think?'

'What's the harm, Hudson? No one's been hurt; give the girl her money,' Andrew said.

Brand didn't reply to Andrew. He wanted out of Kenya and out of this crazy scenario, but the only way he'd be able to get back to Hazyview and live there as a free man was to help Van Rensburg solve the question once and for all of who'd been responsible for killing the women in South Africa and Zimbabwe.

'Kate, tell us, what's your plan if your sister and brother-in-law do get to Kenya?' Andrew asked.

'I meant what I said,' Kate said. 'I'll kill him if I get the chance.'

Brand put his hand up. 'There's no way Van Rensburg can get here and arrest and extradite Peter; there wasn't time to arrange a warrant and as far as she's concerned I'm her best suspect for the murders. We've got no hard evidence against Peter; our case against him is all hearsay and circumstantial. If we can somehow get a confession out of Peter we can help the police put him away.'

A ground crewman came to the door of the terminal and beckoned to Andrew. Brand was grateful that he would be out of the conversation for five minutes.

Andrew paused at the door on his way out. 'Kate, I can't pretend I'm not disturbed by how all this unfolded. I thought you were simply a damsel in distress; I didn't know the police were after you because you were a criminal.'

'I'm sorry, Andrew. I was desperate. I can't thank you enough for what you've done and I'm sure I speak for Hudson when I say we would understand perfectly if you wanted to just turnaround and go back to South Africa. I don't want to get you in trouble.'

Andrew smiled. 'I've always been a sucker for damsels.' He walked out.

Kate drew a breath and turned back to Brand. 'You're right, of course. I can't shoot him in cold blood, but if he gets away then you have to believe me that he's either going to kill me or Anna or both of us, once she learns what he's been up to. You're in danger, as well. Bloody hell, Hudson, he killed a *cop*, as well as this De Villiers guy who he seems to have been working with.'

Andrew came back inside.

'I've got a gun, you've got a gun and Andrew's got one as well,' Hudson said. 'We just need to get Peter somewhere where we can get the drop on him and, to be fair, give him a chance to explain himself. Maybe he's got a sound alibi for the killings, and maybe De Villiers was acting alone or with someone else. His brother Koos is a sick son of a bitch.'

Andrew cleared his throat. 'Right, you two. Plane's ready to go for tomorrow and our chariot awaits outside.'

They left the terminal and got into the bus. The driver, not knowing who they were or why they were there, assumed they were tourists. He delivered a sporadic commentary on Nairobi's sights.

Dusk was falling and their progress slowed to a crawl as the evening rush hour hemmed them in. Marabou storks, ugly birds with fuzzy, balding heads and pendulous goitres, roosted on light poles and shop awnings in the centre of the city. Office workers scooted on foot between the traffic and women in *kikois* slashed the grass by the side of the road. Johannesburg, Hudson reflected, was fast and furious, whereas this African city was cluttered and chaotic, like the thoughts that bounced around his brain.

Kate looked at him. 'Do you really think he might have an alibi?'

Brand shrugged. 'I can check.' He took out his phone and found the number for the Protea Hotel Kruger Gate in his contacts; he did regular pick ups and drop offs there as part of his guiding work. He called the hotel and asked to be put through to the concierge desk. 'Thabo, *howzit*, it's Hudson Brand here.'

Kate listened in as Brand asked Thabo what he recalled of the movements of the male and female guests he'd left at the hotel. Hudson listened, nodding, asked a couple more questions then hung up.

'The concierge said Peter – he didn't know him by name – went to his desk this morning after I'd left and asked if there was somewhere he could go for a walk. Thabo told him he could go down to the Kruger Park entrance gate and across the bridge over the Sabie River, but that he'd better watch out for lions.'

'So he could have met up with Patrick de Villiers on the road?' Kate said. Brand nodded. 'Patrick could have driven him into the Sabi Sand Game Reserve, where they went to the airstrip and killed the detective? Is that what you're thinking?'

Brand exhaled. 'Yep.'

*

The next day they went back to Wilson Airport and flew to the Masai Mara. As they boarded a game viewer at the Musiara airstrip, set in the middle of an open grassy plain, Brand thought about how *best* to catch a serial killer.

'I just want to say thank you, Andrew, for flying us here and picking up the tab for our accommodation,' Kate said as the open-sided Land Cruiser bounced along a black earth road through the Masai Mara.

'It's nothing,' Andrew replied. 'I have many friends in the travel business and you know why I want to help you, Kate. I'm sure Hudson will pay his share back from his expenses.'

'I can't really believe I'm here,' Kate said, bringing Brand back to the present. 'I've wanted to come here and see the migration all my life; I just didn't expect I'd be on the run from the police and my brother-in-law.'

'The migration is almost gone,' said their guide, Godwin, who had picked them up from the airstrip.

'No animals?' Kate asked.

'No, no, no, there are still many animals,' Godwin assured her, 'but the majority of the wildebeest have crossed the Mara and headed back to Tanzania, though some will cross back.'

'I don't understand,' she said.

Brand had led tours to Kenya before. 'The migration's a fluid thing,' he explained. 'Sometimes the wildebeest and zebra will cross the river, and then turn and cross back to this side.'

'Why?'

'It is like now,' Godwin said. 'There was a grassfire on this side of the Mara River and then some unseasonal rains. The fresh grass shoots are good grazing, so some of the wildebeest that crossed to Tanzania and found the grass was still dead there came back this way. As Hudson says, it is fluid.'

'It's like life,' Kate observed. 'Sometimes you take a decision and you think it's the right one, and then you want to go back.'

'You're regretting faking your own death?' Andrew asked her.

She shrugged. 'It seemed like the only way out for me at the time, but Peter had me strung out on drugs. I wonder now if I should have just gone to Anna and confessed everything and asked for her help.'

'She made no secret of the fact that she and Peter weren't getting on,' Brand said. 'Even if she found out about you and Peter, she may not react as you think she will. You said yourself she knows Peter isn't the white knight she once thought he was. What I don't understand is why she stayed with him so long – they've got no kids.'

Kate shrugged. 'My sister couldn't handle being poor and Peter provides well for them. If she's anything like me then she's also scared to put herself out there, to try to trust another man in a proper relationship. She cheated with George, so for all I know she's been having affairs with every man she's met.'

Brand thought that maybe Kate was reading her sister better than she realised, but he decided not to say anything about Anna coming on to him. Godwin picked up the handset of the radio mounted in the dashboard of his Land Cruiser following a burst of staccato

Maasai coming through a tinny speaker. He spoke rapidly into the microphone.

'What is it?' Kate asked.

'Maybe nothing, but we will investigate. In the meantime there are some lions up ahead.'

'Where?' she asked.

'I guess where all those vehicles are,' Brand said.

The countryside was completely different from the thick bushveld of South Africa and Zimbabwe where Brand conducted most of his safaris. Here the gentle, rolling hills and open plains of the Masai Mara and the adjoining Serengeti National Park across the border in Tanzania were covered in short grass. The landscape here was more golf course than bush, though where the plains were bisected by rivers and creeks, lines of dense riverine vegetation sheltered predators.

Godwin took them a short distance off-road to where a queue of a dozen game-viewing vehicles moved slowly in a conga line that followed the course of a narrow stream.

'There!' Kate said, spotting the tawny form that contrasted with the dark green grass. A lioness lay on her back, legs in the air, belly distended. 'Looks like she's just fed.'

Godwin nodded. 'Last night, they killed a wildebeest. The rest of the pride, including her babies, are at the base of those trees there in the shade.'

They peered through the foliage and Brand pointed out the tiny cubs, still showing the spots of their youth. One played with the bushy tip of the pride male's tail until the father tired of the son's antics and sent him scarpering with a short, sharp roar. Kate smiled at the spectacle, but Brand couldn't relax. More than ever he wanted to rid himself of the Cliffs and Kate Munns, and the ghost of Linley Brown, but his own freedom depended on this deadly, twisted human pride's reunion. If he could catch Peter Cliff he could clear his name in the eyes of the police, and put a serial killer behind bars.

Three more lionesses revealed themselves and Kate sat with her elbows on her knees, staring at the big cats, lost in their innocence. 'They kill, but it's the most natural thing in the world,' she said. 'I never understand tourists who feel sorry for the wildebeest or the other prey animals. The cats have to survive and people think they're cruel because they're good at what they do. To kill without remorse, just because you have to, in order to survive . . .'

Brand did not like the direction her mind was heading. 'Do you think you're safe here from Peter, and from the law? I know Van Rensburg; when she checks Andrew's flight plan and finds out you're in Kenya she'll come find you eventually. Where are you planning on running to from here?'

Kate said nothing, continuing to stare at the big cats.

'Or are you planning on staying here in Kenya?' he persisted.

Kate turned from the lions. 'I know I've reached the end of the line, and that there's no point running now. I don't want to be extradited to face the courts in South Africa, though Lord knows I deserve it, but I want this to end, and so do you. The only way you can clear yourself is by taking Peter out of the picture, one way or another,' she said. 'Anna will have called her friend in England, the one you work for, and she'll have confirmed your earlier information, that I'm Linley. Peter will then know I'm really Kate and there will be no stopping him or Anna coming here.'

Brand gritted his teeth. She was right; bringing this to a head was the only way to clear his own name. He was one step ahead of Kate, though; he'd put in place his own plan to monitor the Cliffs' movements. He would know if and when they arrived in the Masai Mara. 'What about Anna?'

'She's in danger, too. I'm assuming you've told your police friends my theory about Peter?'

He hadn't said anything to Kate, but she had guessed correctly. He had called Van Rensburg from Wilson Airport the previous day and told her there was strong circumstantial evidence that Peter was the killer and she should confirm with Tracey Mahoney that

De Villiers had been Peter's guide both times he'd been in South Africa. 'Peter might already be in the police lockup in Nelspruit,' he said, although he would have heard by now if this was the case, and he hadn't.

Kate shrugged. 'If he is, good. If not, he'll come here and it will be up to us to stop him.'

'I'm not a hired assassin, Kate.'

'I've got nothing to lose,' she replied. 'I'm already dead, and as much as I hate what Anna did to me, it's time for me to make amends with her, and to protect her if I can.'

*

Sannie van Rensburg and Tom Furey sat in a raised timber and thatch *lapa*, an open-sided shelter overlooking the Sabie River, at the deck bar of the Protea Hotel near the Paul Kruger entrance gate to the Kruger Park.

'We're missing something,' Tom said as he attacked the last of his steak prego roll. They were taking a short break for lunch after interviewing everyone they could find at the hotel who may have had contact with Anna and Peter Cliff. The Cliffs had skipped out after the failed sting operation in which Mavis and Patrick de Villiers had been killed, and had boarded a flight from Nelspruit to Johannesburg and then on to Nairobi, Kenya, before the police could stop them for questioning.

'I agree.' Sannie drained her Coke Light. Her phone pinged and she checked her emails. There was one from Brand.

'Anything interesting?' Tom asked.

'Huh! Just Hudson Brand telling us what we already knew, that the Cliffs may know Linley Brown is in Kenya and he suspects they may try to follow her there. That doesn't help us.' She tapped a reply to Brand, telling him what she had learned from the airlines, that the Cliffs had taken the midnight Kenya Airways flight to Nairobi. She read aloud to Tom as she typed the final lead: '*Do not try and apprehend anyone but keep us advised of Peter Cliff's whereabouts.*

I have applied for authority from my superiors for an extradition order.' She hit send.

'Do you think you'll get approval to go get Cliff?' Tom asked.

Sannie shrugged. 'You know what it's like trying to get money for a flight from any police service. We need to strengthen the link between Patrick de Villiers and Peter Cliff, and to review the forensic evidence from the deaths of the women at Hazyview and Cape Town. If we can match Patrick de Villiers's DNA to them we'll have a start, but that will take time. The killer was very careful – dare I say it, surgical. Cliff would have known how to minimise the transfer of evidence. And poor Mavis, we'll have to wait for the medical examiner to check her, to see if there is some DNA or other physical evidence to help us identify the other person in her killing.'

'I wish we'd had better luck with the witnesses,' Tom said. They had been over it several times. The security guard at the Shaw's Gate entrance to the reserve remembered Patrick arriving – he was a regular visitor transferring clients to and from the reserve – and the record showed he had paid for himself and another person to enter. The guard hadn't bothered checking inside Patrick's van, and as the windows were darkly tinted he hadn't been able to see Cliff, who was presumably the passenger on board, if Brand's theory was correct.

'We still don't know how Peter got out of the reserve after killing Mavis,' Sannie said, 'assuming it was him.'

Tom nodded. They had been over this, as well. 'Best guess is that he went on foot through the reserve back to the hotel fence and climbed over somehow.' The hotel, where they now sat, was located on the extreme southeastern corner of the Sabi Sand, and shared a fence with the reserve. They had walked the perimeter and found no breaks in the fence, but they theorised that it was possible Peter could have walked down to the Sabie River, along the waterfront, and then made his way back into the hotel complex where the fence had been damaged by warthogs burrowing under it.

'All in broad daylight?' Tom asked. A hippo honked from the river in front of them.

'Not easy, but possible.' Sannie pushed her plate to the centre of the low table in the *lapa* and called for the waiter to bring them the bill. 'Peter had loose ends to tie up; he needed to get rid of Patrick.'

'Are you ruling out Brand as a suspect altogether?' Tom asked.

'I'm still keeping an open mind about him, in case all of this is an elaborate story to throw us off him as our main suspect.'

Tom didn't look convinced. 'He's calling us from Kenya, revealing his location, to try to help us get the goods on Peter Cliff. We need to keep digging; we're still missing some vital piece of information that conclusively ties Peter to the women's deaths,' Tom reiterated.

Sannie knew her husband was right. They would have to go back to the beginning. 'The only person who could have told us, in detail, what Peter's movements were during the World Cup and in Cape Town, and in Victoria Falls, was Patrick de Villiers, and he's conveniently dead. We have to go back to Patrick's boss, Tracey, and get whatever other information we can to recreate those tours that she booked him on. We need more detail – hotel vouchers, soccer bookings – more than just her diary entry that said De Villiers was booked to escort Cliff.'

Tom stood. 'OK, then, love, let's get back to it.'

'Good old-fashioned legwork.' She saw the smile on his face. 'You look like you're almost enjoying this,' she said as she walked down the stairs from the *lapa* to the raised timber walkway above the river's edge.

'I would be if it wasn't for Mavis, but I could follow your legwork all day.'

*

'There is a crossing possibly about to happen,' Godwin told Brand, Kate and Andrew.

'Is it far?' Kate asked.

Brand studied her face. She looked so innocent, so excited. It was hard for him to connect her with what he knew of her, her troubled past and her recent life of crime. Africa, the wild, had a way of bringing out the child in everyone.

'We can get there,' Godwin said, 'and it won't make us too late, as long as the wildebeest don't take too long to cross.'

'I can wait,' Kate said.

Godwin left the lions and they headed south, towards the Mara River. As with the lion sighting they saw the gathering of vehicles before they saw the animals themselves, but this time the number of humans was even greater. There were scores of vehicles, perhaps sixty or more, lining the bank of the river on their side.

'There they are,' said Kate. They saw the procession of black blots on the far side of the river, milling backwards and forwards, and heard the uncertain bleating of the wildebeests above the chatter of the breathlessly expectant humans.

'This isn't what I expected; it's a mess,' Kate said.

Brand had seen it several times before, the jockeying and selfishness of the tour guides, egged on by their clients, who jostled and queued for what they believed would be the best position on the steep banks of the river.

'Every time the wildebeests see a gap on this side of the river some idiot parks his truck there,' Kate said.

'You got it,' Godwin nodded. He had parked away from the river, on a slope overlooking it, and scanned the banks up and down the watercourse as he tried to gauge when and where the animals would cross and the best place from which to view them.

There was a single Kenya Wildlife Service ranger in a green Land Rover, who trundled up and down the waiting ranks of game-viewing vehicles, trying to keep them in some semblance of order and ensure there was a clear space left along the bank for the wildebeest to aim for, so they could exit the river if they made it across safely. As soon as the ranger established an exit point and moved on, the safari vehicles filled the gap like a returning tide.

Godwin drove along the river until he spied a group of wildebeest massing on the far side. 'These ones look ready to cross, but most of the other vehicles are waiting further up the river for that last group.'

'Well done, Godwin,' Kate said.

Brand swatted away a fly. It was a waiting game. He marvelled at Kate's enthusiasm for the crossing. There was a man on his way here, possibly with the intention of killing her, and all she wanted was to see some animals cross a river.

'Come on, come on,' she urged them.

'Look!' Andrew pointed. The lead animal in a herd of about thirty wildebeest took a plunge off a rock, jumping about ten metres into the brown water below. 'He's going for it.'

As soon as the first animal's hooves had hit the water his comrades started leaping in after him. All it had taken was for that one beast to take the plunge. The lead animal was swimming now, fighting the current, his shaggy bearded head jutting forward.

Brand raised his binoculars. 'Croc coming, behind the first guy.'

'No!' Kate put her hand to her mouth. 'It's going to get him.'

A massive reptilian head breached the churning water as the crocodile tried to get its snout around the back of the wildebeest's neck. The herbivore, however, surged on, shaking its head to try and keep the crocodile at bay.

'He's done it!' Kate yelled. The wildebeest had made the bank on their side and was scrabbling for purchase on the red clay. The exit path above him was steep, but he slowly made ground. Behind him the crocodile was drifting downriver and the following animals were making land, bunching up in a bleating black traffic jam at the water's edge.

Godwin shook his head. 'These guys are idiots.' He wasn't talking about the wildebeest, but about several other safari guides who had raced their vehicles to the new crossing point and were now pulling up along the edge of the riverbank. 'Give them some room,' Godwin called to the other operators, but they ignored him.

'The poor wildebeest can't get up,' Kate said despairingly.

Brand watched them through the binoculars and saw their panic and confusion. 'You're right. Look, the lead guy is getting back in the water.'

'No,' she cried.

The wildebeest was swimming again, back the way he had come. Brand saw the knobbly head of the crocodile break the surface for an instant, just to ascertain it was on the correct heading. When it was halfway across the river the wildebeest's head was drawn under. There was a volcanic splash of water and wild thrashing and beating for a few seconds until the wildebeest was stilled.

The croc came to the surface again, all four metres of his ridged back visible as he steered his lifeless prey to the far bank. Kate, who had disparaged tourists who showed emotion over the deaths of animals in the wild, started to cry.

33

Tracey Mahoney's maid said her employer had gone into Hazyview to have lunch with a friend, so Sannie decided she and Tom should pay a visit to Koos de Villiers's farm, where Patrick had stayed in between guiding jobs.

Sannie drove them into the hills from Hazyview towards White River on the R40 and passed their own farm. 'Do you wish we were there now, just sitting on the *stoep* or supervising the harvest?' she asked Tom.

'No.'

'Why not? I know you're always so supportive, baby, but I thought you didn't like me going back to work?'

Tom reached over and laid his hand on her thigh. He gave it a little squeeze. 'I didn't, not because I didn't think it was your place to work, or because I turned my back on the job, but because I was worried about you. But now I know. Now I remember. I wouldn't be anywhere else but here right now.'

She nodded, and though she smiled she felt a little choked up. 'I love you, Tom.'

'I love you too, babe, with all my heart. Now let's go kick this fucker's door in.'

'I'm sure it won't come to that.' She took the turnoff to Kiepersol and followed the narrower, winding road through more plantations until they came to the De Villiers farm. Sannie pulled up at the electrified barbed-wire gate and pushed the button on an intercom on a stalk.

'Hello?' said an African voice.

'Captain Van Rensburg, here to see Koos de Villiers.'

'One minute.'

After a short pause a gruff voice said through the tinny speaker, '*Voetsek*.'

'I'm not going anywhere, Koos. I'm sorry for the loss of your brother, but I have to talk to you about his death.'

Koos said nothing and they waited a couple of minutes. Eventually the big, bearded farmer came striding down the driveway from the ramshackle single-storey farmhouse. His big hands dwarfed the shotgun he carried. Sannie got out of the car, as did Tom.

'What do you want?' Koos said as he approached the gate.

Sannie had her hand resting on the butt of her Z88 service pistol. 'We need to come in and talk to you, about Patrick.'

'You can talk to me through the *bladdy* gate, woman.'

'Show some respect,' Tom said.

'Who the fuck are you to tell me how to speak, Englishman?' Koos spat on the ground.

Tom reached around his back for his own pistol, but Sannie held up a hand to stay him. 'Koos, I know this is a bad time for you,' she said in Afrikaans. 'I'm sorry for the loss of your brother, but we need to come in and talk to you. We need to ask you some questions about people he had escorted in the past.'

'I got nothing to say to you people.'

'Sannie,' Tom said.

'What?' She didn't want to take her eyes off Koos. The big man had a reputation as a violent bully and his eyes were red from crying, presumably over the loss of his equally detestable brother.

'There's smoke coming from the chimney at the house. It's nowhere near cool enough for a fire,' Tom murmured.

'What are you burning, Koos?' she asked the farmer.

'None of your business. Wood.'

'I don't think so. Is it some of Patrick's things?'

Koos shrugged.

He was not the smartest man in town, not by a long way. 'You want to burn some of the things of his so they don't remind you of his loss, is that right?'

Koos frowned. 'Yes, that's it.'

'Right,' she said. 'We're coming in.'

Sannie had noticed that while the gate was closed it was not padlocked. She grabbed the frame and began sliding it. Koos strode to her, but she was through already. Tom was right behind her. Koos had the sense not to level the shotgun at her, but he transferred the gun to his left hand and shoved his huge palm into her chest. 'Get off my land, bitch.'

Sannie reeled back a pace, but before she could draw her weapon Tom was between them. His first punch caught Koos on the chin and snapped his head backwards. As he fell on his arse Koos began to bring the shotgun to bear.

'Drop it!' Tom's foot was on the bigger man's belly and his SIG Sauer, held in both hands, was pointed between Koos's eyes.

'Roll him over,' Sannie said. Tom snatched the shotgun, now lowered, and encouraged Koos to obey with a kick in his ribs. Sannie pulled out her cuffs and snapped them on Koos's wrists. 'Bring him, please, Tom.'

She broke into a jog and kicked open the door of the farmhouse, her Z88 leading the way, 'Police!' she called, but the house was empty. In front of the fire were papers, letters and a stack of magazines. One glossy publication was half devoured by the flames. Sannie saw the contorted faces as she reached the fireplace. Tom pushed Koos into the living room behind her. Sannie bent and picked up the next magazine to be burned and flicked through it.

'Hardcore, foreign stuff. Women being tortured, cut, beaten. Your brother was into some sick shit, Koos.'

'It's not illegal,' the farmer said.

'Then why are you burning it?' Tom asked.

Sannie kicked a shoebox open. A plastic bag full of what looked like *dagga*, marijuana, fell out. Under the box, of more interest to her, was an old-model laptop computer. 'This was Patrick's?'

'I got nothing to say to you,' said Koos.

'Sit him down, out of reach,' Sannie said to Tom. She sat on a vinyl lounge, the greasy imitation leather peeling away, and opened the computer and started it. 'No password needed, I see. He was about as smart as you, Koos.'

Koos wriggled on the battered armchair, straining to get up, but Tom pushed him in the chest, keeping him down. 'You got no right to go through his stuff.'

Whether Koos knew it or not, Sannie knew he was right, but the urgency with which Koos was burning his brother's possessions told her that the older brother knew there was information here that would incriminate Patrick. Sannie opened the email program on the computer. The address of the last email made her gasp.

'What is it?' Tom asked.

She opened it and began to read. 'My God.'

*

Brand, Andrew and Kate sat on fold-out camp chairs in the shade of a lone tree on the short grass plain of the Masai Mara, eating boiled eggs and chicken from lunch boxes that had been provided for them in Godwin's vehicle.

They had left the main body of the migration behind at the Mara River. A herd of a dozen or more topi antelope watched them, warily, from a nearby rise. Godwin was seated in the Land Cruiser, talking on the radio in Swahili. When he finished talking he came to Hudson and said quietly: 'Sir, you asked the lodge to tell you when the other guests have arrived at the airstrip. They are there now.'

Brand had no signal on his phone at this spot in the reserve, but had left instructions before he had lost reception. 'Well, Peter and Anna have arrived,' Hudson announced to the others. 'You're going to get what you wished for, Kate.'

She put her lunch box down, hardly touched. 'I'm ready. Where will we meet them, back at the camp?'

Brand looked to Andrew. The pilot rubbed his stubbled chin. 'Could get messy if this Peter fellow tries something. Might be best not to make a fuss in front of civilians.'

'Out here?' Brand said.

Andrew nodded. 'He won't have been able to get a firearm or any weapon of note onto a civilian airliner, and all three of us are armed. We can cover him, or do you want to call the Kenyan police in first?'

'We don't know how long it would take for them to get to us, plus there would be a lot of explaining to do in advance. Also, to be fair, we've got to hear what Peter has to say for himself. It's all conjecture right now.'

Kate looked down at her fingernails. 'He's guilty. I know it.'

'Godwin,' Brand said, 'do you know a place where we can have a private meeting with these other people who have arrived? Not like here, where all the vehicles stop.'

'*Ndiyo*. Yes. I can find us a quiet place, on the river, but not where the crossings are taking place. There will be no one else there. Will there be trouble?'

'I hope not. Radio the location to camp and please ask them to pass it on to the driver picking up Dr and Mrs Cliff from the airstrip. Say there are some people who wish to meet with them. They will understand.'

'All right,' Godwin said.

Andrew and Brand helped Godwin pack the chairs and they set off, bouncing on the rutted roads. They threaded their way through a herd of several hundred wildebeest and followed the course of the Mara away from a growing gaggle of tourist vehicles and a line of nervous animals on the other side of the river preparing to cross back over.

'Give me your gun,' Brand said to Kate.

'No.'

'Give it to me or I'll tell Godwin to take us back to the camp. You can take on your relatives by yourself.'

Kate stared defiantly at him for a few seconds, but eventually reached into her daypack, pulled out her .32 calibre semi-automatic and handed to him. 'You know I want to kill him, don't you?'

'Yes,' said Brand, 'which is exactly why I'm taking this.' He slipped the small pistol into the cargo pocket of his trousers. He took out his own nine-mil, ejected the magazine, unloaded and reloaded the bullets, then slid it back into the butt, slapped it home and cocked the pistol. He slipped it into the waistband of his trousers.

Andrew took his own weapon out of his bag and checked it. 'We're not going to let anything happen to you, Kate,' the pilot said to her.

Godwin glanced back over his shoulder, his eyes wide at the sight of the guns. 'At least we will be safe from the lions.'

They stopped at a bluff on a bend of the Mara River. The bank on their side had been cut by the river when it was in full flood, leaving a vertical drop of exposed pale sand below them. On the opposite side boulders and rocks worn smooth by the water studded the point on the bend. The river was red-brown, fast flowing. A line of trees provided shade.

'This is fine?' Godwin asked.

'It's OK,' said Brand.

'OK Corral, more like it,' Andrew said.

They sat and waited in the shade, watching the river, occasionally spotting a hippo, or an animal on the shore. 'You might have to testify if Peter gets extradited to South Africa,' Brand said to Kate.

'I'll cross that bridge when and if I come to it,' she said, picking up a rock and tossing it over the bank and into the swirling waters about five metres below. 'I just hope the South African police can link Peter and De Villiers to the murders by other means. I don't want to go to prison, but I do want to reimburse the people I stole from.'

'You know I can't recommend you get the money from the life insurance claim,' Brand said.

Kate nodded. 'I know that. I need to find a proper job, either here in Kenya or somewhere else in the world, and save up to try and right the wrongs I've caused.'

Andrew stood from the chair he'd been sitting on and picked up a pair of binoculars from inside the Land Cruiser. 'Dust plume. Vehicle coming.'

Godwin went to the radio and spoke rapidly into it. 'It is them,' he announced when he'd finished.

Kate stood and Brand noted that her hands were clasped in fists by her side. A muscle pulsed in her jawline as she ground her teeth. Brand felt for the pistol in the small of his back; it was ready for use if he needed it. He thought Peter would try and bluff his way through, but he reminded himself the man was a violent serial killer who had proved adept at covering his trail for several years.

The vehicle grew in size and shape and Brand could see it was a Land Rover game viewer with a canvas awning on top, strung between the bars of a roll cage. Anna and Peter were sitting in the seats behind the driver, who was wearing a traditional Maasai blanket, unlike Godwin who was in khakis. The vehicle stopped about ten metres away and the two guides waved to each other in greeting, as if this was any other ordinary bush rendezvous.

'Kate, my God! It's you!' Peter said as he vaulted from the vehicle.

'He's doing a good job of looking surprised,' Andrew said to Brand out of the side of his mouth. Kate remained immobile, silent, beside him.

Anna climbed down and walked towards her. 'I can't believe it. Oh my God.'

Kate stayed still, arms by her side, as Peter stopped a metre from her. 'Why did you run away?'

Brand heard her faint reply above the rush of the river below and behind them. 'You of all people should know that.'

Peter took a deep breath and ran a hand through his hair. He was lost for words, Brand assumed, overwhelmed to see her even though, by reversing the photo of Kate and Linley that he'd sent Dani, Peter must have known it was going to be Kate who he would meet, and not Linley Brown.

'Why?' was all Anna said to her sister.

'Hello, Anna,' Kate said. 'I'm sorry.'

Anna stared at Kate, not reaching for her, not hugging her, not crying. Brand watched the two women closely. 'Sorry for what?'

'We can talk later, can't we?' Peter said quickly. 'It's just so marvellous that we've got Kate back, isn't it?'

Brand wondered to whom he was asking the question. Kate eyed him coldly; Anna ignored her husband. 'Sorry for what?' she asked again.

Peter reached out a hand, as if to assure himself Kate wasn't a ghost. Kate took a step back, physically shuddering. A hippo mocked them all with its belly laugh.

'Don't you touch me, you bastard,' Kate hissed at Peter, who lowered his arm.

He looked bereft, Brand thought, as though he'd had a prize given to him then taken away. 'I'm sorry,' he said quietly.

'Sorry for what?' Anna demanded. 'Is someone going to tell me what's going on here?'

Kate drew a breath. 'I ran away from Peter, Anna. We were having an affair. I got scared.'

'Scared?' Peter said.

Anna looked from her sister to her husband, but said nothing. Brand noted the older woman's chest rising and falling, the colour rushing to her cheeks, her fury barely in check. Brand felt for her.

'You had nothing to be scared of,' Peter said to Kate. 'I'd never have really hurt you. Kate, no, you must have realised I never wanted to harm you.'

'I was too stoned to realise anything half the time. What I do remember is you using me, like a whore, and that *special thing* you liked to do with the scalpel.'

He looked, Brand thought, like a shamed child, looking down at the ground, his face colouring. 'I thought . . . I thought you liked it . . . liked me.'

Anna turned to her husband, closed the gap between them and slapped his face, hard. 'You really are a bastard.'

'Anna . . . it wasn't all him,' Kate said.

'Shut your mouth.' She rounded on her sister and Andrew Miles stepped between the two women.

'Who the hell is this?' Anna asked.

'A friend,' Andrew said. 'Let's behave like adults.'

They all looked at him. Anna scoffed. 'I can't *believe* this is happening.'

'I've acted appallingly,' Peter said. 'Kate, I love you and I only wanted what was best for you, for me.' He looked at his wife next. 'Anna, I'm so sorry, but you never understood, never accepted me.'

'So you drugged my sister and played your sick, kinky little games with her because I wouldn't indulge your swinging and *cheating*. God, Peter, I knew you were some kind of sex addict, but my *sister*?' Anna turned to Kate. 'How could you?'

'You're asking *me* that? After what you did with George?' Kate spat.

'What about George?' Peter asked.

Anna's cheeks reddened. 'George pursued *me*, Kate.'

Brand wasn't sure where his loyalties lay now. He had found Kate Munns for the Cliffs, but he was also here ostensibly to protect Kate from her brother-in-law, the man whose actions had prompted her to fake her death, and whom she feared was a killer. There was also Anna to think of; she eyed her sister and her husband coldly. Brand remembered her touch and it pained him a little to see her hurt. But perhaps the truth would help her. She needed to be rid of Peter as much as Kate had needed to run away from the destructive affair.

Both of them needed to try and come to terms with the trauma of their childhood, but that would have to come after the current mess was behind them.

'Anna, what do you want to do?' Brand asked her.

She looked at him, seemingly taking a few seconds to register the question.

'Peter?' Brand said.

He looked at Brand and blinked. 'I don't know what to say.'

'There are some things you and I need to talk about. We can do it here, or with the police when we get back to camp. It's up to you.'

'What do I have to talk about with *you*?' he asked, reverting to his normal prickly self, Brand thought.

'We can start with what you were doing in June 2010, in Nelspruit, and in Cape Town in February, and in Victoria Falls a few nights ago.'

'You know perfectly well what I was doing in Victoria Falls, and as for those other trips, I was watching the World Cup and attending a medical conference.' He looked indignant. 'What's all this about?'

'You're the one who should be answering that question,' Anna said.

Brand kept his eye on the humans around him, trying to read them. Unlike animals they were unpredictable. Lions, elephants, buffalo and other dangerous game always gave some hint of an imminent decision to attack or defend, even though it often seemed otherwise. People just exploded.

Anna's face was pure anger, while Peter seemed to have been mentally poleaxed by the events unfolding around him.

'Kate,' Brand said steadily, 'do you want Peter charged by the police for supplying drugs to you, illegally?' It was a start, Brand reasoned, referring to a charge that Peter had already been confronted with and had not denied.

'Don't talk about me like I'm not here,' Peter said from the other side of Andrew.

'You're not, as far as I'm concerned,' Kate said. 'What you did to me was reprehensible, but on some level I know I'm to blame, too. I could have gone to rehab in the UK, or the police, but I was scared of you, and –'

'And what?' Peter challenged. 'You liked it?'

'You're disgusting. No, you kept me addicted to *drugs* after the accident. And you, a doctor; you should be disbarred or whatever they do to doctors. No, Hudson, I don't think the police can charge him with anything, but I just want to make sure I don't end up like those other women.'

'What other women?' Peter asked.

Anna grabbed her husband's arm, forcing him to turn and look at her. 'Those women you raped and murdered, Peter. Don't look so surprised and don't deny it. I was checking the international news when you were in South Africa for the World Cup. For some stupid reason I was worried about you, what with all the violent crime you read about, and I read about the girl who was killed, near where you were staying; she'd been tied up, choked and she'd been stabbed. I remembered all your sick games, how you liked to play with knives. I didn't think it was you, though, until I checked the Cape Town newspapers online when you were there, and there was another girl murdered the same way.'

Peter looked cornered, Brand thought, but then the doctor looked at him. 'Yes, all right, I know about the woman who was killed during the World Cup, and the woman who was murdered the same way in Cape Town, but you're both forgetting that the police already have a suspect, and he's right here next to both of you.'

'So you read about me,' Brand said.

'I googled you when Dani named you as the investigator she had employed,' Peter said, 'and I remember thinking it was scary that a woman had been killed in Hazyview while I was staying nearby. I became suspicious of you after the death of the girl in Victoria Falls and your pressing need to get away from the police, but we needed you to find Linley – Kate, as it turned out.' He looked to Kate. 'I'm just so pleased you're alive. Believe me, I haven't hurt anyone. I have my issues, I know, and it was wrong how I manipulated you, but I never hurt anyone. I *love* you, Kate.'

'You bastard!' Anna lashed out at Peter, trying to pummel him with her fists, but he took a step backwards, towards the edge of the embankment they all stood on, and grabbed her by the wrists. Brand moved to separate them, but Anna used a self-defence move, raising her two hands together then bringing them down and out to opposite sides swiftly. She broke Peter's hold on her then used both her hands to shove him, hard, in the chest.

Peter screamed as he lost his footing and toppled backwards, over the edge, and into the river below. 'Help!'

'Shit,' said Brand. He ran at the drop-off and jumped.

'I'll get a rope,' Andrew yelled as Brand struck out towards Peter, who was flailing in the fast-moving water as the current grabbed him and swept him downriver. He was clearly a poor swimmer.

Brand looked up at the bank above him and saw Anna appear to grab Andrew as he tried to get the rope. Then she broke away from him and Brand saw she had pulled Andrew's gun from the waistband of his trousers. 'Anna, no!' Hudson yelled, as he sucked a mouthful of dirty river water.

Anna pointed the gun not at him but at Peter, and started firing. She didn't appear to be a good shot and the bullets went wide of her target, sending up geysers of water and adding to Peter's panicked yelping. Of more concern to Brand, however, was the V-shaped wake that had appeared on the brown surface of the river behind Peter, making its way straight towards him.

Brand was of no use to Peter flailing about in the water, so he struck out for shore and hauled himself to his feet when he touched the muddy bottom. He moved along the narrow strip of sand at the base of the embankment and drew his own weapon. He lined up on the apex of the wake and fired at it, his round landing dangerously close to Peter. The doctor panicked even more and cried out for the shooting to stop. Brand fired again. Anna's firing had stopped; presumably Andrew had got his weapon back.

A giant, mottled, knobbly head the size of half of Peter's body broke the surface. Brand fired two more shots, but if they hit the crocodile they had no effect. The wicked jaws chomped down on Peter, across his back and shoulders, and the croc submerged, taking Peter with it.

34

A team of Kenya Wildlife Service rangers scoured the banks on both sides of the river, but found no sign of Peter. After the senior ranger took our statements at the scene, we drove to Tipilikwani Camp on the edge of the Masai Mara reserve.

Anna and I travelled in separate vehicles. She still wasn't ready to talk to me, and I guess I understood how she was feeling, even though I felt she had hurt me as much as I had hurt her. We needed to start the process of reconciling with each other, and we needed to go way back to before Peter or George.

I wondered what it had been like for her, back at our home when we were kids. Although she refused to talk about it I imagined she had suffered more abuse, perhaps years of it, before my father started with me. Had she tried to stop him? Had she endured even more to try and save me? I wanted to reach out to her, but didn't know how.

When we arrived at the camp I could see a white man standing next to the Kenyan manager in the entranceway. As we got closer I recognised the mop of curly black hair and the lopsided grin.

'Bryce!'

He came to me as I stepped down from the vehicle and wrapped me in his arms. I pushed my face into his shirt and breathed in the smell of him. 'Are you OK?'

I looked up at him. 'As OK as I can be. You heard what happened?'

'Yes, on the radio.'

'But how did you get here? When?'

'Hudson asked me to follow your sister and brother-in-law. I was on the same flights as them from Joburg and from Nairobi, but they'd never seen me so they didn't know who I was. Hudson told me to come straight to the lodge, in case they decided to come here rather than meet you out by the river. I felt completely helpless here, but it's really good to see you again.'

I had been so cruel to him. 'I told you not to follow me.'

He grinned. 'Yes, but you'll learn I'm no good at following orders.'

'I've got no future, Bryce, no life, no job, no money, hell, not even my real identity.'

'I know, Kate, but I've got friends here in Kenya. We'll find somewhere.'

I hardly believed him. 'We?'

'Sure.' He looked into my eyes, tentative, uncertain, perhaps nervous. 'That is, if you want me in your life.'

I nodded and put my face against him again so he wouldn't see my tears. 'I just need to take it slow.'

He stroked the back of my head. 'Sure. No problem. You're safe with me.'

Bags were unloaded and Hudson sorted out rooms – permanent tents on wooden platforms overlooking a narrow stream – but no plans were made to meet up for dinner, even though it was nearly dark. It was hardly a time to be socialising. I made my way over to Anna and took her hand. She looked at me blankly, and I realised she must be in shock. 'Can we talk, please? Maybe later?' I asked her.

'Yes,' was all she said. A porter came to her and she followed him to her room.

In my own tent I showered – it felt like a week since I'd washed – and changed back into the clothes Rina had paid for, which were now as dirty as the ones I'd replaced. I felt like I was going backwards in life and already I missed Bryce. I left the tent and walked down a pathway to the bar and dining room, an open-sided affair that looked over a wide lawn. A fire was burning in a brick pit out there, and I walked to it and pulled up a wooden camp chair. A shadow alerted me to movement behind me and Andrew stepped into the ring of light. 'Mind if I sit down?'

'No, of course not,' I said. 'I never thanked you properly for all you've done for me.'

'My pleasure. I can't imagine how horrible this has all been for you.'

No, he couldn't. No one could.

Andrew cleared his throat. 'I've got a friend who works near here. He runs balloon safaris. I called him from my room; we're catching up for dinner soon.'

'That's nice,' I said, not really interested in Andrew's social plans.

'I asked him if he had space on any of his flights. He said he had two free for tomorrow morning. It's a pre-dawn start, but it's one of the most amazing flights you could ever take in your life.'

He was sweet, but I wasn't in the mood for sightseeing with him and his old chum. 'Thanks, Andrew, but perhaps Hudson might want to go with you.'

He laughed. 'No, no, no. I told my chum that I had a couple of young friends, a man and a woman, who might like to go. He says there's no charge – he owes me a favour. I thought that you and Bryce might, well . . .'

My heart softened at his simple kindness. I reached over and laid my hand on his, on the arm of his chair. 'Oh, Andrew, thank you, so much.'

'Right, well, I'll let him know you're keen. In fact, I should go back into the bar, as he's due soon.'

I thanked him again, silently grateful that he had to go. As much as I appreciated his offer, I was in no mood to make small talk. It was after eight and I was already dog tired, exhausted by all we'd been through, and tormented, in spite of my hatred towards Peter, by the image of him being dragged under the water. I forced it from my mind, and got up and walked back to my tent.

When I got there I noticed that the mosquito mesh door was unzipped, and I heard the creak of floorboards from inside. 'Hello?' I called.

A form appeared at the door, then stepped through the open zip into the light of the balcony. 'Anna,' I said. 'You startled me.'

'Sorry.'

'It's all right. I'm glad to see you. Do you want to talk?'

'I don't know.' Her face looked drawn, tired, and I wondered if it was the mirror image of mine. 'I don't know if I ever want to say another word again.'

'You must,' I implored.

'Must I? I don't know what's left to say. We've hurt each other, and the man I once loved, the man I thought would make everything right, is dead. I should just disappear, I think.'

I reached out and took both her hands in mine. 'Come, sit down. No one's going to disappear. We can't let this, or what happened to us in the past, beat us. I know that now. I was wrong to try and run away. I should have gone to the police with my concerns about Peter; I should have been braver, like you.'

She looked at me like she didn't understand a word I'd said, as though I was speaking some foreign language. 'Yes, let's go inside,' she said, and stepped back into the tent. I made it to the threshold but couldn't see her. The lights were off and I couldn't remember where the internal switch was. Perhaps she'd disappeared into the en-suite bathroom at the back of the tent. Nearby a lion called, the sound low and full of longing.

'I can't find the light switch,' I said, trying to make a joke of it, and failing.

'No,' said my sister. 'Leave the light off. I don't want to see your eyes.'

She was a shape in the dark. I had seen her unhinged today, trying to kill Peter. We'd all said the same thing to the rangers, that she and Peter were having an argument, but that she had not deliberately tried to kill him by pushing him at the edge of the riverbank. I knew that wasn't true, but deep down I felt that Peter deserved what had happened to him, as terrible as that sounded.

'Hudson wants me to leave in the morning, early,' Anna said. 'He has to fly back to Zimbabwe to pick up his truck. He's going to get the police in South Africa and Zimbabwe to talk to each other about Peter, which will get him off the hook.'

There were bigger issues at stake than Brand's Land Rover, which he had mentioned he'd left in Zimbabwe when he'd picked up the larger touring vehicle to transport Anna and Peter, but the move was timely. Anna wouldn't want to be facing a lengthy Kenyan police investigation and the local rangers had not had the power to confiscate her passport. 'Anna, let's put on the light, I'll order us a drink, and we'll talk.'

'No,' she said forcefully. 'I've tried talking, it doesn't work.'

'Dad did terrible things to you, didn't he, Anna – more than just the beatings he gave us both and the way he used to touch me.'

Anna pursed her lips and wrapped her arms around herself. 'He deserved to die.'

She started moving from the gloom towards me. I wanted to rush to her and hug her and thank her for being my sister and to tell her we *would* be OK, we *would* come through this.

'Kate?' a voice called from behind me, at the external steps.

'Bryce. Just a minute,' I said. Now that he'd found me I couldn't bear the thought of turning him away again, but I had to try and make things right with my sister, or at least begin the process.

Before I could say anything, however, Anna rushed through the tent and brushed past me on her way out. 'Anna, wait!'

'No,' she called as she ran down the stairs. 'I'll see you tomorrow before I leave.'

I went outside and saw her running off down the pathway. She didn't turn. Bryce stood there, looking confused. 'Sorry, I didn't mean to interrupt.'

'No, it's fine,' I said. 'It's probably too early, still too raw.'

'I'll go, if you like. I wasn't going to come, and I'm not looking for anything, but I just wanted to make sure you were OK before I went to bed.'

I looked down at him, at the honesty and goodness in a face that had not known the terrible things that Anna and I had been through, that had only known a loving family and a carefree life in the African bush. I wanted that life, and I thought that maybe, just maybe, that life was still out there for me. I reached my hand out and he took it. I led him into my tent and, once inside, he took me in his arms and kissed me.

*

Brand had gone looking for Anna, and bumped into her, literally, as she ran down the path. He caught her in his arms to stop her from falling then held her out from his body. 'Hey, hey, are you all right?'

She looked up at him. 'I don't know. I don't think I ever will be.'

'How's Kate?'

'She's fine,' Anna said quickly. 'She's with Bryce. He's a good man; I've only just met him, but I can tell.'

Brand nodded. For what it was worth he agreed with her assessment of Bryce. 'Good. Are you going to your tent now?'

Anna sniffed and looked into his eyes. 'I am. Please don't take this the wrong way, but I don't want to be alone tonight. I'm scared.'

'Of what?' Brand asked.

'The past.'

'I'll stay with you.'

'Thank you.' Anna broke from him gently and walked ahead, leading him to her tent. Brand followed her up the stairs and inside.

He looked around the interior as she went to the bathroom. When she came out she undid her blouse and unzipped her skirt. In her underwear, she climbed into bed. 'I'm so very tired.'

He went to her and pulled the covers up to her chin, bent down and kissed her forehead. 'I'll be here.'

Anna closed her eyes and Brand went to the chair in the corner and sat in it. He watched her as the lion continued calling, until she fell asleep. Brand walked quietly to the dressing table and found a pen and a piece of paper. He sat back down in the chair and, glancing at Anna every now and then to make sure she was still sleeping, began to write.

35

Bryce, with his safari guide's eyes, was pointing out animals faster than the balloon pilot could, but it wasn't the wildlife that amazed me, it was the incredible sense of peace and freedom I felt. It was, I think, a feeling I'd never truly known.

It was the way the sun burnished Bryce's cheeks a beautiful red-gold, and the way the zebra herds made swirling psychedelic patterns in the grass below. It was the complete absence of sound as we floated above the Masai Mara's endless plains, and the warmth of the burners on my back when the pilot fired them up. All of it produced a feeling of being in a weightless cocoon, made all the more comforting when Bryce put his arm around me and squeezed me, as he did every few seconds.

I had wanted to see Anna before she left, to make one last attempt at beginning the healing process, and I wanted to thank Hudson Brand and Andrew Miles, but when I got to Anna's tent in the pre-dawn blackness after Bryce and I had dressed for the balloon flight, I'd found her gone. Andrew, I knew, was flying them back to Nairobi, from where Hudson and Anna would fly back to Zimbabwe. From there, Anna would return to Britain.

Bryce kissed me, just before the pilot gave us the command to sit down and brace ourselves for landing. I remembered his touch from the few short hours we'd spent together earlier: tender, caring, yet strong and passionate. We didn't chat much with the other passengers over the champagne breakfast on the plain. Instead, we spent a lot of time staring into each other's eyes.

I was feeling pleasantly mellow when we returned to camp, and I was looking forward to peeling off my safari clothes and getting into a bath with Bryce. When I entered my tent I saw an envelope on the freshly made bed.

'I need to use the loo,' Bryce said.

I picked up the envelope, which had my name on it, and opened it. It was hand-written and my eyes went straight to the bottom. It was signed, Hudson Brand. I began to read it.

Dear Kate, by the time you get this we will be in Nairobi, and there is something I must tell you. It won't be easy for you to hear . . .

'Hey,' Bryce called over the noise of the toilet flushing as I read on quickly. 'Is this yours? I just found it on the floor in the bathroom.'

I looked up from the letter, my vision swimming and my heart pounding. Bryce was holding up a folding hunting knife with a wicked-looking blade that glinted in the morning light streaming in through the open tent window.

*

Andrew taxied the Beechcraft to a hangar at Wilson Airport. 'Here's our ride,' he said into the intercom.

Brand looked out and saw the black car with tinted windows. He undid his seatbelt and opened the door. Anna, who'd been quiet during the flight, got up. Brand led the way down the stairs as soon as Andrew had cut the engines. The car drove up to meet them.

'Quite the royal reception,' Anna said as the car door opened.

Brand moved behind Anna as Sannie van Rensburg got out of the car and introduced herself by rank, name and service. 'Anna Cliff, you're under arrest for the murders of Nandi Mnisi and Juliette February in the Republic of South Africa, and Melanie Afrika in Victoria Falls, Zimbabwe. You'll also be questioned about the murder of police Warrant Officer Mavis Sibongile.' As Sannie began to read Anna her rights, Anna tried to talk over the top of her.

'This is outrageous. I've done nothing . . . my husband, my late husband, Peter, he's the one you need to –'

'Mrs Cliff,' Sannie said, brooking no further interruption, 'we searched the lodgings of Patrick de Villiers yesterday afternoon and found a number of emails between you and him in which you discuss the planning and execution of these murders – and rapes – in graphic detail, along with your desire to kill your husband's lovers and to set him up at some point in the future. We found some long strands of hair at the scene of Warrant Officer Sibongile's murder which look very much like they came from you. I believe you were with De Villiers when Sibongile shot him, and that you killed her. You also discussed with De Villiers a plan to frame this man, Hudson Brand.'

Anna looked at him, and around her, but two uniformed Kenyan police officers emerged briskly from the hangar. Tom Furey, Sannie's husband, had also got out of the black car and was standing by to restrain Anna. However, she looked nonplussed now as Sannie put the handcuffs on her.

Anna turned to Brand. 'You knew.'

'Captain Van Rensburg called me yesterday. My phone was flat and I only got power and signal when we got back to camp. I came to find you as soon as I heard.'

She looked at him, realising he had known about her and her crimes all night long. He'd had a job to do, making sure she didn't harm herself or anyone else through the night, but he had learned of her childhood and her marriage and he felt something for her, though he wasn't quite sure what. None of that excused the horrific crimes she and De Villiers had committed, but it told him he was dealing with a troubled, damaged soul. Brand had debated, in his own mind, telling Kate, but he figured she and Bryce needed a few hours of peace and happiness before she learned the truth about her sister. He'd opted for the letter instead. Also, if Sannie van Rensburg found Kate she'd do her best to extradite her to South Africa as well.

Van Rensburg and her husband had done well to organise the extradition and arrest warrant as well as passage on the overnight flight from Johannesburg to Kenya. It saved him having to deliver Anna to South Africa.

Tom and the Kenyan police ushered Anna into the back seat of the hired limousine, which would take them all to Jomo Kenyatta International Airport for a return flight to South Africa later that day. Sannie walked over to Brand and extended her hand.

'Thank you for your help, Mr Brand. No hard feelings, I hope?'

'No.' He shook her hand.

'I don't suppose you can tell me where Linley Brown is?'

'Linley Brown?' Brand said. 'I think you'll find she passed away.'

Van Rensburg smiled. 'Can I give you a lift to the airport?'

Andrew Miles was standing by his aircraft. 'When is the owner collecting this crate?' Brand asked.

'Not for about a week,' Andrew replied. 'He said I can use it up here until he gets back.'

'I kind of like the sound of Zanzibar,' Brand said. 'So, thanks for your kind offer, captain, but I think I'll pass. I can pick up my Land Rover later.'

'Zanzibar looks nice,' Sannie said. 'In fact, my husband and I were just planning a trip there on the flight last night. I hope you're long gone before we get there.'

Brand smiled, 'Me too.'

Van Rensburg got in the car and they drove away.

*

I read the rest of the letter out loud to Bryce. Brand explained the evidence against my sister, and the final sting he had planned with Van Rensburg, to arrest Anna in Nairobi. He apologised for leaving me in the dark last night, but I understood why he'd done it. I would need to find a way to communicate with Anna in prison, but that would take time. I also had to look after Lungile; she had kept my secret, even around her brother. I had told Bryce about her while we waited to board the balloon.

Brand said De Villiers's computer and emails had revealed how he and my sister had acted as a devilish team. Anna had pretended to go on overseas trips to Thailand and Singapore while Peter was away, and had sent me postcards from the airports of these countries before catching connecting flights to South Africa. There, she and her safari guide lover, whom she had met in a sexually based internet chat room, had tailed Peter and stalked and murdered the women he had slept with. Anna, it appeared, was motivated by revenge and a grand plan that would eventually lead to Peter being blamed for the murders and imprisoned. De Villiers hated Brand and after the incident with the rhino poachers, when the Cliffs decided to engage him as their guide, Patrick and Anna hatched another plot to set up the American as a backup scapegoat, in case he found out the truth about Anna. De Villiers and Anna had also discussed the search for Linley or Kate, and Anna had bragged how she had set up a fake email account in Peter's name and used it to send the reversed picture of Kate and her friend to Dani Russo. Anna had been tailing Peter and she had found out about our affair. They had thought they were clever, but Patrick de Villiers's lack of computer security had undone them.

'The knife,' I said, looking at the wicked weapon Bryce still held. 'I wonder if she came here last night planning to kill me, just as she killed the other women Peter slept with.' Something else crossed my mind. 'Our father was a monster, Bryce, and he made Anna what she is. He was stabbed to death and no one was ever charged with the crime; I wonder if it was her? She told me he deserved to die.'

'Maybe if she gets some kind of treatment or therapy in prison it might come out; it might help her.' Bryce put the knife down on the side table. 'She would have had time to stab you before I arrived, so maybe she thought better of it.'

Dear Bryce, I thought. He *would* think the best of Anna. If she had wanted to kill me then he had saved my life.

'There's something you don't know about me,' Bryce said.

I felt a moment of dread. I hoped there wasn't a monster lurking beneath his gentle, loveable exterior. 'Go on.'

'My family's loaded. I do want to find work here in Kenya, but we won't starve, Kate. Also, seriously, if you need legal help for your friend Lungile I'll find a way to help, likewise if your sister needs counselling or anything like that.'

I kissed him, then went back to reading the final paragraph of Hudson's letter.

One more thing. I've decided not to make a final report to the insurance company. They may pay you, but they're notorious for finding ways not to pay claims and making that call, as you did, may have voided your policy. I figure that I'm done with hunting people after this case and by the time they work out the truth I'll be on a beach somewhere out of contact. If you do get your money, I do hope you're true to your word about giving something back to the people you stole from and making amends with them. If Bryce is reading this he'll make sure you stay on the straight and narrow.

I looked across at Bryce and he grinned.

I wish you the best of luck, Kate. You've got a good guy and a good guide there in Bryce Duffy. He'll show you the right way.

Acknowledgements

It was a conversation over a beer with a man in Zimbabwe, John Woodward, that gave me the premise for *The Hunter*. John, the managing director, special services, for the Safeguard Security Group, was telling me how he had investigated many cases of people faking their own deaths.

John, a former police officer and member of the World Association of Detectives and Association of British Investigators, later talked me through the intricacies of this particular crime, and agreed to read the manuscript that was born of that first discussion. I'd like to pass on my thanks to John here, and my apologies for any embellishments I've added or any slipshod work on the part of my fictional investigators.

Likewise, I'd like to thank former South African Police Service officer Sonnett Scholtz for kindly agreeing to read through my story, and for her input and corrections. Thanks also to Adrian Kitchin of Insurance Advisernet Australia for answering my questions about insurance claims.

I'm indebted, also, to a very helpful team of African experts who read the manuscript with an eye to cultural, linguistic and geographical errors. My deep thanks go to Annelien Oberholzer, Sue Fletcher, Hilary Hann and Ayesha Cantor.

In the course of writing this novel, as with my past books, I was lucky enough to visit some truly beautiful places and I'd like to thank the following people and places for their hospitality: Garth Jenman of Jenman Safaris and Elephant's Eye lodge in Zimbabwe; Duncan Rodgers of Leopard Hills in the Sabi Sand Game Reserve (who also read the manuscript for me); Don and Nina Scott of Tanda Tula Safari Camp in the Timbavati Game Reserve; Chris Harvie of Rissington Inn in Hazyview; and Brett McDonald, Managing Director of Flame of Africa holidays and owner of the *Lady Jacqueline* houseboat on Lake Kariba

As with many of my previous novels, I've devolved the (often tricky) responsibility for thinking up character names to a number of deserving charities and NGOs. The following big-hearted people paid good money to their respective causes to have their names assigned to characters in *The Hunter*: Linley Brown, Peter Cliff, Vanessa Fleming (for Geoffrey Fleming) and Bev Poor (for Andrew Miles Poor) made donations to Painted Dog Conservation Inc, an Australian-based charity supporting in-situ wildlife conservation projects in Africa; Kate Munns, who works for the NGO Worldshare, made a generous personal donation to Heal Africa, which funds a hospital in the strife-torn Democratic Republic of Congo; and Kevin Gillett (for Daniela Russo), generously supported ZANE, Zimbabwe, a National Emergency. I hope you all enjoy your fictitious identities.

The character of Bryce Duffy is named after another real person, Captain Bryce Duffy, Royal Australian Artillery, who died in the service of his country in Afghanistan in 2011. Bryce, like his mother and father, Kerry and Kim, and his sisters, Cassie and Samantha, had been to Africa and had read some of my books. I became good friends with the Duffys when writing Bryce's story for the book *Walking Wounded,* written by Brian Freeman and me. The Duffys have had much to do with supporting and helping other families who have lost loved ones in Afghanistan, and with soldiers suffering physical and psychological wounds from the war. I never knew Bryce, but wish I'd met him and it was my honour to name a character in his memory, on behalf of his family.

A number of other people have helped me and my wife, Nicola, in so many ways during our travels in Africa, and special thanks go to Dennis and Liz in Zimbabwe, for introducing me to John Woodward; our friends and neighbours in Hippo Rock (my fictitious name for the place Nicola and I now call home for much of our time in Africa); Greg and Tracey Meaker (not Mahoney); and Wayne Hamilton, of swagmantours.com.au who helps me explore new places and also organises safaris (escorted by me) for my readers.

If you have enjoyed this book then a large part of that is down to my devoted unpaid editors: Nicola, my mum, Kathy, and my mother-in-law, Sheila; and, at Quercus Books, Fiction Publisher Jane Wood, Editor Katie Gordon and Publicist Margot Weale. I'd also like to thank Nicky Stubbs, Jean Pieters and the rest of the team at Book Promotions in South Africa, and my hard working agent, Isobel Dixon.

Lastly, whoever you are, wherever you are, and no matter how you're reading this story (as long as you haven't illegally downloaded it), thank you: you're the one who counts most.